The Highest Mountain

Death and Life
in the Adirondacks

For Tim
Keep climbing!

David Pitkin

ALSO BY DAVID J. PITKIN

Spiritual Numerology: Caring for Number One

Haunted Saratoga County

Ghosts of the Northeast

New York State Ghosts, Vol. 1

Aurora Publications E-Mail:

pitkinaurora@aol.com

The Highest Mountain

Death and Life in the Adirondacks

David J. Pitkin

AURORA PUBLICATIONS
Chestertown, NY

Aurora Publications
P.O. Box 690
Chestertown, NY 12817

PUBLICATION DATA

Pitkin, David J. 1939-
The Highest Mountain: Death and Life in the Adirondacks
ISBN 978-0-9663925-5-5
Published August 2007

1. Law enforcement   2. Adirondack Mountains   3. Metaphysics
4. Near-death experience   5. Environment

Library of Congress Control Number: 2007922792

Cover Photo Credit: Jamie West, "The Top of Mt. Marcy"

Verleih' uns Frieden gnädiglich,
Herr Gott, zu unsern Zeiten!
Es ist doch ja
Kein And'rer nicht,
Der für uns könnte streiten,
Denn du, unser Gott alleine.

Martin Luther (1483-1546)
Felix Mendelssohn, 10 February 1831 (op. posthumus)

Grant us merciful peace, Oh Lord!
For there is no one else to protect us
in our time of strife except you,
the one and only God.

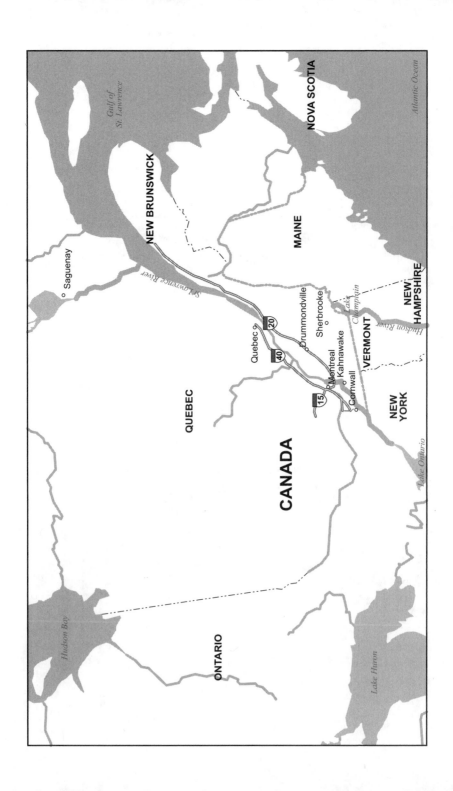

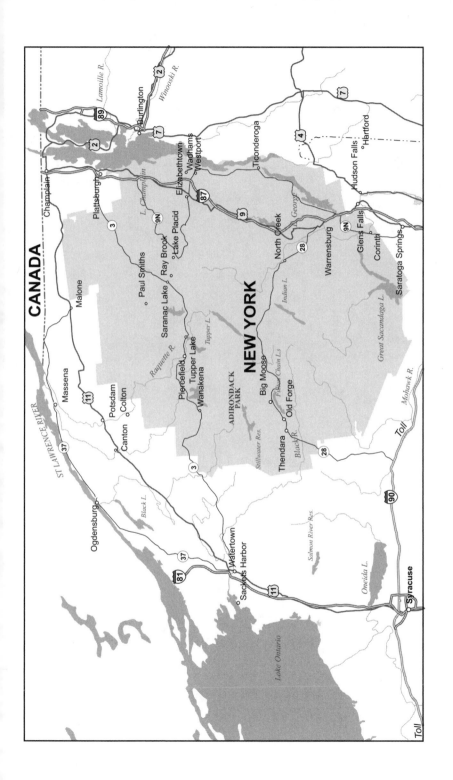

CHAPTER ONE

Bitter cold! Another damned icy Adirondack winter night, thought BCI Sr. Investigator Dennis Girard as he shuffled his boots in the drifting snow. Why don't I have the smarts to retire and go south, like sensible people? Temperatures here numb a man's skin right into the marrow of his bones, then straight to the soul. My body's getting too old for this! The radio says this 2008 winter is the coldest in years!

It had been 18 degrees below zero at 2:00 a.m. when he left home in Chestertown, NY, and the mercury kept dropping. Now, doing a slow and silent shuffle to keep his circulation going, Girard scanned the silhouetted old farmhouse and barn, at the moment barely visible in the night's darkness across the field outside Chilson. No lights. Nothing moved. Nor did he expect movement for a while yet. The place had seemed deserted for weeks, but the State Police Bureau of Criminal Investigation intensified its surveillance after a usually reliable source in Ticonderoga indicated something big would happen there soon.

Pretty quick, Tommy Delehanty will come in to join me, he reassured himself, exhaling a mist of warm breath into the frigid air. The pair hadn't been due at what was now the Charbonneau property until 4:00 a.m. but Girard had been restless, sensing that something *must* break soon, and he had come over to the stakeout early to watch and listen. His brief and fitful sleep had been punctuated with dream images of earthquakes and tumbling, black stone walls, strengthening his anxiety now in the mountain darkness. The prey couldn't be allowed to escape the snare *this* time.

He poured and sipped a Thermos cup of coffee, which turned ice cold almost instantly as it was engulfed by the frigid early morning air. In police investigations, stakeout work was always tiresome and boring, and seldom yielded the dramatic outcomes for which one hoped. But right now he needed not just a development, but *results*.

He'd given up attempting to sleep after those troubling dreams, had risen at 1:00 a.m., smoked two unfiltered Camels while warming some leftover coffee on the stove in his small apartment, then filled the Thermos and headed northeast to watch the dark farmhouse in the mountains west of Ticonderoga. He sure could use a smoke right now, but didn't want its glow to give away his position if Charbonneau suddenly appeared. Finally, we have an arrest warrant on that bum, but unless I can catch smuggler Louie Charbonneau red-handed, I'm likely to lose my shield

1

and sorry professional life, and in the end, what little remains of my self-respect, he fretted. I've made too many professional mistakes in recent years, so there can be no more blown investigations. Major Sincavage had made *that* clear enough at the last disciplinary hearing. Maybe it's all for the best if I just get out, he concluded. Who needs this kind of life? Who needs *any* life? I sure haven't made much out of this one.

Girard's career had gone downhill since 1992, when he'd lost his comfortable investigative job on the State Capitol Building Detail in Albany. But trying to be a good soldier gets you nowhere anymore, he often chided himself since those days. People can stand just so much truth, but not the plain bald-faced truths he had uncovered.

Since 1992, he'd gone through a divorce and a voluntary transfer to Troop B, which covers northern New York State. His investigative skills of the 1980s had dulled and now were no longer as precise, and his formerly sharp, analytical mind was now sluggish. He'd moved from case to case in the past two decades from one reassignment to another, from one rebuke by his superiors to the next—one dirty detail after another.

His marriage had ended in '93 and the tiresome bickering with his ex-wife, Irene, then grew even colder and more vicious in its legal intensity. With that collapse, he reflected, had vanished all his remaining hopes for a decent retirement or happiness in old age. He'd ceased to care about his health and began drinking more heavily to bury his emotional pain. His grown-up kids no longer came around or called, depressing him terribly, and he had ceased his perfunctory attendance at Sunday Mass. Now, it usually took three or more stiff shots of Black Velvet just to fall asleep at night, though he always awoke exhausted before dawn, needing nicotine and strong black coffee to pump up his weary body for another day's work. From time to time he remembered lines from Peggy Lee's old song, "Is That All There Is?"

The coldness and isolation of the stakeout mirrored his alienation from family members and fellow Troopers. The young go-getters in Troop B viewed him as a wheezy boozer, an over-the-hill cop. His superiors treated him as a screw-up who could no longer be trusted to pursue important investigations to a successful conclusion, and Girard knew they wanted him out. He could no longer muster the "good soldier" idealism he'd had after Vietnam, and there seemed no reason to even *want* to improve his lot anymore. *Almost* no excuse, he reminded himself, snapped back to his shivering present reality by a wind gust spraying icy snow crystals into his face as he peered at the frozen landscape. There was still

Charbonneau, the only man who'd ever put a bullet into him.

Louie "Two Claw" Charbonneau was probably still away somewhere to the north, maybe in Vermont, maybe Canada. The informer in Ti had indicated that Louie's new strategy was to return via secret routes from pick-up runs into the Green Mountains, upper Adirondacks, or Canada (no one knew exactly where) before dawn that Tuesday morning, his pickup laden with another load of untaxed contraband cigarettes, and Girard wanted to be there *this* time to get the goods on him. And the snitch had suggested that maybe Louie was carrying an even more valuable cargo on this run. State Police road patrols had been instructed not to stop Charbonneau's old pickup during this trip so he could return to his cigarette-filled barn and be arrested red-handed.

Despite their best efforts, the BCI had been unable to rein in Two Claw's cigarette-smuggling operation. Using connections among the St. Regis Mohawk Indians, his wife's people, Charbonneau had run a lucrative cigarette traffic across the Canadian border since the late 1990s, when the state's tax-take on cigarettes had gone to $1.25 a pack. Now, Governor Pratie was gearing up for a higher government post—maybe in Washington—and wanted to establish a strong "get the tax cheats" résumé, which obviously didn't include his cronies. Such a tough pose would also distract public attention away from his excessive spending programs and lackluster administrative record. These facts were acknowledged by Maj. Sincavage when Girard and his old friend, Investigator Tommy Delehanty, had been assigned to the Charbonneau case.

What a farce, Girard ruminated. He was among the few insiders in law enforcement who'd worked the State Capitol and knew that the whispers about former Assemblyman, now Governor, John Pratie's luxurious vacation home in the Bahamas, his mistress in Scarsdale, and his cohort of powerful and greedy corporate financial backers weren't just political idle talk. Pratie's private lifestyle had been too opulent for a state lawmaker, and the capitol media, seemingly no longer interested in investigative journalism, had stifled any suspicions of the man and devoted themselves to robotic rewriting and printing of press releases from the Governor's Office.

Girard, however, had momentarily pierced Pratie's good-government facade when the Assemblyman's private jet arrived unexpectedly at Albany International Airport in the predawn hours back in 1992, on a night when Girard was waiting at the State Police Aviation Unit to pick up and transport a convicted felon to Dannemora State Prison. Trying to comprehend what he'd covertly seen emerge from that plane, and asking his friends in Governor Cuomo's office quiet but sharp questions about Pratie had gotten Girard into trouble with Pratie's political and financial handlers, who engineered Sgt. Girard's exile from the State Capitol post. This move stressed the investigator's already fractious marriage, which then collapsed. After the divorce, he welcomed a move away from his home in Latham, and transferred north to Troop B in the Adirondacks.

Snow—goddam deep snow and icy air—that's *my* reward, he mumbled. Pratie became Governor and, expecting a 2010 victory, wants increased cigarette tax revenues to show the state's "little people" he's watching their every revenue penny after years of his support for increased state borrowing and levying higher fees and taxes. In the meantime, playing on the voters' apathy and disgust with politics, his administration continues to funnel state contracts, consulting fees, and sweetheart deals to cronies and magnates who backed two previous campaigns, Girard reflected. Some pundits figure that if he can gain re-election Pratie might be his party's candidate for President in a few years. So, under pressure from the Governor's Office, the word had come down in the Division, much more strongly this time: Catch tax evaders and smugglers—make a splash in the news—catch *somebody*. Show the people the Pratie administration is tough on crime!

The dark clouds broke for a moment and February's full moon briefly illuminated the snow-covered Essex County farm in this coldest winter in 20 years. At the edge of the field a fox pranced daintily over the white blanket and quickly ducked into a thicket, while a miniature whirling dervish of powdered snow rose and blew itself toward the barn. An even colder, biting wind was building now, and Girard snuggled more deeply into his parka and heavy Malone pants, scuffing his feet in the snow boots. Global warming, my ass, he sneered. In the distance he saw the glare of lights and a plume of steam seemingly frozen in mid-air over Ticonderoga's International Paper Company mill in the valley below. His Thermos cup was empty now, and so cold that his lip almost stuck to it. He dropped it into his carry bag.

What was *that*? Was he missing something? He brought his binoculars to his eyes and scanned the field and house; nothing. Did he hear someone running? As clouds sped over the moon's face once more, there was the illusion of moving figures against the white landscape, but Girard guessed these were darting shadows cast by the fleeting moonlight. He relaxed once more against the timeworn door of the old chicken coop in which he'd taken refuge and, in the sub-zero cold, the wooden frame gave a tired squeak. Delehanty would be in soon, and they could chat as they waited for Two Claw's truck to appear on the snow-drifted farm road. Yesterday, the pair had executed a search warrant and found perhaps a ton of cigarettes in the Charbonneau barn. Fortunately, the drifting new snow had obliterated their tracks.

Tommy and he had been buddies in college and then served in Bravo Company, 3rd Battalion of the 101st Airborne Division in those final days in Vietnam. Both forestry majors at Syracuse University, and although it meant a delay in their degree program, they'd enlisted together in 1968, determined to preserve democracy for South Vietnam's peasants. Even today, each of them still sported the no longer fashionable "sidewall" crew cut that the 101st had favored.

In the end, quickly disillusioned with the graft-driven "democracy" that so many friends had died defending in Vietnam, they'd been glad to escape Southeast Asia with their tails intact. Throughout the war they'd watched each other's back, and countless times saved one another's lives. The corruption Girard had seen in Vietnam's government became immediately obvious when he encountered it again in the New York State Legislature, among lawmakers who prostituted their public trust in a lust for personal power, money, and gifts.

Together, he and Tommy had joined the New York State Police in 1975, following their discharge from the Army. Working with Delehanty throughout the years was about the only joy remaining in his police work career. After State Police Academy training they'd both been posted to Troop G in the Lake George area. That first year Girard had been responsible for catching night nurse Ruby Overbaugh in the act of poisoning senile adults at the Loomis Nursing Home in Fort Edward. Posing as the night janitor, he'd caught her with a cyanide-filled syringe, poised over the infusion line of Minnie Buffardi, mother of State Senator Michael Buffardi. The grateful and powerful senator, chairman of the Senate Finance Committee, had later spoken a few quiet words in the right places and Girard's career began to ascend.

Afterward, he was posted to the Malta barracks, just south of Saratoga Springs and Tommy had gone to the Duanesburg barracks. Malta was a hectic post for catching speeders on I-87, but also a place of frequent special assignments, protecting the notables of New York State and federal governments when they visited the popular Saratoga Thoroughbred Racetrack in August. Until he realized that the glitz and glitter of the incredibly wealthy was a veneer over so many putrid private lives, Girard had been dazzled by those glamorous figures. Eventually, however, he had become jaded by celebrities, power seekers, and show people who led hollow personal lives of never-ending greed. Life had to be about more than *that*, he'd concluded.

By the mid-1980s he had become a State Police Sergeant, and later, in 1992, an Investigator in the BCI where he achieved the rank of Senior Investigator 10 years after the transfer to Troop B. Back then, freed of endless hassles with Irene at home, he thrived on North Country detective work and its demand for sharp wits, especially when he could work in plain clothes. How had he devolved from all that early professional success to this hangover-troubled stakeout in the icy Adirondacks? he wondered.

Licorice! He could have sworn that he smelled licorice in the cold wind. Must be the frost is turning my brain to jelly—not enough "antifreeze" last night, he mused sardonically. Icy particles of snow became airborne, lifting into the air and faintly colliding with the faded red paint on the clapboards of his lair. It was as if a million pins were now bouncing off the wooden surface. Then suddenly, in that faint drumming, he knew he was not alone.

Behind him, he heard "*Bâtard!*" Spinning, he almost lost his footing in the drifted snow of the doorway. In the darkness stood the bear-like, hunched figure of Charbonneau, and the man had an old .410 shotgun leveled at Girard's chest. "You want *more*, you sonofabitch? I shot you once in Chazy, Girard, and I got *more* for you now! Why couldn't you just leave me alone? All you sonofabitch white men got your rackets, why pick on a poor Indian like me?"

Girard dropped his right glove into the snow. "You're no Indian, and you're sure not poor, Louie," he responded. Girard shifted a quarter-turn to his right, partially obscuring his right side from Charbonneau's view. "I saw your inventory over in the barn. There've gotta be tons of cigs there, and the state wants your butt *and* your butts. We've got you *this* time, you miserable shit, and you're going away for the rest of your god-forsaken life. The lapel on his parka flapped in the wind, obscuring for a second the slow movement of Girard's hand inside toward the 9mm. Glock pistol in his belt. Three more inches and he'd have his hand on its grip.

"What have you got against *me*?" spat Charbonneau plaintively. A short twist of black licorice abruptly shifted to the right side of his mouth. "You guys took down my operation in Chazy, and now that I'm making some nice money again, you want to put me out of business for *good*. Goddammit!"

"Come on, Louie, give it up, this place is surrounded with troopers!" Girard bluffed. One more inch, he thought, one more inch and my Glock *will* put him out of business. But Two Claw was too crafty. His paranoid, defensive nature caught the slight shift in the trooper's stance. Without warning he fired into the left side of Girard's chest. And that was all the investigator knew.

There was blinding light from the gun's explosion, though no sound, simultaneous with a stab of pain as his life exploded within him. Then, nothing. Investigator Dennis André Girard lay dead in a snowdrift at the Charbonneau farm. Dropping his .410, Two Claw backed away for a moment, then lunging forward, spat licorice juice on Girard's body. Then, backing away, he ran out the back door of the chicken coop, disappearing into the snowdrifts where he had parked his truck.

CHAPTER TWO

Investigator Thomas Delehanty was early. He pulled into the sheltering hemlock grove on the back side of Charbonneau's farm, and noted that Girard's car was already there. The unmarked Chevy Impala was covered with a thin layer of wind-blown snow. He also noted the almost-drifted-over profusion of tire tracks and footprints alongside Girard's vehicle. Den must have been here for a while, mused Delehanty, but who else? As he moved toward the flat dark shape of the chicken coop rendezvous, he noticed the trail of footprints both to and from the coop in the low drifts. Can't be *that* long ago that Denny got here, he puzzled. Before Delehanty left the cover of the trees he scanned the old farm. Nothing moving. No one. Good. He eased into the coop and staggered at what he saw. There was Denny Girard, face up in the snow. Pools of black ice on the white surface were surely blood. He immediately knelt over the body. It was cold and unresponsive.

Delehanty grabbed at his cell phone and called the State Police barracks in Westport. "This is Delehanty. We have an officer down at the old Anderson farm in Chilson. He's been shot! Call Essex County Emergency—get me some help in here fast!" His fiancée Janice Howland

7

took the call at Westport Barracks, but Tommy wasted no time in small talk with her. He abruptly pocketed the phone and tried to rouse his friend with CPR. Nothing. He tried chest compressions again and again, ignoring the coagulated wound, into which he pushed his handkerchief. Not even the flicker of an eyelid—no response. "Come on, lad, come *back* to me!" he implored. Resuming mouth-to-mouth resuscitation on Girard's cold lips produced no result.

Despite his parka, Tommy Delehanty shivered, more deeply now in his soul. Was it the cold, or was it him recalling Vietnam and the hot January day in 1971 when their patrol was ambushed outside Hué, when Denny had taken a piece of mortar shrapnel and appeared dead? Girard had been breathless and had lost a lot of blood, Tommy remembered. The Medevac chopper had gotten Girard out of the rice paddy that time, though Tommy figured he'd lost his best friend. Looks like Den bought it big time *now* though, he groaned. Suddenly there came a gush of emotion, filled with feelings of impotence, of dashed hopes and his loss of a brother. Dammit, it was Nam all over again! He sat down briefly in the snow and wept bitterly, all the while rubbing his friend's wrist vigorously. Then he jolted upright, slammed a gloved fist onto the ground, and frantically resumed CPR.

The cell phone in his pocket rang and he found Sgt. Paul Chartrand from Westport Barracks on the line. "Essex County Emergency has only one ambulance in service this morning, and they're at a bad accident with multiple casualties in Wilmington. LifeFlight and Dartmouth-Hitchcock air ambulances are busy too, so we have MedFlight already in the air from Albany Medical Center. ETA is 18 minutes—hang on. How's your partner? Delehanty mumbled a vague commentary, ending in "doesn't look good," then signed off, falling once more into despondency. If anyone could help now, it would be the emergency medics. He knew their helicopter was a flying Intensive Care Unit. He resumed chest compressions on Girard's body.

The *hup-hup-hup* of the airlift chopper roused Delehanty from his grief and he dove out the chicken coop door into the snowy field. The chopper's searchlight was probing the buildings as it approached from the south, and it came straight in toward Delehanty's signaling flashlight. Westport had given excellent GPS coordinates, and Delehanty indicated a flat spot in front of the building with his light. Flight Nurse Alma Wooding, NY State National Guard medic and trauma nurse at the Albany Medical Center, jumped into the knee-deep snow and ran to the building's doorway, even before the chopper's skids touched ground. Medic Sandy Renfrow was right behind her, bringing a backboard stretcher and his kit.

Dashing to the inert body, where Delehanty had already loosened the bloody flack jacket and shirt to expose Denny's bare chest and gaping wound under the left arm, right at the edge of the jacket armhole, Alma knelt. There was no more bleeding in the cold. Her stethoscope was immediately on the cold flesh, quickly here, then there, pausing and moving on. She puckered her face several times, frantically searching for a heartbeat in the cold body. Nothing. "I tried CPR, but no go," Tommy informed her. He and Renfrow lifted Girard's body to remove the parka and flack jacket in order to fully expose the wound. Wooding found a neck vein and started a saline infusion. Handing the drip bag to Renfrow, who held it high, she bent over once more to listen and puckered her face. Thirty seconds later, she sagged. "No good," she said, "Let's get him in the air. In this business we say you can't be cold and dead. We've got to get him to Albany Med fast. If he's a goner we'll pronounce him there in a warm trauma room."

With those words, Tommy Delehanty felt the salty tears start again, but he quickly swallowed them and regained his composure. He helped the pair attach a cervical collar and cover the body in blankets, then he and Renfrow lifted the stretcher into the helicopter. Delehanty jumped inside as the skids lifted off the icy snow, and slid the door closed behind him. Following standard procedure for gunshot deaths, he began to bag Girard's hands for the gunshot residue test during the autopsy later.

This is a fellow trooper and my dear friend, he reminded himself, and I'm going to do this last stuff for *him* by the book. Maybe from the hell that Denny's put himself through, this is a fitting end. Nothing has gone his way for a long time, and management would surely throw him out now for disobeying regulations so many times. No man was supposed to go on this kind of stakeout and arrest without a partner. And that last broken regulation would likely have gotten him canned whether or not he'd captured Charbonneau.

Girard's body was quickly covered with another blanket after Nurse Wooding inserted an airway. Delehanty buckled into his seat and, using his cell phone, called the Westport barracks again, urging the issuance of an APB for Charbonneau and informing Sgt. Chartrand that they were airborne to Albany. Then kicking the bagged shotgun in its plastic sack beneath his seat, he settled back as the chopper sped over Warren County. He peered intently at Girard's unresponsive face beneath its mask.

9

Delehanty's mental refuge in times of trouble had always been procedure—what do *regulations* require next? Stay focused! Mentally, he stuck to that chore...think, *think*! There would be hours of paperwork ahead, and the unimaginable grief of losing the man he thought of as "brother." This dead man was his closest buddy and steadfast friend. This was the man who, with all their company officers dead in a Nam ambush, assumed command of B Company and called down an air strike on their surrounded position after having his men dig deep shelter holes, back in December 1971. The next day, most of their outfit had walked out of that carnage alive after the napalm fires cooled. Thousands of Viet Cong had died trying to overrun Bravo Company's position. Our boys were sure named right, he reflected, "Bravo the brave!" The NVA called us "chicken men," from our bald eagle insignia, but there was never a "chicken" among *our* Screaming Eagles!

He returned to the present, hearing the flight nurse speaking into her mike phone over the engine's roar as they swept southward over Wilton.

"Base, this is MedFlight. Here's what we've got right now. Patient is intubated, on oxygen, and had a shot of epinephrine. We're dripping saline and Lactated Ringers. We're ready to defibrillate right now."

A sharp hospital voice responded "Roger,"which echoed over the engine's roar. Base then asked her two more questions that Delehanty couldn't hear. To both of these she responded, "Negative!"

Renfrow now had the de-fib unit paddles on Girard's hard, cold chest. Calling "clear!" he administered a jolt. Girard's frozen body jumped against its restraints but there was no response. Again, the procedure was repeated with no result. Adding another blanket to Girard's covering, Wooding and Renfrow continued to work over Girard for 10 more minutes, mumbling to one another and searching for even a small sign of life. They began their descent into Albany, having been cleared through all commercial traffic at Albany International Airport. The helicopter set down on the D Building helipad at Albany Medical Center at precisely 4:00 a.m., ironically, the time when Girard and Delehanty were supposed to have begun their surveillance in Chilson.

Now there was no hurry, Tommy concluded. Denny was clearly dead and Charbonneau, almost certainly his executioner, was long gone. Tommy grabbed the bagged shotgun to deliver it to the criminology lab, and they'd say for sure. They'd also have to identify some unrecognizable, frozen black substance on Girard's parka, which Tommy had bagged along with the bloody flack jacket. Inside the hospital, while a dozen trauma team members struggled to revive Girard behind the curtains, Delehanty first called in his report to the BCI captain at troop headquarters in Ray Brook. Sgt. Chartrand had already notified them that Girard's body had gone to Albany.

He then called Denny's ex-wife, Irene Karamanlis, at her home in North Bennington, VT, where she taught art at Bennington College. Irene well-remembered Tommy from the old days, when she'd resented his intrusion, almost as a rival, in her married life. She had no close friends of her own, and envied Dennis, who was befriended by many, though she never dared permit her envy to rise to full consciousness.

Irene was clearly irritated at this middle-of-the-night call, and showed no distress at the death of the man she blamed for all her apparent failures in life. "He was just a sorry excuse for a husband, Tommy," she said, "and an even worse father—I won't miss him. The war burned him out and you know it. Then the state of New York owned him." Her voice became shrill. "I never had his heart, and most of the time I didn't even have his *attention!* He never understood my art and creativity, and he never understood *me and my suffering!*" There was a moment of silence while she composed herself. "I'll call the kids, Tommy, when I get around to it, but don't expect sympathy from *us*, and don't expect us at the funeral. He was a jerk, a loser, and just no good, *I owe him nothing!*" she concluded, as the phone line clicked dead.

Delehanty was sure that headquarters would detail an officer to Irene's home in North Bennington anyway. Even an ex-wife and grown children were given the dignity of an official notification. This process validated her former-wife role and that of the State Police itself, which had lost one of its own. He returned to the trauma room cubicle. As he'd suspected, Girard's body was now covered with a sheet, having been pronounced D.O.A. by a haggard attending physician. Girard's toe tag was now visible outside a corner of the green drape. The nursing assistants maneuvered the corpse into a white body bag, then moved the gurney out for its journey to the morgue over in F Building. There'd be a coroner's exam at 7:00 a.m.

Tommy took a deep breath, fought down the pain and sorrow in his gut, and looked up to see Trooper Gil Romaine outside the Trauma Unit. Gil would sit with Denny's body in the morgue until the autopsy, another dignity for a fallen officer. The two men shook hands and exchanged a few words, then Delehanty set out to arrange transport back to Troop B in Ray Brook. There were papers to fill out and more calls to make.

11

CHAPTER THREE

Snowdrifts almost blocked the road in many places on Route 30 as Charbonneau drove, slipping and sliding, relentlessly speeding north. Since leaving Saranac Lake an hour before, he had taken almost impassable county roads to reach the hamlet at Paul Smith's and Route 30. He knew for certain that an all-points bulletin would be posted for his capture and he relied on his craftiness and the cover of the growing storm to reach the safety of Akwesasne. There was no traffic except an occasional snowplow, so he felt secure in making his escape. His pickup truck looked ancient and incapable of facing severe weather, and that's the way he wanted it. He had added a heavy-duty radiator and battery, helper springs, an oversize gas tank, heavy-duty snow tires, and police scanners to the vehicle, and now felt invulnerable.

Invulnerable outside, anyway. His stomach hurt, and hurt bad. Every time he had an emotional upset, such as having just killed Girard, sharp pains assailed him to the point of feeling faint. Sometimes he coughed up blood, and Charbonneau couldn't imagine how much more painful death could be. A large pack of black licorice lay on the seat beside him, along with a filled cashbox he had taken from his farm. There was also a .357 magnum pistol that would be somebody's way out of this world—either his or someone else's. After his three-year prison term years ago, he had vowed that no white man would ever take him alive again.

Just ahead were the lights of the Route 11 intersection and he slowed so that he could time his passage straight through a green light, thus lessening his time in the crossroads illumination. A Franklin County Sheriff's patrol car with lights flashing shot through the intersection, going eastward on Route 11. Some poor bastard was probably off the road or maybe dead. Tough shit! He had no compassion for white men. They were there to be *used*, to profit from, and he'd get along with them if he could, but he also could pull a trigger if he had to. He thrived on his image as a modern Mohawk warrior.

The light changed to green as he approached it, and Charbonneau sped through the glare and into the darkness of Route 37. Only a few more miles, and he'd be home free. Using his cell phone he called Dark Eagle, letting his business partner on the reservation know he'd be there within the hour.

In Fort Covington he made a quick right onto Pike Street, then slid onto Drum Street, buffeting the snowdrifts out onto Hopkins Point. The Border Patrol, if they were out in the storm, was invisible. The narrow road was too drifted to go farther now, so he turned the wheel over and careened down the riverbank, shooting out onto the river ice and slip-sliding on the new snow that obscured the frozen surface. Fortunately, his helper springs took the jolt and he floored the truck past the vacant ice-fishing shanties, westward now, and along the shore of the Reservation land. At this point, all he'd have to watch for was the Mohawk Nation police, but he felt certain he could finesse them.

Two Claw found an old beach and gunned the truck through a drifted snow bank and up onto the hill. After a few quick turns, he swung into the old garage that Jim Tarbox, also known as Dark Eagle, owned. The blizzard winds were ferocious now, more than 30 miles per hour, and they concealed his tire tracks almost as soon as he passed. Free! He knew Dark Eagle would have a case of Molson's ready for the celebration party. He turned off his lights and sat in triumph. He had killed an enemy—like his heroic ancestors of old, *he had counted coup* on the oppressors!

CHAPTER FOUR

Something. Barely something. Not motion, not sound—what was it? Not a sensation or feeling, because he recognized that he had lost all sense of touch. Perhaps a breeze, but no, not that. Just the faintest suggestion of movement. Whatever it was, he observed it to be taking place in absolute silence and darkness. There was no sense of heat or cold. From time to time there was an indication that something grayer than black had just shot past his vision, though it wasn't as if he could *see* in the normal sense. He had no ability to move any part of his body, and what was odd, he didn't really think he *had* a body, but none of that really seemed important. Girard was just a mute witness to events he couldn't control or comprehend.

He was on a stunned journey of sorts, and more charcoal-gray patches flitted past. The consciousness that had been Dennis Girard seemed to be moving gently, yet at a breakneck speed, surrounded more often now by a faint, but increasingly eerie light. There was no vibration; no wind, just the certainty that he was rocketing at a terrific speed toward something—a gigantic *something*! He kept trying to assess his location and

13

what was taking place, but his investigator's intellect wouldn't work anymore. All he could do was watch and submit.

All at once, he could see ahead to his journey's end. Streaks of brilliant white light shot past him now, emanating from a pinpoint way in the distance. That was his destination, for sure, but what or who *was* it? The term "warp speed" seemed to fit his present experience, but Girard couldn't remember why. He hurtled toward the light, eerily and even more rapidly now, in absolute silence, but with a growing sense of alarm. Brilliant streaks exploded past him like meteors. Whatever this portended, he knew he was terribly unprepared. There was no weapon he could load and aim—he couldn't even position his hands or body for the impact. He flashed back to memories of Nam, where he'd always been able to set up a good perimeter defense around his position, but now he was helpless—no longer in control of anyone or anything. If he had hands and arms he couldn't see them or make them work, and he possessed no physical strength. Suddenly the journey reached its terrible conclusion—he erupted into brilliance and was absorbed. Then, nothing. Just being.

Twenty-four year-old Neftali Temu slowly swung his mop back and forth across the old floor tiles deep in the cellar of Albany Medical Center. Mopping tiled American floors was new to him; he'd grown up in a dirt-floored *tukul* stone house in the Ethiopian highlands of East Africa. Only the kindness of his Uncle Mogus Brook had allowed him to escape the goatherd life that would surely have been his destiny there. Uncle Mogus had emigrated to the United States back in the early 60s when he'd gotten into political trouble with the Haile Selassie regime. And Uncle had made a success of his life in this new land, now owning several apartment buildings in New York State's capital city. Temu was grateful that Uncle had brought him to America, and he worked hard at night to become the success that his family expected him to be.

Cleaning floors and bathrooms, even at 5:30 a.m., was where it all started, he had been told, and if that's what it takes, that's what I'll do, he assured himself. Only *this* floor in F Building, I don't like. This is where they keep the dead bodies in the morgue, which will open in another half-hour. Look at this one coming in on a gurney, he mused, covered with green cloth over the body bag and awaiting the coroner's exam at 7:00. Some kind of policeman walked alongside, holding the side-rail of the gurney while an attendant pushed. Rinsing his mop once more in the mop pail, Temu followed the two men into the morgue and commenced mopping as the attendant left. The policeman remained, seated at the foot of the stretcher. Temu's heavy, full mop pail spun and banged against the gurney, causing it to slam against the wall near which it had been placed. Trooper Gil Romaine, seated nearby, angrily jumped at him. "Watch what you're doing, you idiot! This is the body of a dead hero! Keep your distance!"

"Okay, okay, sorry!" Temu responded sheepishly in broken English. He then reflected, it's okay, *he* doesn't care, *he* can't feel anything now. That body once was human, but now it's a thing. We *bury* our dead quickly in Ethiopia. Why Americans want to study them for hours is beyond me; it seems savage. Looks like this one was a male, he observed, seeing the hairy, tagged toe splayed from the partially unzipped body bag opening. Temu recognized the letter G on the ID tag, but cared little what name the rest of the letters spelled.

Turning away, Temu took a minute to rinse his mop again, squeezing its braided cotton strands in the plastic pail's yellow wringer attachment. The thud of the opening wringer jaws seemed to echo and re-echo from the hard walls of the morgue—strange, how could that be? He was no longer pushing the handle down. Then he realized the sound came from just behind him, from the gurney he'd just passed! Wide-eyed, he swung around and saw that the bagged corpse had fallen to the floor. Trooper Romaine had run to it, trying to catch the body and stop Temu from approaching all at the same time. The bag was moving slowly and turning onto its side, like a giant white worm!

Temu shot out the door, down the hall, careened left around a corner, and took the stairway upward three steps at a time. On the second landing he collided with an x-ray technician coming downstairs in green scrubs, knocking the man off his feet. "That man! He's alive!" he sputtered. "That man down there! He's not dead!" Regaining his feet, Temu sprinted upward and out of sight.

X-ray technician Burton Vandervelde regained his footing. "Those *people!*" he sniffed. He'd had enough of the superstitious Jamaicans and downstate Latin-Americans who now held many of the menial jobs at Albany Med. They just didn't have any boundaries or sense of procedure—they'll be doing Voodoo in here soon, he snorted to himself. Everybody *knew* there were no living beings except the night cleaners down here in the morgue—not this early in the morning. No! Why, of course they are all dead!

Vandervelde carried his films down to the cellar storage room and turned right, only to stop dead in his tracks. A bleeding naked man, supported by a state trooper, was being helped from a body bag beside a gurney thrust into the hallway! The man, groaning pitifully, was painfully attempting to stand upright, while the trooper tried to ease him back down onto the gurney, which kept rolling away from them. The two struggled in a macabre dance alongside a growing pool of blood on the floor.

Vandervelde's first impulse was to run, just as the black Ethiopian had done. He was torn—here was a patient in distress, but here was a *dead* man! He had been *pronounced* dead, for God's sake, how can he *not* be dead? And why is there a trooper here? Oh, why do I get into such things? Vandervelde anguished. I got into radiology because it's *clean*. I don't want to deal with this messy stuff, like *other* people here have to.

Burton Vandervelde's humanity, however, quickly won out over his esthetics, and he rushed to the pair's side, helping hoist the corpse back onto the gurney, amid groans and a new gush of blood from the man's left chest wound. Vandervelde, dropping his x-ray files onto the floor, took his handkerchief and pressed it firmly into the wound, stanching the blood flow for the moment. He knew he couldn't let go of the man and fumbled his cell phone from his shirt pocket, punching in the one hospital number he could remember—the x-ray office. He caught Shirley Wernicki, his fellow night technician, still in the office, and gave her the startling news. In just two minutes a trauma team was rushing from the elevator, through the hallway, pushing a crash cart with all the cardiac resuscitation paraphernalia, drugs, and equipment they'd need. Mercifully, Dennis Girard knew none of this, as he had passed out when they hoisted him onto the gurney.

CHAPTER FIVE

The trauma team, led by Surgeon Richard Walker, worked on the investigator for three hours, stopping the bleeding and removing the shotgun slug lodged against Girard's heart. After the blood flow had been stanched, drains inserted, and the tissues sutured, Walker explained to his staff that the slug apparently had lost much of its velocity upon hitting the Kevlar flack jacket, then tumbled over the edge of the jacket's left armhole, shattering two ribs, puncturing the pericardium and slamming against the heart itself, stopping its rhythm. Neftali Temu jolting the gurney in the morgue most likely stimulated some residual seed of life buried deep within Girard's body/mind, starting a weak and irregular heartbeat that led to his revival. The freezing Adirondack temperatures had evidently coagulated much of the blood flow, preventing him from bleeding to death, so that Girard had died of shock rather than loss of blood. The killing shotgun slug would normally have remained in the body until the autopsy, but since Girard had showed he wanted to live, Walker smiled, they obliged him by taking it out.

Everyone in the OR smiled at the miracle of life returned. They were cautioned, however, that Girard almost certainly would have suffered permanent brain damage, and likely would be unable to speak after he had awakened from surgery. His physical revival was astounding to all the medical staff.

At 3:00 p.m., after Girard regained consciousness in the SICU recovery room, Walker entered to speak with him. "How are you doing, Dennis Girard? You're something of a sensation. Everyone in the Med Center is talking about the miracle man who came in dead and is now alive." He waited for a response from Girard but got none.

"Channel 13 News has dubbed you 'The Super Trooper.' But you're not out of trouble yet," Walker continued. "There are still serious problems. We patched up your ribs and did a lot of stapling and suturing inside you, but we expect more internal bleeding, so we might have to go in again. We're trying to get your blood to clot a bit, but not too much. Your heartbeat is still irregular, so we've got you on a monitor and are watching that carefully. You're going to be very sore in the days ahead, but I think you're going to make it. What do you remember? Who shot you?" Walker, watched the patient's flickering eyes and probed with his patter to discern the almost certain severe brain damage.

Girard stared vacantly at Walker's mutton-chop whiskers that enveloped a compassionate face. Who *did* shoot him? *Why?* It was all a blank. Nothing in him really cared whether he'd been returned to life or not. For a split second he recalled a brilliant light in some other realm, but that image quickly vanished, leaving him apathetic, though he couldn't understand why. Shouldn't he be as happy as the surgeon? The painkillers held him in a chemical buzz, so he felt no pain or strong emotion of any kind, just lassitude. "Sorry, Doc, I can't remember anything," he mumbled.

"Good, you can speak! Well, do you know your name?"

"Sure, Dennis Girard."

"What do you do for a living?"

Living—now isn't that ironic, Girard reflected. I don't think I have been *living* in any real sense for a long time—I've just been holding on, existing. But for what purpose "I've spent a lot of time doing police work, Doc—chasing bad guys," he pushed the words out. "I'm a washed-up state trooper." He was weary now, and a vague force began to summon Dennis Girard away, as if his essential self had already departed to a distant place, and was now beckoning the remainder of his essence to leave the conversation and to take flight to another abode.

"Well, Dennis Girard, you *will* eventually be able to return to your police work, if that's what you want. You're sure a lucky man—only one in a million ever walks away from a chest wound like this one. Why that slug didn't blow your heart out your back, I'll never know." He paused a minute and fixed his patient with a piercing look. "Someone or *something* was watching over you. I'll be in to see you again this evening. Now, get some rest." Dr. Walker departed from the SICU, noticing that Girard had once more slipped beneath the veil of consciousness.

Twenty minutes later, Nurse Greta Freylinghausen sat at the nursing station desk, monitoring the 12 units assigned to her and checking meds reports. A bank of video screens gave read-outs on the vital signs of a dozen very sick patients. This evening she felt sick to *her* stomach. It was always that way after a fight with Rudy, her sometimes boyfriend. She was glad to get away from her home in Delmar and to pursue the more manageable excitement of the Medical Center. Suddenly she heard the alarm and saw the flashing light of unit #3, patient Dennis Girard—he'd straight-lined. She called a code and the team responded. Dennis Girard had died again.

Violet mists streaked with razor-edged blinding shafts of white light surrounded him, and it was as if he could inhale and taste the color. Wherever he was, it was an electric place, almost like the midway at the Altamont Fair when he was a kid. He drifted silently upward, past formless objects, as the light show persisted around him. For a second, it occurred to him that this display was a welcome home parade, punctuated by fireworks. Sometimes the surroundings took on the appearance of giant silver-gray redwood trees. At other levels they resembled the huge columns he'd once seen in photos of the cathedral at Chartres, France. Gradually the columns morphed into hieroglyphics-adorned pillars he remembered from pictures of an old Egyptian temple. Looking upward, he saw that these columns supported a luminous ceiling, into which he was rapidly ascending. He *knew* that brilliance—he remembered it from somewhere, and knew it had a personality. But *how* did he know this? As he rose through this roof of light, all about him was The Presence. The entire layer of radiance descended to meet him as he ascended and it gently engulfed his being. Whatever body he had was now totally at peace, fully blended with its surroundings, which he remembered with awe and reverence. He *had* come home.

The Presence surged through him as if he no longer had boundaries. He was in It and It was in *him*. "We must resume our dialogue," The Presence informed him. For a moment it was as if a smile appeared on the brightly glowing, formless mist before him. How it communicated with him, he wasn't sure, but a comprehension of Its ideas seemed to resonate in his head and expand his heart. An indescribable, invisible, and compassionate force now held him firmly but gently in an overwhelming sense of belonging, as if he had finally reverted to his true identity. He viewed the bright light from outside, but at the same instant experienced its benevolence from within. "What do you *want* from me? Who are you?" Girard's faltering sense of separateness demanded.

Instantaneously he was flooded by waves of the most powerful passion and peace that he'd ever known. "You've forgotten us so soon? We just *are*," came the response. "You know that. Look!"

Again came the images he'd witnessed just recently—but where? Scenes appeared from throughout the span of his life. He looked upward into the most beautiful pair of brown eyes, which he suddenly recognized as those of his mother, Colleen Girard. He'd just been *born*, he realized, and felt unconditionally loved by this woman. At the same time, he looked down into the eyes of a tiny baby boy, only a few minutes old. He was now his own mother and experienced great joy at delivering a healthy second son. He was in her consciousness, and yet was alive within the baby's utter vulnerability. Still, from a third perspective, he stood apart from the scene, viewing mother and child gazing lovingly into one another's eyes, like the Madonna that he'd seen in church. And it was as if Christmas had returned!

Once again he stood outside the door of Mrs. Thomas' second grade classroom in elementary school, his fist cocked to punch Billy Kirk, his childhood enemy. As he punched, he felt the pain of his knuckles hitting the bone of Billy's cheek, though he felt the impact on *his own* face. He saw the angry, red visage of Billy's assailant and recognized it as his overwrought juvenile self. And he knew he'd get a licking from his dad that night for fighting in school. Another part of him observed the conflict from the hallway ceiling, watching two little boys scrapping, and he sensed the futility and stupidity of it all.

He felt and observed himself winning a cross-country race in high school and, passing the finish line, Dennis felt the exhilaration in his father's chest—he *was* his father! He watched it all from 50 yards away too, a father and son sharing the same glory in an instant.

In the next moment, he crouched in a stinking grove of swamp trees. Nam again, with all its cold terror, waiting for the enemy to rush Bravo Company's position! A small, black-garbed man jumped from the bushes and ran at him, yelling in English. Some kind of trick! He blew the Viet Cong away with his M-15 and scanned for more attackers, just as another dimension of his desperate consciousness broke from cover and ran toward a crouching American soldier who would protect him. He knew he was Vinh Hung from the city of Hué, educated in the U.S. and returned to Vietnam, then captured and impressed into service as an ammunition carrier for the Cong. Hoping for an American rescue, Girard instead felt American bullets riddle this small body as life ended. And above the swamp, Girard's higher vision, soaring as an eagle over-flying the jungle, surveyed the sorrow and emptiness of one human wasting another's life, and the resultant destruction of a part of that soldier's soul.

Then he stood at the door of St. Agnes Roman Catholic Church in Lake Placid, smiling with pride at finding love with his new bride Irene, his "Greek goddess." Well-wishers showered them with rice and cheers. He simultaneously stood in white lace, gazing admiringly at the tall soldier in dress blues whom she'd just married. What devotion that was, he marveled—he'd forgotten all that! And momentarily he stood in a crowd of faceless, formless, rice-throwing people who thrilled at the marriage ceremony just concluded before them. What unity of hearts that all was! He'd forgotten the *joy* of that day.

Then it was gone, replaced by the sensation of his drill instructor, Sgt. Oren Vinson, hovering over him as he did push-ups at The State Police Academy. Simultaneously he felt determined to discipline the cocky, alleged war hero doing one-handed push-ups in front of him. Concurrently, from overhead, he viewed a class of men engaged in vigorous physical activity 30 feet below. Scene after scene flashed through his vision, and he was both doer and doee in all of the imagery. Curiously, he had the capacity to dispassionately stand aside from the action and watch his life happen, as if he were a voyeur, as if it were all a hologram.

Finally the kaleidoscope of color and action faded, blending once more into the bright but not blinding luminosity of The Presence. He was awed by all the energy, activity, and emotion contained in a single life span. All the events of that physical life had been assessed or judged from within himself, and he was paralyzed between shame and joy. Was *this* The Last Judgement? The story of his life all made sense, but something was missing at the end. What was its *purpose?* What was its *goal?*

Now, before him stretched an endless, suffused whiteness, like Irene's minimalist paintings—white on white. Only *this* rendition was truly beautiful, and all the imagery made sense somewhere deep within him. Streaks whiter-than-white pulsated now through the alabaster landscape. Formless light communicated answers to his questions even as he tried to compose them in his mind. "Am I all right?" he questioned. "Am I dead? Is this Heaven?" Lastly, "Am I going to be punished?" He felt so desolate and exposed, as if he had reverted to the susceptibility of infancy. Then he saw—or imagined—a smile forming again in the flow of opalescent energy swirling slowly around him. Lousy as he felt, he instantaneously understood that The Presence not only accepted his flaws, but *treasured* them—he was as a product under development and inspection. "You must return, Dennis. There is still much to do," It intoned solemnly.

"What? *What* do I have to do?" he demanded. No response that he could grasp came forth.

He slipped once more down a lazy stream of cream-colored water flowing between enormous chalky mountains, toward a vast glacial lake of blue-tinted whiteness that soon enveloped him. In the distance he heard someone calling his name. Was it Timmy? No, Timmy couldn't be at this lake; his brother had died at age 11 in 1958, hit by a speeder on Route 7. But indeed, he could now make out the form of his long-dead older brother Timmy, dressed in the cowboy suit they'd buried him in, though this sibling now seemed to be in his *30s*!

"Hi kid!" Timmy offered, extending a hand that Dennis couldn't quite grasp. "They're going to let me work with you," he said with a jovial smile.

"Work? Where? *How,* Timmy?" he shouted, "You're dead! How did you grow up?" Timmy just grinned at him without a word of response. A warm and gentle arm seemed to embrace his back, as Timmy slowly faded. Dennis Girard stood alone at the shore of a vast, powder-blue lake. Then even that certainty faded.

Other voices now called him, and this time he opened his body's heavy-lidded eyes. Many people in white and green stood over him. Nurses? Doctors? One still held the electric paddles that had just shocked him back into the body and physical life. He felt as if he weighed a ton. Everyone was grinning and some had tears running down their cheeks. Dr. Walker beamed. "Thought you'd go traveling on us, huh?" he grinned, and stroked his whiskers with satisfaction. The voices hovered over him for a while longer, but Dennis Girard slowly drifted into a void—a limbo he welcomed, as it numbed the emotional pain of the present and the looming humiliation of a law enforcement career about to end.

CHAPTER SIX

Irene Karamanlis cancelled her classes for the day. It was all really just too much—so much more than any *artist* should have to bear. First, there was Tommy Delehanty's early morning call yesterday, which opened up so many old, bitter feelings that she had thought were safely locked away. Then, knocking at her door at 11:15 a.m. was a NY State Trooper who identified himself as Trooper Bill Cobb—she really hadn't expected *that*. Just as he introduced himself, his cell phone rang and he turned away to take the call, letting snow flurries blow into her freshly waxed foyer, so she had to let him in to close the door. God, how she hated that grey uniform! A minute later, Trooper Cobb smiled at her. "Mrs. Girard, I came over here to notify you of some sad news...."

Irene interjected testily, "I am *not* Mrs. Girard. My name is Assistant Professor Irene Karamanlis, and it's *been* that for quite some time. You'll please address me correctly!" She was winding up for a fight, and she could feel it.

"I'm sorry, Mrs. Karamanlis, I didn't know...."

"And, I'm not *Mrs.* anybody anymore either, get that through your thick head! I am a *Ms.*!" Irene snarled coldly.

Trooper Cobb was unflappable. He began again in a professional monotone, and resumed his notification: "Ms. Karamanlis, Assistant Professor Karamanlis, I was sent to notify you of the death of your former husband, Sr. Investigator Dennis Girard," he smiled, "but the captain just gave us wonderful news. Investigator Girard revived at Albany Medical Center less than an hour ago—he's alive! I know you'll rejoice with the rest of us at that good news. If you'd like, we can keep you informed of his medical progress." A veteran trooper, Cobb smiled broadly at Irene, showing off a new set of brilliant white dentures.

Irene stood in the half-light of a snowy morning, stunned. "Please stand on the mat—you're dripping water and leaving footprints all over my freshly waxed floor," she snapped while trying to collect her thoughts. Here was the state of New York jerking her around *again*—first he's dead, now he's alive! Who *cares?* Now they've sent me this dripping, damned Chessie Cat standing on my doorstep, grinning me to death!

"Okay, Trooper Cobb, thanks for coming over here; consider me notified," she responded with great self-control. "If I want to know anything more about Investigator Girard, I'll call in, okay? Watch your step on the sidewalk outdoors, it looks icy," she said, ushering Cobb toward the door and outside. She swiftly closed and locked the door. Smiling, Cobb walked to his cruiser. God, I so love to jerk divorced women around, he thought, and it's something I'm so *good* at! Every time I get to do it, I can see that witch Miranda's face, he chortled, remembering his second wife.

First he's dead, now he's alive! I never could get any consistency from that rat, Irene fumed when she was alone. Why don't these troopers say what they mean and mean what they say? I bet this Cobb came over here just to upset me. Well, I *can't* get upset; artists *can't* get upset or they lose their muse, she thought, tossing her head of long, silver hair. Walking to the kitchen, she put the teakettle on the stove and sat down to brood. What did all this mean for *her* life? she agonized.

As Irene waited for the teakettle's whistle, she switched on the television and found herself looking at Channel 10 News from Albany. Him! The Girard story dominated the noontime local news. "Girard this" and "Girard that;" "Girard Defies Death—Trooper Restored to Life!" Her stomach knotted and the old feelings of abandonment arose again. She snapped the remote button off in disgust and gazed at the snow falling peacefully outside.

She slowly surveyed the interior of her tastefully decorated room. On a large easel next to the hanging spider plant was a six-square-foot canvas with the faintest aquamarine tint. In the upper right corner of the canvas she had daringly placed a small red dot. Completing this, her latest work, the previous week, Irene expected to enter it in the New England Minimalist Art Show in Boston in April. She had chosen the title *Iceberg Flow* for this work, and was quite proud of it, expecting praise from her mentor, Les Izmore, at the State University in New Paltz. Izmore had brought minimalism back from near-death in 2005 and was now recognized as a genius by some art authorities. An adherent of a Zen sect, he

23

strove to deemphasize form and line, requiring the viewer to draw upon his or her own instincts to find "meaning" in the imagery.

Irene clearly remembered Izmore's words to her during his first critique of her work at New Paltz in 2001, "You aren't painting for the *common* mind, you know. The ordinary person is completely incapable of understanding the cosmic energies that you want to channel." Inwardly, Irene comprehended that her life had become one of drifting in a vast ocean of feelings and that she had grasped at this new man, this piece of inspired driftwood, to sustain her, and restore meaning in her life—reconnecting her to Eternity. This was a union that she felt certain she had enjoyed somewhere ages ago, but one which others had seemingly stolen from her. In Izmore and his principles she again found a purpose greater than herself and, swallowing it all, had assimilated it in order to *use* this overpowering energy. She also vaguely comprehended that even Izmore was not the fullness of Truth, which still continued to evade her.

Assistant Professor Karamanlis believed she had finally discovered her life's work in artistic creation. She imposed rigid guidelines on herself, however, so that she risked as little of her vulnerable soul-self as possible in these works. With each new painting came the difficult decision: What to put on canvas that would gain recognition yet avoid unfavorable criticism? Too much honesty with her inspirations, if she permitted it, might lead to condemnation by the trendsetters, which would be even worse, as it would cause her to feel a rebuke to her very essence. Izmore had found the secret of pleasing the esthetes and had garnered great acclaim. Now *she* must fearfully and carefully tread the road that *he* had paved to gain the praise of the cultural nabobs.

Absentmindedly, while staring at the falling snow, she rearranged the silk flower arrangement on the Ching Dynasty table that she used as a buffet. She hated Chinese furniture and pottery, but had recently learned to affect a love for these because so many of her new, fashionable friends in New York City and Boston were collectors. An introvert by nature, and strongly dependent on others for personal identity, she *needed* friends at this time in her budding career, sincere ones or not. Her students at Bennington College were much easier to finesse than the critics. Most of her freshmen came straight from private high schools, expecting to study at the feet of real artists and, as she made few demands on their imagination, or willingness to take risks, she got along on her title.

Many of these young adults were dull and uninspired, and morning classes were usually filled with students staring vacantly, hung over from late-night drinking binges or bouts with recreational drugs. Her class, The History of Art, was only another mandatory check mark in a long list of "accomplishments" that these students would later use in self-marketing after graduation. Teaching the works of others helped Irene avoid any integration of the disparate ideas in her own life and work. The adventurous masters of the past created the structure of the present and were now idols to be unquestioningly venerated by all. Her freshman students wanted no daring inspiration for the 21st century and got nothing unorthodox from her. She suppressed all thoughts that these students were so like her own fragile self in high school and married life.

The teakettle gave a piercing shriek, severing her train of thought. Dead and then alive! She weighed the alternatives: if that jerk had *stayed* dead, she'd finally be able to let go of the guilt about her marriage. But now alive, she knew that she would continue to be irritated by his increased publicity. She had always hated that her husband was in the news, occasionally seen in crime scene interviews or at vehicle accident scenes on television news. Each mention, each picture of her former husband served only to remind her of how little she'd made of *herself.* And she already felt like such a failure—the daughter of Leonidas Karamanlis, Adirondack furniture tycoon.

The family patriarch, Leonidas Karamanlis, had arrived in America from Greece in 1946 with just $3 in his pocket. He began work as a furniture salesman in Glens Falls and learned the English language quickly. Within five years he owned a small furniture store in Tupper Lake, and in the 1960s had purchased three more small furniture stores to create an Adirondack mini-empire.

Leo, as his friends called him, believed that success was the result of backbone and hard work, not emotions, and he died bitterly disappointed in his two daughters, Irene and Jean, who were much more sensitive and less aggressive than he. Leonidas had tried shame, ridicule, and sarcasm to push his daughters into achievement, but those tactics had created just the opposite result, Irene decided. It made me afraid to fail in any way, and Jeannie avoided success of any kind. Her sister had never married, though Irene felt that she, herself, might achieve a safe, secure life with a war hero to provide for her, and so took the risk of marriage. No, neither girl had ever dared to risk much. Not much, she seethed, until *she* got rid of that crazy workaholic husband—just like her father—work, work, work!

Irene remembered Dennis calling her his "Greek goddess," and idolizing her beauty during their courting years. He never did see that I'm no goddess—I'm made of straw! But that bum finally *made* me strong, and I got mad enough and strong enough to tell him to go to hell! And now I'm on my way, if I'm careful and don't make mistakes.

For just a minute the idea of Izmore being another father figure flashed through her head, but she immediately stifled the thought. Irene flipped the television on to the Home & Garden Network and watched a San Francisco woman cultivating bonsai trees, offering terminology and ideas that would come in handy on her next trip to New York City. She took notes.

CHAPTER SEVEN

When Girard awoke again it was dark, and against the translucent curtain he saw the silhouette of a morphine drip easing his pain. Extremely weak and unsure at any given moment whether he was asleep or dreaming, Girard strained to remember where he was, cautiously scanning the space around his bed. In the hospital, he reckoned. The SICU room was quiet except for the faint hum of the machines that monitored his life energy, as if all other sounds in the universe had ceased. The faint late-night illumination showed his cubicle to be shrouded in shadows and darkness, lit only by the red and green fluorescent lights of the monitors. All at once, he had a foreboding of something ominous about to pull his stomach out of his body. Although Girard couldn't hear it, he could *feel* it—just as he used to sense when the Cong were readying a sneak attack.

There—he spotted it! In the dark shadows of the farthest corner—someone or something. It looked like a giant man whose head touched the ceiling—what would that be—eight feet? Nine? Ten feet? His listlessness vanished and he immediately went on guard. And what's on this giant's back—some kind of apparatus? Girard tried to force his inner state to return to the sharp analysis he once could summon so easily, but the effort failed. Despite a surge of adrenalin pumping through his veins, Girard's arms and hands, encumbered by surgical tape and drip lines, were almost immobile, yet they trembled of their own will. Through the thin fabric of the apparition's dark cloak there was a faint silvery gleam, as if the fabric covered a metallic garment. The figure moved slightly.

"Jesus Christ—who are *you?*" Girard panicked, "You sure scared *me!*" No answer—the looming figure didn't move or respond. Girard's heart was racing now and, despite the oxygen tube, he felt he was suffocating. Nurse Emily appeared, "What's going *on* here? You hurting, honey? Your readings are going crazy out at the desk." He nodded an assent and closed his eyes tightly, trying to blot out the terrifying figure in the corner. Unable to do more than mumble to the nurse, he tried raising his hand to point out the intruder, but could not. He hoped desperately that this was all a nightmare. Emily's body obscured the figure in the corner for a moment as she adjusted his oxygen, checked his blood pressure and drip lines, and then, watching the readings return to near normal, left the cubicle.

The ghoul was still there. Quietly, then more sensed than heard, came the intense words, "How easily the Name of The Anointed One rolls off your tongue. Such a vulgar insult to the One who sinned not!" Girard, jolted into a dialogue he couldn't escape, suddenly felt ashamed, but couldn't fathom why. I'm in some deep shit now, he concluded.

"Who *are* you? Some Quasimodo night janitor? Are you on the staff here?" Girard demanded in alarm, fumbling to find his nurse call button and to draw himself into full consciousness.

"You might say instead that I am on *The* Staff, and obedient to it. It is the staff that gathers in *all* the sheep," came the hushed reply. The intruder's eyes seemed to glow red in the shadows. Then, for a moment, Girard thought he saw a benign smile cross the shadowy, fierce face of the figure, though he could make no sense of the words that had just been spoken.

"What do you *want?*"

"It is time we met openly, Dennis. I have been working with you for a long time, though you haven't cared to notice me. You enforce *your* law and I enforce a Greater Law, a path you've been trying to evade for a long time, only to suffer for it."

"Did the superintendent send you here? What for? To prove I'm crazy and push me out the door? Are you some Division bogeyman or shrink?"

"Dennis, I was assigned to you at birth. You may think of me as a guard or guide." With that, the figure turned slightly and Girard beheld gigantic wings folded behind its back.

"Goddam! Now I *know* I'm done if I'm seeing angels!" He kept unsuccessfully trying to sit up. "Must be that morphine! Or else I'm *really* dead for good. Damn! Damn! *Damn!*"

"Where there is life, love, and will, *nobody* is damned!" the figure retorted. "When you were a child at St. Gabriel's Church in Rotterdam, don't you remember your religious instruction that all souls are granted a guardian angel when they put on flesh? Don't you remember seeing a bright light behind the altar one day when you were serving as altar boy at the 7:00 a.m. mass? *Your thoughts were moving energy,* drawing my essence from the light plane, and I tried to encourage you to *think* about the words you were mumbling in response to the priest. You were so often half asleep at that time of day, and I tried to rouse you to understand what your activity was really about."

Girard did in fact remember the incident, but had rationalized that he'd gotten something in his eye that morning in 6th Grade, and the light had vanished after he'd rubbed his eyes. "What *are* you—nuts? You expect me to believe in *angels?* I'm an adult now. I've been a soldier—a state trooper. If you were there guarding me or guiding me, then why did you let me *die?* Twice!" he demanded in disgust. "Why weren't you with me in Nam? Why didn't you give me help to keep my marriage going? I'd say you're doing a damn lousy job."

The angel now glowered at him, with fierce eyes, which seemed to become electric, and Girard suddenly felt a dread so deep that he feared for his newly restored life. "You have been almost dead *spiritually* for a long time, Dennis Girard!" The angel's eyes bored deeply into his soul. "You have ignored most of the many opportunities and teachers sent to you. You've been living on the doorstep of a personal hell. This must not continue, as there is now *much* expected of you, not only for your own good, but for that of your nation.

"Nevertheless, The Creator has given you the choice of responding to these opportunities or not. Your life is really not about *your* personal comfort, but rather involves the resolution of a profound, ages-old problem facing humankind." The voice now seemed to thunder, shaking the walls and curtains around him. "Your gift of life in the flesh again is truly about *justice,* but not in the narrow form into which you have constricted that word. When you are ready, we *will* meet again."

With those words—or rather thought impressions—the apparition dissolved, leaving Girard drained and speechless.

"What's up honey, you hurting again? I think Albany might have just had a little earthquake, because my desk was shaking." Nurse Emily stood chattering beside him, checking his drains. "I heard you talking—were you dreaming?" She checked her watch because she had just notated being with him two minutes before. Emily moved to check his infusion lines and to readjust a bandage, then took his right hand in hers. "Dreaming again?"

"Yeah, that's for sure," Girard responded reluctantly. "I've *really* been dreaming!"

After Emily left, the quiet humming of his unit lulled him back to sleep, and this time he had vivid dreams of swimming through snake-infested waters toward a distant shore. Throughout the remainder of the night his dreams were interrupted by flashes of lightning from somewhere in the far reaches of his unconscious mind.

CHAPTER EIGHT

He slept throughout the next day, and on the third morning Girard awoke much more aware of his surroundings. He heard Nurse Greta conversing quietly with the resident outside the door, and the words that he could discern involved the miraculous survival of the man who had died twice in 24 hours. Nurse Greta opined that Girard's brain had suffered irreparable damage in the almost three hours of clinical death. "The night nurse said this guy was arguing with himself all night and, despite his wound and pain medication, he was constantly tensing muscles and clenching his fists. His eyes exhibited the rapid eye movements we observe in dreaming patients—seems like he dreamed all night long." The resident murmured something about watchfulness and left. For a moment there was quiet, then he overheard Greta in brief conversation with a familiar male voice. Quietly, the smiling, friendly face of Investigator Tommy Delehanty popped into his cubicle.

"Hey Den! Man, am I glad to see *you*...awake!" For a moment he choked up, then, "I've been in here every day since you started this vacation, lad, but you were always zonked out!" *Lad* was a calming term of support they'd copied from an old British movie, and used with one another when trying not to lose self-control or panic during combat in Vietnam. It meant, 'Stiff upper lip, it's all going to be okay.' Delehanty's eyes filled with tears, despite his resolve not to get emotional. "All the guys back at troop headquarters were sending their uniforms out for dry cleaning just so they could look spiffy at your funeral," he joked, pushing away the gravity of the situation.

"You won't *believe* the stories they're telling about you outside. There are reporters all over the place! The *Times-Union* did a front-page feature story on you this morning, called "The Thin Grey Line," about troopers who have been injured or died in the line of duty. The superintendent's office is swamped with PR requests. A hospital spokesman is downstairs talking to Channel 6 right now—you know, about how unbelievable your survival is. Your story was on all the networks last night. It's created a tremendous interest in the State Police from all over the country. People are realizing that we're an undermanned and underappreciated army. I just saw a science reporter from BBC talking to a reporter from Canadian Broadcasting downstairs. And there's just one subject—*you*! There are almost no records anywhere in the world for a guy being dead for three hours, even *if* you were frozen stiff, and coming back without becoming a vegetable," said Tommy in his usual tactless style. "The publicity about this case has spread so far that even Governor Pratie lauded your devotion to duty in a press release this morning, and you know how little praise he gives to *anybody* except his fat cat campaign contributors."

Throughout his adult life, Delehanty had been Girard's link with order and sanity and, with Tommy's appearance now, he was jolted back to full awareness of the crisis he was in. Girard remembered now that he'd been shot after recklessly going on stakeout alone and badly underestimating Charbonneau's desperation. This final bit of bad judgment was sure to get him canned by the superintendent, and old fears began to overwhelm him.

He'd met Delehanty, a live-wire downstater from Westchester County, at Syracuse University. Lovers of nature's beauty, he and Tommy had become inseparable chums, eschewing the fraternity scene for the Cycling Club, skiing, and other outdoor activities, as if some "greater truth" could be found in nature. Delehanty, from a wealthy suburban family, was trying to escape the sorrows of an alcoholic upbringing, and Girard was attempting to flee his father's rigidity.

As the Vietnam conflict escalated, both idealistic men feared for the future of America, and after their sophomore year both enlisted and were sent to intense infantry training at Ft. Benning in Georgia. Before Christmas, both were assigned to the 101st Airborne Division in Vietnam at Camp Eagle near Hué. Within a month, Girard was promoted to Corporal in Bravo Company, 3rd Battalion, which had taken heavy casualties. Immediately, the unit was involved in fire fights along Highway 1, operations that took many lives. It had all happened so fast. Bravo Company took heavy losses again in early 1969, and Girard was promoted to Sergeant in September. "Getting ahead" was Girard's watchword, and every obstacle to success in what he thought then might become a full military career dissolved under his energetic touch. He worked with Delehanty, just promoted to Corporal, and together, they whipped Bravo Company into a first-rate bunch of buddies, and not just fellow soldiers.

It had all been a roller-coaster ride of thrills and horror and, upon their discharge in 1974, each having served a minimum tour of duty and having suffered serious wounds, both men were separated from the Army. Disillusioned with the hideousness of war and the duplicity of national politics, each hoped to find some durable, personal meaning in the upstate places they both knew and loved from their college days. Seeming chance led them to a New York State Police recruiter in Albany, and the result was a lifelong profession for them both, after they proved they could pass the background checks and tough physical exam, which only 1 out of 12 applicants can do.

From Syracuse through Vietnam, through his early years in Troop G, then through a failed marriage, Tommy had been his unwavering comrade. Delehanty had been through a divorce of his own, and experienced troubles with the church because of it. Later, Tommy voluntarily transferred to Troop B, tired of the routines he'd fallen into in the Albany area. Having a friend in the northern New York State troop provided Girard an incentive to likewise ask for a transfer to Troop B after his own divorce. The two men understood much of each other's suffering.

"What's happening up north? Has anyone seen Charbonneau?" Girard asked Tommy.

"No, he seems to have vanished without a trace—him and his pickup," replied Delehanty. "Capt. Telfer has a team going over Charbonneau's place with a fine-toothed comb, and they already confiscated about 10,000 cartons of cigarettes. Everyone thinks he's gone to ground up at Akwesasne or some other Mohawk lands in Canada, and our relations with those Mohawk tribal leaders aren't that good right now. So, if he's in there, nobody is going to give him up. And it'll be too easy for him to slip across the St. Lawrence River into the Canadian parts of the reservation. Nevertheless, the Quebec provincial police have patrols out watching the ice for river crossers. Maybe they'll get lucky.

"Homeland Security has detailed another three men to the Hogansburg area on the Reservation to keep an eye on the local hangouts and to watch the Ontario shore and the woods along the Quebec part of the border, along with the ICE patrols, just in case. But we think the Feds did that reinforcement because of some *other* hush-hush investigation that they won't share with us. They wanted to know if Charbonneau is involved in something bigger, but we told them he's just a small-time operator. You and I know what a jagged shore that border is, and if Two Claw wants to cross into Canada he'll probably do it. Anyway, all he's got to do is walk into the woods on snowshoes to cross into Quebec, now that it's winter. With all this snow and ice, he'll probably be able to avoid all those new sensors the Feds installed. We're hoping the Mounted Police or the *Sûreté* can intercept him.

"They told me I can only take a few minutes with you today, so take care of yourself, lad. I've got things to attend to, so I'll be in tomorrow." And Tommy left.

CHAPTER NINE

After Tommy left the SICU, Dennis Girard reflected on his life. He was born on December 9, 1949 in Cohoes, NY, the son of an Irish mother and a French-Canadian father. Both parents were immigrants and imparted their sense of life's urgency to their sons. "Making good" was a priority in the family. Henri Girard was a welder by trade and, upon his return from combat with the 100th Division in Germany in 1945, found a job at the Harmony Mills textile plant in Cohoes. Later, the family moved to the Rotterdam section of Schenectady, where Henri worked in the steam plant at General Electric. Dennis received his grade school and junior high school education there, but in 1966 the family moved north to Corinth, on the Hudson River, where Colleen worked at the Cluett-Peabody shirt factory and Henri worked as a welder at the Hudson River Mill of International Paper Company. Although Dennis knew his parents to be hard-working, strive as they might, they never got ahead because they had a too-narrow outlook about life, he judged. And that embarrassed and repelled him.

In his high school years the young man often biked alone into the West Mountain area, especially around Hunt Lake, where he could be at one with nature. "Getting somewhere" was his youthful ideal, and that meant travel. He became a standout on Corinth Central School's cross-country team and established some New York State scholastic track records that still stood. He began to discover that the world was much larger and more complex than many of his village friends seemed to understand, and his desire for greater knowledge and personal expansion were fostered by several inspiring teachers. Marion Armstrong taught him respect for the history and literature of past civilizations, and Tom Perlmutter expanded his consciousness in English, especially in American literature. Howard Homan had stimulated his strong love for the mysteries of the natural world. Girard's desire to enjoy nature and yet know more of faraway places became overpowering and, upon graduation, he chose the School of Forestry at Syracuse University, hoping for a career as an environmental conservation officer or perhaps a timberlands manager for International Paper's vast Adirondack holdings. Back then, he was proud to be called a "stumpie," a tree-saver.

Funny how things work out, he reflected as he awoke the next day. So many times a person starts down one road and soon finds himself on another, but exactly where the switch-over took place, is hard to say.

Tommy was true to his word, and right after his new doctor, Dr. Kristopher, finished his morning examination, Tommy reappeared. "Hi Tommy! How do I look?"

"Piss poor, Den. Looks like you went on one of Dick Gregory's weight loss programs. How do you feel?"

"Some pain, but my head is still foggy. You *did* tell me that it was Charbonneau who shot me?"

"Yeah, Den. He was gone when I got to the farm, but he had dropped his shotgun and the crime lab says we've got his prints all over it. There are APBs out on him in the U.S. and Canada, but so far, nothing. He and his pickup seem to have vanished without a trace. Capt. Telfer has a team still going over the rest of Charbonneau's property right now. As of today, we've confiscated almost 14,000 cartons of cigarettes, and after dusting and printing the barn, they found his prints on the merchandise and everywhere in the farmhouse too. So we know it was his base, but we've found many other prints that don't show up in any database in the U.S. We're stumped on those. There were lots of documents in French in the house and we're getting those translated now. There was even a book of Persian poetry written in Farsi, but we don't know how that fits in. Without the profits from this cigarette stash, I don't see how Two Claw can survive."

"Sure, Tommy, he's gotta be near broke after losing that inventory, and nobody is going to front him more purchase money now. If the Border Patrol and ICE patrols are beefed up outside Akwesasne, and the Quebec

Provincial Police, the *Sûreté*, do their thing, maybe someone will get lucky. Girard tried to shift onto his elbow and felt a horrendous stab of pain beneath his left arm, and fell back onto his pillow.

"I don't know whether or not *I* was lucky to come back from this one, Tommy. I've had some very weird visions and experiences since I woke up, and I wonder if I've lost it."

"Sure, that's to be expected with the pain killers they're pumping into you, lad. Remember when I got that back wound just before we left Nam?" Tommy queried, "Boy, that Demerol had me singing to myself for a week…and you're on morphine! Of course you're going to be in la-la land for a while, but everyone says you're going to recover to almost the same as you were."

Girard was silent for a minute before he spoke again. "Tommy, I hope that's not true. I was in bad shape even before getting shot, and you know it. Funny thing though, I haven't had even the *slightest* desire for a smoke since I've been awake. You know me—been a two-pack-a-day man for years. Even stranger, somebody outside my door was playing classical music earlier this morning, I think. And I was actually *enjoying* that sound! Go figure."

"Well keep your mouth shut about any Twilight Zone stuff if you expect to come back to work. They won't let a man they think is nuts back on the job and you know that. It's a quarter to 10 now, Den, and I wanted you to know there'll be some brass coming over from Division Headquarters at 10:00. Outside, they told me the Superintendent himself was on the phone with your surgeon right after they sewed you up, so they sure have kept an eye on you, lad. Get yourself ready. I don't know if they'll read you the riot act and hand in your papers for you, or whether they'll pin a medal on your chest. But it's to your advantage that the publicity about this case has spread so far that even Governor Pratie had to laud your devotion to duty, *again* yesterday. After all, you're chasing the tax cheats! The two looked at one another and grinned. "Well, take care of yourself, lad, I'll be in bright and early tomorrow," Tommy added and left.

CHAPTER TEN

Superintendent of State Police Oliver Hazard Perry Simcoe walked quickly from his car at the far end of the Albany Medical Center parking lot, where he hoped to arrive, transact his business, and then leave anonymously. He scanned the path ahead and was relieved that there was no media lurking around the side door today. Usually he'd have delegated this task, or have had an aide with him if he was to do it in person, but he wanted today's meeting with Girard to be without witnesses. As he entered D Building, he surveyed where *his own* career had gone since his days at Annapolis. A graduate of the Class of 1952 at the U.S. Naval Academy, he had had come to love surface ships, especially carriers.

A native of Edgartown, MA, on Martha's Vineyard, O.H.P. Simcoe came from a long family naval tradition. His brightness and eagerness eventually took him to Capt. John Iarrobino's ship, *USS Oriskany*, when it deployed to the Tonkin Gulf in 1966. As a Damage Control Assistant Officer on Yankee Station, he had gained recognition for efficiency and bravery and received the Navy Cross for his heroic rescue efforts below decks during a tragic fire in October that year, which took many sailors' lives. At great personal risk he had gone repeatedly into the flames of a bomb storage bay with a hand fire extinguisher and pulled out several badly burned men, while his comrades dumped bombs overboard. The experience of losing 44 valued men had seared his memory for life.

Continuing with surface ships, he eventually deployed with the 7th Fleet in the Pacific with the rank of Lieutenant Commander on the intelligence ship *Stony Point,* picking up a fluency in both Japanese and Chinese during long cruises through the Taiwan Strait. Then came a painful deployment aboard the *Fallen Timbers,* another intelligence-intercept ship, in support of the U.S. Marines in the Multinational Expeditionary Force sent to Lebanon in early 1983. More than 200 Marines died that October when a terrorist explosion destroyed their Beirut barracks, and Simcoe often berated himself for not having been able to get or decipher the single intelligence intercept that *might* have foiled the assassins. He'd developed a special hatred for terrorists since then.

Returning to the U.S. later that year, he requested transfer to The Presidio Language School where he studied Arabic, a language whose value to a naval officer many of his superiors questioned at that time. In

35

1985 he continued graduate study and served as intelligence instructor at the Naval War College in Newport, RI. Then, in 1994, Simcoe retired with the rank of Vice Admiral, anxious for a life in which he could still command men, but see fewer of them die in action.

For a few years he held an executive job at IBM in Poughkeepsie, but found himself longing for action. His expertise in organization and chain of command, as well as a reputation for "having ears," led to his appointment as Superintendent of New York State Police by Gov. George Pataki in 2005, even though he was well past the normal retirement age and required a special legislative waiver to be hired. He'd run a taut ship since then and was known as a no-nonsense leader. Few of his associates had ever seen him smile, and some lower ranks referred to him as "Old Iron Bottom," his Navy nickname.

Now, he strode quickly toward the hospital elevators, struggling with mixed emotions. A few days ago he thought he'd lost *another* man, a subordinate who years before had been a valuable investigator, though Girard hadn't shown much in recent years. That agony of loss was at first mitigated with the relief that Girard's murder had saved Simcoe from having to force the investigator's retirement. Now the man was *alive*—alive and making international headlines. Simcoe had even had to field inquiries about Girard's health from friends in Scotland Yard! So how was he going to finesse Sr. Investigator Girard now? And in what direction? Retirement? Reinstatement? He just didn't know.

The elevator sped upward and Simcoe soon stood beside Girard's bed. The patient was dozing but awoke quickly, as if inwardly warned that he wasn't alone. "How are you, Girard?" Simcoe tried to make his question sound as impersonal as possible.

"I'm okay Superintendent; they say I'm going to recover fully, but I'm sure being rocked by the medication right now. It leaves me feeling goofy a lot of the time."

Briefly, Simcoe's heart opened wide. Here was the earnestness that he'd first found among *Oriskany's* young airmen and crew. Here was a fallen comrade and not a screwed-up investigator. "Girard, anything you need...*anything,* you have your doctor let me know. We're going to get you back and in good shape!" Then, worried that he had been too effusive, Simcoe paused briefly to regain his composure and said, "When you're...*ready*...to come back to duty, of course, there will have to be physical examinations and your doctors will have to sign off that you're ready for full duty status. Picking his words deliberately, the superintendent added, "And Girard, it wouldn't hurt to get a psychiatric evaluation. You've been through an unbelievable experience and we want you 'balanced' when you get back." He intentionally emphasized the word *balanced*. "If you want out of Troop B we can fix that too," Simcoe concluded with a forced smile, while massaging the brim of his Tyrol dress hat.

"Thank you, Superintendent," Girard heard himself responding, as his mind suddenly saw the new forces arrayed against his continuing as an investigator. He'd been verbally escorted to the firing squad wall, and the Superintendent had done it personally, without delegating it to underlings. In spite of himself, Girard smiled at Simcoe's integrity.

"It's nothing." The Superintendent drew himself up stiffly, as if to justify both his vulnerability and power. "It's what I have done my whole life for *all* those under my command, Girard. Well, I had to see you, and see what your intentions were. As you get closer to discharge, give a call to my deputy, Lenny Mueller. He'll keep me informed." With that remark, Simcoe was swiftly through the curtain and out the door. The hall outside Girard's room returned to absolute quiet.

The entire dialogue had taken just six minutes. Descending in the elevator, Simcoe ruminated that those six minutes had seemed six hours long. As he walked rapidly to his car, his inner turmoil began again. What to *do* with this man?

CHAPTER ELEVEN

When Nurse Greta came back on duty at 7:00 a.m. the next day, Girard noticed a red welt on her left cheek. She'd tried to cover it over with pancake makeup, but hadn't succeeded very well.

"Hey, what happened to you?" he inquired. "Someone push you down the stairs?" Greta looked wide-eyed at Girard. The look said, "How did you *know*?" and "I'm so ashamed," but her lips mumbled something about slipping on a carpet.

"You okay, though, Nurse?" asked Girard.

"Sure," she responded. "There are some things in life you just get used to. I'm just clumsy, that's all." Maybe it was the painkillers, but on some internal screen that he'd never known before, Girard suddenly "saw" a taller man viciously slamming a fist into her face. She likely

37

wouldn't corroborate it, he knew, so he didn't debate the matter with her.

It was relatively easy to slip once more into a restful haze, part awake and part asleep. Nurses and doctors came and went, but he dozed. Later, he was awakened for dinner—Swiss steak, mashed potatoes, and pumpkin pie—and he found his appetite strangely ravenous. He slept all night and remembered no dreams in the morning. Maybe my nightmares are over, he thought. No dreams is good dreams.

After breakfast the next morning he met Denise Bills, who introduced herself as his physiotherapist. "You know, Mr. Girard, you can't favor that left arm too long. You're healing real well, and when the last drain is taken out and they've closed you all up, we're going to get you going on gentle movement exercises. We've got to work on restoring your lung capacity too, so get ready to start walking. We've got a great big toy here called a UBE Arm Bike that you're going to *love*."

Great! thought Girard, here I'm enjoying this pleasant buzz every day—my morphine haze where nobody can really reach me, and now they're going to cut me off. I just *knew* it! He wasn't sure he was ready to emerge from his cocoon of not thinking or feeling much. Also, he didn't want to face the certainty that he had a strong addictive streak deep within. He remembered the occasional case of drug use in Bravo Company, and how he'd condemned those men as derelict in their duty. Now, here *he* was about to become a junkie, if a medically prescribed one—ironic!

The morphine drip ended that night, but in the morning a small infection was discovered, requiring two boring weeks of antibiotics to subdue it. The nurses put him on a regimen of blowing into large plastic bottles in order to restore his lung capacity. The first week, he thought the strain of pushing would pop all his stitches, and the pain of exertion was almost unbearable. Only Tommy's sporadic visits brightened the routines during that time. Several "Get Well" cards came from folks he knew well in Troop B, but not too many from the guys at headquarters. Wonder why? He pondered the matter.

Then, true to her word, and after Dr. Kristopher removed his last drain and did the final patch-up, Denise was there, radiant and chirpy. "Okay, here, let's go for a walkie," she said, and slid him into a sitting position. I could get to hate this girl and her cheeriness real quick, he decided. Girard was surprised at the lethargy that overwhelmed him, almost as a resistance to involvement in the world again. A moment later, his feet hit the floor and some foam hospital slippers, and it occurred to him that this would be the first time he'd stood in three weeks. Weren't the memories and dreams of flying more attractive? Walking was so much *work*! Dizziness and weakness were his companions throughout that first stroll.

Throughout that week and the next, there were two daily walkies on the arm of his beautiful physiotherapist, also, x-rays, a painful left arm, shoulder, and upper body therapy exercises, including work on the UBE Arm Bike machine. Sitting into that exercise apparatus and taking the first few turns on its handles caused him to feel that his left side would immediately fall off. The exercise left him winded very quickly and he was additionally tortured by blowing into those damned plastic bottles to strengthen his lungs.

Girard was continually reminded of a hamster running in an exercise wheel every time Denise had him exercising. Before the end of the fourth day, however, his weakness and dizziness passed, though his left rib cage hurt terribly. His entire body and mind felt stretched to the breaking point. Despite the soreness, however, Girard began to feel stronger after one week and more confident by the end of the second. Maybe I won't have to spend the rest of my life flat on my back, he speculated wryly.

They moved him out of the SICU and into a regular room and gave him a roommate. As Girard quickly noted, however, this roommate wasn't long for the world, as nothing more could be done for him except to provide oxygen. Family constantly visited the other man's curtained bed and came away weeping. Stuart Knopka, a volunteer fireman from the town of Schodack, had a brick wall fall on him while fighting a fire. His chest had been crushed, Girard learned, and the man had almost no respiration without the oxygen. The investigator felt sorry for the firefighter, a fellow public servant, and Girard found himself praying that God would take this patient from his suffering existence.

About midnight, Girard was roused from a sound sleep by faint tinkling sounds, as if from thousands of glass chimes being struck with tiny pins. He couldn't locate the source, and scanned the dimness of his room, finally glancing toward his roommate's half-curtained bed. Vapor seemed to rise from the man's body, coalescing into a vague, horizontal human shape in the air above the bed. Somewhere in the hall outside, he could hear an alarm, and the nurse entered quickly, hurrying to Knopka's bed and placing her stethoscope on the fireman's chest. Mechanically, she looked at her watch, then turned off all the monitoring devices and ventilator, and partially pulled the divider curtain between the beds.

Through the narrow curtain opening Girard watched the nurse pull the sheet over the fireman's face and leave the room. He continued to watch the transparent material shimmer in the air—hadn't the nurse *seen* it? Microscopic meteors of light darted like shooting stars through the gossamer mass above the corpse. For almost five minutes more, until a doctor entered with the nurse to pronounce the man dead, the miniature pyrotechnics continued. Gradually, the vapor rose to the ceiling and dissipated while the tiny lights faded. Girard was unable to comprehend what he'd seen. It had been more than two weeks since his last unnerving experience—had something new broken inside his head? Was this experience some morphine flashback? Was he crazy now? What *could* that have been in the air? For a split second, a voice within him insisted, "His life energy—his soul!" Girard fought to silence that voice, refusing to listen to such rubbish, wherever it came from, and the inner prompting finally ceased. Sounds like more of Sister Concordia's nonsense, he sputtered mentally.

Dennis Girard slipped once more into sleep, but not a peaceful sleep. His unconscious mind was racked by a frightening dream. In the drama he was driving a large black car, vaguely like his father's old Buick Roadmaster. Everything in and on it was black and he was driving happily when, suddenly there came a flash from the left. A gigantic, brilliant white Porsche slammed into his car and black blood began spurting everywhere. He could feel his life ebbing and began screaming for help. Then the night nurse was there comforting him, and he realized he was still alive, soaked in sweat, but alive. He soothed himself with the suspicion that his medications were somehow to blame—again. Either it was the drugs or he was going nuts.

On Thursday that week he received a surprise Get Well card from his youngest boy, Patrick. Inscribed were the words, "Dear Dad, Glad the bad guys didn't get you. Love from us all, Pat." It meant the world to him, to know that one of his estranged adult children could see him as another suffering human being, instead of a patriarch, and could muster compassion for him. I'll have to follow up on this and give Pat a call when I get out of here, he promised himself. At least I have *one* kid able to open his heart, he rejoiced, and Pat has troubles enough in his marriage. Maybe it's a good omen, he continued, maybe I'll hear from my other two kids. But Clara and Joey, absorbed in their own lives, remained silent, alienated from their father and, supporting their mother's neediness, incapable of acknowledging their father's brush with death. Scanning the wall calendar in his room, Girard noted that more than a month had elapsed since his shooting and March had pretty much been a painful blur. He wryly recognized that Pat's card had come on April 1—April Fool's Day. I hope there's something to be said for fools, he reflected, because I've sure *become* one.

His physical therapy had succeeded well enough that he now didn't need further therapy except daily walking and upper body exercise. For the latter, he walked to the PT unit, where he began daily physical workouts. He was also sent to the mental health unit for examination, which seemed simple enough. He had fun playing with the doctors' heads during the Inkblot Test, then finally informed the psychologist that he was joking about seeing a UFO attack in the shapes. Simple tests were administered over several days and the psychiatrists seemed pleased with his physical and mental coordination. They also appeared content with his responses to the talk therapy, though Girard didn't volunteer any information about his visions, dreams, or reveries.

Dr. Kristopher praised him for the spectacular recovery that had taken place in half the time originally estimated. Dennis Girard sensed he was nearing release, and was increasingly nervous about being evicted from his comfortable foxhole. An avalanche of responsibilities would descend upon him soon, and he wasn't sure he could handle them. Glumly, he sat on the bed and dialed his bedside phone, making a call to Lt. Mueller's office, notifying the Deputy Superintendent that he was almost finished with his recuperation at Albany Medical Center Hospital.

Release day came on April 16th, and Girard said goodbye to his nurses and doctors. He'd gained a new and deep respect for those in all aspects of the healing profession while at Albany Med, people he'd pretty much taken for granted in previous years. Asking the nursing staff to distribute the few bouquets that had accumulated in his room to patients without friends or family, he took his pile of cards, many from North Country well-wishers in Troops B and G. He had already arranged to stay for a week with an old Troop G friend, Eugene Sprague, who now worked in the Albany Crime Lab, in order to reassure himself of his own physical, mental, and emotional soundness. It did occur to him, however, that this week in Albany might be a subconscious excuse to prolong his avoidance of the inevitable.

During that time Lt. Mueller provided him a list of psychotherapists approved for the State Police medical insurance program. Although there was nothing in writing, Girard knew that his eventual return to full-duty status depended heavily on the reports of a physician *and* a psychologist.

On one hand he resented the additional layer of bureaucratic snooping now hovering over his head. On the other hand he was relieved, hoping a shrink could help him understand all his visions and other aberrant experiences since the shooting.

On several days during his stay with Sprague, he went with Eugene to visit the crime lab as a way of returning his consciousness to the tasks of analysis and investigation. On two occasions, while watching a technician work with blood samples, he "knew" what the samples would reveal. In another instance he "saw" the man whose semen had been found in a raped murder victim. Girard couldn't understand these intuitions and felt compelled to remain silent. Eugene offered to drive him home at the end of the week, but Girard rented a car instead, deciding to take his time returning to the apartment in Chestertown.

CHAPTER TWELVE

He traveled up I-87, the "Adirondack Northway, to Exit 12 in Malta, had coffee and a blueberry muffin at a small diner there, and later passed his old state police haunt at the Malta barracks, but didn't stop in. They were all young guys in there now, and he felt nothing in common with them.

Swinging north on Route 9N in Saratoga Springs, he then traveled through his old hometown of Corinth and drove on some familiar streets, seeing the old high school for the first time in more than 30 years. So much that he remembered had changed or gone. The shirt factory had closed long ago. Even International Paper, the village's mainstay industry for over a century, had pulled out, leaving no major employer. He thought he saw despair and defeat in the faces of many young people on the streets. Too bad they couldn't have grown up here when *I* did, he mused; there was so much to do and so much hope for the future back then. He continued north to the Route 28 turnoff north of Warrensburg, eagerly anticipating his next stop—Lucy's.

Driving with his car window open, he enjoyed the fragrant smell of the Adirondack pines that drifted through the car's interior. Pine trees had always filled him with a sense of renewal, as if he could draw on their electric energy, which seemed to be a pale blue in his mind. He didn't miss the medicinal smells of the hospital and the stench of Albany's commuter traffic. Traveling up Route 28 to North Creek, it seemed as if there was a shimmer on the needles of the pine trees as he passed. Must be the sun's angle causing that, he decided. North Creek was off the direct path home to Chestertown, but he liked to eat lunch at Lucy's whenever he could. The regulars there were like distant relatives who knew one another by name.

It was no surprise, then, that he was greeted by an ovation from the regulars as soon as he entered. Everyone had seen television news coverage of his story and many had sent cards. There were a lot of pats on the back and comments such as, "Can't keep a good man down!" and "You're the *man*, Inspector!" as they called him, though the State Police had no such rank. Everyone knew him as Dennis, but none ever addressed him informally, always calling him "Inspector." At one time several years before, he'd wondered if they were teasing him with memories of Inspector Clouseau, Peter Sellers' comedic film detective; but he had since dismissed the thought. Most of the regulars had memories of cases he'd cracked, favors he'd done, and bad guys he'd hauled away during his years in Troops G and B.

Roy Guzik, Emmett Pierce and Stan Rogers all waved and gave big smiles from the counter stools. He had everyone's affection and admiration as a human bridge between their humble lives and the overwhelming power of crime. Nellie Brower came over and gave him a big hug and kiss on the cheek, despite her five-foot height. Peg and Roy Sullivan, who usually lunched at Lucy's, also gave him big handshakes. This was more affection than his now-vulnerable insides could process all at once. His stomach cramped and a tear crept into the corner of his eye. He abruptly brushed it away.

He strode to his usual corner booth and ordered the regular pre-accident breakfast: cayenne scrambled eggs, pork sausage, two English muffins, and Lucy's bottomless cup of coffee—no more bland hospital food and no more of Eugene's restricted diet! After the customers' attention shifted to joshing local author Graham McGill, another regular, Girard sat mulling the enormous decisions before him. *Would* he return to his old job? Did he really *want* to? Troopers younger than him had already put in their retirement papers, though some had died of boredom once off the job. His old trooper friend, Jason Black, had developed a good private detective agency over in Old Forge, and had gained a beautiful, young new wife and child to boot. So what was *he* trying to prove by hanging on when he had the injury ticket to retirement—why not take the easy way out? Then, sudden flashes of Charbonneau's weasel face in the moonlight just before the shooting jolted his mind and momentarily enraged him, and Girard *knew* his decision. If his doctors and the superintendent allowed, he'd return to Troop B, by God, and get this last job done. And *then* maybe he'd consider retirement.

George Edwards, the logger, stopped by his booth and asked, "Those doctors take the smokes away from you, Inspector? Huh? You ain't lit up since you come in. I got so used to seeing you with a weed in your hand and a cloud of smoke around your head when you was sippin your coffee," he grinned.

"Yeah, well, I've made some changes, George," Girard muttered dismissively, as Edwards walked away smiling. Girard's inner purification, if that's what it was, had taken place by *choice*, he was sure, but he didn't know *why* he'd made those choices. No smokes and no booze since he was "reborn," and he couldn't understand why he had not even had the *desire* to imbibe. Even more puzzling, all the way north from Albany, he'd listened to an overpowering choral piece by Mendelssohn on WMHT-FM Public Radio, and now inspired by the mountain scenery along the way, he felt elevated and transformed in his deepest being. He'd never liked classical music, especially choral music—it all had sounded like stuffy church music. He didn't really know who Mendelssohn was, but he now knew he hungered for a deeper experience of the energy in that man's music. Today sure has been an odyssey of sight, sound, and inner feelings, he observed. Somehow he'd bypassed his old favorite country-western music on the radio dial and never missed it, and he wondered why.

A slight pressure dropped onto his left thumb, and Girard looked down to see Oscar. Oscar, the housefly, was another of the regulars at Lucy's. He had hatched there long before anyone could remember, and was the only insect in Lucy's otherwise spotless diner. Every one of the regulars called the ageless fly by name, as if he were an old friend and not a nuisance. "Move along, Oscar, I've got some thinking to do," said Girard absently.

As if on command, Oscar zoomed off. The next thing Girard knew, a strange young man seated himself across the booth. There was something vaguely familiar and foreboding about him, but Girard couldn't place the face and didn't remember a name. He straightened in his seat and put on his investigator's poker face. This wasn't anyone he'd ever busted, he was pretty sure. They looked at each other silently for a moment, taking one another's measure. The red-haired stranger wore jeans and a white sweat-shirt with big maroon letters—UNION. He sported a baseball cap whose A-shaped logo seemed familiar to Girard, though he couldn't immediate-ly recall which team it was. In a strange sense, this man with piercing blue eyes was beautiful, though Girard was more impressed by the fierceness and intensity behind the placid countenance.

"Hello again," the stranger said ominously, as if Girard had just entered the other man's office for an interview. Something in that voice, thought Girard—what *is* it?

"How are you?" Girard responded impersonally.

"I thought if I dressed this way, it would be less frightening for you" said the stranger, whose eyes took on an electric red that immediately van-ished.

"Oh, shit!" hissed Girard, as the color drained from his face. "Shit, shit, *shit!*" He pounded his fist on the table. Immediately, those old feel-ings of unworthiness and vulnerability gripped his intestines. He felt absolutely helpless because he now *knew* this character, who wasn't, as far as he could reason, human. "Okay, wise guy, where's your armor?" he rebuked the figure.

"Oh, that's just a projection, you see," the angel spoke solemnly. "It's not a genuine part of me." He leaned forward and said confidentially, "Still it *is* a symbol of the powers I've been given and the Greater Power I serve." Girard's stomach muscles began to cramp again and his healing ribs suddenly ached. It was as if he sat across from an electric dynamo and the skin on his arms prickled. It was all too close.

"Where's your wings, wise guy?"

"We don't have wings and bodies, as you know them. Something within humans elicits this visual metaphor because your souls *know* who and what we are. Thus, wings become apparent when we manifest visual-ly on the earth plane. They indicate that we move between the heavenly state and the physical vibration," responded the angel.

"If you're so exalted, then why do I feel so shitty when you show up? And what's your name, anyway?"

"I have no need of a name. Each of those like me knows who *we* are as a self, but we also know our abiding unity with The One. We know who *we* are, and what energy called us into being. How about *you?*" The angel smiled disarmingly, though his increasingly fierce eyes probed Girard even deeper than an x-ray. "Those of you encased in flesh seek your pur-pose as *separate* entities, so I'll say this: some among you might call me

"Apsara" or "Malak," though on your level, the knowing ones would most likely prefer "Israfil."

"Well, why are you picking on me, Izzy," Girard retorted, increasingly nervous as, one by one, the lunchtime customers left the restaurant. He had to go on the attack. "Are you going to give me more of that God stuff? You know, I really don't believe *any* of that crap anymore. I think you are just another hallucination and maybe I've just got some serious brain damage that the doctors didn't find. All that religion nonsense just weakens a man's resolve and prevents him from being strong and decisive. It's a drug that weak people need—some bogus life raft to cling to in order to feel good and avoid deep thinking. If there *is* a god, he's cantankerous as hell, and totally untrustworthy!"

"Yes, for some, religion has become a drug against fear. Ah, yes—and trust—just the same as faith. We must discuss that soon," said the stranger. Suddenly it dawned on Girard—the team's logo on the stranger's hat—the Anaheim Angels! He buried his head in his hands, as if his defensive perimeter had once more been overrun by the enemy. Jerking his head upward once more, Girard said, "Look, maybe you escaped from some institution. Why not just go back there and leave me alone?" he begged without much conviction. Sr. Investigator Girard began to perspire; this sudden intrusion into what has been a happy day wrenched him. He knew he'd have put any collar of his in a mental ward if he heard them spouting off even half of the stuff he was witnessing and saying.

Though he had appeared real enough until now, Israfil began to harden in texture. The more Girard pursued his skeptical and recalcitrant stance, the more the angel became transformed. It seemed as if each molecule of Israfil's body had become a pulsating dynamo of energy; a veritable light show, controlled, yet dynamic. The angel began to emit a faint, electric-blue aura of light; short bursts of lightning seemed to emanate from his pores. The angel glowered and short flashes of red energy leapt from his eyes. The hair on Girard's arms tingled in trepidation.

"I serve I AM and minister to those I'm sent to," he thundered. "What brought me to *you* even before your birth was a desire deep in *your* soul for new life—new physical and spiritual life! I was appointed to, and must fulfill, the mission assigned to me. I will *not* disobey!" Girard nervously scanned the room. Nobody seemed to notice the awesome pyrotechnics that engulfed the booth. How could that be? Girard's hands continued to tremble and drops of perspiration fell onto his placemat.

"We're alike, Dennis," the angel softened his wrath. "We both serve organizations larger than ourselves. All you need do now is to enlarge your perspective as to what the fellowship of that service *is*. Surely it's not just your police organization. You also have responsibilities to a *greater* order, springing from every action you've taken thus far in your life and from every word you've ever spoken. You cannot walk out on these responsibilities without harming your eternal self. To do so would betray your essential truth…would betray the energies that set *you* apart at present from others. Shall we get down to business now?"

"Jeez, you sound just like Sister Concordia all over again!" Girard lamented, wiping sweat from his brow and grey hair with his hand. "Okay, lay it on me," he abdicated. "I guess I can at least listen to you." Dennis Girard felt like a small child again, abjectly surrendered to someone "more adult." At least this angel isn't carrying Sister Concordia's discipline ruler, he reassured himself silently.

"We don't need rulers," Israfil's eyes flashed, "we know the *true* measure of all life. In the end, you have your free will—even The Creator will not deprive you of that. You'd know the deepest meaning of Love if you could understand *that* truth. If, in the end, you choose not to see the Divine Face, you won't. But there is so much misery in such a choice— and a deep soul sorrow that you haven't even begun to know. You and every living person have been summoned to return to the high state that you all once had, higher even than mine. It is your decision whether or not to cooperate and co-create with The One who will permit you to claim that inheritance."

"Look, Israfil, I really don't understand this. Do you want me to start attending Mass again?"

"Dennis, we desire that you now *become* the Mass! Within you lie both the bread and the wine that must be sacrificed, don't you understand?"

"I don't even know what you're *saying,* for God's sake! Sister Concordia never taught us any of that crap at St. Gabriel's. Sunday Mass is where I used to *go*. As an adult, I genuflected in church. I memorized all the important prayers. I said 'Amen' when I was supposed to, and I stayed awake during sermons…well, most times anyway. What *more* must I do?"

"Dennis, dear Dennis," the angel whispered tenderly, now radiating a profound compassion. "Your spiritual life is what you must become *inside*, not what you do by rote. Earth life is a process of being continually reborn." Israfil's eyes now brightened and he laid a steel hand on Girard's arm.

"Most humans live their lives without considering what they are doing or why. Their life is consumed with just going along and seeking the approval of other weak humans. You must now become more conscious of your *full* existence and purpose, more mindful. You are a son of The Most High! He has called you. Your essence or soul chose birth in this place and time of opportunity because it was best suited to the growth *you* must accomplish.

"When you were among us, 'dead' you would say, some of your innate God-given powers were released because it pleased the I AM for you to accelerate the comprehension of your true identity. You agreed to that shift way back on Culloden Moor. It's not that difficult a maneuver if you are willing to take up your burden."

Overlooking the geographic reference, the investigator responded, "Yeah, burden—you got *that* right." Girard leaned forward in desperation. "Look, I'm just trying to stay alive. You got that? I have to go back to work and try to catch the bad guys without getting killed again. Even an angel should understand *that*. Don't you know the difference between 'good guys' and 'bad guys'?"

"You suppose it is that simple to discriminate, do you? At your level, you don't yet comprehend who or what you are looking at when you see another human being. You can't know its past or its future or the experience it has chosen to undergo in the present life experience."

"Are you saying you know *my* future?" Girard demanded. Then, not waiting for a response, "Look, Israfil, or whoever you are, I've been around—I've busted rapists, murderers, counterfeiters, smugglers, bunko artists, porno magnates, ATM robbers, and speeders. This world is full of assholes, and only a small bunch of men and women in uniform, and even fewer in plain clothes, are there to keep the corruption of this world from destroying *everybody!*"

Marlene, the waitress, brought his eggs, sausage, English muffins and coffee. "You okay, Inspector? It looked like you're over here talking to yourself. At first I thought you were talking to Oscar, but he's over playing in the sink right now." She never looked at Israfil, and before Girard could ask why, she left to wait on a new customer.

"Can't she see you?" Girard asked Israfil.

"Well, yes and no. Part of her knows I'm here, but her conscious mind isn't anywhere near ready to actually see me, or to contemplate the tasks that will descend upon her when the day comes for her to enter the greater truth of *her* reality. Right now she's engaged in simple survival. Leave her to her illusions."

"Why can't you do the same for me? Do you mean I'm lucky to see you?" Girard said sarcastically, stabbing at the eggs with his fork.

"In truth, I say that. Now, I must tell you a Truth that was written long before you and I ever existed, that you will return to your police work, and that, if you can bear the burden, you will be most successful—as if a reborn man. Finish your bodily nourishment now. I will lead you to new nourishment for your eternal self in the days ahead, and many in high places will be thankful." And Israfil simply disappeared, as if the vent fan had suctioned smoke from the booth.

Girard sat in a daze munching his English muffin for the next 20 minutes. He couldn't stomach the pork sausage, which was Lucy's specialty and had always been his favorite. Maybe that's what's making me sick to my stomach, he figured, all this angel illusion. He waved off Marlene when she offered a refill on the coffee, a gesture she'd never seen before. The Inspector was always a guaranteed second, if not third, refill. Eventually, he threw down an extra-large tip, paid his bill at the register, and left Lucy's. He headed south to Route 8 and an apartment he hadn't seen in months.

CHAPTER THIRTEEN

The emotional party continued through the night in Jim Tarbox's garage. He and Charbonneau had consumed a case of Molson Export, and although the pair had lost their investment in the cigarette stash, the crafty Charbonneau had escaped. And, as usual, Tarbox had another scheme that figured to net the pair a great amount of money, recouping their loss.

"Two Claw (Dark Eagle always called Louie by his chosen Indian name, as it made it easy to manipulate him), I've met a new source for funds. The guy isn't Mohawk like us—he's white—but he hates New York State's and America's greedy governments as much as we do. I think he told me he's a Bavarian count, or something like that, because he has quite a dialect. But he's also got money. He's got a place down near where you shot that trooper—Port Henry? Charbonneau, still pumped up with the adrenalin of killing an officer, and mellowed by the alcohol surge, grinned, "Bring 'em on, Eagle, we can handle any task he has for us!"

"If he has money and helps us regain our pride as warriors in the land

49

of our ancestors, I say we include him. My work here in this chop shop isn't making us much, but it gives me a legitimate presence on the res," Dark Eagle offered. "I want to hear this guy out before we invest in any more smokes, okay?"

Charbonneau, warmed by the woodstove fire, and sedated by Molson's, nodded in agreement, but soon was lost in a stupor.

CHAPTER FOURTEEN

His landlady, Hannah Morgenstern, profusely greeted Girard after he parked and pushed through the picket fence gate circling the Knapp Hill Road rooming house. She had a large bouquet of daffodils in a vase at his apartment door. He felt truly at home and, as soon as he entered the apartment, Girard turned on the stove, filled the teakettle with water, and set it on the burner. Now was a time to plan.

Dr. Kristopher had determined that Girard should continue physical therapy and could do so at the Hudson Headwaters Health Center in Warrensburg. On this first day home, Girard called and made an appointment for the physical therapy, though he also knew he'd have to face psychotherapy and mental probing before he could return to work and finally settle scores with Charbonneau. The investigator was restless, stymied by the enforced idleness of the weeks ahead. He was also frustrated by the state police policy of never assigning a trooper to work on cases in which he had a personal interest. Maybe, somehow, I can overcome that, he mulled.

Sleeping late each morning, he collected and read accumulated mail, watched national news programs, and read magazine articles that he had months ago set aside for perusal; lots had gone on during the waning winter months, and he was determined to recapture it all. He talked with Tommy each day on the phone. During the next week, he found little else to do around the apartment. He was too restless to read anything in-depth, feeling he must be up and doing *something*. So from time to time he took walks up Knapp Hill Road, which was pretty much undeveloped above Mrs. Morgenstern's house. When not engaged in physical therapy at the Health Center, the investigator spent countless hours slowly walking the village streets, something he'd had little time to do while working long hours up north. He realized it was just a mile to the supermarket from his rooming house. On his way home, he saw that a new outfit called Aurora Publications now occupied John and Joan Conway's old house. He wondered who they were and how long they'd been in the house. Girard also yearned for the familiar routine of investigative work, where every thought and action "counted."

For now, however, he had no official role to play in Troop B and he knew the guys at the barracks could only slap him on the back so many times if he visited. They all had road patrols to run, hard work and investigations to do, and lots of evidence to compile. He was certain that he'd be in their way if he went back without a specific job to do. He also knew that some called him "Denny the drunk" behind his back and worried about ever overcoming that appellation.

And, this proved correct on his first "re-visit trip" to Troop B Headquarters, and he came away feeling humiliated. When he entered, after many effusive greetings and the traditional back-slapping, the guys at the front desk introduced him to Richard Ramirez, a new trooper graduated last year from the Academy. "How ya doing, Ramirez? I'm sure you'll like it up here," Girard offered.

"Thanks, Girard. Glad to be here. Also glad to meet *you*—you're something of a legend to me and my buddies—you walked away from The Bad One!" Ramirez grinned, and they chatted a few minutes more, then Girard turned to go. In the doorway he involuntarily halted, feeling an invisible arm wrap gently but firmly around his waist. The unseen presence whirled him around and propelled him back to Ramirez, and he heard himself say, "Oh, one more thing, Ramirez. Have they got you mainly on traffic enforcement?" Ramirez nodded yes. In spite of himself, Girard blurted out, "Look, if you make a traffic stop today, stay well back from the driver's door and window. *More* than they taught you at the Academy. Don't let that driver get his elbow out the window, you hear me?" He puzzled where the idea and words that rushed unbidden from his mouth came from. Girard, why did you let that out? This kid's going to think you're nuts! You're not even his superior, he chastised himself.

Lt. Lou Gregory looked up from his nearby desk with a quizzical look, having overheard Girard's uncharacteristic order. It hadn't even been a suggestion. "Okay, Girard, I want to do everything here right," Ramirez responded nervously, taking one step backward, "but why are you asking me to be overcautious?"

Girard wondered about that himself, and could only grumble, "Never mind." Then, totally befuddled by uncertainty, he countered, "Remember what I *told* you!" and with that he fled the building feeling like the jerk that Irene had always claimed he was.

Investigator Tommy Delehanty wasn't in when Girard arrived at Headquarters in Ray Brook, but he knew Tommy had made many shift changes during Dennis's operation and recovery, and now was working long hours to balance it all out.

What can I *do?* he pondered. There had to be some option that he could take while deprived of the full investigative resources of his State Police job. In any case, it was certain that his superiors would never reassign him to a case involving the man who'd shot him. That was an absolute operational rule of thumb in the State Police. This is going to take something creative from me, Dennis concluded.

Charbonneau had tried so hard to think and act *Mohawk*, Girard began to reason. But only Two Claw's wife, Marie, had been the *real* Mohawk, hadn't she? And most of the time she had resided on the Canadian reservation at Kahnawake. Girard began to plot. Aha! I've got it! Maybe I can cross into Quebec as a tourist. Yes, and then…Luc Gosselin! The face of his old acquaintance from Nam suddenly sprang to mind.

More than thirty years before, Lt. Luc Gosselin had been the Canadian Forces liaison officer with the 101st in Vietnam and the two had had many discussions about the beauty of the Adirondacks and Laurentians during those Vietnam days. At the time, Gosselin had been an avid outdoorsman and rock climber and had vowed that when he returned to Canada he'd never again be far from the Laurentians and Gatineau Hills he loved. Like Girard and Delehanty, Gosselin had found his way into law enforcement after the war. Girard recalled from a "touching base" Christmas card some 20 years before that Gosselin had joined the *Sûreté du Quebec*, the principal law enforcement unit in Quebec Province.

When he returned from Ray Brook, Girard phoned the 418 Area Code Information and learned that an "L. Gosselin" lived in Quebec City. He called the listed number but received only a curt, "*Bonjour*/Hello. *Laissez un message*/Leave a message," then a beep. He left a brief communication that Gosselin should call him at home, which was now his base of operations, and gave his Chestertown number. Two hours later, as he consumed his fourth cup of coffee in the kitchen, the phone rang. Gosselin had returned home briefly, found his message light flashing and was absolutely delighted to hear from Girard again.

"*Ça va, Denis?*" Gosselin had loved teasing Girard's poor conversational

Québécois back in Nam and since. Though his father, Henri Girard, had often spoken to him in that Canadian French dialect, Dennis had absorbed only a stumbling knowledge. He had taken Bart Lindsey's French classes while in high school however, and could make himself understood in Quebec, although his dialect was more Parisian French. *"Ça va bien, Luc!"* Dennis responded, and then lapsed into English.

"Luc, I'm on medical leave from the State Police right now," he said, downplaying the serious events of the past three months, "but I'm unofficially working on a case. I remember your mom was part Mohawk. Didn't she live at St.-Régis?"

"Not exactly, *Denis*, she worked in the hospital on the Kahnawake Reservation about an hour north of St. Regis/Akwesasne until she died 15 years ago."

"I...I'm sorry, Luc, I didn't know," said Girard, realizing how badly he'd lost touch while immersed in his own losses.

"C'est bon," Gosselin responded, "she had *une bataille terrible* with alcohol and, in the end, lost the war. But, she did have some really good sober periods along the way, and I often used to visit her while she worked there. *Maman* was always concerned I'd be too hard on the Mohawk lawbreakers we caught."

"Luc, did you ever meet up with a guy named Louie Charbonneau up there? Kind of a barrel-chested guy, white, 230, about 5'10"?"

"Sure, I remember him. Crafty as a fox! RCMP and *Sûreté* both watched him when we could, because we *knew* he was up to something. But we never could catch him red-handed. A slimy bastard—watch out for him! Both his parents were whites born in Saguenay, you know, but he masquerades as a Mohawk. The tribal leaders don't acknowledge that or respect him, so he hangs out with only the worst elements on the reservation. He probably moves from one part of the Mohawk lands to another, making it hard to keep track of him. *Maman* nursed his wife, Marie, who died of breast cancer, in *her* last days at the hospital in Kahnawake. I used to encounter Louie in the corridor near Marie's room, though I don't think he ever knew or cared who I was. Charbonneau became very bitter after he lost Marie, I heard. You think old "Two Claw" is your man?"

"Yep. He put another bullet into me, Luc. Killed me, in fact!" Gosselin gave a belly-laugh, not comprehending the severity of Girard's casual comment.

"Look, *Zhee-rar* (Gosselin had always loved to tease him by overemphasizing the Gi first syllable of his French name, as if to remind Dennis he was now something less than Quebecois because he'd abandoned his father's Habitant heritage), I'm usually off on Tuesdays. Why don't you drive up and I'll show you around the office and we'll take a little trip out to Kahnawake. Then we can go over to Akwesasne if you want to."

"Sounds good, Luc, I'd love to see Canada again." His mind was suddenly back flying among the exhilarating blue and white mountains of his death experience. "It's been more than a dozen years. How about we make it for *next* Tuesday, though. That fit your schedule? I'm getting antsy and don't know when I'll be reinstated. I have to get *something* moving on this case."

"*Très bien, Denis!*" Luc responded, "got my address?"

"Still living in the Old City?"

"*Oui.* 169 rue St.-Jean."

"Yep, see you! *Au revoir!*"

Chuckling, Gosselin hung up the phone and went back up the hill to work.

The next four days seemed like four months. Girard busied himself on Saturday by walking over to the market to pick up hot dogs and beer. He missed the taste of beer and hadn't had a drink since being shot. He tried to spend some time every day admiring Mrs. Morgenstern's crocus flowers, so as he exited the house, he stood for a moment to observe. They were just coming into bloom, like children shedding their winter wraps to enjoy the warm spring sunshine. He so appreciated the feisty colors this cool morning. It had been a very cold and snowy winter and all the spring flowers seemed late. He admired the intermixed Dutchman's-breeches and Scilla blue and whites next to her sidewalk. She had deep purple Trilium plants next to all her shade trees. By the first week in May they were usually in full bloom. He was happy to see living flowers again, as if he was revisiting old friends.

Girard crossed to Riverside Drive on a slow stroll to the store. The window boxes at the bank would soon add color to that Main Street corner, he expected. Later, after leaving the market and heading downhill toward home, he reconnected emotionally with his great love of nature, and he reflected how deeply he had buried that link since leaving Syracuse University.

When he got inside and began cooking the hot dogs, he found the aroma to be strangely nauseating, and his first sip of beer made him gag. He was unable to eat the hot dogs or drink the beer, and exclaimed aloud, "Now I'm *sure* I died, and here I am in a dietary hell!" He settled for a miserable substitute of shredded wheat and tea, then took a nap. When he awoke, he watched The National Geographic Channel on television until bedtime arrived. He was frustrated and bored, and he knew it.

Sunday morning he awoke with a sense of foreboding. Was something wrong? Why was he so edgy? The sky was slate grey at 7:30 a.m. and the clouds had dropped to mountaintop level after last night's rainstorm moved on eastward. What to do this early in the day? He sat down to a breakfast of scrambled eggs with chives and a cup of mint tea. Then a wild thought gripped him. It would be hard, he knew, but why not go to *church?* Maybe he was now ready to find some answers there, and maybe he owed it to whatever mysterious light had restored his life. Strange, he pondered, earlier in his life, going to church had just been routine, but now he was filled with so much doubt and apprehension. At least it'll pacify that damned angel, he thought, smiling grimly to himself.

Too many recent events were pulling him back to the old questions about life and its meaning. And he feared the trap snapping shut on his recently-freed mind if he set foot in a Catholic church again. He hated being preached at—it was always "Don't this" and "Don't that." Where was the joy and good news that people were supposed to find in God? Why was God so far away and so invisible? How could scaring the hell out of parishioners be considered 'good news?' Nevertheless, he reasoned, how else can I deal with angels, misty valleys, a dead brother returned, and all the other spooky experiences? Maybe that's some Heaven stuff I missed out on as a kid! Then, for a split second it occurred to him that there were some things about Heaven that *he* might share with the Church. The preachers essentially wasted years of my life, he glowered, harping at me to be nice, but this isn't a *nice* world!

Dennis Girard had pretty much had it with religious hierarchy and a clergy that seemed to make people's lives harder and more repressed, to say nothing about hanging guilt on the faithful ones. In grade school they said it was all about love, but look at those pedophile priest scandals of a few years ago, and the bishops were *still* covering it up and protecting their own asses! Weren't the clergy supposed to lead people *to* God? Those guys and their "good old boy" superiors drove people *away* in hordes and destroyed the faith of the simple people in the process. Good, ordinary people became bitter and disillusioned and gave up the search to find and understand God, it seemed to him.

Those remaining in the priesthood had the audacity to pressure the few self-directed seekers into guilt for having deserted the Sunday collection basket! The priesthood now seemed more a hideout for anti-social people than a fraternity of way-showers for those seeking inner peace. Nevertheless, he hadn't set foot in St. John the Baptist Church since moving to Chestertown so he'd be just another stranger to the regulars there. He picked out a new shirt and slacks and put on his NYSP windbreaker, screwed his courage to the sticking point and, looking for inspiration, left his apartment.

At the 10 o'clock Mass Dennis Girard sat in the rear-most left seat. As in most Catholic churches, the bulk of the congregation sat toward the rear of the church. Was it that they feared too close a contact with God, or did they fear something else? He squirmed, expecting the same old, routine Mass from his childhood. "This one's different," a voice behind him said. He swung around reflexively, but nobody was there. Whose voice was that? He tried to remember. Could that have been Timmy?

Promptly at 10:00, Father Bernie McCabe and one altar boy came into the sanctuary. The priest bowed and kissed the altar top, beginning the prayers in English that Girard had once known so well in Latin. In a way, he missed the "mystery" of the ancient language, but found that modern English left no illusions about what the priest was praying, and he was now obliged to pay attention. It was routine at first, kindness and blessings, call and response from the congregants, until Father McCabe stepped to the lectern and, after reading the Gospel selections from John 14—16, began his sermon.

"Friends, in Chapter 14 of today's Gospel, Jesus says that those who have faith in Him will lead their lives in the manner that *He* was living. He also promised that those of us who came after him would do even greater things than He'd done, because He was going to leave them and go to the Father. Think on that for a moment. How could He help them by *leaving?* Is there a secret in those words? Do you know what He implied? Think about it for another minute. His followers would be doing things *greater* than helping the lame walk, curing those with the detested leprosy, restoring sight to the blind, and finally, even raising the dead man, Lazarus! Was Jesus a liar, or should we take this promise seriously? If the latter, then you and I must work to read, study, and know *more* about the life the Master lived if we're to be His equals. Equals you question? Yes, He didn't want slavish followers, but instead wanted us to become like Him!

"And we must consciously work and think deeply about it every day if we're to call ourselves Christ-ians. Life is a gift, and we can't continue to drift through this gift unconsciously, just letting things happen to us. For a moment, Girard remembered those as being Israfil's words. "He knew His students would be unable to find their inner godliness as long as they were dependent on Him to be the holy one. In essence, Jesus implied that they couldn't mooch off His holiness, but had to find *their own* relationship to God, and then *live* it each day. Jesus showed us the path, but *we* have to choose to walk on it." Girard nodded in assent; he now fully understood that life returned was a gift to him, at least.

"Notice that Jesus later commanded His followers to love one another in the same manner as He had loved them. And you know," the priest continued, "His was an unselfish lifestyle, based not on fear, but instead on a certainty of what His role was…teacher and loving example for us to follow." McCabe then repeated the Gospel words, *"There is no greater love than this, that a man should lay down his life for his friends."* Girard thought of so many of his friends in the 101st who had lived and died heroically, but for what, in the end, if not to aid their buddies? Then he recalled the several troopers he'd known, men and women, who had died enforcing laws that could, at best, guarantee only a temporary peace and justice in society. "And you don't have to die to help your friends," McCabe went on, "because most times it's harder to *live out* your highest beliefs."

Girard tuned in again as Father McCabe ended his sermon with words that the investigator had never heard before: Jesus telling His students, "I call you servants no longer; a servant does not know what his master is about. I have called you friends, because I have disclosed to you everything that I heard from my Father. You did not choose Me: *I chose you.* I appointed you to go on and bear fruit, fruit that shall last, so that the Father may give you *all* (the priest emphasized that word and held it for a moment) that you ask in My name. This is My commandment to you: love one another."

McCabe closed with "My friends, Jesus's name was His *purpose.* It was Emmanuel—heavenly love descended to earth and *lived!* I dare you to follow this, giving your love and compassion generously to as many people as you can each day. It's hardest with family, isn't it? But you must begin where you are. Do that, and He'll give you even greater work to do." The sermon ended and, for just a moment, McCabe stood smiling, looking into each face in the church. Then he walked swiftly back to the altar.

Girard didn't stay much longer. When the priest turned, Girard made a quiet exit. The sermon had caused so much turmoil in his conscience and mind that he could no longer sit still. "Friends, not servants! Nobody ever told me He said *that*," he muttered aloud as he walked homeward. He kicked at a small white stone in his path. "It sounds as if Jesus wanted us to be His equals. For a second, he had the image of Jesus as the older brother he'd only briefly known. Man, if He could only have known that the image-makers would turn Him into cutesy statues with sappy eyes! Girard wondered why so many ministers and priests had made Jesus into an unapproachable perfect being, so that those like himself, the Girard who stumbled and bumbled so often, could no longer look the Teacher in the face. Jesus had sought the "brother" relationship with the true seekers who wanted more from life. Now, Girard felt more bitter than happy at this exposition of the Gospel's words. He felt suddenly obligated, but to whom he couldn't fathom. Surely, not to *everybody*! Surely not to the bad guys!

As he approached his rooming house, Girard scanned Mrs. Morgenstern's hyacinths, and was startled to note the opening flowers' purple color stood out more than three inches beyond the buds. It's gotta be my eyes, he thought, something in my brain has gone dead. My wiring is screwed up—maybe my vision is going. They're *never* going to recertify me for duty. On my next checkup at Albany Med, I gotta see the eye doctor.

On Monday he searched for the old family Bible, which had become buried among boxes of belongings from his married life. Inside, he found his parents' signatures inscribed beside his and Timmy's birth records. He spent several hours scanning the thick book, reading bits and pieces from the Old and New Testaments. For a while, he sipped his mandarin orange tea and pondered the role of religion in peoples' lives. Why was there so much disagreement over the Truth? After reading, he kept his PT appointment and was pleased that Keith, the physical therapist, said he'd be finished soon, but should maintain regular physical activity.

He was restless for the remainder of the day and decided to walk down to the ice cream shop on Main Street for a double fudge cone. Mikki, his favorite server, was on duty and, sporting a radiant smile, added just a bit extra on his double scoop treat. Girard felt appreciated, touched by a teenager's generosity; a girl who didn't even know him. He hit the hay before 9:00 p.m.

Finally, Tuesday morning rolled around, and he eagerly arose at 3:00 a.m. to slurp some fresh coffee, his only remaining vice, he assured himself. The whiskey bottle hadn't been opened since he'd returned from the hospital, and a cobweb-covered, stale pack of Camels lay on the kitchen shelf untouched. So much had changed inside him! How? Why?

By 4:00 a.m. he was turning into the North Country on I-87 and headed for Canada. One hour to the border, one more hour to Montreal, then two hours up "The 20" (why didn't the Canadians call it Route 20, like we do here? he wondered). The first leg of the trip was uneventful, and he listened to Vivaldi, Finzi, and Holst on North Country Public Radio from Canton. The music lasted almost all the way to Montreal, where he picked up the booming signal of CBM-FM. Their early morning music was mainly baroque and very orderly in its style, aiding his thinking and reminiscing.

Only later did he reflect that he hadn't listened to his old country-western favorites Garth Brooks and Travis Tritt in three months. Bluegrass music, his other old favorite, just didn't reach his core anymore either, maybe because, though happier fare, its message wasn't courage. It was as if a more structured and formal music, a deliberate cadence and harmony, now dominated his consciousness, permitting his imagination or mind to roam eternity, seeking inspiration while his ears were involved in listening. Girard's soul also seemed to need the nourishment from more uplifting, less-chaotic music now, a harmony that could vibrate his heart of hearts. And he didn't care if he ever heard another song lyric, except from massed choral groups. Maybe that *is* what is found in Heaven, he concluded.

Outside Montreal, as he turned onto The 20, moving northeast in the direction of Quebec City, he was overjoyed to see a beautiful sunrise in the east. Crimson and gold light, with violet cloud layers above and below. He felt invigorated by and more positive about the sight than about anything he'd seen in a long time. He hoped it prophesized a final resolution of the Charbonneau problem.

An hour and a half later, as he neared St.-Nicolas, Investigator Girard noticed an increasing tremble in his hands. Must be I'm gripping the wheel too tightly, he thought. Maybe I'm tensing up—gotta stop *that* or they'll never recertify me for duty. Nevertheless, as he continued driving and made the big northward swing toward Quebec City, his body went ice cold. Pinpricks stabbed his back and a throbbing headache started at the base of his skull. What *was* this? An infection? Then he remembered that almost the same thing had happened back in 1999 when he'd driven the same route on a brief vacation to Canada with his then girlfriend Lydia.

Back then, he'd thought it was the start of the flu. No flu today, he decided, what *is* this?

He finished the coffee in his mug, and fought nausea all the way to the Pierre Laporte Bridge. Once he passed beneath the second high arch of the bridge and into Quebec City, however, all the symptoms vanished. He didn't question his good fortune. Healing is healing, he decided.

Despite the rush-hour traffic, which hadn't yet subsided, he found the correct turns and zig-zagged to rue St.-Jean in the Old City. On the street in front of number 169 he saw a tall, heavy gentleman chatting with a dark-haired young woman beside a small red car. The familiar face was still that of Lt. Luc Gosselin, though the body now belonged to a slightly paunchy, balding man. Gosselin's spine, nevertheless, was still ramrod stiff, the way Dennis remembered him from Company HQ in Vietnam. Luc kissed the young woman, who then skipped several feet to her little red car, got in, and drove away. Gosselin, spotting Girard, waved as he walked to the car door, extending the hand of friendship to his old comrade. "Hey, you sure got grey! Let's get some coffee, *mon ami,*" suggested Girard, and the pair walked to a nearby coffee shop to chat.

CHAPTER FIFTEEN

For more than an hour the pair reminisced about mutual acquaintances from the war—guys who made it out and those who didn't. They choked on memories of the foul-ups endemic in any large government operation, especially in wars, where innocent people are killed and maimed. Somewhere, they found humor in the most awful memories, too, and there were stories of wonder also.

Gosselin, without prompting, told Girard of a tale he'd heard in the JUSPAO press office before he left Saigon. It involved an American infantry patrol up near the Ho Chi Minh Trail, where the squad had walked into an ambush. Every man was shot and only one badly wounded survivor remained—with an unbelievable tale. The soldier later told of being hit, falling, and fainting. When he semi-awoke, the VC were stripping the American bodies of personal effects, wristwatches and money, tossing treasured family photos on the ground. Then the enemy patrol left the jungle clearing. Soon after, the wounded American, lying with one side of his face on the ground, and staring at his buddies' dead bodies, noticed a dead comrade getting up on his hands and knees *out of his body*! The semi-transparent soldier looked at his fallen friend, waved, and walked off into the jungle, leaving his mangled physical corpse behind. "No matter what I do, *Denis*, I can't shake the memory of that story. The guy who told it was somewhat embarrassed to pass it on to me, because he feared I'd laugh at him. But I know *he* believed his source."

"Luc, after we get better reacquainted, I got a story that'll top that one," Girard smiled. "Are we off to the *Sûreté?*"

"*Oui*, come on, it's not that far, just on the north side of the city. You probably knew that your State Police also have a liaison man working full time at our headquarters in Montreal; helps us both," said Gosselin as they got into Dennis's car.

Girard asked, "Luc, tell me about that woman—your daughter?"

Gosselin smiled wryly. "*Non, Denis*, she is my *petite amie*, my sweetie. When Janine died in 1991, my heart was broken and I vowed never to marry again. Then, six years ago, I met Marguerite, who was a postgraduate student at Laval University. She's only 25, and probably just looking for a father, but she made *me* feel alive again. And...she got me interested in Impressionist art—in painting, actually. She has an assistant professorship at the university now, and we just live together. We love one another, so who thinks of marriage anymore? *Comprennez?*"

Gosselin took his old friend on a tour of *Sûreté* headquarters on the Boulevard Pierre Bertrand. Girard was impressed with the array of international communications and information systems available to their officers, instant contact not only with the FBI and NYSP, but also with Scotland Yard and MI5 in Great Britain and, of course, Interpol. The roof of *Sûreté* headquarters bristled with a forest of antennae and satellite dishes. Girard murmured his approval at the extensive and modern crime lab, with a forensics unit much better than was available at Ray Brook and at least as modern as the state lab in Albany.

The pair toured the bomb squad facility, the electronic crime detection unit and met Lt. Armand Gazaille, the chief trainer of the tracking and drug-sniffing dogs. Gosselin told him that the *Sûreté* facility was totally independent of the electric power grid, noting that the headquarters building had been constructed to survive earthquakes, so they would remain operational in the worst disasters. The pair then toured the new investigative unit "safe rooms," established after the terrorism incidents of 2007, when it was discovered that international terrorists had somehow pene-

DAVID J. PITKIN

trated the Canadian law enforcement establishment. Other investigation rooms' access was only by iris scans for those working in particular secret investigations.

"Guess that's about it," said Gosselin. He introduced Girard to several of his friends, and Commandant Raoul Mercier. Each Canadien spoke French to Girard, who blushed and responded in English, though he usually got the drift of the comments addressed to him. Luc then inquired, "What do you say, *Zhee-rar*, are you up to a trip upriver to the Mohawk reservation?"

"That's okay by me, Luc, I want to see where Two Claw hangs out." They drove south for the next two hours, again reminiscing about their sacred and profane experiences in Vietnam and the noble plans that each had envisioned then, now dashed for them both.

Turning into the Kahnawake Mohawk lands south of Montreal, Gosselin urged Girard to drive directly to a large, old stone church whose steeple stood above the small community. "This is a place that I've always loved, Kateri's Shrine," he told Dennis. "When I was stationed at the *Sûreté* office in Delson, I came over here many times. Park there, beside the fence, and let's get out." The pair walked inside the black wrought iron fence to the large, granite gravestone of Kateri Tekakwitha. A costumed Indian woman stood waiting for them behind the stone, the trace of a smile on her face. Gosselin told Dennis of Kateri's early life in the Mohawk Valley village of Caughnewaga in New York State. "She was partially blind as a youngster and had many scars from disease. She became one of the early Christians among the Mohawks there and suffered much from the traditional tribal members because she was so devout and loving according to the white man's religion. She later migrated to Canada and died here at age 24 in 1680...see here on her stone." Gosselin gestured at the date. "The miracle was that, as she lay dying, all the scars left her face and she became radiantly beautiful beyond belief!"

Girard kept waiting for the young female guide to speak to them, but she stood silently, holding a lily in her hands. "Hey, *Denis*, try this. Put your left hand on top of her stone." Girard complied and instantly felt a low pulsation of energy rising in his arm. He looked questioningly at Gosselin.

"I know, *Denis*, doesn't make sense does it? But *you* can feel it too! That's why I like to come here—I walk away feeling cured of all my cares. This lady is going to be made a saint one day soon. They call her 'The Lily of the Mohawks.'"

At the mention of the flower, Girard looked up to spot the lily in the girl's hands—but she and the flower were *gone*—vanished in an instant! Oh God, my sickness is back, he thought. He didn't mention the vision to his friend as they returned to the car.

Luc then took him on a tour of the Mohawk village and showed him the modern hospital where his mother had worked, and where Charbonneau's wife had died. Luc spotted René Pine, a member of the Tribal Council, and had Girard pull over in order to renew an old acquaintance. After introducing Girard, Gosselin asked Pine about Two Claw's location. Pine smiled a strange smile and told Luc, "He has new friends now, so we seldom see him over here at Kahnawake." After a few more pleasantries, René moved on.

"Well, looks like your man isn't in this town today, *Denis*. Right, then. One more stop," he said. They crisscrossed the village's narrow streets, finally arriving at a small, weathered cottage. "Let's go in, Grandmother Thompson is home, and I'd like you to meet her. Grandmother is a term of respect we give all Indian women elders."

They climbed the steps and Gosselin rapped on the door. *"Entrez, mon petit!"* came the strong voice from within. Girard saw a wrinkled old woman wearing black-framed eyeglasses and a print dress and apron, seated in a recliner chair. Her unkempt, long grey hair fell behind her back, and in her hand she held an unfiltered cigarette whose smoke rose above her head. "So, Luc, you've brought your friend. I knew you'd come today; the voices told me."

"Grandmother, this is *Denis Girard* from New York State," said Luc.

"Ah, New York State," said the elderly woman, adjusting her eyeglasses. "I have family near Syracuse. Why are you here?" she asked.

"I'm glad to meet you Grandmother," said Girard. "I'm trying to find a man."

"Oh, the one who shot you?" asked the old woman. Girard gave a quick glance at Gosselin, who shook his head in amazement, as if to deny tipping off the old woman.

"I didn't tell her, *Denis*," he said in awe. "Grandmother Thompson was my mother's close friend and has a way of knowing things, which always surprises me."

"If you are the friend of Luc Gosselin, that's good enough for me," said the elder. "His *maman* and I were best of friends, and she helped me get my cataract operation. I was going blind, you know? Sit down and let's see what the voices can tell me about this man you seek. She adjusted her glasses again, then slumped forward as if she'd had an attack. Concerned, Girard again looked at Luc, but Gosselin wasn't worried and gave his friend the high sign. They waited.

The old woman sat nodding for five minutes, then straightened. "You won't find *him*, he'll find *you*—at the place of the bells, the ancestors told me. The man is dirty and under the control of the birds of darkness. He will make you search your soul, *Denis Girard*."

"He's already made me do that, Grandmother," Girard replied. "Where are the bells? In a church? A city hall?"

"I don't know, but there is much water nearby. Even *I* have difficulty in hearing and seeing in that other world sometimes, but that place is secure with the love and protection of my ancestors, so I trust it. You *will* meet with this dark man again. And you must search your soul when you do. That which is hidden inside you *must* come out."

Gosselin produced a jar of honey from a paper bag he held. "Grandmother, the honey bees have produced this just for you, and I'd be pleased if you'd accept it from them."

"Still your mother's son, Luc! You know I have a sweet tooth," she grinned, grinding her cigarette into the ashtray. Girard was just as happy, as the cigarette smoke had begun to make him queasy.

"I waited for you to arrive before taking my nap," said Grandmother Thompson, "but I'm old, and you'll pardon me if I sleep now. Unsteadily, the old woman got to her feet and clasped both men's hands, staring deeply into each one's eyes. "*Au revoir,*" she said, and pulling aside a curtain, went into her bedroom.

"We'll let ourselves out," Luc called, moving toward the door.

Outside, the pair walked for a while. They discussed a person's capacity to know the future with any accuracy. Girard was surprised to discover how open Gosselin had become to the belief in extrasensory perception since they'd last visited. "Looks like our man isn't here," Gosselin concluded. "If Two Claw has new friends of some sort, it probably wouldn't avail us much to go down to Akwesasne today. That's a trip you can take on your own. Come on, let's head back to Quebec City. Marguerite should be finished at the University when we return, and we can go to dinner."

Gosselin directed Girard to return to Quebec City on The 40, which runs on the north side of the St. Lawrence River. He pointed out several landmarks as they drove, some historical and some personal. Arriving at rue St.-Jean, they found Marguerite already home and dressed in a sleek, black dress with pearls. Gosselin introduced them and Girard made small talk with her while Luc got dressed. Very attractive, smart, and sweet, Girard decided, but much too young for me.

The trio spent an enjoyable evening dining at the Resto Parisien, overlooking the river. The air was balmy and the conversation encompassed many facets of their individual lives. The entertainer that evening was something of a new Canadian singing sensation named Véronique Lebrun, who had once been a nun, but had left the religious life to become a jazz singer. The three sat mesmerized by her mellow alto renditions of old standards.

Girard was fascinated with Marguerite, who was much less than half of his and Luc's age. She had a sophistication and wisdom that belied her years. Still, he thought to himself, I wouldn't be in Luc's shoes—I'd need a wise partner with the experience of age to keep *me* on course. Again, Luc and Dennis reminisced about their first experiences in Asia and how that environment had left indelible influences on their views of life, and their unshakeable memory of the gentle Vietnamese for whom they fought. Eventually the trio discussed art and the great difficulty that artists often have in translating their vision into a form that can inspire the masses. Marguerite offered some ideas from her study of Chinese Taoist art and its growing influence on other nations' art styles.

At the end of the evening Girard wasn't tired and decided to drive south toward Montreal and to spend a night in a motel along the way. "I want to go down to Akwesasne tomorrow, so I'll cross over the bridge at Cornwall because I want to scout out the territory where Charbonneau might be hiding. I want to see where he comes from. In all my work in Massena, I never got into Akwesasne for very long, so now I want to take the day to explore." Outside the restaurant Marguerite gave him a wonderful hug and Gosselin gave him his warm hand in friendship. Girard promised to come north again when it wasn't "work." He took leave of the two, who seemed radiantly happy together. Girard turned south on The 20, spending the night at the Motel des Deux Amis, in Drummondville.

When he crossed onto Cornwall Island the next day, still in Canada, he reflected on the many jurisdictions that make up the Mohawk Nation at Akwesasne: the U.S. government and New York State to the south and the two Canadian provinces of Ontario and Quebec to the north. The Mohawk lands comprise several islands as well as the mainland, making the issue of law enforcement a nightmare for the two nations if it wasn't for the goodwill and cooperation of the Mohawk Tribal Council.

Continuing south on Akwesasne International Road, he turned west, driving to the end of Cornwall Island, then all the way back to the east, sizing up the many businesses and homes. He found the population of this Mohawk reservation both more numerous and poorer. Evidence of alcoholism was clear, yet he was also inspired by the smiling faces of the children he saw along the way, several of whom waved at his car. I hope their lives will be better ones, he thought.

He then crossed from Cornwall Island onto the southern shore, driving at medium speed through the communities of St-Régis and Snye, observing as he went. As he turned south out of Snye, he noted a black pickup truck tailing him. He took several side roads to be sure that he *was* being followed. No doubt about it, someone wanted to know what he was up to—but why *him?* Why would someone follow an unmarked car, unless he'd been under observation for quite some time? Girard didn't stop, but did note several old semi-trailers sitting among the trees. Were his pursuers protecting those? He didn't get out to investigate, however, because of his "friends." Finally, he swung eastward on Route 37 toward Malone, and as he did so, his pursuers disappeared from the rearview mirror. He chose to let these observations "perk" for a while in his mind, certain that he must have noticed details that hadn't yet come together into a conscious understanding. "Right you are," said a voice from the rear seat. He pulled to the side of the road, stopped, and looked behind him. Nobody was there.

CHAPTER SIXTEEN

Upon his return to Chestertown he noted the Superintendent's list of psychotherapists on his kitchen table. Funny, he thought to himself, I'm sure I put that paper in the bedroom. Okay, that just proves I'm losing it, he mulled good naturedly, and shrugged. So now I need to have a shrink prove *that* to my superiors—that I *am* nuts!

He brewed a fresh pot of coffee and sat in his battered, old recliner chair, picking up the list to peruse. Lots of names with letters after them: PhDs, MEds, MACPs, MDs,—what a maze! How can an ordinary person know who has the best qualifications? Is one degree any better than another? One thing is for sure, there aren't any high school diplomas like mine in there!

Scanning the page he stopped at Bernice Epstein, PhD, a psychiatrist in Plattsburgh. He was sure he didn't know her or anything about her. Yet something fascinated him about the name, which seemed to radiate a golden glow on the page. It was as if he could visualize a tall, slender, middle-aged woman with flecks of grey in what must have once been jet-black hair. Well, if I've got to confess my sins to *someone*, it might as well be an attractive lady, he decided. Girard called Dr. Epstein's office and was surprised to learn she'd just had a last minute cancellation for tomorrow and the pleasant female voice said Dr. Epstein would see him at 2:00 p.m. He made the appointment.

The next day, as he stood in the doctor's office at 1:50 p.m., he found himself reading the diplomas and credentials that she had posted in the waiting room, rather than authoritatively behind her desk like so many therapists do. All diplomas were in black frames except a gold one from the Jungian Institute in Zurich, Switzerland, indicating that she had studied dream therapy there. "Jung-ian," he said slowly, pronouncing a hard J. He puzzled at the word; it reminded him of the jungle and wild animals.

The door opened behind him and a friendly female voice asked, "Are you Mr. Girard?" He turned to see an exact duplicate of yesterday's vision of Dr. Epstein. Figure that, he taunted his inner self. "Yes, I am," he smiled in return. "Hey what's Jung-ian? Some kind of zoo?" Again, the hard J.

Dr. Epstein laughed. "Sometimes I think so!" she chuckled. "No, it's German or Swiss. The J is pronounced as a Y, so it should be pronounced 'Young-ian.' Jung was the Swiss disciple of Dr. Freud, the first great psychoanalyst." At Freud's name, Girard wrinkled his nose in distaste. "I know, I know," she said. "Still, we must thank Freud for showing us how important the unconscious mind really *is* in everyone's daily life. However, Carl Jung knew he couldn't continue as Freud's disciple because Dr. Freud's atheism blinded him to an even more marvelous truth. A part of *every* human being's unconscious mind seeks full development and eventual union with the Eternal Purpose or the universal forces. And likely, that part of our unconscious is not only in constant contact with the Higher Power, but also connected to the unconscious minds of *all living people*. Jung believed dreams are a direct pipeline between the Infinite Mind and our finite sleeping minds. Isn't that neat? Now, come on in and sit down, and we'll get to work."

Girard entered the rather plain office and sat in a red leather armchair. Either she's poor—in that case, probably a pretty bad doctor, at these prices—or else an interior decorator's nightmare, he mused. Dr. Epstein took 20 minutes to record all the elemental information about Dennis Girard, from a medical history, childhood through high school, college, Vietnam, state police work, his divorce, his brief affair with Lydia, and finally his experiences with death. "Let's work with each one separately and carefully," she said, "then see where the wholeness is—where the healing is, and how they all come together. We want to assess the work you have to do yet to become *you*. Jung called it 'individuation.'

"You didn't say much about your religious background or practice; would you do so?" She listened for almost the entire remaining 30 minutes, and Girard left nothing out. He ranted and raved about pious clergy, and was near tears of frustration twice. He suspected she was Jewish and wouldn't understand his Christian foundations, but he poured forth the experiences of his visions and of Sunday's stunning turnaround in his new thoughts about the Christ message.

At the end of the session he made the next week's appointment, left her office and Plattsburgh, and headed home on I-87, feeling that he had opened some private vault to Dr. Epstein, thus rendering himself permanently vulnerable. But what the hell's life about, he pondered, what have I got to hide anymore? Izzy is there to protect me, right? "Are you there, Izzy?" he called loudly into the back seat. No response.

On Wednesday morning he began walking. Up until then, his walks had taken him along the streets and roads in and around the village of Chestertown. Now, knowing he had to rebuild his lung capacity and lower body strength, he decided to walk eastward along Route 8 and past Brant Lake, toward Graphite Mountain, maybe all the way to Hague on Lake George someday. He came back winded on his first day, having traversed only two rather level country miles to the Schroon River Bridge, before his legs weakened. However, he managed four miles the second day, and four miles back, recognizing that he had become a slave to his car. In the hamlet of Brant Lake he celebrated by buying a deli sandwich at the small country store there.

The next day, he made six miles over and six back, walking on the road close to the lake shore. Every outing he extended his walk another mile or two, and as he did so, he reaped the physical and esthetic benefits. Dennis Girard loved the still-cool mountain air of morning and the red buds of the maple trees now exploding into an almost fluorescent green on the upper slopes of the mountains, while green buds had already opened into deeper green on the lower elevations along the lake. Nature displayed a most beautiful spring—light yellow-green willows down at lake level were fully leafed-out and dark green pines intermingled with the wood tones of the forest higher on the mountainsides. Flowering dogwoods and shad punctuated the wash of color throughout the woods.

Each day he walked and pondered, inhaling great gulps of mountain air as he trod the shoulders of Route 8. After three weeks he would be easily able to reach the far end of Brant Lake where many vacationers had begun cleaning or opening their summer camps. The trip over and back from that point was about 19 miles, and he was returning home each day feeling stronger and only occasionally short of breath. He walked at about two miles an hour at first, and his only difficulty was along the narrow shoulder of the road, especially on the highway turns along the lake beyond the Point of Pines, where traffic zoomed dangerously close. Troop G has to get a radar unit in here pretty quick, he observed. All these people speeding—I wonder if they ever take the time to *see* the beauty that's all around them. I wonder if most modern Americans *ever* take the time to see it. He recognized how much he, himself, had blotted out the Lord's handiwork during all those years of concentration on family and career.

Girard's second appointment with Bernice Epstein had yielded something new. Upon entering her office he had noted a strange, bearded man with long, black hair who wore a long, black coat and rounded-crown hat, seated behind Dr. Epstein. In his late 50s, he judged, the man seemed to be silently observing her, and Girard took him to be a psychology intern of some sort, perhaps someone from Plattsburgh's ethnic community. The man sat quietly, listening, as Dennis and Dr. Epstein conversed. The pair worked first on his "car crash dream," which had recently so frightened him. Dr. Epstein seemed anxious to discuss his recent dreams before they got down to the therapy questions he expected.

"Dreams," she reflected after a while, "are the medium through which an all-knowing universal healing force entices us to better our lives, showing us both practical and cosmic applications of eternal truths. Jung called this force 'the Self.' Dennis, the Jewish sacred scripture called *The Talmud* says that 'a dream un-interpreted is like a letter unopened.' Think how many thousands of dreams you have had—we've all had—since birth, and how much of that knowledge and insight we've deprived ourselves of. Dreams are largely symbols, yet filled with powerful energy and emotions. They draw on our emotional experiences to form pictures that are loaded with energy, memory, and meaning. If you can honor each dream and not be put off by the pictures, but analyze the greater *meaning* of a color, a shape, number or person, you can discover you have an inner teacher. And that teacher always shows you the truths in your life—even when you don't know you want to look." She leaned forward earnestly, "And *all* dreams have but one aim—your wholeness, your healing, if you'll cooperate consciously."

"So, let me get this straight," he responded, "dreams are an inner hard-wiring system that encourages us not to lie to ourselves?"

Bernice laughed, "Something like that." She then drew his attention to the color of the dream automobiles: black and white. "That alone should get you thinking," she prodded. "What do you think white and black represent?"

"Well, I guess it's about opposites. Good and bad, isn't it?" Dennis responded.

"Consider that one is light and the other dark, but you would not recognize light unless its opposite, darkness, also existed," Bernice said. "They're really a team, working in you and for you. Light can be a metaphor for what is observable, and dark, what is not. Light can represent what you know, and the dark can represent what is still unknown. Light is illumination; dark might be confusion or that which is obscured. What things were dark and which ones were light at that point in your life, see? Now, what is a car? Is it not a 'vehicle?'"

"Yes, I guess it carries or transports us," Girard conceded.

"Yes, transports or carries the real you, maybe, though if you're a taxi driver or stock car fanatic, maybe the symbol has a different individual meaning. Is there a hint here that you have been 'driving in darkness, living your life, and thinking you were happy?' If your life's essence is soul consciousness, might the vehicle containing it not be your physical body?

"And what has recently crashed into your physical body besides a bullet? What ideas, themes, or energies have collided with your former understandings?" They paused in silence to reflect. "And the number of the cars is two, a classical symbol for choice or dichotomy, maybe self vs. others, even the paradoxes in your life. Which vehicle was bigger, the dark one or the light one? Maybe even the German name Porsche has a meaning. From my college German studies, I seem to remember it means 'offering.' So what might be the 'offering' here in the collision? The gentleman behind her moved his lips silently and slowly raised his hands and eyes toward the ceiling as if in supplication, but no sound came from him.

"Well, Doc (he felt safe in seeing her as a professional and didn't want any personal relationship to form, though she was a fine-looking lady and her laugh continually uplifted him), I've been hit with so *many* things.

Look at my career, for instance. I've been going downhill for a decade; I'm surprised the state police didn't throw me out long ago. And my body health is lousy; I've finally been able to look at that, and started exercising. I stopped smoking and can't stand alcohol anymore. I'm even drinking tea on occasion. Last night I had frozen *quiche* for dinner!

"But you know, with all the strange hallucinations I had at Albany Med, I've also come to recognize that there are men and women in my life that I truly *love*, but not in a romantic way. Now I can see so many of them as strugglers and stragglers like myself. In my 'dead time' I believe I went to some place where the powers-that-be looked at me and found my lousy life acceptable—at least for where I was at *that* time.

"Still, I've continued to have so much anger inside at thinking my rigid Catholic upbringing would bring me happiness. It didn't. They posed as 'the one true church,' but dropped the ball. When I was in that Light Place I expected some guy to show up at any minute and order me to 'Go to Hell!' Instead, I felt such love there that I wanted to cry. Every time I remember that place I weep. Why?" His eyes misted up and the therapist proffered a box of Kleenex. "Yeah, I've sure been impacted by an awful lot of stuff."

"Now, Dennis, notice the direction from which the car's impact came—the left," Bernice said. "In dream work we often consider objects on the left to be 'the unknown,' and the Latin for the left side is *sinister.* So much of what we don't know *can* hurt us, can exert a sinister influence—like an ambush—in our lives if we won't wake up to our truths. Do you think this dream can represent a 'status report' on what you've undergone since late February? And maybe it can even hint at where you're going. Most good dream doctors believe each dream in some way forecasts an outcome or next step in our present struggles."

And so the give-and-take session continued. At the hour's end, Dennis stood, signed an insurance paper for Dr. Bernice, and left, saying, "See you guys next time." Bernice gave a puzzled, uncomprehending frown.

The next Tuesday, fresh from an exhilarating morning hike to the foot of Graphite Mountain under cloudless blue skies and in 78-degree weather, all done in a little more than five hours, Dennis noted the strange man was absent from Bernice's office. "I meant to ask the last time who your observer was, Doc."

"What do you mean? I'm not being observed."

"Who was the strange man sitting over there last time?" he pointed and gave a description of the man's appearance.

Bernice went slightly pale, then brightened, and Girard saw a tear in her eye. Out came the Kleenex box again. "Dennis, that's my dad. He was a wonderful man, an Orthodox rabbi in Forest Hills, NY, in Queens— Mordecai Epstein. People were mesmerized by his great wisdom and illuminating sermons. When I fell away from Judaism at Columbia University, I broke his heart. First, I went into atheism and a lot of ego inflation, then I toyed with Marxism. I was so idealistic—there was so much I was seeking to understand, and I couldn't find it in tradition. I'm a Sagittarius, you know. A year or so later I felt a need to explore Christianity, whose dominance is so strong in this country. But, you know, I found most Christians confused or rigid, arguing about Jesus's message, when it seemed so clear to me. I couldn't decide who was right, but I knew for certain that Jesus began life as a Jew and *that* fact seems missing or ignored in all the Christian churches I attended. How can any true Christian understand Him without knowing the depth of his Jewish-ness?

"Then I found Buddhism. I struggled hard to find my own truth back in the 70s, and ended up being what I now consider a Buddhist Jew. I don't keep kosher, though I still profoundly observe the High Holy Days and try to *live* the *Torah*—our holy book of Law—like the first part of your Old Testament. Jews don't like that term 'Old,' you know, because we feel Christians treat Jews as if we failed in some way and are passé— old-fashioned and out of date. When I left my Judaism, Father refused to see me any more, and I was heartbroken when he died in a traffic accident in 1988, still a young man. I've always thought I could feel his presence around me here, and you just confirmed it for me." She gave Girard a dazzling smile.

"Well, whatever he was doing here, he seemed to be right in your corner, listening to you talk to me, Doc, and occasionally nodding at your statements," Girard offered. He paused for a moment and reflected, then said, "Oh God! Now I'm seeing *ghosts*! And do we both think that's *okay*?" Both laughed and Dr. Bernice asked Dennis to talk about his early life, especially his attitudes toward his parents as individuals. In 40 minutes she noted the hour was up again too quickly. They made next week's appointment and just before he left, Bernice took his hand in hers. "Thanks, Dennis, you've given *me* more today than I think I've given you. I'll see you next time."

What a warm woman, he thought, not like any shrink I've ever heard of—a real woman who is filled with a real strength of knowledge and understanding, but still willing to be vulnerable though she is in charge here. And her life is certainly based on a whole lot more than hairstyles, shopping, popular music, and soap operas.

Descending the steps to the street outside, Girard wondered if he was still in the real world. How could he allow himself to get into all this touchy-feely stuff and still retain a tough investigator's unemotional command to uncover criminal activity? He liked Bernice, even found her attractive, but what woman wanted to be close to a loony? He was pretty sure she was just tolerating his tales of visions and voices. He just couldn't understand these inner experiences in the light of anything he'd ever been taught in high school, college, or church, and certainly not in the military or at the State Police Academy.

Dennis Girard gazed toward the beauty of Lake Champlain off in the east. Remembering his naval history, he recalled how American Commodore MacDonough had defeated the British fleet out there in the War of 1812. Men had died violently and in anger, blown apart or drowned. So much turmoil once, now it looked so peaceful. Wonder if I'm ever going to find that kind of peace?

CHAPTER SEVENTEEN

Appointments came and went, and Dr. Epstein's weekly dream work seemed to make more sense each time. She made Dennis struggle to find his own symbolic connections before she would offer her orchestration of the material. Eventually, he came to see himself as a steaming cauldron of feelings, thoughts, buried memories, and experiences, all going somewhere, but making him neurotic because he hadn't integrated them into a comprehensive personal truth or lifestyle. Together they covered his experiences and aspirations in his youth and high school years before college and Vietnam. But the question that nagged at him was: where was it all *going*—was there a plan or intention, and if so, whose, for his unique life? He was now recording his dreams daily in a notebook and evaluating them with Bernice, who was still "Doc." He had grown fond of her and sometimes wondered whether they'd ever become lovers, but there was too much inner work to do, and above everything else, he wanted her professional certification in order to return to duty.

Dr. Epstein usually kept the sessions impersonal, disclosing just enough from her life to support Girard as he poured forth his inner hopes and fears. He felt good about his life now, better than he'd felt since graduating from the Academy years before. Now, as in his State Police Academy graduation, he felt that this therapy was a task that he *was* eminently qualified to perform. Because his PT at Hudson Headwaters was completed, he was also now driving down to the YMCA in Glens Falls once a week, to swim and work out with light weights. His wound had completely healed except for some ugly-looking red marks and the surgical scars. There was seldom any pain from his mended ribs, though he was still wary when lifting weights with the left arm. It looked as if he might be physically fit for duty soon. He made another trip to Albany to visit with Dr. Kristopher and to undergo a follow-up examination.

Back in their third session, Dr. Epstein had introduced Girard to the concept of "the Shadow," a Jungian term for all the qualities and behaviors in life that might have been incorporated into his personality and conscious mind, but for one reason or another, he had consciously rejected, repressed, or even condemned them. So many of these traits or urges had been taught to him formally or learned experientially and when they appeared to be "bad" or didn't serve his ego's plans, he buried or submerged them as he grew up. She said that many of those qualities had kept him from becoming the fully integrated, balanced personality that he might have become, though he still had time to be open to them and individuate.

Dr. Epstein continued, "When a person will not face his Shadow tendencies, he becomes neurotic and projects his own evil onto others, Jung said, leaving us seeing darkness and confusion everywhere in the *outer* world, but never inside ourselves. In such behavior a person's life is continually filled with 'enemies,' and the individual isn't inclined to examine the rot of his or her own inner state because it is so enjoyable and seemingly safe to constantly see one's enemies and ugliness as being in the *outside* world. In other words, let me quote from an old Hindu aphorism, 'What we detest in ourselves, we hate in others.'"

Girard was silent for a while as the force of that statement hit home. So, all the qualities he had condemned in criminals and acquaintances were more than likely lurking within *him* too. And, since he wouldn't face these tendencies or failings, he condemned the people in whom he found them. So where, in fact, does evil lie? he wondered. He was also fascinated by the back side of the proposition: Those elements or traits that we admire in others are very likely a part of our own potential if we'd work to assimilate and grow them. At least that is what Dr. Jung said.

At the fourth session they had entered the minefield of his failed marriage, something only touched on in the earlier therapy. He came to see how the "hero role" had so appealed to him in his marriage, and he had found Irene Karamanlis' vulnerability so appealing in their early married life, as she represented the "damsel in distress, the woman to be saved." Bernice suggested that the "outer woman"—Irene, really might represent the "inner female"—the intuition and soul qualities of receptiveness in Girard himself, which was the real consciousness that needed "saving." "We in psychology call it a man's 'anima,'" Doc said. Even when Irene had developed "nervous problems" and chose to stay home to raise the kids, Girard had felt validated because he could now work even harder, filling the role of hero/husband, and struggling longer and harder to earn money to provide for his family. Unfortunately, his obsessive work patterns had deprived him of so much enjoyment in his children's development, and left his kids under the strong influence of Irene's neurotic behaviors and those of their peers.

Irene eventually became totally dependent on Girard for strength and support, eclectically taking art courses in high school evening classes to busy herself, but refusing to challenge her comfort by then getting a job or putting her fragile ego to the test of daily interaction with society. Only after their divorce had she begun attending formal college art classes and, upon graduation from Skidmore College in Saratoga Springs, had taken an adjunct professorship at Bennington College for a summer session. It turned into her first full-time job.

When he and Bernice finished reviewing those issues and the maladaptations that he'd made, it all seemed to have been for nothing. He'd ended up with three kids and an ex-wife, all hating or resenting him having busted his guts for them. And they resented his breaking apart their comfortable illusions about a happy family. He then had turned to more smoking and drinking to bury his angst, and the only thing he could give himself good marks for was not seeking another woman while his marriage still had a chance.

Doc and he also studied the brief affair he'd had with Lydia Roberts, a dancer and artist that he'd met in a bar in 1999. A seductive and lively woman at first, he soon came to see her essential neurotic, critical, and negative nature, which spoiled any real chance for a lasting romance. Bernice quoted him a relevant old saying, "When criticism comes in the door, love goes out." Lydia had learned to be a user of men, mining their resources and ideas, then casting them aside. She found imperfection in each human she met, and had no long-term close friends, never understanding that it was her own shadow of imperfection that repelled her. Dennis told Doc that he later found out that Lydia had suffered parental abuse as a child and now was consumed with a personality disorder, keeping her the adult victim of her own un-faced trauma. Their affair had ended in anger and devastation to them both.

Dr. Epstein's insights helped him validate the hard work and motives in his relationships and career, while showing him that *his own* behaviors were as neurotic as Irene's and Lydia's. He and Irene had placed one another on unassailable altars. Only Dennis's had crumbled so far. Irene remained ensconced on her mountaintop, as yet unwilling to acknowledge any personal fault in the marriage or divorce, and likewise with Lydia. Therefore, until these women could face their own motives and illusions, they could not save themselves from the hell of an ego-centered existence, which always leaves the individual overwhelmed by his or her own fears. While Irene might yet perceive the root of her difficulties, Lydia probably will never be able to wake up in this lifetime, Dr. Epstein decided; and maybe it would be too painful for her to do so. She told Dennis that the woman likely suffered from what was termed "a borderline personality disorder."

Doc suggested that such an ego-centered existence was the true goal of conquest in all people, regardless of their religion. "It's like a hill or mountain that we have to climb continually," she said. "From my Christian studies, I wonder if the concept of original sin isn't the same thing—the drive to elevate our ego self above our need for a humble and spiritual connection to the Source of all life," Bernice said. "Many of the world's mythologies tell that story."

From time to time during the middle of May, with Major Sincavage's permission, Girard also visited the state police shooting range in Ray Brook to take practice. Girard wanted to re-qualify with the pistol, shotgun, and assault rifle *before* he returned to duty, just to assure his superiors that he was ready. Using both the indoor and outdoor practice ranges, he wanted to do more than merely *qualify* on the first time he went for record.

With practice, he found that he had lost little of his former accuracy, and on the fourth trip to the range, decided to go for his pistol qualification. He fired a perfect score, and only at the end of his targets, did he realize all the other men on the range had ceased firing to watch in awe at his demonstration. Is this still the same Denny the Drunk? Lou Gregory asked himself. When the range officer announced he had a "possible," a perfect score, the assemblage gave a great round of applause. The following week he again fired perfect scores with both shotgun and assault rifle. The Superintendent's Office would get Girard's official scores.

Dr. Walker and Dr. Kristopher released him from their care on May 19, though he was urged to come back in three months just for a checkup. Girard determined to keep up and even expand his daily hikes now so that he could return to work in better health than he had enjoyed in years.

CHAPTER EIGHTEEN

Dennis Girard awoke at 8:00 a.m. and made a pot of coffee. Coffee— my only remaining vice, he mused once more, as he looked at the untouched, open and stale pack of cigarettes on the end of the shelf. Sipping the brew from his extra-large cup, he heard the happy voices of children outside and looked out the window. Two uniformed Boy Scouts were calling excitedly to one another as they walked down Knapp Hill Road. Wonder what's up today? he asked himself. Oh yes, today is Saturday, the 31st—Memorial Day. Someone at the store had said the three-town parade was in Chestertown this year, and he remembered that in alternate years it was in Pottersville or Brant Lake.

Pouring his second cup of coffee, he reminisced about the many comrades who had fallen around him in Vietnam, and in his dad's generation in World War II. Guess I owe those guys some tribute; maybe I ought to go watch the parade and memorial service. I haven't done that in 30 years. So long ago, wasn't it? Nam seemed like a hundred years back. Yes, it'd be right for me to go over to the Main Street monument and attend the ceremony.

He poured the remaining coffee into a carry-mug, pulled on his NYSP windbreaker, and stepped outside. Strolling downhill past Mrs. Morgenstern's fading jonquils and narcissus, he walked along Church Street on his way to Main Street. Father Bernie McCabe was just closing the church's front door after the morning's Memorial Day Mass and gave him a hearty wave, though the two men didn't really know one another. Girard raised his palm half-heartedly, but didn't seek a personal encounter

77

with the priest, as it might have been embarrassing to them both. He walked toward the General Store on the corner. Neat stores and shops made life in Chestertown enjoyable, and he could remain anonymous for the most part, as the village wasn't in Troop B's patrol area.

Outside the General Store, he encountered Norma Hicks in her Legion Auxiliary uniform, selling memorial poppies. He smiled, gave her a dollar, and hooked the paper flower into the zipper pull of his jacket. These poppies, he remembered, were a reminder of the slaughter of World War I memorialized in that famous poem, "In Flanders Fields," a tear-jerker if he ever allowed the words to flow back into his conscious mind.

Here and there were Boy Scouts, American Legion, and Veterans of Foreign Wars members, all in uniform and headed for the parade formation point down toward the high school. Throughout the Adirondacks, he mulled, in small towns just like this one, the organizations that held the American social fabric together were cooperating today to honor those who struggled and died to preserve that society. Most of these small-town commemorations were modest, not a lot of pomp and ceremony, just a red, white, and blue acknowledgement of gratitude to the war dead, as well as to the families that sent their sons and daughters away to fight. And there were fewer and fewer veterans to march each year.

He walked uphill toward the Panther Mt. Motel, as it was a great vantage point from which to view the passing parade near the Legion war monument, where the final ceremony would take place. As he walked, he was surprised to see individuals in authentic uniforms of other wars standing stationary, as if frozen, along the parade route. All were young and handsome, in the bloom of life.

The first one to catch his eye was a beautiful young woman in an 1800s Florence Nightingale-type military nurse's uniform, staring uphill. Somebody must be really dedicated to get so many re-enactors into those uniforms. He spotted at least 20 such figures around the hilltop: a World War II soldier in the infantryman's uniform, a Civil War soldier with his bayonet-fixed musket, a Mexican War cavalryman standing at attention, hands on the pommel of his saber. A World War II WAC holding a clipboard. A Gunnery Sergeant from the First Marine Division in Korean War winter gear. And all of them stood at attention, as if in anticipation of a momentous experience.

That takes training and discipline to get such an effect, Girard mused. Must have cost a pretty penny to outfit them, but it sure depicts the history of our country's wars—wonder where they're from? He passed an alert young woman in a World War II WAVE uniform who, like all the others, stood at attention, looking uphill toward the memorial stone. And there stood a carbine-carrying black cavalryman in the uniform of the Tenth Cavalry, the famed Buffalo Soldiers of the Indian Wars. Against the background of slowly moving people, these re-enactors stood out because not one moved or even blinked. In brand-new uniforms, each was in the physical perfection of early adulthood. He looked down and punched the overhang of his own gut, grunted, and continued walking uphill.

It was a sunny day and crowds thronged the village sidewalks. Many sat in vans and family cars along the parade route while others stood or sat at curbside in folding lawn chairs. More active spectators, especially boys, whizzed through the streets on crepe paper banner and flag-decorated bicycles while balloon vendors worked the curbside crowds. A group of Girl Scouts walked together downhill, carrying the troop banner and happily chatting.

At the top of the hill, where a World War I Doughboy stood holding his Springfield, Girard decided to cross over toward the gas station at the intersection of Main Street and Theriot Avenue where a World War I sailor stood at attention with semaphore flags tucked under his arm, directly in front of the Dead End sign. As he passed the man, Girard realized that the re-enactors had an eerie, vacant stare but, he reflected, that was probably a calculated and sobering effect they were expected to portray for the occasion. For a small village, Chestertown has done a great job with this spectacle, he reflected.

After a while, a flashing red light caught his attention down the hill and he recognized the Warren County Sheriff's patrol car clearing the parade route. The driver would probably be Deputy Mo Tremblay, an old acquaintance in the department who loved parade duty. Then came a sound that both chilled and excited him—the deep thump of the bass drums, still far out of his sight. Drums had always had that paradoxical effect on his emotions; when he heard them—a sound that produced deep anxiety, as if the world was going to end in the next minute or so—the concussions also invigorated him, creating the desire to move proudly. Whenever he heard a drum, for some strange reason, he felt he should also be hearing shrill bagpipes skirling over the muffled, rhythmic thud.

Then, rounding the corner, up the hill they came—the massed flags of the Legion and VFW color guards, and the lively marching step and flags of the North Warren Central School Band in their gleaming green and gold uniforms—almost Irish looking, he reflected. The honor position in the line of march was held by a unit, Charlie Company of the First Batallion, from the 10th Mountain Division from Fort Drum, a division that had taken heavy casualties in both recent Middle East and Afghan wars. A great ovation of applause and cheers issued from the crowds as the men of Charlie Company passed. *These guys* know we love and respect them, Dennis assured himself.

As they reached the foot of the hill the band struck up "The Battle Cry of Freedom", an old Civil War tune that had always inspired him. He remembered the regimental band had played that march when the 101st main group returned from Viet Nam and passed in review at Ft. Campbell, KY. Today was special and Dennis felt proud that he'd served his country as best he could back then, though the politics of the war had been so muddled and the national goals so obscure, and the conflict had been predicated on a deliberate lie. Instinctively he reached down to the dent in the back of his right thigh, where North Vietnamese shrapnel had nearly cost him his life.

Then, the three towns' fire companies marched past, followed by emergency vehicles with flashing lights. And at the parade's end were members of the next generation that he prayed would be spared the horrors of war, the Boy and Girl Scout troops and Little Leaguers. American flags fluttered everywhere.

It would have been nice to have Tommy Delehanty here reminiscing with him, but Tommy had drawn holiday duty back at Troop Headquarters. Girard pondered how often he, himself, had been on Memorial Day duty in the past, never having the time to remember America's war dead in any overt, meaningful way. The boy in him thrilled at the blare of the brass section far down the road now, nearing the Municipal Center. They'd have a traditional prayer there at the VFW and Legion flagpole and the honor guard would fire a salute volley in testament to America's fallen ones. He decided to wait for the parade's return and the final placing of flowers at the Legion monument.

Two little boys in coonskin hats, carrying toy muskets, ran past him making *bang-bang* noises at one another. I guess little boys never change, he thought, seeing himself noisily celebrating at the parades in Rotterdam when he was a child. Three volleys of gunfire snapped in the distance and reverberated off the side of Panther Mountain at the village's south end. Soon the parade returned uphill to the monument, with the band playing Sousa's "El Capitan." The throng then became silent when the band came to parade rest in front of the Legion Memorial. Lee DeNike, the Legion chaplain, offered a brief prayer and the Post Commandant, Walt Heins, placed a wreath of flowers at the base of the memorial plaque.

A slight movement to his left caught Girard's eye and he noticed the World War I sailor had just disappeared. How'd he *do* that? He glanced toward the Marine in Vietnam camouflage battle dress who had been on his right. The man was right before his eyes *dissolving* in mid-air! What's *wrong* with you, Girard, he agonized. You've been pretty good for a couple of weeks now—no vision problems and almost no haunting dreams. Now, here you go again. You've never seen people fade into nothingness before! You've gotta share this with Dr. Epstein.

For a moment, an awful thought seized him. Are those figures ghosts, like the bearded man I saw in Doc's office? Dead soldiers, sailors, airmen, and nurses attending these ceremonies? Why? *How?* And why should *I* be seeing ghosts? I'm not one of those goddam television psychics! *I* don't see dead people. He realized he'd dropped his empty coffee carry-mug and bent to retrieve it.

"See, kid I told you we'd get to work together," came from behind him.

He straightened abruptly but there was no one who appeared to be speaking to him. Hearing a voice over loud band music, Girard? He could see the Cougars' green and gold uniformed band marching at the end of Main Street now, headed back to the High School, and he could make out the fading music of "Stars and Stripes Forever." The thought persisted, how *could* he have heard that voice and whose was it? On a deeper level, he *knew*—it was Timmy's voice, though he couldn't consciously admit it. How can I report to work in two weeks and think I still have my full faculties? I can't *allow* this crap to overtake me anymore. I've got to turn it *off,* he resolved.

Maybe I need some sleep, he reasoned, and abruptly turned homeward. For the first time he focused on the name of the Catholic church as he walked past it again: St. John the Baptist. Yeah, that guy got killed doing *his* job too. At least, *I* got to come back with my head!

"Great parade, wasn't it?" a cheery voice called out. "Brings back some of the few good memories of Nam," Father McCabe called out. Girard saw the priest working alongside the stone wall of the church, and crossed the street to respond.

"You in Nam too?" he asked.

"Yep, door gunner in a Big Red One Huey. That certainly was a time wasn't it? Where'd you serve?"

"101st—Screaming Eagles. Up in I Corps. Never thought we'd make

81

it out. My name's Dennis Girard," he said, extending a hand.

"Bernie McCabe," came the response, and the two shook hands. "I know what you mean," said the priest. "Lots of times it *was* grim. But if I hadn't gone *there*, I certainly wouldn't be here. In Nam we attended lots of simple Masses in the field, as I'm sure you did. Lots of times they used the hood of a Jeep for the altar. I got inspired," he confessed with a grin. "You *are* Catholic aren't you I think I've seen you once or twice at Mass."

"Just once," said Girard glumly, "I have a room up on Knapp Hill Road. Mrs. Morgenstern's house?"

"I know her well," said McCabe. "The lady has a genius for gardening."

"Yes, I've seen some small miracles in her garden," responded Girard with a reflective smile. "What do you mean about Nam and Chestertown?"

"Our unit was on R&R near Cam Ranh Bay once, and I met a South Vietnamese priest that the Cong had tortured, a Father Truc. He had no hands—the VC chopped them off because he said Mass for the villagers. He had to get a special dispensation from Rome to say the Mass, because he might drop the chalice. I was stunned at the man's holiness and gentleness—he had no bitterness toward the Communists at all. And, during mass, when he raised that chalice with his stumpy wrists, I was always awed.

"Dennis, I killed a lot of people over there—that was my job, though not all of them were certified Charlies. I could spray the LZ with the best of them—anything that moved, I killed it. And I didn't care *who* got hit, as long as we could put our troops in there and get out in one piece. But, when I got home to the U.S. of A., I knew I had to square some things in my soul and after a lot of counseling and self-assessment, I went into the priesthood."

"That's quite a story about that priest," said Girard thoughtfully, overlooking McCabe's personal revelation. "I don't get to Mass much any more. I'm on medical leave from my state job. Still am sick, I guess, after today's experiences."

"How's that?" inquired the priest.

"I got hurt on the job and I've got vision problems, some kind of head trouble," Girard replied, masking his law enforcement role. "I'm in counseling to get it fixed. I'm supposed to return to work in a few weeks, but I'm not sure that I'm ready."

"I often wondered if a combat veteran like *me* was ready for this parish priest job," McCabe offered. "I'm not really the Bishop's favorite guy, if you know what I mean. I've been in bad places and seen lots of bad things in my life, so far. I've *done* bad things too—too many bad things. And there's lots of darkness still inside me. And if I didn't believe in God's grace and forgiveness, I'd probably be robbing banks somewhere today," the priest said with a broad grin. "Not really serious about that last part, but I felt so much love welling up in me during my seminary studies—like I finally found what I was meant to do. And I've never had a second guess about my calling to the priesthood. You were in the service and you work for the state, so you know about bureaucrats and bullshit. And in the priest business we get both so, as much as I can, I try to do this job my way. On second thought, maybe I should say *His* way.

"There are good and gentle people here in town, Dennis. Struggling people, tortured people, soul-sick people who can still find a deeper capacity to love if someone can help them find out how, *show* them how, and not just preach at them. Life is all about loving, and they need to experience that love in their lives if they're going to act in a loving way toward others. I've learned I can bring that love to some of them. I can help some find their dignity again, so they can take responsibility for their own individual lives and their relationship with God. I *can* help them let go of their expectancy that some organization or church can save them without *them* having to first cleanse their inner lives. I can help them see that Christianity, as it's been taught for centuries, has really buried some real life-giving truths. So, I am really happy working here," he said contentedly, "and I hope the Bishop lets me stay until I retire in a few years. Well— here I am gushing! Sorry."

Girard smiled and thought he understood some of what McCabe was saying. He'd never heard a priest expound so earnestly. But he was simultaneously distracted by memories of a sailor just vanishing and a Marine disappearing before his eyes.

"Think about this, Dennis. I have a friend, Father Don Lee, who is Spiritual Director at Holy Cross Friary in New Hampshire. He gives the most magnificent spiritual retreats—ones that make a man really think and dig into his innermost feelings! He's a Nam vet too, and he's really down to earth. Here, let me jot down his name, address, and phone number for you. Why not consider spending a few days on retreat with him? He'll be good for your head, your soul, and your heart." With that, the priest wrote quickly on a slip of paper, which he gave to Girard. "Let's see more of you around here, too. You know you can always talk to me, whether or not you ever attend Mass or read the Bible. I care about an old soldier like you. Like *us*!"

"Thanks, Father McCabe. Maybe I'll do just that." Girard gave a wave and started home.

"And soon?" the priest queried over his shoulder, returning to work.

CHAPTER NINETEEN

Girard never got to nap at home, however. He couldn't—his mind was racing a-mile-a-minute and he found himself absentmindedly changing into his hiking sweat suit. He pushed Father McCabe's scribbling underneath the sugar bowl on the kitchen table. It was almost noon, but he could still do the hike up to North Pond Parking Area and return to town before it was too dark to see. He needed a lot of walking to calm his mind right now. What did Doc call it—integration?

He had the 30-mile round trip down to just nine hours so he'd be home before it was pitch dark, and he needed time and space to think. Walking had the effect of tiring his physical body gently, allowing his mind to roam over many profound areas of life as he moved along. In nice weather he often discovered he had walked miles, as if in a daze, without remembering specific spots. He could walk and just *be*, as if on autopilot, without a memory of where the last half hour had gone. He wouldn't get much of that leisure once back in Troop B.

Girard had rediscovered the order and beauty in nature that he'd treasured as a young man, and now it surged more and more to the forefront of his older consciousness. All this beauty, he observed, striding and carefully avoiding the speeders and trucks on Route 8's narrow shoulders, and humanity rushes past it day after day. Brant Lake, which bordered half of his route, was beautiful in the late springtime, and he knew it would be so again in the fall when the foliage changed color, turning the mountainsides into a kaleidoscope of earth tones.

I'm sure becoming a philosopher, he mused. How did all this natural beauty get created? Was it created in an instant of the Creator's imagination? Or did it evolve slowly by itself over the millennia? And if so, was there a mind behind that evolution? And why, then, was it all created? What's it all *for*? Can beauty just exist for its own sake? Or does it need a human being to see and react to it? Maybe it serves some greater purpose that human beings just can't fathom. He felt a hunger to know the most profound of truths, to experience some breakthrough realization, and not just attempt to live life by the rote scientific explanations of the church and college courses that he'd relied on for too long.

On his previous hike Girard had begun seeing what he understood was a flowing of energies along the lake's surface and among the trees— not anything intimidating like the ghosts, but a normal coursing of nature's forces from here to there, often in a violet or deep yellow color. Is there even *more* that I can't yet see, he wondered.

His watch showed exactly 4:30 p.m. when he reached the North Pond Parking Area, where he was accustomed to turning around. Made good time, he concluded. The parking strip made an arc southward from Route 8, in the direction of the large pond, then gradually swept back north to rejoin the highway east of the parking pull-off area. Walking into the strip, and with traffic now obscured behind trees, Girard scanned westward, out across the quiet pond and its swampy borders. This must be how it all looked before humans arrived here, he figured, and no wonder the Indians revered the Creator's spirit in this beauty. The sun began to sink below the highest treetops on his right as he watched its lingering and solemn rays mirrored in the water—blues of the sky and blacks of the reflected forest intermingled with the oranges and pinks of the fading daylight. A late-afternoon, warm breeze swept over him as he stood in reverie. Senior Investigator Dennis Girard decided to surrender to these sensations for the moment, just letting them be, without judgment.

A piercing shriek overhead broke the spell, and simultaneously a dark shape was upon him, descending from over his right shoulder, pummeling Girard's body with rapid gusts of air. Defensively he ducked and, squatting, backed onto the pavement with his right arm raised to shield his eyes. He whirled to focus on the creature—an American bald eagle, which had landed behind him on a rocky outcrop across the pond road. Now perched, it sat unmoving, staring intently at him.

Cold sweat dripped down his back and his head began to pound. He had never seen an eagle up close like this, since there wasn't a bald eagle population in the Adirondacks when he was in Syracuse Forestry School. The two stood about 25 feet apart and stared fixedly at one another. Girard moved toward the middle of the road, expecting the bird fly off at any minute. He wanted to see; he wanted to *experience* this wild creature, this lord of the mountain skies, and his heart pounded within him. The eagle's gaze remained fixed on Girard, whose anxiety began to subside. Awestruck by the bird's beauty, he recognized that this was not a threatening situation; it seemed more a propitious event. What did Doc call such moments? Numinous experiences?

After a few minutes he became amused by the standoff. Out loud he said, "So you're a Screaming Eagle, too?" The bird blinked as if in assent, and took one forward hop to the edge of the rock. Girard countered with two slow forward steps of his own. This creature sure isn't timid, he marveled. "How beautiful you are!" he called out. "How exquisite you must find this mountainside from way up there in the air. I envy your freedom. Why did you just land *here*?" Quietly he added, "Do you have something for *me*?" The bird slowly unfurled its wings to a full six-foot span and gave one gentle flap, hopping laterally to the stump of a fallen tree before folding its wings once more to its side. By now Girard had fully crossed the road and stood in the sweetgrass ditch along the shoulder, his eyes at a level just below the bird's eyes. No more than 10 feet from the eagle now, it was close enough for Girard to see into the dark depths of the creature's unafraid eyes; it was as if he were peering into deep pools of some truth higher than he could comprehend.

He suddenly began to tingle and heard a deep voice say, "Your people!" Girard wasn't sure if the sound had come from within himself or from the bird.

"Did you just say that to me? Did you just say, 'Your people'?" He took another step forward. Now, with the pair no more than eight feet apart, Girard leaned upward toward the eagle demanding, "What *about* my people? Who do you mean? My family? My fellow troopers? Who? Are they in trouble? Are they doing something wrong?" No response. It was as if the eagle was waiting for the gravity of its message to register within him.

Then, with a powerful lunge, the bird broke its hold upon the earth and thrust its wings rapidly to gain altitude. Reflexively backing away, Girard remembered the Navy A-4 Skyhawks shooting upward after dropping their napalm canisters in Vietnam. From a great height the bird called out its piercing cry three times, then flew off and over the mountain to the north. For a moment Girard stood in awe, then regained his self-consciousness and groaned aloud, "Jeez, now I'm talking to the birds! Probably the bees will be next! Then, probably the Little Folk that Grandma Kelly used to talk about. If I told anyone about how screwy my life has become, they'd Section 8 me right into the funny farm!"

The sun had dropped down in the sky now, and Girard took his cue to hit the road westward, over and down Graphite Mountain to Chestertown. He jogged for a half mile then settled into a strong military cadence. As he walked, he reflected that he must have been totally immersed in a unity with that bird for at least 15 minutes, and sensed this was a gift from the cosmos unlike any event he'd ever experienced before. Vaguely, he remembered Professor Rafferty at Syracuse scoffing at the prospect of interspecies communication. He let out a loud, "Ha!"

Taking stock of his mind and body now, he noticed the absence of sore muscles, even under the left arm. His breathing was no longer forced and he took in great breaths of the spruce and pine-scented mountain air, knowing that his body had recovered its full strength. He couldn't remember feeling this healthy in the last 20 years, but it was what was taking place inside him that made him cautious. The sky above the mountains to the west was becoming increasingly crimson, with deep layers of purple amid cloud tops fringed with gold. Maybe some rain tomorrow, he mused.

The trip home was uneventful and he arrived back at his Knapp Hill Road dwelling at precisely 9:55 p.m. As soon as he entered the apartment, he started heating hot water for chamomile tea, a sure drink for sleep. By 10:30 he called it a day and slipped into bed.

But it wasn't the end of that day—far from it. Dennis Girard found himself running across a beautiful green meadow with a brilliant sun directly overhead. He could see his dark running shadow flitting beneath him and he was somewhat puzzled to find sandals on his otherwise bare feet. He then noticed sandals running on his right side and, glancing upward, saw a group of perhaps a dozen other young men wearing white garments, all running toward the left in a jagged line. He looked down at his own body and noticed a similar white garment—some kind of toga? Exhilarated at his regained youth and the effortless run, he was emotionally buoyed by the comradeship and the sun's warmth on his head.

As he ran, he looked once more to his right. "Holy shit! I know that guy—it's Jesus!" Immediately he felt conflicting emotions. First, there was the joy of being in Jesus's company. Then the profound embarrassment of having just used vulgar language, something he was sure the Messiah never did. He felt the urge to "cop a plea" and, running a bit faster than Jesus, suddenly turned to block the bearded man's path, facing Him. Jesus pulled up short and gave Girard a pleasant smile. "You're not going to hold that against me, are You?" he begged earnestly. "It's just cop talk. Army talk. I got excited when I saw You."

"Many are surprised to recognize me in unusual spots, but I, too, have spent much time in the dark places and have heard all the thoughts and words that human voices can utter. Darkness doesn't intimidate me, as I know what it *is*," came the reply. At that thought, Jesus threw back his head and laughed heartily. "None of it is *real*, don't you see?" he asked with mirth. "Only your love for one another is real and lasting," He offered. Girard could see both strength and compassion in those sparkling eyes. This wasn't the wimpy character of the statues or the Bible fairy tales he had learned as a child. This was a living, joyous, mature man, not a plaster saint.

"Look, I just got excited—You gotta pardon me. You know, I really stopped believing You ever existed, and now I meet You out in this field—damn! It really *did* shake me up."

"We have taken the field together, don't you see? Let's run farther as one," said the Teacher.

"Okay, fine. I'm glad I can run, You know, I've been hurting lately," he complained. Instantly, Girard felt ashamed of so blatantly seeking Jesus's sympathy.

"Where are we going?" Girard's dream-self inquired as they sped onward.

"Up there," responded Jesus, motioning to a high hilltop on their left, where Girard could make out the silhouette of three crosses. "We're going up to be crucified."

"Uh, okay," responded Dennis Girard contentedly, and the two of them continued on cheerfully. He didn't see what happened to the rest of the runners, but the next thing he knew, he was flat on his back. His garment had disappeared and he didn't know if he was naked or not. His back hurt and he felt wooden slivers puncturing his spine. He was on a rough wooden cross that lay upon the ground! Why wasn't he scared? To his left a man with a lifted maul was about to drive a nail into the palm of his left hand. But what a strange nail it was—a long thin red-colored cylinder with a white band around it. Placing the point of the cylinder on Dennis' palm, the executioner struck his blow. There was a loud explosion, which deafened them all. As the smoke cleared, Girard looked down past his feet. There, on another cross, was Jesus, though now He wore a crown of thorns and red blood dripped from His head onto the earth. Girard was overwhelmed with grief and loving gratitude, thinking, He didn't *have to* do this. He didn't have to! But He did do it—why? To help *me*?

Deeply disturbed, Dennis Girard awoke to find his digital clock registering 1:01 a.m. He stood and shakily sipped the remainder of his now-cold chamomile tea, then fell back into a dreamless sleep.

CHAPTER TWENTY

On June 10, at the end of their regular session, Dr. Epstein signed the requisite NYSP forms, asserting that BCI Sr. Investigator Dennis Girard was in better psychological and mental shape than any client she had—now physically, mentally, and emotionally prepared to return to the full, strenuous duties required of a state trooper. And she added that he had voluntarily agreed to continue in therapy, a fact that should please his superiors. Coupled with the reports from the doctors at Albany Med, all faxed through channels to the Personnel Office for review by the Division physician, the Superintendent's Office should soon order him back to work at Ray Brook.

Although this therapy was completed, Girard chose to avail himself of the state medical insurance policy and remain a monthly client of Dr. Epstein. He liked dream work, understanding that there was much inside him that still needed exploration, and that he had found a dignified, if also beautiful, fellow-seeker for truth in this woman. At his last weekly appointment—after they'd decided to make their sessions monthly—he left the office with a big smile, saying, "July 15, it's a *date!*" Bernice gave him a genuine, if curious, smile.

Two days later a certified letter arrived from the Superintendent's Office, stating that Sr. Investigator Dennis Girard was now classified as "fit to return to full duties and able to take on the responsibilities of a trooper." From somewhere in his apartment he heard a good-natured laugh, but he knew he was alone.

He called over to BCI Captain Alex Telfer in Ray Brook for permission to return to work. Capt. Telfer, uncharacteristically jovial, said, "Come on back next Wednesday, the 18th. We'll give you a short week and the 10 piles of work that have been waiting for you since February!" It pleased Girard that Telfer seemed not to have completely written him off, but he was curious about what work they'd give him. Senior Investigator Dennis Girard wanted to continue his pursuit of Two Claw, but understood that no such permission would be granted. Maybe Izzy could help him get that task finished.

On Wednesday morning he entered the doorway at Headquarters. Most of the secretarial staff and Headquarters personnel were busily moving about, and only a few nodded to him as he pushed through the double doors. He went to his office and sure enough, there was a file box in the middle of his desk. Removing the cover, he found the paperwork files for a cold case, the Elmore murder back in September 2006. Muriel Elmore had been found strangled in her apartment in Crown Point and the Forensics Investigation Unit (FIU) had found no good prints or other clues. Ligature or rope marks were found on her discolored throat, but no rope was discovered at the crime scene. There were also plenty of grisly photos taken by the detectives.

Troop B had given the crime top priority for a year or so, as there are few such vicious murders in their zone, but no witnesses came forth and no leads developed, even after investigators canvassed door to door in the village and throughout the Port Henry-Ticonderoga region. The autopsy had showed nothing unusual except the typical evidence of strangulation. Apparently the woman hadn't resisted, because no skin tissue was found under her fingernails. For almost two years the case had languished and then was placed in the "Don't Hold Your Breath" drawer—the "cold case file."

As Girard read the file, something happened to his left—he looked up and found the entire Headquarters staff assembled outside his office door, the entire BCI crew and many uniformed troopers, all grinning. They broke into "For He's a Jolly Good Fellow," and finishing, each one came inside to wish him well, even if more than a few had their fingers crossed. Last in line was his old Army chum, Tommy, who gave him a big hug, a gesture not often seen at Headquarters. "Tommy, Captain Telfer gave me the Elmore Murder to start with," he said when they were alone. "What do you know?"

"Well, Den, Management is saying, 'Show us what you got.' Maybe dying screwed you up somewhere deep inside, where the doctors can't find it. You're going to have to prove your investigating is much better now than it was when you left, and you're going to have to try to bring this case to a better conclusion. How're you going to start? Maybe if you can turn up something new—*anything*—it will show them you still have your stuff. Want my help?"

"No, that's okay Tommy. It looks like a nice day. I think I'll drive over to Crown Point and take a look at the scene of the crime for myself."

"Hey, Den, you'll want to know that Capt. Telfer has put me on the Charbonneau case full time. We'll get that scummy guy, you wait and see," Tommy grinned. And with that, Girard hefted the Elmore file box and left. First day, first job for the new Girard, and it all took just 25 minutes.

He found the flat where Muriel Elmore was murdered. There was a "For Rent" sign on the upstairs apartment window, so he knocked at the downstairs door and, showing his ID, asked the landlady to see the apartment. The white-haired woman who answered the door reeked of alcohol and peered at him through red eyes. "Funny thing 'bout that apartment—I jush can't keep it rented. People move in for a month or so, and then they're gone. It's empty now, so take your time up there, you ain't scaring anybody away," she slurred, handing him a passkey.

Girard let himself in and found the room bright but foreboding, even with the morning sun shining in the east windows. His scalp began to tingle and he got the old "electric field" sensation again. He walked slowly into the kitchen and was startled by the apparition of a gaunt, pale, and dark-haired woman standing in her housecoat. She reached a hand toward Girard, then gradually faded into nothingness, which reminded him of the Memorial Day ghosts in Chestertown. So *that's* how this is going to work, he figured. Well, I'm just going to slam *that* door. Can't let Headquarters know I'm also seeing ghosts while I'm working. Now, where to start?

The only piece of furniture in the main room was an old captain's chair with a broken armrest. Pulling it into a shaft of sunlight, Girard sat and began to meticulously read the file, so that no detail was overlooked. Muriel Frances Elmore, female, 36, Caucasian, unemployed. Never married, apparently. No visible means of support, and not listed on Social Services assistance either. She'd lived alone there for more than a year before being murdered. Witnesses had only ever seen one man entering her apartment, but it was always at night and their visibility was poor. On September 29, 2006 the landlady had heard a crash overhead and went upstairs to investigate. She had seen and heard nothing except the noise from above, but found Elmore's body sprawled beside the bed when she let herself in through the locked door. Simple—that's all there was. The Forensics crew had photographed the scene, mapped the site with the new electronic workstation, vacuumed for debris, and sought usable fingerprints, apparently to no avail. Quinn and Shaloub had done the forensic job and they were top-notch. It sure would be some kind of magic if he could solve *this* one!

91

The room was warm because of the sun streaming through the windows. Mrs. Wilke, downstairs, seemed to like the place about 78 degrees, even though it was June. Girard unbuttoned his blazer and closed his eyes. Momentarily, he slipped into a defeatist mood, Why me? Everyone, good investigators, had done their best on this one; why give it to me? Unless...maybe they want me to strike out, he worried. Yes, that's it, maybe they gave me an unsolvable case just as a pretext for putting me out to pasture.

There was an almost inaudible click and the apartment door opened. Without moving in his chair, Girard opened his eyes. A dark-haired, dark-complexioned, young man about 27, eased into the apartment. The fool—housebreaking! Can't he see I'm here Girard sputtered to himself. He watched the man cross to the window, which for some reason, was now dark. The room's interior was suddenly gloomy and furniture abruptly appeared from nowhere. How'd that happen? The intruder crossed to a figure sleeping on a bed that wasn't there a few minutes ago. He wasted no time in looping a cord around the inert woman's neck and yanking it tight. This isn't real! Girard panicked—he *knew* that, but had to fight down every officer's normal impulse to help in order to continue observing a crime without interfering. Goddam head stuff!

On one level, he knew this was another of his ghost visions, like the lady in the kitchen. Nevertheless, there was nothing he could do to stop a certain murder—he felt paralyzed in his chair. His heart was beating rapidly; he *knew* it wasn't real, but he still could *see* it happening. His head began to throb and cold sweat broke out on his brow. The murderer gave one final, prolonged yank on his cord, jerking the woman's body up from the bed and backward, before loosening the cord, which he then stuffed into a small hole in the wall near the door as he prepared to exit. The cord pulling had almost tugged the body off the bed, and the woman was now sprawled half on and half off.

This must be Muriel Elmore, thought Girard. Did I just watch somebody *murder* her? How can that happen? More ghost stuff? Angel stuff? Okay, take your time, Girard—look at the guy's face before he leaves—get a complete description. He did so. Then the intruder slipped out the door, setting the lock as he left. Elmore's unstable body, sprawled more off than on the bed now, slipped and fell to the floor with a resounding thud.

The scene vanished and he was once more in a bright, unfurnished room. The perfect crime...almost, but the murderer didn't know there had been a witness. Girard, still suspended between the past and the present, heard a motorcycle rev up and speed off into the night outside, though it was daytime. He sat stunned, as any person, law enforcement or not, would have done after witnessing the vicious taking of a life.

He glanced around and realized that it really was daylight. What *was* this? Was he crazy? His perspiration and throbbing head suddenly vanished. Well, Girard, I think you're nuts, he mumbled, you're just nuts—a goddam wacko! The investigator walked over to find the hole he'd seen in the wall. It was no longer there, though he could locate its position from the crime scene photo in his folder. It was obvious that someone had patched the wall since the initial murder investigation, but he took his pen and made an x to remind him where the opening had been. Walking downstairs, he again rapped on Mrs. Wilke's door. "Did you ever see anyone who rode a motorcycle around here when Muriel Elmore lived upstairs?" he asked.

"No, but once when I was driving up Route 9, I spotted her in front of Skippy's Cycle Shop just as you come into Port Henry."

The prospect of this inebriated woman behind a car's wheel staggered Girard, and he asked, "Do you remember ever telling the investigators that fact back in 2006? It's not in the investigators' notes."

"I don't think I did. I'd see that girl around town lots of places, but the cops didn't ask me about those things, and I just answered their questions. I run a nice place here and I didn't want to get into trouble or get a bad reputation," she cooed.

"Well, this house seems to have a bad reputation *now*, right?" Girard countered dryly. "I'm going to have some other investigators come back, because there may be some new evidence up there. Do I have your consent to do an official search of the premises again? Okay?"

"Sure, officer. Like I said, I want to cooperate with the police." Geraldine Wilke staggered against the door and had to catch herself while closing it. All this cop talk made her nervous and she needed another drink.

Investigator Girard used his cell phone to call Headquarters in Ray Brook. Knowing he'd need a search warrant now, he informed Capt. Telfer that he had Geraldine Wilke's consent for another investigation. At Girard's request, Telfer switched the call to Frank Whitson, of the Troop B Forensics Unit at Headquarters. Whitson noted that the FIU was finishing an investigation in Rainbow Lake that night and would be free first thing Thursday morning. "I'll make that our priority tomorrow," said

Whitson. Girard mused that "the Goo Crew," as he called them because of all the blood and body parts they usually had to handle, was often the biggest single factor in solving "impossible cases." Enjoining Mrs. Wilke to stay out of the apartment, Girard crossed the street to the Save-a-Lot gas station for coffee. *My last remaining vice,* he reminded himself.

There was still some good investigative time remaining, though the skies were clouding over rapidly; maybe a storm was coming. Girard was now energized to such a high level that he felt like a bloodhound on the trail. He decided to follow up Mrs. Wilke's other clue about seeing Muriel up at Skippy's. He secured the apartment, crisscrossed the locked door with yellow "Crime Scene" tape, and went to his car. He was happy that he'd been re-assigned his former Chevy and settled in for the 10-minute drive up to Port Henry.

He'd known Skippy Perrault, who built the place in the 1970s, but remembered that Skippy had retired, and now someone new was in there, a guy with a foreign name. The noontime sun beat down and the glass front door at Skippy's was open for ventilation when he arrived. Out in front of the shop stood a big Honda 2200 CVT cycle in iridescent green. Girard entered and found nobody at the counter, but hearing voices out back, he walked toward the repair shop door.

"Goddam cat!" came a man's loud voice, as a frightened tabby cat came skidding from the repair shop doorway and shot out the front door. "Oh, hi, didn't hear you come in," the mechanic said to Girard, as he suddenly appeared in the doorway. The investigator found himself looking into the cold, blue eyes of the dark-haired man in his Crown Point vision—no question about the identity. Suddenly, he knew how to open the gambit, but was puzzled at how quickly the inspiration had appeared in his mind. He showed his identification.

"You have a break-in here last week?" he inquired, all the while wondering how and why *that* question was on his lips.

"Yeah," the man replied quizzically, "but we didn't report it to anybody."

"Well, do you want to make an official report now?"

"Sure, why not?" came the mechanic's reply.

"Sorry, I didn't get your name," said Girard.

"Oh, yeah. I'm Paul Hochlitzer. I run this place, but my uncle, Faust Hetzer, owns the shop."

"Let me get a report form from the car," Girard said. He left briefly to retrieve a report form from the front seat file in his car. Hochlitzer watched him go, wiping greasy hands on a rag tucked into his belt.

"Okay, here we are," said Girard, returning and handing over the form. "Not that hard to fill out." Hochlitzer reached for the paper and his still-greasy hand left fingerprints on the sheet. "Oh, that won't do," said Investigator Girard. "Headquarters won't accept complaints that are dirty. Here, take another, and wipe your hands before handling it. Thanks." Dennis Girard carefully tucked the spoiled copy into his folder and between two sheets of plastic inside. Hochlitzer quickly filled out the sketchy information: a rear door had been found open in the morning. No footprints outside either the front or back door. After a quick inventory, they'd found nothing missing. Girard knew that by now, there was little likelihood of finding the burglars unless they'd left fingerprints, but the State Police had *this* suspect's personal information and, most important, good prints from his right hand.

In a minute, the mechanic returned the form to Girard, who responded, "Thanks. We'll see what we can do about catching these bad guys. We'll get a fingerprint team in here pretty soon, just in case the robbers left prints. But at least, you have this report on file with us, in case you *do* find something missing and want to cover it under your insurance. Well, good day."

"Hey mister, what made you stop here? We hadn't reported the break-in."

"I was working on another case in the area, and someone down in Crown Point must have mentioned it to me. I forget." Girard dissembled. He waved, got into the Impala, and departed north. As he turned westward, the grey skies opened up in a drenching downpour, but Girard was buoyant; he knew he was onto something solid. And it was going to save his career!

CHAPTER TWENTY-ONE

He arrived at work at 7:30 on Thursday morning, ready to put his intuitive vision, or whatever goofy experience it was, to the test. Before doing anything else, he closed his office door and stood in silent prayer for the moment, asking Whoever Runs This Show to bear him out, to not let him come away from this day looking like a fool. In the FIU room, he could see Whitson's team of Shaloub and Quinn readying to join him in Crown Point, going over their equipment and materials. In the hallway near the front door he met Investigator Alice Gaudreau, who was readying to join the pair, preparing to carefully inventory whatever they turned up, sealing the materials in carefully marked evidence bags, and depositing them in the evidence vault at Headquarters upon the team's return. She was carrying her palm video camera, with which she would record the opening of the wall and whatever the team discovered after they did it. Palm videos were very helpful in showing the chain of custody for all evidence, just as it was being plucked from its *in situ* discovery site. They said hello and "I'll see you soon," to one another. Then, picking up his notebook, Girard headed over to Crown Point.

At two minutes before 9:00 a.m. the black van of the FIU team rolled up to Mrs. Wilke's building. The investigators got out and shook hands with Girard again. "What you got here, Denny? There can't be anything new here after so many years. We went over this building with a fine-toothed comb following the murder."

Walking the team to the upstairs apartment and unlocking the door with Mrs. Wilke's passkey, Girard said, "Kenny, I'd like you guys to punch a hole in the wall there below that x, but nicely—no dirt and no dust. Look at this crime scene photo from 2006. See that break in the hard wall? It's been fixed since, but I'd like you to open it up again, gently. I think something might be down inside the wall. Maybe some evidence."

"OK, Denny. We'll do it, but what makes you think something's in there? How about getting us some coffee while we set up?"

Girard was only too glad to ignore the first question, and walked quickly over to the gas station to get "three all blacks, no sugar," and a cream and sugar for himself. We're getting to the sticking point really quick now, and it won't be long before they all know how nuts I really *am*, he figured.

Five minutes later he returned to the upstairs apartment with the coffee and found Kenny Quinn and Tom Shaloub hunched over something on the floor. Alice was standing close, using her zoom lens to capture it all. A bright, miniature floor light illuminated a 9-inch square cut they'd made in the wall at floor level. Moving closer, Girard saw Tom, with latex gloves, lifting an old pull cord with the stub of a broken handle attached into one of Alice's evidence bags. Turning, Kenny exclaimed, "I'll be damned Girard! How'd you know this was in there?"

"I didn't *know*, Kenny, I just saw that little hole in the wall in that crime scene photo, and wondered if someone might have jammed a garrote, a belt, or rope of some kind in there," he lied. The four then compared the pattern of twisted strands on the pull cord with the pattern or twists showing on the victim's throat in the old forensic photos. It seemed a dead-on match.

"We vacuumed all the dust out of the bottom of that space and are bagging that for the lab too," said Tom. "Now we're going to cut the entire panel between the wall studs right up to where that hole was, and see if anything else is in there. As he said this, Quinn turned on a small electric sawing tool and began his cut. In five minutes he'd finished, the panel was lifted out, and the wall space examined. "Nothing else inside, but at least it's *something* new," said Tom. "And we just might get some good latent prints off this cord handle. Seems like it's impregnated with something oily, so maybe we'll get lucky. Looks like it's off an old snowmobile or lawn mower."

Shaloub promised to put the prints into the hands of the trooper scheduled to make a noontime run to Division Headquarters in Albany where the fingerprints would be entered in the Statewide Automated fingerprint Identification System (SAFIS). The "Goo Crew" packed up and said their goodbyes, leaving for Ray Brook and some microscopic and chemical forensics work of their own that might even turn up some usable DNA.

This is good, Girard concluded, really good! I don't know how I did it, and it's scary to think that someone I can't see might have helped me, but dammit, we're going to crack this one! Feeling exhilarated, he decided to detour to where his misery began—Chilson, and the old Anderson farm that Two Claw now owned.

It wasn't a long trip down to Ti—maybe a half hour if he didn't push it, then west on Route 74. Part of him dreaded seeing the site where he'd died during the previous winter, but something more powerful now demanded that he confront this mysterious new vulnerability which had begun there.

Near the top of the mountain, he turned right onto the gravel road that led to Two Claw's place. He parked in the muddy driveway, still slippery from last night's cloudburst. Walking toward the house, he remembered all the buildings as if it was just yesterday that he'd stood there in bone-chilling cold. All at once, as he approached the side door of the old farmhouse, a sudden movement back near the trees caught his attention. He stopped in his tracks—it was Two Claw, walking away from him! Charbonneau apparently hadn't seen Girard, and the investigator quickly moved to put a screen of bushes between them. He drew his pistol and stealthily approached. Gonna get that sonofabitch today and put it all to an end, *right now,* he resolved angrily. His heart hammered within his chest, his brow was suddenly covered with sweat, and his hands turned ice cold.

Moving forward, he could see Charbonneau's back clearly. The man was bending over a trash pile, apparently ready to burn something. Now only 20 feet behind his quarry, Girard went into a shooter's stance and called Charbonneau's name loudly. "Stop and raise your hands, you bastard. This is the State Police," he shouted so loudly that even *he* feared the voice that seemed to emerge from a deeper, angrier place within him than he'd ever known before. Charbonneau simply vanished before the reverberation of Girard's voice stopped.

Girard stood stunned; how'd he *do* that? His shoulders sagged and his pistol dropped to his side. Aw, shit! Is this more of that damned angel stuff? Is my mind finally cooked? Was that sonofabitch real or *not?* He walked cautiously toward the trash pile, as if expecting Charbonneau to suddenly reappear. It didn't happen. The investigator stood looking down at a rain-soaked pile of old, wet papers and ashes. There were no footprints in the mud. Nobody had been standing there. Yet, somebody, sometime, had tried to burn a lot of stuff there—to destroy evidence of some type. He wondered if the burn pile had been visible to the investigators back in February, and made a mental note to have Whitson get his crew down again to preserve whatever evidence might remain.

In disgust at his vision and failure to put Two Claw away for good, Girard kicked a rock as hard as he could. The rock bounced away toward the old chicken coop. Aw, the hell with this goddamn job and this damn fried brain of mine! "Goddammit, angel, why are you *doing* this to me?" he screamed at the top of his lungs.

Turning, he retraced his steps to the car. He now had lost all enthusiasm for revisiting the old chicken coop where he had died. What had begun as an uplifting day was now filled with feelings of disgrace. To have seen Charbonneau so clearly and then have him disappear had taken a great toll on his emotions. Girard headed north to Ray Brook, feeling almost as shaky as the day he had awakened after dying.

He arrived back at Troop Headquarters at 4:15 p.m. On his desk was a copy of a still-warm fax which had originated at the Albany SAFIS office. Kenny Quinn's attached note with a 4:10 time notation said, "Denny, this was just *too* easy!" The report sheet indicated that there had been a quick match of the pull-cord fingerprints, when SAFIS accessed the U.S. Army fingerprint database. The prints on the pull cord from Port Henry belonged to one Paul Michael Hochlitzer, Male, Caucasian, 31, 5 feet and 11 inches tall, a naturalized American citizen born in Bonn, Germany. Last known address was in Moriah, NY. He had two prior arrests for vandalism at age 18 and for possession of stolen goods at age 22, after being dishonorably discharged from the Army, and finally for assault and battery on a Westport woman in 2005. All three cases were pleaded down to fines and probation, but Hochlitzer was still on probation at the time of the Elmore murder. Kenny's note also stated that there were microscopic skin cells found in the twists of the cord, and he was sending the cord to the FBI Lab in Washington, DC, seeking usable DNA, if it was identifiable.

Girard then had Shaloub fax the spoiled burglary inventory sheet prints to SAFIS, assuming that he'd have another hit when he returned to work the next day. Okay, that's it, Girard concluded with a grin of satisfaction and suddenly reinvigorated. One I.D. from the pull-cord is probable cause for Hochlitzer's arrest, anyway, so my first job will be Skippy's when they open in the morning. He stopped by Capt. Telfer's office, and the officer broke off a phone call as soon as Girard laid the Elmore file before him. Breaking into a big smile, Telfer said, "Right now, get an arrest warrant from Judge Bogle, so we can bust this one. Investigator Girard called the Judge, then faxed the necessary evidence from his investigation to Bogle. A couple of minutes later, the judge said, "Come right over, Investigator Girard, I'll have the warrant ready for you when you get here."

All in all, despite the crappy afternoon, not bad for my second day back at work, he congratulated himself. Girard headed home to Chestertown around 5:30 p.m., then suited up for a cathartic evening hike up Graphite Mountain, hoping to exhaust himself before his nightly cup of tea. This was going to be a good, if late, night.

CHAPTER TWENTY-TWO

At 8:30, in his Friday morning mail, Girard found a second positive identification for Hochlitzer's prints from the spoiled form he'd sent the

99

previous night. Now, armed with the arrest warrant and accompanied by Trooper Dick Ramirez, Girard left Ray Brook. As they started on the southeastward journey to Port Henry, Girard began making small talk with his companion. Ramirez was gazing at him in a funny way, and finally Girard called him on it. "What's up, Richard? You've been giving me the fish eye ever since we left the office."

"Girard, tell me something" the young trooper replied. "A month or so ago, on the day we met, you gave me a warning about making a traffic stop. The first thing out, I caught a guy doing 85, not uncommon for New Jersey drivers on the Northway, so I thought it would be routine. But you made me more nervous than I usually am, and when I stopped that BMW, I expected trouble. I remembered what you said about staying well back behind the driver's window, and you were right. When I came up behind that guy's front door and asked for license and registration, his hand came out with the documents in it, but he had a small syringe hidden behind those papers. He stabbed at me, but I was just one foot too far away. I arrested the bastard at gunpoint, cuffed him, and called in the info. I could see he was wild-eyed. Later, when we booked him, they said he was high on meth. How could you have *known?*"

Realizing he had to fudge this one, Girard countered, "Well, Richard, when you've been a trooper as long as I have, you hopefully develop a sixth sense, and if you listen to it, I mean really *listen* to it, you'll usually find it helps. In this case it probably saved your life. Nobody at the Academy *really* prepares you to listen to your intuition, but I'm sure it has saved *me* many times. And I suspect that's true for most of us old-timers."

"Yeah, I see what you mean," said Ramirez thoughtfully. "But all that intuition stuff—isn't that really horseshit? Some kind of psychic hogwash? My grandmother in Mexico was what they call a *curandera*, like a witch woman, and I never believed in *her* stuff."

"I don't think it's nuts, Richard. I think it's a God-given, inner warning system that even the cavemen had. Check it out and you'll see." Silently, Girard wondered where *these* words, which made so much sense right now, had come from.

The conversation then changed to the recent increase in summer drunks on the roads, with colleges and high schools now on vacation. The rest of the journey down to I-87 was filled with good-natured banter. Both men expected their careers to improve before the day ended. As they approached Port Henry, Girard went over the case once more to be sure his partner understood what was expected of him.

The investigator swung his unmarked car down into Skippy's parking lot, and the two disembarked. The trooper uniform coming in the door unnerved the 18-year-old female receptionist. Before Girard was able to speak, the girl, Earlene, called out in a shaky voice, "Pauly, wanna come out here?" Ramirez seemed to remember her from somewhere. Maybe a recent traffic stop?

"Hey, did you catch my burglar?" Hochlitzer emerged from out back, wiping his greasy hands on the rag at his belt. He eagerly walked over to the two men.

"We caught more than that," Girard responded gravely and moved closer. "Paul Michael Hochlitzer, I arrest you for the murder of Muriel Elmore on September 29, 2006." The mechanic panicked and turned as if to run. He hadn't reckoned with Trooper Ramirez, who had been slowly shifting to Hochlitzer's left and quickly seized him, spun him, and had him handcuffed behind his back in 10 seconds. "You have the right to remain silent..." Girard began the Miranda Warning.

"You bastards! Coming in here to catch my burglar, huh? Bullshit! Well I didn't do nothing. You hear me I didn't do *nothing*! I didn't even know that whore!"

"Do you understand these rights as I've read them to you?" concluded Ramirez.

"You bet I understand them—I know a frame-up when I see one. You rotten bastards—I'll sue your asses! You can't make that charge stick. Earlene, honey, you lock up. I'll be back, and I'll see you tonight. They can't hold *me*!"And with that, Hochlitzer was placed in the right rear of the Chevrolet and taken to be booked at the State Police station in Crown Point. Then the mechanic was taken to the Essex County Jail in Elizabethtown to be held until arraignment on Monday. When they returned to Ray Brook later, Trooper Ramirez was jubilant. His first murder collar! Girard was also ebullient; he hadn't lost his stuff, and now his fellow investigators would *know* it.

Major Sincavage, who had been summoned to the booking area by Captain Telfer, gave Girard a hearty handshake, but also a strange, piercing look. He had known the Elmore family and rejoiced that this incident was so much like the victories he and Girard had shared during the first few years they worked together in Ray Brook. Leaving the celebrating men, Sincavage went to his office to make a short, late-evening phone call to Lt. Lenny Mueller, deputy to the Superintendent of State Police in Albany.

"A murder a day, eh Girard? Congratulations! How many are you going to nab tomorrow?" Frank Whitson crowed. He'd known Girard for years and was extremely happy to see the old smiling face back on the job.

CHAPTER TWENTY-THREE

Dennis Girard slept well Friday night and bounced out of bed early on Saturday morning, filled with vigor and with the anticipation that he would score another success soon. I'm on a roll now, he congratulated himself. Today he'd ponder the whole case from beginning to its quick ending as he took his new "Saturday morning regular hike" up Graphite Mountain. After a small breakfast of poached eggs, coffee, and toast, he hustled down to Route 8 and began his trek.

Leaving Chestertown and walking in the direction of the morning sun, he exulted at his relatively quick first victory. Passing beneath the Northway bridges and headed east on Route 8, he now felt better about his job and the manner in which he'd performed it, just as in the old days when he was young, strong, and quick. And, he'd helped bring in a murderer who might otherwise never have been caught. Girard, his voice, veiled by the roar of Northway traffic overhead, yelled to his invisible caretaker, "You see *that*, angel? I did it! Just as you said!"

"Really? All by yourself?" came an androgynous voice from the roadside. He whirled to see who had spoken, as he hadn't passed anyone. There stood a tall, lean, elderly, grey-haired black woman with a flowered hat, holding a black patent leather purse. Her outfit reminded him of that used by Grand Old Opry star, Minnie Pearl, of years ago. "Lady, you could get hurt out here on the shoulder of this road. What are you doing there all alone?"

The woman drew herself up to her full height and looked intently into Girard's eyes from 15 feet away. The voice deepened and said, "I keep trying to communicate with you in a manner that won't lead you to anger, like last time." Now he could see the details of her face more clearly, though the woman's eyes were obscured by steel-rimmed eyeglasses. Girard was jolted by the slight reddish glow behind the glasses, because he knew that this was Israfil again.

"Oh God!" he exclaimed. "Not again. Can't you just stay invisible?

Just when I thought things were going right, I have to encounter *you* again!"

"Oh, things are going well, considering the circumstances," the lady said, straightening her dress. "You are no longer the same man as when we first met. But time is of the essence in your reality, and you must fortify your inner and outer mind to prepare for the work that is set before you now. I am here to assure you that you had *much* help in catching the law-breaker." A large RV zoomed past headed downhill to the Schroon River Bridge, creating a strong gust of air.

"Yeah, I thought I'd gotten pretty damn lucky, bringing that guy in so quickly," Girard said dejectedly. "But he was one of the *bad* guys I told you about," he brightened. "They're everywhere. And they're not goody-goodies like you!" In his sudden irritation, Girard took a step toward the woman, close enough to see that, despite her wrinkles, she had the soft, clear skin of a girl.

"Some time ago I promised that your career would improve *if* you shouldered the burden of your hidden gifts," the woman said, smiling to reveal a perfect set of teeth, despite her 80-ish appearance. "You are now opening to many new dimensions of this strength, but with these comes a grave responsibility, and you must not be dismayed or deterred by it. Now, *I* provide you with assistance that improves your perception, but soon you will be able to access that force from within yourself, without assistance. And society will be the better for it. That's all I have to say for now." And as quickly as she had appeared, she vanished, leaving the roadside grasses waving gently in the breeze.

Girard stood sweating, astonished at Israfil's sudden return and rapid disappearance. The only way to steady his nerves was to break into a quick-march gait, almost a power walk. He mused that his route was taking him uphill, the same metaphor that the angel had described for his life.

At the North Pond Parking Area he lingered and walked slowly around the turn-off, hoping for the reappearance of his eagle. He was edgy because his future seemed both assured and unpredictable. After an hour of walking meditation, he went out to the highway and started home. Taking his time in returning to Chestertown, he stopped at Suzy Q's restaurant in Brant Lake for a lunch of un-spiced scrambled eggs, coffee and an English muffin.

He went to bed early Saturday night, but awoke suddenly at 1:01 a.m., feeling compelled to write a puzzling dream in his journal. He knew it was important and that he would need Dr. Epstein's help in making sense of it and then finding out how to apply it.

In the dream imagery, Girard viewed himself on a flat, dry desert with only a very dim pre-dawn illumination. He lived the dream as both participant and observer, from time to time visualizing himself as a stooped old man in a raggedy cloak and broad straw hat that seemed Chinese in design. He was engaged in fulfilling a task that required him to grope along the shadowed, sandy desert floor to find a barely visible piece of crystal glass, then grasp it in his bare hand and transfer the shard to a large basket that he carried. The sharp edges of the glass hurt his hands, and he soon realized that the crystal sliver was covered with his blood. As he painfully grasped a second piece and placed it in the basket, the horizon grew a bit lighter, a result that he experienced with the collection of each new fragment. He understood that a great crystal had long ago been shattered, and that his task was to gather, then reunite some, if not all of its bits. And he dimly sensed that it was *his* blood that was to be the binder in restoring the fractured object. His labors seemed endless in the dream, and his only indicator of progress was the gradual illumination of day. End of dream.

Finishing the journal entry, he sipped the last few drops of cold tea from a cup on the table and returned to bed, where he slept until almost noon on Sunday. Awakening, he started the coffee pot and snapped on the television to catch the CNN noontime news, whereupon he pursed his lips at yet another in a seemingly endless chain of terrorist bombings in the Middle East. I wonder where all this killing will end, and why does God keep *letting* this happen, he puzzled. It's the innocent people on buses and street corners that die, and less often the soldiers. And they keep telling me that God is a God of love! If there's love in all this death, I've got to dig a whole lot deeper than I know right now. After that news report, CNN aired a two-hour special on the major Middle East terrorist groups, which he found compelling.

At that point, taking a break from the stress of the news reports, he poured a cup of coffee and sat down to read a copy of Dr. Carl Jung's book, *Memories, Dreams, Reflections*, which Dr. Epstein had loaned him. So much of it made sense. Jung wrote of each person's *need* for an ego to provide strength in making his way in a threatening world, but also of an equal necessity for linking this ego's consciousness to a Higher Power, so the person doesn't live continually in self-worship. We have to have a relationship to the Higher Self if humans are to escape neurotic living. People were meant to maintain a link, maybe something like a sonship with God, while recognizing and developing their uniqueness in the world. I've sure been neurotic, he reminded himself, probably most of my life. He read until 10:30 p.m. and then turned in, hoping for another superlative day at work on Monday.

CHAPTER TWENTY-FOUR

Faust Hetzer was angry. He slammed his way out of his house in Westport that Saturday morning and drove south on Route 9N to Skippy's Bike Shop in Port Henry. That imbecile kid! That bastard son of my sister! I should never have brought him to America and trusted him to do his part, even though he *does* speak perfect English, he thought. Now Paul has screwed up the whole operation, which was supposed to run precisely, like a good engine!

As Hetzer drove south, he remembered his narrow escape from the German BKA police that night in Düsseldorf back in April 1991. The juggernaut of capitalist bankers and multinational corporations had ensnared post-war Germany, and even that April 21st execution had not slowed its onslaught. Detlev Rohwedder, the director of the government privatization agency, was an enemy of the people, a tool of the fascist capitalist structure, and therefore *deserved* to die. But he was only an underling and not the master puppeteer. No, those powerful strings were pulled from outside Germany—in the United States! And that *scheisskerl* oil magnate, George H.W. Bush, was the master capitalist who organized all the large industrial nations to keep the world's working nations perpetually poor and powerless, and he also used America's military to maintain western domination of Middle East oil. When impoverished nations wouldn't submit to the capitalist overlords, they were denied development loans or were invaded.

When he was President, Bush was too hard to hit, but it could be done *now*—it *must* be done, so that his son likewise might suffer before relinquishing the presidency! The Bush Dynasty in America, a power that dominated the poor Third World and worker nations for the wealth of the few, had to end now. It would be a first step in demolishing the G-8 conspiracy.

The network had gotten him out of his East German homeland, providing a false passport in the name of a long-ago-deceased East German boy named Faust Hetzer, an identity that he'd converted into American citizenship in 1999. He appreciated the meaning of the name, "the rabble-rousing fist," which he now believed to be his destiny. Once in the U.S., he used the new identity to become a low-profile good citizen of Essex County and a small capitalist himself, with a motorcycle shop. The groundwork had been laid, and now the "tools" were coming. And it looked like there were new, non-European members willing to work with the organization. But that stupid boy had murdered a woman, throwing the entire enterprise under scrutiny, and worst of all—he'd gotten caught!

The *verwünscht* American authorities mustn't suspect the prize that Faust Hetzer really sought! Now he had to assemble the broken pieces, and quickly, to see what could be salvaged. Likely, that Jim guy from up north could still be counted on. He and another man named Louie had another network that would help get "the tools" in place. First, Hetzer needed a good lawyer to defend his nephew, making sure the boy didn't disclose any secrets under questioning. Yes, unfortunately, that had to be done right now. Then, close the shop and journey north to see that Jim guy today, before they get onto *me*.

At Skippy's, Hetzer called the prestigious Albany law firm of Hoover, Herrnkind, Sloger and Robinson, which took even the dirtiest cases and turned them into gold for defendants. Dick Robinson agreed to interview Hochlitzer at 7:00 p.m.

Hetzer's second call was to Willy Adlerschild, one of his co-conspirators in Frederick, MD. Though, he didn't know the man's real name and didn't care, Hetzer knew the man needed to be near Ft. Detrick. And he knew that Adlerschild had contacts to other cells of the network, cells that fomented the still-unsolved anthrax scare of 2001. This network had men and women with communications know-how, and what seemed most important right now, was to know what the cops knew or suspected. First, did they know about the network? Did they know about Hetzer's role in it? Were they watching Skippy's? And, most important, did they know about "The Plan"?

CHAPTER TWENTY-FIVE

Sr. Investigator Girard completed the journey to Ray Brook deep in thought on Monday morning. Some of Carl Jung's ideas circulated and recirculated just below the level of consciousness, occasionally popping to the surface for recognition. Clearly, if Jung was right, each person had to do the inner work of fending off the illusions that continually plague his or her unthinking personality. It seemed obvious that each individual was then responsible for saving *himself* from meaninglessness. But then, what role did God play? And what part of a human being was it that needed salvation?

Entering his office, he received congratulations for Friday's success from some, but not all, of his fellow workers. A few of the investigators on the BCI wing seemed to avoid him that morning, and he wondered if there was some professional jealousy or resentment at the quickness of his "comeback." Capt. Telfer had left two Post-It notes atop a second file on his desk: the first said that the DA, Merton LaBarge, decided to hit Hochlitzer with a Murder One indictment at his arraignment at noon that day. Girard was to be in attendance at the courthouse. The second note taped to the file box said, "Try this one as soon as you are able. Can you do another miracle?"

The file label identified the contents as "Bortiatynski" and gave a file number and date, though the name didn't ring a bell in his memory. He set it aside for Tuesday, as there was plenty of paperwork to do on young Hochlitzer. Right now, he knew he could cover the damned angel stuff by using Mrs. Wilke's memory and his own sharp eye that spotted the hole in her wall, as justification for reopening and quick success in the case when he wrote his report.

Girard completed some paperwork and at 10:45 a.m. took the slow drive to the County Courthouse in Elizabethtown. He parked at the Stewart's store and got himself a large coffee, then walked across the street to the courthouse. Stopping at the state historic marker in front of the building, he refreshed his memory of John Brown's body. After his trial and hanging execution for the failed pre-Civil War raid on Harper's Ferry in 1859, Brown's body was brought to the Essex County Courthouse, where it lay in state before being carried for burial to Brown's farm in the nearby hamlet of North Elba. Another martyr.

The noon arraignment was short and sweet. LaBarge, up for re-election in the fall and something of a showman, entered the courtroom with a scowl on his face, slamming his briefcase upon the table and looking menacingly at the prisoner, who was represented by counsel in an expensive suit. The assemblage rose when Judge Diane Conlin entered, then seated themselves for the reading of charges. Hochlitzer was instructed to make his plea, which predictably, was "innocent." Judge Conlin ordered him held without bail, pending an indictment by the grand jury, though Richard Robinson, Hochlitzer's attorney, strongly protested, saying that the prisoner was not a flight risk. During the brief drama, Girard scanned the almost empty room. Mary Deltry of the *Post Star* was the only press representative there.

But there was one other observer in the courtroom, an individual unknown to the investigator, an unsmiling and tense-looking individual with close-cropped, grey hair and steel-rimmed eyeglasses. As Girard turned to look at him, the man shot a menacing glare in return, which immediately put Girard on guard. "You can't imagine how dangerous he really *is*," a voice pronounced. Did it come from within *him* or from Timmy? Or from Izzy? Before young Hochlitzer was led away, the steely-eyed stranger requested a few moments with the prisoner, and it became clear to Girard that the man was Faust Hetzer, the young man's uncle, and the owner of Skippy's Bike Shop. Girard unconsciously reached a resolution on the matter, though he didn't understand it fully until the next day. The arraignment quickly concluded; Girard hit the road for Ray Brook and a few more hours of work.

When he checked in on Tuesday morning, Girard set to reading the new crime file—another cold case. The date of the initial report, February 17, 1983, fell during the period of his service in Troop G to the south, so he probably had been too intent on advancing his career and dealing with Irene's criticism at the time, he surmised. Opening the box, he found a précis of the investigation. Young Walter Bortiatynski, age 14, 5' 4" and 110 pounds, light brown hair, from Potsdam, had disappeared without a trace and no sign of him had ever been found. The boy was on a high school winter vacation when he disappeared that Thursday.

The only child of Walter, Sr., and Mary Lou Bortiatynski, the former honors student had become introverted in 8th Grade, and by the start of school the next September, had few friends. A guidance counselor had notated at the time of Walter's disappearance that "it was as if he suddenly felt himself to be a leper." The boy's school grades had fallen off badly at the beginning of 9th Grade and he was twice referred to the school psychologist, who could not determine a cause or remedy for the boy's apparent depression. The father, a machine tender at the local paper mill, disdained psychotherapy and refused to send the child to a private counselor in the city. Mary Lou worked as a cashier in a local supermarket, leaving the boy to his own devices after school.

There was also a notation that the Potsdam Police Department had briefly held the boy for marijuana possession in 1983, then released him into his parents' custody in January, about six weeks before the boy disappeared. Walter, Sr., and Mary Lou had been warned that young Walter was known to be in bad company, and that they should assert stronger control to ensure the youngster's safety. On the morning of Thursday, February 17, the teenager told his mother that he was going to the bowling alley to see if he might find an after-school job. The parents both went to work as usual, and young Walter never came home.

The case was referred to State Police Investigator Phil Rusin, who, with the Potsdam P.D., doggedly followed all potential leads. Girard nodded approvingly as he read the list of contacts that Rusin, aided by detectives Joe Popovich and Rick Albert, had chased down. All three men were stymied at the paucity of hard evidence. Rusin had done it all by the book in the days before Amber Alerts.

The investigation included a search of the boy's bedroom at home and interviews of a few of his school associates as well as teachers, and of course, the story ran for a week on WWNY-TV, from Watertown, and WPTZ from Plattsburgh, the local television stations. Area newspapers made the story front page fare for three days, then gradually ran it farther back in each succeeding edition as no leads turned up. By March 1st they had dropped the story pending further developments.

Curiously, Potsdam High School 10th Grader, Michelle Carpenter, had also disappeared on Monday of that week. Investigators could turn up no link between the girl and young Walter, though. Michelle showed up early Wednesday morning when the local cops busted an all-night vacation pot party on Depot Street. Michelle was unable to give any credible information relative to Walter's disappearance and likely did not know him, though both were marijuana users. The only conclusion, absent any suggestion that the boy had met with foul play, was that he had run away from home.

Walter was placed on a national list of runaways, and well into the summer of 1984 letter-size posters offering a reward for the teen's whereabouts could still be found at local stores and libraries. As the 1980s came to a close, apparently even Walter's parents had forgotten him, as cold-case investigators conducted an unproductive and unemotional re-interview with them in November 1989. A flash of presentiment struck Girard as he read the latter fact. A phantom hand was laid lightly on his left shoulder, and although he understood Timmy was probably working with him full time, he didn't even turn around.

The 65-mile drive across northern New York State to Potsdam was a sober one for Sr. Investigator Dennis Girard. He always got steamed when parents didn't safeguard and guide their children. In spite of his severity, Henri Girard had been a good father to *him*, and a good, if unimaginative, role model. Dennis concluded that, to the best of his own ability, he also had attempted to do that for his own kids. Parents today...he left off thinking.

How to get started on this one? Of course, the courtesy visit to the P.P.D. would come first, though both detectives Popovich and Albert were now likely retired and unavailable. Then what? Probably a trip to the high school and interviews with any available former teachers and guidance counselors, but then what? Where to go? There was no physical evidence at all, just the files of interviews and a few photographs in the case box. It seemed a cold trail, and he had little expectation that he could ever reach a better conclusion than Phil Rusin had, unless some new physical evidence emerged.

Cold northern New York and another cold case, he ruminated, though it was a hot day. Phil Rusin—now there was a guy: still young and handsome, a macho ex-Marine, and *smart*, who had retired early from the State Police in 1994 along with Girard's friend Jason Black, soon after Girard had been posted to Ray Brook. Both investigators had gone into private businesses and had found success...and new loves. At least their departures had opened the door for *him* to move up in rank to Senior Investigator. Why didn't *I* have enough smarts to quit when *I* turned 55? he berated himself.

Girard spent an hour renewing acquaintances with Rick Albert and two old friends at the Potsdam Police Department, but gained no helpful insights. P.P.D. had done little on the case since 1989, as there was nothing *to* do. He left the police station and drove to the high school on Leroy Street, where he took a Visitor's Parking spot and entered the building, spending the remainder of his day doing staff interviews that turned up absolutely nothing new. He stayed another hour, interviewing Ken Keast, the about-to-retire director of guidance. Before leaving Keast's office,

Girard called Walter Bortiatynski, Sr., and made an interview appointment for the next morning.

It was a long drive back to Chestertown and Dennis Girard was emotionally down when he arrived home at 9:00 p.m. *Wish I owned a pet, some simple creature I could tell my frustrations to,* he mused. Then he smiled. *Well, I do—I've got Izzy and he doesn't require a litter box cleanout!* Girard put the teakettle on the stove, popped a mandarin orange tea bag into his waiting cup, warmed up some week-old beef stew, and settled in to watch CNN. Paula Zahn was hosting a special program relating the increasing difficulties American women had in conceiving children in the 21st Century.

He took a message from Capt. Telfer from his answering machine, requesting him to come in to the office before returning to Potsdam on Wednesday—his signature was needed on some paperwork. The tea refreshed him as he struggled with the case's apparent dead end. *Yeah, that's sure the term, I bet, dead,* he grumped again.

Finishing off the stew, he waited to see Jay Leno's monologue on the *Tonight Show* before hitting the hay. The comic was ridiculing President Bush again. It was a night of troubled sleep in which he dreamed, over and over, about being unable to open a door underneath which a bright light shone.

CHAPTER TWENTY-SIX

His alarm buzzed at 7:00 a.m. as usual and, after a breakfast of shredded wheat and strawberries, he dressed and left the house. Mrs. Morgenstern was already at work among her perennials and the two exchanged smiles and waves as he backed from the driveway. As he pulled into the Headquarters parking area an hour later, yesterday's insight constellated. There was something about Faust Hetzer that he had to uncover, and it was something that the angel and Timmy would not reveal, though he sure had asked.

Once inside, he strode to the FIU and found Frank Whitson sipping his morning cup of mint tea. "Hi Frank. Remember the paperwork on the break-in over at Skippy's in Port Henry? Have you set up a date to do the fingerprinting there?"

"Sure, Dennis. Quinn and Shaloub are scheduled to be there tomorrow morning. We called the owner just now to be sure the shop will be open. Mr. Hetzer, the owner, said the business was closed, so I had to persuade him, suggesting that he was blocking the investigation of a crime, and I asked if he wanted to take that responsibility. He then said he'd meet us there at 9:00 a.m. Why?"

"I can't really explain it, Frank, but there's more to the boy's uncle than meets the eye. Kenny Quinn is pretty good with a camera. Do you think he might get a head shot of Hetzer without the man realizing it? Maybe he could shoot some possible 'fingerprints' on a door frame, but catch Hetzer's face in the background, or something like that? I don't know how he'd do it, but I want to try a hunch. What do you think?"

"Sure, Dennis, you're the Golden Boy here now," Whitson jibed. "Kenny has that Irish sense of humor and just loves to put one over on people, especially if they're possible bad guys. I'll make sure he has some prints for you, too, on Friday morning."

"Thanks, old buddy, I knew I could count on you."

He left the building and started the long drive to Potsdam. Another "something" kept nagging his subconscious mind about the Bortiatynski case, but it refused to immediately surface. Maybe today the interview with the boy's parents will uncover some new shred of evidence, he hoped. Walter, Sr., retired and now sits around the house most of the time except for hunting and fishing trips with friends, the P.P.D. had informed him. Mary Lou still works at the market, but had taken the day off to meet with the investigator.

Finding the address on Arlington Street, Girard exited his car and knocked on the door. A burly, unshaven, and cigarette-smoking man in an undershirt and slacks answered the knock and gruffly invited Girard to enter after the investigator identified himself. Curious, Girard observed, and made a snap analysis. Just briefly he felt the hand on his left shoulder again, as if in confirmation that he'd spotted something important. So, what was it?

Mary Lou came from the kitchen with curlers in her hair and in a dirty pink bathrobe. Curious, Girard again observed. If I were to meet with someone who might find my lost kid, wouldn't I be on my best behavior and dress? They all shook hands and Girard was offered the recliner chair, which he knew was the seat of power in the room. Though Walter, Sr., sipped from a cup of coffee, neither parent offered him any refreshment. No *coffee*? You folks are in deep trouble, he joked to himself.

Girard reviewed the case from his notes and attempted to take Mary Lou and Walter, Sr., back a quarter century to the teenager's disappearance. "Let's see, young Walter would be almost 40 years old by now," he observed aloud. His eye caught Mary Lou's quick, tight tug on her bathrobe belt. Both parents had forced smiles on their faces and Girard knew there was more to learn. Clearly, they were nervous, but where was their grief? The pair reminded him of a fidgety couple he'd known years before in Queensbury, a man and wife who he'd interviewed in a theft case. He'd later discovered that they had stashed the stolen cash box beneath the couch on which they sat during his interview. He smiled to himself, maybe *these* folks are on a hot seat of some kind too.

"Took you long enough to get to *that*," a voice behind him said. Apparently, the Bortiatynskis hadn't heard it. More of Timmy's pranks, Girard judged, and didn't respond. "Tell me, Mary Lou, did the boy have any relatives who he liked?" Where did *that* question all of a sudden come from? There was a slight push from behind him and he now knew that Timmy was again his point man. Mary Lou looked away, toward the television set. "Just my brother, Freddy. The two of them used to go off camping when Walter was younger. They'd go up to Canada sometimes. Freddy isn't married and always wished he could have kids of his own." She glanced quickly at the investigator as if to see how her statement satisfied him, and then quickly looked away.

Walter, Sr., pulled a new cigarette from his pack of Marlboros and lit it from the old butt. The energy in the room had unmistakably changed— Girard had broken through something, but *what*? Obviously, the couple had not expected the question about relatives. He kept up the pressure.

"Tell me Walter, where's Freddy now? Does he live here in Potsdam?" The husband's jaw set tighter and he took a moment too long to answer, "Aw," Walter drawled, "he lives over in Norwood, but he probably isn't around today. He goes off hunting and fishing a lot, you know?"

"How does he make his living?" Girard pried again.

"Aw, he does construction work, you know? Whenever he can *get* work." Girard noted Mary Lou crossing, then recrossing her ankles. Needs to shave those legs, yuk! Girard observed. So, *this* was it. Something here—walk carefully, Girard. You're on the threshold. Clearly, this pair knows a whole lot more than they've ever let on before.

"Would you give me his phone number and address please, Walter? If he camped with the boy, maybe he can remember some insights about Walter's behavior or ideas at that time, even though it was long ago. Did the police interview Freddy back in '83?"

"Aw, probably not," said the husband. "He'd just been fired from a job and was away at the time."

"You mean he didn't even come back to help search for his *nephew*?"

"Aw, well, you see, Freddy's got a temper, you know? Probably he was off drunk somewhere. We didn't see him when the investigation was going on," said Walter, Sr., as he handed Girard a piece of paper with the requested information.

Mary Lou interjected, "What makes you think you can do any good *now*? Why not just let the matter drop? Little Walter is never coming back for one reason or another. Why stir things up *now*?" That's a pretty cold comment, Girard thought. Let's warm things up.

"Well, you see, Mrs. Bortiatynski, I've never lost a case yet. I *always* get my man...or woman. Back at the station, they call me 'Tiger' because I never let up." Mary Lou seemed to blanch at the answer.

Suddenly an insight came to him, but from where only God knows. "Mr. and Mrs. Bortiatynski, have you ever had dreams of the boy since he disappeared?" Mary Lou let out an involuntary, short cry. "Jesus! Why on God's earth would you ever ask such a question?" the woman demanded. There was a long silence before she gruffly responded. "Yeah, I dreamed of the boy. For a while there, he often showed up in my dreams, always behind a set of iron bars, like he was in prison. I figured it was just my sadness, you know? Maybe he's really in jail somewhere, how do I know? I tried taking sleeping pills so I wouldn't dream anymore, but I'd have those awful nights so many times anyway. Now I don't dream about *nothin'* anymore!" She gave a smirk of self-satisfaction.

Nevertheless, this is pay dirt—somewhere in here. "And you, Walter, have you ever dreamed about your son?"

"I don't hold with that sissy stuff, you *hear* me? I don't dream because I don't *want* to dream! Dreamin' is for sissies, and I used to tell the boy that. I told him to be a *man*; start working out and build up some muscle—get a job in the mill, like me. But he just kept doin' sissy stuff, like trying to write poems. His marks went bad in school, and he hung around with dopes. Lotta good *I* could ever do with him."

Wow! Bernice would have a field day with this pair, Girard observed. A field day for all kinds of unconscious stuff—even a beginner like me can see that. "Well, Mr. and Mrs. Bortiatynski, thank you for your help. If anything turns up, I'll get in touch with you. Thanks for giving me your time. Here's my card if you need to get in touch with me. If it's possible,

I *will* find your boy, or whatever has become of him." Glancing at Mary Lou, Girard could see tears on her cheek as she stood with tightly folded arms, as if hugging herself, and she didn't extend a hand to him to give a goodbye handshake. Girard entered his car, briefly scanned the road map, and swung the car northward toward what he knew intuitively was the answer to his quest in Norwood.

Just outside Potsdam he stopped to get some food at Bonnie Mae's Gustatorium, a small roadside stand. Most of the fare was greasy, though it all smelled appetizing. He settled for a bottle of apple juice and the small-size portion of what was billed as "Bonnie Mae's Famous Fried Chicken. Just the way Mom cooked it!" Sitting in the car, he quickly decided that Mom would have been better off getting a job in the paper mill than feeding anybody's family. The juice was cold and enjoyable, though.

The 12-mile drive to his destination went quickly and, as he knew the village of Norwood quite well, within 20 minutes he had parked across the street from Freddy Holochuck's house. Instead of crossing to knock on Freddy's door, however, he decided on a ploy that had served him well in the past. He was parked in front of a small variety store, and decided to play "stranger in town," a role that invariably turned up new information.

"Good afternoon," the female store clerk greeted him. Hmm. 28—30, twice divorced, and dangerous, he sized her up. He didn't know *how* he knew, however.

"Yes, how are you?" Girard ventured. "I'm looking for an old acquaintance of mine, Freddy Holochuck. I think he lives in town, but didn't get an address. Do you know him?"

"Friend of *yours*, mister?" the woman responded bug-eyed, deliberately scanning Girard from head to toe and stepping back. "You don't look like *his* type."

"Oh, what type *is* Freddy's type?"

The woman peered intently at him; perhaps she smelled The Law. Girard somehow knew she had two priors for prostitution and one for petty larceny. She sensed a trap—the investigator knew. "You see, I haven't seen him since we got out of the army," he lied.

"You and him in the armeee?" the woman again sneered. "Like, what army is *that*?"

"Vietnam. U.S. Army."

"Yeah, well, okay," she said vacantly, not taking the time to recognize the improbability of Freddy having served in Vietnam more than 35 years ago. "You come to the right place, mister. See that brown house over there? That's Freddy's house. And it looks like you're in luck. I just seen him throwing stuff in his car, kinda sudden like. Probably he's headed out somewhere. Like, real fast, ya know?"

"Well, okay, thanks for that. I'd better *catch* him before he leaves," Girard responded with a smirk, "don't know when I'll see him again."

"Like, it's none of my business, mister, but you ain't one of them cute little boys that hangs out over there. What do you want with him?"

"Oh, didn't I tell you?" Girard's intensity at closing in on a quarry often made him sarcastic. "I work for State Lottery now, and Freddy's number just came up." He strode out the door, hearing the girl call after him, "*Freddy* did? Well, goddam!"

A thin man with shoulder-length, dirty blonde hair moved quickly down the steps with a duffle bag clutched in each hand. Girard strode rapidly to intercept him. "Freddy Holochuck?" he called out.

The man turned visibly pale and had a cornered look in his eye— Freddy somehow knew he was done. Girard, in the middle of the street, could tell the man was frozen between fighting and fleeing. The subject dropped the duffle bags and reached under his sport shirt.

"Stop right there!" Girard drew his pistol and went into a shooter's stance aiming at Holochuck. "Raise your hands and turn around! Let me see those hands—*now* or you're dead!" he shouted. "It's your call, Freddy. Make up your mind *now!*" he commanded. The man seemed undecided. "Hit the ground, prone, *now!*" You have to catch these rabbits before they decide to run or else someone always gets hurt, he reminded himself.

Girard closed the 40 feet between them in seconds, reaching beneath the man's shirt and removing a silver .38 Smith & Wesson pistol from Freddy's belt tossed it on the grass. He then hooked a toe in front of Holochuck's leg and pulled back. The clearly frightened man lost his balance and fell forward, partly onto the lawn and partly onto the sidewalk. In falling, he hit his chin on the cement and started to bleed. The sight of blood threw some inner switch in Girard and he heard his hoarse voice yelling, "Fred Holochuck, I'm arresting you for the rape and murder of Walter Bortiatynski."

How the hell do I know *that*? He'll get me for false arrest now for sure. Yet, he's up to *something*—wish I knew for sure what. Girard slipped the .38 into his jacket pocket. At that moment, the phantom hand fell once more on his left shoulder. "Okay, Timmy, thanks for that," he said without turning. It didn't do any good to look back anymore, anyway, because nobody was ever there.

He kicked his prisoner's feet apart and knelt on Freddy's shoulder blades while snapping handcuffs onto his wrists. Holochuck, now restrained, began to weep and thrash about at the same time. Girard stepped back and let the man go through what was obviously a tantrum. Then, as Freddy's frenzy subsided, Girard jerked hard on the handcuff chain. "Come on, pervert, let's get up on your feet, real nice now. That's it, nicely, we wouldn't want you to get *hurt!*" Uttering that final word, he yanked so hard on the chain that the man cried out in agony. This is not good, Girard, knew instantly, some part of me is out of control here. He felt slightly ashamed of his sudden roughness, but he had never apologized to a prisoner in his life and wasn't going to begin today.

Frisking Freddy, Girard found a plastic bag of marijuana and another bag of a suspicious white powder. As he touched the bags, he suddenly knew all about the case. It was as if, on some inner screen, he was reading—yet seeing enacted—a horrible crime. He ushered the still-weeping man to the rear seat of the car and locked him in. He called the Massena Barracks on his radio, notifying them that he'd be there in 15 minutes with a prisoner. As he closed the driver's door he was stunned at how quickly it had all happened. He had acted almost entirely on intuition, with a dose of training and past experience, and sure hoped he was right or the whole case would blow up in his face. Girard was also plagued by doubts as to how he could write up the report or testify as to his probable cause in this arrest. "Maybe you'll help out on that, Timmy?" he said aloud. No answer.

CHAPTER TWENTY-SEVEN

Sr. Investigator Girard drove to the State Police barracks on Sterns Street in Massena where the prisoner would be booked. As he drove, Girard gave Holochuck his Miranda Rights and made sure Freddy understood them. Girard escorted his collar into the station where Sgt. Samuel Priebe took him in hand while Girard signed in on the station blotter with his name address, and the charges to be preferred against the prisoner.

Sgt. Sammy Priebe was a tough old-timer like Girard, and escorted Freddy into the booking room to begin the paperwork and fingerprinting. Before he sat down at the computer, Priebe called one of the road patrol to secure Holochuck's house prior to getting a search warrant for the premises. The Sergeant then called City Judge Peter Baycura for a search warrant. Baycura, seemingly delighted that another "doper" was arrested, said he would personally deliver the document to Girard when Freddy was arraigned in an hour in a rare and hastily scheduled night court session. Things were coming together!

After cuffing Freddy to the interrogation table, Girard sat opposite the prisoner, snapped on the recorders, and began a conversation with his prisoner.

"Fred Holochuck, I've read you your rights, so you know you have the right to a lawyer. Nevertheless, do you want to talk with me about how you murdered young Walter Bortiatynski?"

"Murdered? You gotta be crazy, cop. He was *asking* for it. He teased me and teased me until I couldn't stand it no longer. Don't you understand? I couldn't *stand* no more teasing! Whenever we'd go camping, he was always skinny-dipping and showing off his ass and it drove me crazy. It was pure teasing because he knew I was weak. So, he got what all them slutty kids end up getting. He come to my house that day, when I come home from work at the Clarkson University construction site. He knew I just got paid and wanted money from me so he could buy dope. I told him take off his clothes and I'd give him money. Well, he called me a queer and lots of other names, and I hit him with a lamp and he just fell down. I tried to help him up but the back of his head was broken and bleeding, and I knew he was dead. He was *dead*, you hear me? He got what little teasey-ass boys always get!"

Girard wrote furiously, even though the interview mike was on and the video/audio recording system was running. He needed these notes if he was to attempt a recovery of little Walter's corpse. "Okay, Holochuck, but I think you're lying. I think something even *dirtier* and scummier than that was going down. You were selling him dope, *too*, right?" Again, Girard sat astounded as the words simply sprang from his mouth. How did this happen?

"Yeah, you probably read my record," Freddy responded sourly. "You know I got priors for dealing."

"So, let's see if I got this right. You were dealing to the kid and screwing him too. That right?"

"Look, cop, he deserved it *all*, you got that?" The Sergeant, poker-faced, interrupted to escort Holochuck to the new digital fingerprinting station, where Priebe placed the prisoner's fingertips onto the electronic surface, each finger pressed into its template section. The device made instant laser impressions of the fingertips and translated these to a printed hard copy.

Girard continued during that process. "You know, Freddy, it just might go easier for you if you can show us where Walter's body is. You have to know his folks are anxious."

"Anxious? You gotta be kidding!" the prisoner responded, twisting away from Priebe's bearlike hands. Sgt. Priebe stoically pulled Holochuck's hand back onto the machine surface. "Mary Lou, she *knew* I wanted that boy. And she didn't *care*, because he was always a problem between her and old Walter. She knew I done him in. And old Walter was so ashamed of the kid that he didn't even want the cops to *look* for him. Ha! Well, they're never going to find him, and you know why? Nobody wants to tear down the Alumni Hall at Clarkson, that's why. I took the boy's body over there that night and slid him under the rebar rods because I knew we was gonna pour concrete over that spot first thing in the morning, and I was the man on the chute, see? Then I threw a piece of construction felt over him. So, you know, we covered that spot first in the morning and the driver never saw where our cement was going, because it was a cold day and he wanted to stay in the truck. So now, hundreds of people walk all over little Walter every day, and the little sonofabitch *deserves* to be walked on. That's all them little teasies deserve! And I ain't gonna tell you no more, cop!" Holochuck set his face and refused to comment further. Sgt. Priebe pushed a button and the print machine spit out the digital fingerprint form.

Tomorrow I'll transfer the taped words onto a statement and maybe get Freddy to sign it, Girard concluded. He bundled Holochuck into the car, along with the charge sheet, and transported him to City Judge Baycura, who enjoyed arraigning the worst of the worst. Eager to quickly put away another miscreant, Baycura had already informed the DA's office of the arraignment, and a rather irritated Assistant D.A., Bill Getz, arrived at Baycura's house just as Girard pulled in. The judge, a Slovakian immigrant, had a love for tough law ever since he saw his first American movie about Judge Roy Bean, the "hanging judge," in 1948.

At the arraignment, Holochuck was ordered held without bail on the Murder Two count requested by District Attorney Chris Clark. Girard then transported the prisoner to the St. Lawrence County jail, where he'd be held pending the search of his home and the scheduling of the Grand Jury inquiry. It was nearly 3:30 a.m. when an exhausted Sr. Inv. Dennis Girard fell onto his bed in Chestertown and immediately was asleep.

Four hours later, on Thursday morning, he arose from bed, began brewing his morning coffee, but then surprised himself by sinking into his old recliner chair to pray. For a moment he felt unmanly in begging a Great Power that he couldn't see for help in doing the impossible, but he knew he was no longer a proud man. You have borne me up so far, he said silently to the Lord of All That Matters, and left it at that. It had been years since he felt humble enough to pray sincerely to The Maker of All. He realized that God and Jesus had been his favorite swear words for years.

With his carry mug filled with coffee and with a cold piece of French Toast from breakfast in his insulated bag, Girard ventured forth one more time to confront the forces of darkness, both in the world and in himself. He was tempted to call out to Israfil for help, but worried about re-establishing contact with an entity that was proving a difficult know-it-all taskmaster.

On his way to work, as he approached Saranac Lake, Girard found himself turning east instead, toward headquarters in Ray Brook. Why am I doing this? he wondered, but someone or something ran a finger up his spine. Okay, that's the way it is, Timmy. I'll just tell the guys I forgot a folder. When he entered his office, there was a photo envelope from Frank Whitson on his desk. Inside were three views of Faust Hetzer. Boy, Kenny Quinn is a true artist, he concluded. One of the photos was almost as good as a mug shot. "You're going to need this one," said a voice behind him. He didn't bother to turn. This seemed to be why he had come to headquarters.

Capt. Telfer commended him for the Holochuck arrest, and several other investigators wanted to pump his hand. Within law enforcement circles, news of an officer's victories or failures travels very fast.

Girard hit the road once more for Norwood. He had requested a young trooper from the Potsdam Barracks to help him conduct the search of Holochuck's house, and introduced himself to Trooper Charlie Clements at the barracks in Potsdam. The pair headed over to Holochuck's house in Norwood. When they arrived, the two men found the FIU "Goo Crew" just finishing their forensic work and ready to return to Ray Brook. They exchanged professional pleasantries and the investigators left. Girard and Clements went inside.

It was a squalid place with pornographic magazines strewn throughout the house. All the shades were pulled, and dirty and torn plastic drapes adorned the windows. There were several well-used bongs on the dining room table, as well as a residue of white powder and crushed marijuana leaves. Girard knew the FIU boys had samples of everything in their kit when they left. The dirty and cracked linoleum kitchen floor was littered with wine cooler and beer bottles, and the stove was covered with grease and dirty dishes. An overstuffed couch and arm chair seemed to be the only furniture, though both were ripped and covered with dirty blankets. There were several DVD discs on the living room floor in front of the television, and the titles indicated they were almost all porn. As he bagged them for evidence, Girard noted curiously that there was one other title, *Mysteries of the Great Pyramid*. The two men couldn't understand that subject being of interest to a sexual predator.

Girard enjoyed showing Clements the way an investigation was conducted. The young trooper was quick, insightful, and ambitious, and Girard knew the man would one day be BCI. They took notes of all that was observed. Freddy's phone book was impounded for its potential evidence. Secreted behind a false panel in the upstairs bedroom, young Clements found a stash of Canadian currency, $10,000 worth. In another part of the bedroom, underneath a loose floorboard, the pair discovered another $18,500 in American money. Likely all drug proceeds, Girard assumed, and bagged it as evidence.

Aside from the money and pornographic items, the house was unremarkable and the pair left at 2:45 p.m., securing the building with crime scene tape. Each man had a report to make and Clements invited Girard to the break room back at the Massena Barracks. His promise of quality coffee convinced Girard to do some further "investigation" there.

It was 5:50 p.m. when Girard left Potsdam and the western sky was a beautiful, dark purple-gray. Obviously a thunderstorm was coming in from Lake Ontario, but the face of the cold front was illuminated from beneath, giving the entire horizon a magical tone.

Back in Chestertown, Girard was rather pensive and not especially hungry. He made a salad from some fresh greens that Mrs. Morgenstern had left for him—a sweet lady, he mused. Instead of watching television, as he often did, he finished reading the symbology book that he had begun a few weeks ago. At 9:00 p.m. he chose to go "hunt some symbols," as he had begun to term the activity, and after showering, dropped off to sleep. And an interesting night it was.

He was a youngster again, dressed in his cowboy suit. He had his cap pistol and spent the night shooting Indians. Suddenly, from the sky came a jet-black crow with huge talons, which swooped down, attempting to

121

lacerate him. Glancing down at his garments, he found himself in his Army uniform again, running across the field directly at the NVA, who were shooting RPGs at him. He awoke in a cold sweat. He had faced death once more without knowing the outcome. What's trying to get me? He went to the bathroom, then took time to record the dream in his journal. Doc is gonna love this one, he surmised.

The rest of the night was peaceful and he awoke at the regular time, fried a couple of sunnyside-ups with toast, filled his big mug with coffee, then drove once more to the courthouse in Canton. Assistant DA Bill Getz, puffing on a large cigar, greeted him outside. "Damn county buildings. We can't smoke a good smoke inside anymore. You ever smoke, Girard?"

"Yeah, but I quit four months ago, Bill. And it sure has enhanced my sex life," he joshed the Assistant DA. Getz quickly stubbed his cigar on the brick wall and shot a smiling Dennis Girard a curious look as the two entered the building for what was a 55-minute ordeal. Several members of the Grand Jury seemed partial to Freddy and tried, by their pointed questions, to suggest that Freddy was in actuality gay, and that Girard was homophobic. Without becoming angry, Girard patiently answered each question from the panel and tried to smile. He kept thinking of Trooper Bill Cobb and his new dentures and tried to emulate the old-timer he'd known back in Troop G.

After he finished his testimony, Girard returned to Headquarters to do a bit more work on his report. A good way to finish the week, he figured—catch a crook a week, wrap 'em up in cuffs and paper, put 'em away, and clear the decks for another upright citizen to take that bum's place next week in the Wonderful World of Crime.

He looked forward to his Regular Saturday Morning Hike as a heart-and-mind-clearing sacrament. He felt impelled to return to Port Henry once more, if only to gloat at the scene of his first big case since returning to work as he headed home. He found Skippy's shuttered, locked and abandoned. Serves them *all* right, he decided.

Then he saw movement and a flash of color across the railroad tracks. He judged it to be on the end of Harbour Lane, where Nick Quatro ran a boat shop. Girard had always been fascinated by the big old PT boat that Nick's father had purchased after World War II, and which was now displayed on land in front of the shop as a business sign. He circled around into Harbour Lane and down to its end. "Hi Nick" he called out without seeing anyone.

Nick emerged from beneath a Sea Ray Luguna, whose fiberglass hull he was inspecting. "Hey, Dennis Girard! Haven't seen you in a lake sturgeon's lifetime," he quipped. The two shook hands and Girard told his longtime acquaintance of his continued fascination with the old PT Boat. Nick looked nostalgic, as it reminded him of his father, who had served on PTs in the Pacific during World War II. The old craft was no longer usable, but had become a monument to his parent, who had died of throat cancer in 2001. "Yes, that's my father's favorite boat, for sure. No matter how cold the winters got here, all he had to do was look at that boat and he was instantly back in Leyte Gulf. What can I do for you, Dennis?" It seemed that Nick was quite busy and anxious to return to work, realizing that, for all his value to the State Police, Girard just wasn't a boat guy.

"Oh, not much, Nick. I just saw some movement over here when I swung by Skippy's, and remembered this old relic, and thought I'd just stop by," the Investigator said.

"Aha! I thought you stopped over to see my new toy," Quatro returned. "Come on over here and I'll show you." He led Girard to a large tarp-covered object on a long boat trailer, and whipped the tarpaulin off. There stood one of the most magnificent boats that Girard had ever seen. "What *is* it, Nick?" he queried, "a guided missile?"

"This, my friend, is a big Fountain Lightning. Thirty-eight feet of zoom. You know my dad left me some money, and I banked it until I knew just what I wanted. I'd like to believe his spirit is happy as hell with this choice, and sometimes I feel he's riding with me. You probably think that spirit stuff is hogwash, don't you, Girard?"

"You'd be surprised, Nick," Girard responded. "It sure is beautiful, though. Looks like it wants to leap off its trailer and into the lake."

"Dad would have loved this even more than his PT," Quatro replied. "If you ever want to go to war, come on down and I'll give you the thrill of a lifetime," Nick laughed. "I'm going to put it in the water tomorrow and do some playing on the weekend. This sure is a babe catcher. Too bad you're here *today*."

"It's good to see you're doing well, Nick," Girard said, holding out his hand to Quatro. "You never know, maybe I'll take you up on that offer one day." As she said this, Girard felt a hand on his shoulder and, instantly, an icy cold current ran up his spine. Aw shit, he mumbled inside as he walked back to his car. Really? Timmy? Izzy? "What the hell are you guys planning for me?" he asked out loud. The only response was the sound of power boats on Lake Champlain. Girard looked forward more than ever to the Saturday Morning Hike as he headed home.

CHAPTER TWENTY-EIGHT

Girard pushed through the doors at Headquarters early on Monday. Several BCI men congratulated him on solving a second cold case; one that resolved a previously baffling disappearance. He entered his office and sifted through the phone messages and faxes that had accumulated. Nothing there that he was seeking. He spent the next three hours on paperwork and more than one trip to the coffee carafe in the break room.

After one of his return trips, Kenny Quinn entered with a big smile on his face and tossed a file folder on Girard's desk. "Damn you, Denny, you should be a fisherman with your luck. Wanna come down to the Saratoga races with me some afternoon? I could use some help betting."

Opening the file, Girard saw a summary of the fingerprint identifications taken at Skippy's. There were identifications for young Hochlitzer, his counter girl, Earlene, and other IDs for local bikers, some of whom had felony records, suggesting who might have done the break-in. Another set of unidentified prints had been taken down to Division in Albany because SAFIS couldn't identify them. "By the way, Denny, I had Hetzer sign a document verifying that we had done the burglary follow-up, and then kept it safe and clean so we could look at his prints too."

"But the big news," Quinn continued, "because you were away Friday, I asked Frank to have Hetzer's prints run through the Interpol ID system too, after I lifted them, and guess what? The reply from Division and the FBI is that you got a real bad guy here, and I already talked with the captain about how to proceed. I hoped you'd be here to initiate that notification, Dennis, but Division *has to* involve the Feds in this, so it's bigger than Troop B. We'll be lucky to hold on to even a small part of this investigation—looks like the FBI will run the whole thing.

"Interpol identified Hetzer as Dieter Ohnesorg, a wanted former member of the RAF. Remember the Red Army Faction in West Germany during the 70s and 80s? They were sometimes called the "Baader-Meinhoff Gang," a bunch of leftist murderers and assassins who killed more than 30 people in business and government, trying to destroy capitalism single-handedly. The Germans identified this guy's prints on shell casings found outside the home of an assassinated German official, Detlev Rohwedder, back in April 1991. But Ohnesorg disappeared and hadn't been heard from until now. We're obligated to share this with the Feds because it's an international fugitive case, and Major Sincavage is right now at work on that with Division. There's an outside chance that the FBI or the State Department or the German government will let us play with Hetzer and dangle him a bit, so we can watch where he goes. This is an oddity; we've not had such a case in Troop B since 1983."

Major Sincavage joined the pair, having already talked with Division and the FBI about the new developments. He told the two investigators that the matter had gone directly to the Superintendent's office to relay to the Feds. It was expected that the FBI would run the investigation because it was a national security issue all the way; in this new world, Hetzer was a terrorist. The Major asked rhetorically, "Why is such a revolutionary *here?* He doesn't do the mechanical work at Skippy's and the business is almost certainly a front. But for whom? For what? This isn't likely a one-man show either—there must be a group or organization supporting him. What *other* agenda do these guys have?"

Capt. Telfer joined the trio and informed them that he had already put Trooper Joe Ellington in an unmarked van watching Skippy's since 8:00 a.m. Ellington's job, pending a decision on jurisdiction in the case, was to keep watch on the cycle shop itself, taking photos of any and all activity at the otherwise closed business. Trooper Tom Ellis was also dispatched in an unmarked unit to the Hetzer home in Westport to watch from a distance and to tail Hetzer whenever he showed up and wherever he went, though his present whereabouts couldn't be ascertained. "We've run his license and registration, and know that Hetzer's got a big black '06 Navigator, New York plates CZZ 321. All road patrols are on notice to not intercept the SUV, but to report its location as soon as he's spotted," Telfer said.

The memory of those Red Army Faction assassination teams, which had conducted killings, bombings, and bank robberies to finance their anti-capitalist operations now surfaced in Girard's mind. Though his personal life was in a shambles during those years, he had been buoyed up by the possibility of the USSR's downfall, and the RAF seemed like a last desperate gasp against Free World ideology. Somewhere in the depth of his memory he recalled the FBI catching one of the Baader-Meinhoff members smuggling explosives into New York State from Canada in 1983. He remembered also that the RAF simply vanished from the news in the early 90s. So here's one that was never caught, Girard mused, now what's he doing in *Port Henry?*

He resumed filling out and filing the Holochuck papers and received notice that a date had been set for his appearance before the Essex County Grand Jury that was summoned to indict Paul Hochlitzer for the Elmore murder—9:00 a.m. on July 3. What's wrong with human beings that they want to kill *other* imperfect human beings like themselves—where is it all going to end? he wondered. For just a second, as he worked on the Bortiatynski report, he visualized himself in a Roman helmet, but laughed it off as an overactive imagination. He looked over his paper mail and the new e-mails. Nothing special.

Capt. Telfer entered again and quietly said that the Superintendent, himself, had just called and asked that Girard be assigned as an *ad hoc* member to the joint task force working on the case, and Telfer asked if Girard agreed. "This operation will be run by the Joint Terrorism Task Force (JTTF) and all kinds of federal departments will have a hand in the pie," Telfer said. "You comfortable working that way, Dennis? As part of a *team?*" Again, something ineffable had passed between them. Usually the captain used his surname, and Girard quickly noted the discrepancy. And what did he mean about the team question? Does he think I couldn't *do* that?

Telfer continued, "With Skippy's under observation and Hetzer's home staked out, there doesn't seem to be anything cooking today, Girard, so get on down to Albany. See Lt. Mueller in the Superintendent's office; he'll send you to this afternoon's JTTF get-together. You'll be our main man there for the Hetzer case. I want you to coordinate Ellington and Ellis, and study their daily surveillance reports, okay? If you need more men on this, let me know."

"Hey, Captain, if there's one thing I do *well*, it's surveillance," Girard said jokingly, grabbing his left armpit and grimacing. Telfer smiled and uncharacteristically teased Girard in return, "We may have lots of time, boring watching and waiting, ahead on the Hetzer case. So, after you check in with the JTTF, there is another old file box I just dusted off, just begging for a top investigator, Girard. When you have your necessary paperwork and Albany trip caught up, would you take a look at the LaRose case?"

The LaRose file box was quickly brought to Girard's desk. Here you go, Dennis Girard, he thought to himself—haven't even got the paper-work finished on Bortiatynski, and now they want *more* out of you. For just a second he wondered if management was pushing him *too* hard, maybe to see if he'd break. He smiled to himself. If they only knew....

Girard remembered the LaRose investigation—one in which a six-year-old girl in Ogdensburg had disappeared while returning from school back in November 2005, much like the Bortiatynski boy had years earlier.

The investigator remembered that he hadn't worked that case, as it had been given to Ole Nielsen, now retired and living in Florida. Nielsen had organized search teams and had gotten local businesses to offer rewards that eventually reached $85,000, but with no result. As in the Elmore case, no clues were turned up; no credible witnesses came forth. Hundreds of house-to-house interviews had been conducted but it was as if the child had vanished from the earth. There had been Amber Alerts posted within three hours of the disappearance notification, but nobody had seen anything.

The file contained no crime scene photos, just a second grade school photo of the youngster, along with copious investigative notes and street diagrams. A Social Services Department investigation had revealed no history of child abuse or neglect in her family. He noted that little Janet LaRose lived with her single mother, Darlene, on Paterson Street when she disappeared after leaving Sherman Elementary School on Friday, November 1. Darlene, totally distraught, was on public assistance and investigators found no major blemish in her past, unless it was her addiction to daytime television soap operas and being at the scene of several violent disturbances at Solomon's Bar on Ford Street. The father, Seaman Second Class William LaRose, had died in the terrorist bombing of the *USS Cole* in Yemen in October 2000, and apparently Darlene hadn't found a replacement for him. Without a provable crime or crime scene photos, Girard felt it was going to be even more difficult to get his intuition going on this one. It would all be there waiting when he was ready.

He stowed the box and went to his car for the two-hour drive to Division Headquarters, where Lt. Mueller filled him in on the latest information and speculation. From there, it was over to the FBI Building on McCarty Avenue at 3:00 p.m., to meet with Supervisory Special Agent in Charge (SAC) Joe Zarr, who was coordinating the Hetzer Investigation for the JTTF.

This was his first opportunity to observe a JTTF operation and Girard was excited about stretching his imagination beyond the Adirondacks. It was also exciting that he'd play the double role of State BCI and a federal officer, as quickly as he could be sworn in. This case likely would have global ramifications. Entering the FBI building through the security doors, he showed his ID, was handed a visitor's pass, and then was escorted to the third floor. When he entered the JTTF office, he was joined shortly by SSA Joe Zarr, who introduced him to five strangers: Chuck Kuenzel, of the Bureau of Alcohol, Tobacco and Firearms (ATF), Secret

Service Agent Cindy Parker, George Proctor from the U.S. State Department, Bill Hershfield from the CIA, and Curtis Brainerd from the regional Homeland Security office. First, Girard was sworn in as a Task Force Officer (TFO), which now made him more of a JTTF brother than an NYSP Investigator—he was now a federal officer, if only until the Hetzer Case was resolved, as there was already a full-time State Police member of the JTTF, Trooper Peter Kurto.

Zarr asked Girard to brief the group on the current status of the Hetzer investigation. All assembled took notes quietly and several members made marginal notes on Agent Zarr's handouts. It was clear that each intended to immediately begin rattling their own department's cages to see what they could shake loose on the situation. The meeting was short, as there were no current developments. Girard would notify Zarr via telephone at each new development and Zarr would decide when the team should meet again on this particular issue, though Girard realized the team met almost daily on the dozens of other cases they handled. Everyone shook hands; they knew they would have a lot of meetings regarding Hetzer in the future. An hour later, Girard was on his way home, to eat, read, and dream.

CHAPTER TWENTY-NINE

Although Tuesday promised to be a scorcher, Girard drove with his window half open rather than run the air conditioner, and drank in the pine-scented mountain air. He recognized that if Israfil was correct, something totally new was being revealed to him about the mysteries of nature, and he realized he had been given no apparent preparation for this phenomenon. Maybe even now, as he took in nature's sights and scents, he was inhaling that force. And if so, what was it doing to him?

As he neared his Ogdensburg goal, he switched on the car radio to catch up on the hourly news, something he rarely did while on duty. The main story was the upcoming Republican National Convention in St. Paul, MN on Labor Day weekend, and the question of who would emerge as the party's standard bearer. A curious final story involved the disappearance of a UPS truck in St. Regis Falls. The driver had found it gone when he returned from an early evening delivery. It was one of the mid-size P700 models, and there was an APB out for the vehicle with no results so far. Girard continued on to Ogdensburg.

It was a familiar route: up State Street and right onto Ford Street, so he could visually remind himself of the LaRose's proximity to Solomon's Bar on the corner. Then right on Paterson. As he turned that corner, in mid-turn, he noticed a slight, smiling girl swinging around the street sign-post on his right and staring at him, as if she'd been waiting for him. Until he completed his turn he couldn't look down at the crime file lying open on the seat beside him, but that little girl sure looked like Janet. As he straightened the car after the turn, the child vanished. His file didn't say Janet had a twin.

Girard parked across the street from Number 399, the dilapidated LaRose bungalow, and exited the car. A stylishly dressed, middle-aged blonde carrying a briefcase was just leaving the house. She looked up once, then twice, smiled and said loudly, "Dennis! Dennis Girard!" It took just a second to recognize the beautiful face beneath the still-blonde hair—Arlene Hubbard. They'd known one another at Syracuse U. more than 30 years before. Back then, everyone called her "Tizz." He gave her a warm handshake and for a second they just looked at one another. "Why are you *here*, Dennis?" she asked. "This is a house of death."

"Why are *you* here, Tizz?" he returned, slipping quickly back into his investigator persona. As he did so, he noticed a pink light around her head and shoulders.

Slowly shaking her head, she said, "I work for St. Lawrence County Social Services, and Darlene was assigned to me two years ago. I came over here to see how she's doing today, and it's not good. She's a sad case—do you know her? She doesn't have long to live, you know. We have her set up with a home health aide and are trying to make her comfortable. She's only 45." Arlene seemed distressed.

"Thanks for the insight," Girard responded, "I'm just following up an old case. I'm a State Police investigator now."

"Her daughter's disappearance?"

"Right, the state's just about given up any hope of solving that one. They only give me the *impossible* cases," he said disarmingly and grinned.

"Will you be around town long, Dennis? It'd be great to see and chat with you again."

He noted no ring on her left hand. "I can't say, Tizz. A lot of today's work depends on how this interview goes. Maybe Mrs. LaRose can supply some new lead that was overlooked years ago. But if you and I don't connect this time, I'll make it a point to call ahead on the next trip up here, and we'll get together, okay?"

Arlene flashed her charming smile, and in that split-second he wondered why they had never become more serious in those college years. "Okay, Dennis, this is kind of a busy day, anyway. I'll hold you to that promise." Then the smile left her face. With great seriousness she placed a hand on Dennis' forearm. "Dennis, there's something terribly *wrong* here. I've been helping Darlene since she was diagnosed as terminal. But I just can't find what's missing in this story. Maybe you can." Then she straightened, again flashed her million-dollar smile, ducked into her county car, and sped off.

Almost at Dennis' feet, a little boy about five rode his tricycle slowly past on the sidewalk in front of the LaRose house. With an innocent smile and brown eyes, he looked up at Dennis and sang, "Open your eyes *and* your heart," and pedaled away rapidly, making beeping noises and repeating the mantra. Stunned for a moment at the maturity of the words, Girard faltered. Something in that voice, he thought…that's not a *kid's* voice…but whose? Who's telling me how to do my job? He looked again at the little boy, now half a block away on the street, just to make sure the child was real. The way things have been going lately, he concluded, I don't know *who's* real anymore!

He pushed the dirty yellow button of the doorbell and waited for a response while surveying the chipped, flaking grey paint on the porch and the uncollected bags of trash stashed behind the porch railing. Then, he heard a weak voice inside say, "Come on in." He entered a gloomy room and saw a thin woman with tousled hair and wrapped in a faded blue corduroy bathrobe, staring at him. Smoke curled from an ashtray in which he could see about half a pack of old cigarette butts. The television was on. "You Mrs. LaRose?" he asked.

"Darlene. That's me," came the laconic reply. "How can I help you?"

"Mrs. LaRose, I'm Investigator Girard from the New York State Police," he said, closing the door. "I'm following up on your daughter's disappearance. It's such a sad story that I couldn't leave it alone. Just wanted to see if there had been any new developments on your end. Any new ideas about what happened or how?"

"The local cops came back two years ago, but I couldn't help them then, and I can't help you now." The woman never looked directly at him as she spoke. After Darlene's response Girard noticed a slight movement in the dining room behind her. The small girl from the street corner, a dead ringer for Janet, stood watching them.

"Mrs. LaRose, how many children did you have? Just Janet?"

"Yes, that's all me and my husband could produce," she said ruefully, taking a long draw on her cigarette. Girard saw no emotion in the woman, who was now gazing at the ceiling. Apparently she had resolved all her grief and was resigned to the finality of a lost child and the impending end of her own life. For a moment he felt guilty about intruding on the double tragedy. He looked behind Darlene once more and the child remained in the shadows, staring. Goosebumps rose on his neck. Suddenly he realized what was taking place, and was certain he wasn't prepared—more of that damned angel stuff! The child said something softly; Darlene didn't hear, or didn't react if she had.

"Mrs. LaRose, I'd just like to go back over the information we have in our file. May I read it to you? Perhaps just in listening to the words, you'll think of something."

Darlene began to fidget in her chair, slowly wringing her hands. She was gaunt and certainly in bad health, but nevertheless, stubbed out her short cigarette and lit a new one. Dennis opened the file and began to read, "Friday, November 1, 2005, 4:35 p.m. Darlene I. LaRose of 399 Paterson Street, Ogdensburg, reported the disappearance of her six-year-old daughter Janet, who failed to return home at 2:30 p.m. from Sherman Elementary School, just a few blocks away." He continued, noting that investigation had shown the school authorities had released the child at the normal dismissal time and that she had been in the company of two girlfriends when she left the school grounds. The two other children had gone directly home safely, believing that Janet also had returned to her house. When Darlene called the police at 3:30 p.m., all available Ogdensburg Police Department officers had conducted door-to-door interviews along the child's normal school route. Officers were posted at all local intersections to question neighborhood motorists. At 6:00 p.m. the Ogdensburg P.D. called in an Amber Alert, believing the child had been abducted. As he summarized the few specifics, Girard heard the child in the background say something softly that sounded like "…sold me." He looked at the girl and realized that she was semitransparent, as he could see the dining room table through her body now.

Again it came, this time louder and more pathetic, "Mommy, you *sold* me!" the girl said forcefully, with tears streaming down her cheeks. Girard looked at Darlene—there was no indication she'd heard. If she had, the woman remained remarkably unmoved, though she now began to wring her hands continually. The child stood unmoving. Darlene made no comment on the material that Girard had read, and took another puff on her cigarette. The ash fell from its end onto her bathrobe and rolled to the floor.

It was silent in the living room. A car drove quietly past the house, and somewhere in the room a clock ticked away noisily, relentlessly. The girl glided alongside Darlene. This time she was crying and screamed angrily, "*Mommy, you sold me to that man!*" Girard could no longer stand the unrelieved tension. He sat down in an armchair, leaned forward to Darlene, and said, "Mrs. LaRose, don't you think it's time you told me about selling your daughter to that man?"

Darlene LaRose turned white and gasped, seeming to lose her breath. She reached to stub out her cigarette but missed, hitting the edge of the ashtray, and flipping the accumulation of butts and ash all over the floor. Covering her face with her hands, she shrieked loudly in agony and collapsed back into her chair, crying and coughing uncontrollably.

Eventually the woman was reduced to gut-wrenching sobbing and coughing, hunched forward over her knees. Girard waited quietly, suspecting these were the first real tears that Mrs. LaRose had ever shed for little Janet; or were they for herself? Finally, Darlene looked up at Girard with red eyes and said gaspingly, "It's okay, mister, it'll be better this way. I gotta go before God soon and He'll kick the shit out of me if I can't finally *admit* what I done."

Girard took a small digital recorder from his pocket and placed it on the footstool between himself and the woman. He spoke quietly into the recorder, giving date and time and identifying himself. He asked Darlene's permission to record the interview and recorded her assent. He gave her the Miranda Warning, to which she responded affirmatively. Then, for the next half hour Darlene LaRose gave him all the details. She'd been lonely after Billy died in Yemen, and often, when Janet was asleep, she'd stroll over to Solomon's to have a few beers, hoping to find a sympathetic man.

One evening in June that year, Darlene said she had gone to the bar and met a strikingly handsome Lithuanian sailor called "Stig." His ship, the *Kapitonas Kazimeras,* was loading corn pellets about five hundred yards away from the bar, downhill at the Port of Ogdensburg on the St. Lawrence Seaway. With his blonde curly hair and accent, he reminded her of some old-time Hollywood actor, maybe Fernando Lamas, her childhood idol. After heavy drinking they had walked the few blocks to the Port fence and made love in the tall, dark grasses alongside the gate, illuminated only by the work lights a hundred yards away on the dock. He offered her some white powder, which he placed on her tongue. In an instant, all her tensions vanished, and she felt whole again, and loved.

"Stig" became her Prince Charming, like one of the beautiful men on the afternoon soaps. Darlene at last felt that she *could* be a good mother to Janet, she said. She asked Stig for more of what she called "magic powder." He asked her for money and she gave him all she had in her purse, about $151, even though it represented her food budget for the next three weeks. From his shoulder pack, he gave her a large packet of the powder wrapped in brown paper, promising to return to Ogdensburg in November on his last voyage of the season. Then he walked away, down to his ship, which was preparing to cast off its lines.

"I tried, mister. I really tried not to use too much of that powder," Darlene told Girard. "I tried to just swallow some when my sadness got too strong, but I couldn't stop. It was good. It was *soooo* good, and it kept me happy, at least for a while. By the end of August it was all gone, and it was almost two months more before Stig could come back. Then I heard of a girl in Massena who could get me some more, so I'd go over there to buy it until Billy's death benefit money ran out. But that lady got busted in late October, and I had stomach cramps all the time; I couldn't sleep and was so cranky with Janet. My nose ran all the time and my heart would beat real crazy-like some of the time, you know? So, you know, it was so good to see Stig's ship come back on November 1st.

"I went down that morning and asked for him. When he came down to the dock three hours later he suggested we go to my house, but he wouldn't give me any magic powder from his duffle bag. He was angry that I didn't have much money. I cried and I begged him. Then Janet came in at 2:30. He said 'I'll take *her*, then.' Stig gave me some powder and I went to the kitchen to swallow it, so Janet wouldn't see. I heard a scuffle noise, but when I came back he and Janet were gone. I was feeling *so* good; maybe I imagined it all, I thought to myself. I just couldn't handle those complicated ideas. Yes, maybe I *hadn't* seen her; maybe she really *hadn't* come home. Yes, I was *sure* she hadn't come home.

"Now Stig was gone and I had three months' supply of powder, and I was happy for the first time in a long time. But when Janet didn't come home by 3:30, I knew something was wrong and called the cops. Maybe I'd been mistaken; maybe I had *imagined* her coming in, I just couldn't think clearly. No mother could swap her kid or sell her kid, could she, mister?" Darlene implored him, looking into Girard's face for the first time.

Inside, he felt both pity and revulsion. He'd seen too much of drug and alcohol addiction and what it does to devastate a person's life and a family's existence. Outside, he heard the clatter of the little boy's tricycle and his beeping sounds, and it snapped Girard back to the task at hand. He wanted to punch Darlene—he was that angry! He visualized little Janet, probably knocked unconscious and stuffed into Stig's duffle bag, carried down to the port and then...where?

"Mister, you got kids?" Darlene implored.

"Yeah," he responded automatically, and was silent for a minute, reflecting on his own kids and staring at the small pink roses on Darlene's faded green wallpaper. Then his investigator's circumspect demeanor returned. "Yes, I do. Three. And *they* all got to grow up," he remarked harshly. His investigator's mind attempted to compute his next legal step with the woman. He had to arrest her, that was for sure, but then what? Did he want to transport a basket case to the nearest barracks? She could hardly stand, so how could she flee? But she had to be charged and booked.

His human emotions, on the other hand, were aroused and he felt compelled to subdue them. His emotional urge was to lay into this wreck of a woman with his fists to rip her up one side and down the other. He was disgusted by what he saw, an almost skeletal woman killing herself with cigarettes and who knows what drugs—a pitiful wretch who didn't deserve to live, while her daughter was long gone—fish food somewhere out in the Atlantic. The horror of what Darlene had admitted to made him nauseous. What would it have taken in *him* to sell Clara, Joey or Pat? What scum could do that to one of her own kids?

Another part of his mind watched his body as it sat tensely on the chair. Wasn't he overreacting? And why? Why again, after the inner ferocity he'd experienced in the Bortiatynski case? He'd seen men cut in half in Nam. He'd had to clean up a decapitation crime scene in Malone once. He'd also helped load charred bodies into the coroner's ambulance after the big fire in Saranac Lake, and there was the Jordan shotgun murder/suicide in Wanakena a few years ago, where just about every inch of the cabin's interior was splattered with blood and guts. How did he get through all those and only *now* feel so devastated by a murder that had no corpse? And what was it that Doc had once said about inordinate anger overwhelming a person? That some such sin lay at his own doorstep? I can't look at that crap right now, he resolved.

Girard excused himself to walk into the kitchen. Taking out his cell phone, he called Headquarters and briefly reported his findings to Capt. Telfer, asking for advice. Telfer agreed to call Christopher Clark, the St. Lawrence County DA, and to discuss the situation. There would have to be an arraignment to charge Darlene, but Telfer wanted to see how Clark wanted to handle the rest of it. The DA was up for re-election in the fall, and law enforcement officers learned to walk carefully in election years.

Telfer said he'd have a female officer from the Ogdensburg barracks there by 7:00 p.m.. "Dennis, we'll probably arraign Mrs. LaRose in the morning, after stopping by the barracks to book her, but I want you present at both of those. No problem staying overnight?"

"None at all, Captain."

Girard returned to the living room and found Darlene staring at the television. Her favorite soap opera, *Lust for Tomorrow*, was on, and having muted the sound, she sat transfixed, apparently unaware that he was there and that she couldn't hear the dialogue. Then, as he rounded the corner into her field of vision, he was taken aback. Janet, still visible, had moved to Darlene's right side and was stroking her mother's hair with compassion. Girard felt his gut tighten, and a tear sprang to the corner of his eye. He had to look away, as none of the imagery could be contained in his heart anymore. He reflected that his death a few months ago had left him a weeping wimp. *How on God's earth was he ever going to tell somebody about this*? How was he ever going to write an accurate report of his interview with Darlene LaRose?

CHAPTER THIRTY

While waiting for the woman trooper, Girard calmed himself in order to re-engage in conversation with Darlene. Obviously, she was no longer an addict, though she was deathly ill. The dark circles under her eyes gave her the appearance of one of the voodoo ghouls that he used to enjoy in high school, from the days of black and white TV horror movies.

"Mrs. LaRose, how did you get off drugs?" What he was fishing for was the answer to a nagging question. Why didn't Darlene's addiction show up in either the Social Services files or the State Police crime file? They might have gotten onto her much earlier if they'd had that information.

"Mister, I finally got sober last year. One of the ladies on this street who works over at Catholic Charities, got a caseworker to visit me. I was in bad shape, but the woman knew I was hooked on bad stuff and suffering from the loss of my kid. She didn't know how *much* I was suffering, you know? They got me connected with Judy Baker, an addictions counselor, and Billy's military insurance paid the bill, so I didn't have to talk to the welfare people *or* the cops.

"But, there's a problem, you know? When a lady gets sober, she has no place to hide. Who she is and what she's done is always there 24/7, and I haven't really been able to forgive myself. I've had horrible nightmares ever since I got sober, and I'll have to die knowing that I'm the wickedest mother in history—I swapped my baby for dope. Darlene coughed several times and at the end, wiped a small smear of blood from her mouth. "Janet was really a good little girl—she didn't deserve *that*. And how can I make amends now for my wicked behavior? I'm scared to die because I really don't think God can forgive me."

Girard felt compelled to say something comforting, but remained silent. What could he say? What did *he* know about God and forgiveness, he wondered. Too bad I can't get Izzy in here to talk to her; he's got an answer to everything, dammit! "Look, can I get you something from the kitchen? You haven't eaten since I came in," Girard offered.

"Mister, I just drink juices and that stuff in cans out on the shelf. My stomach is dead from all the shit I poured into it. You can't put your stomach on stun for years, then expect it's gonna be okay afterward, you know? I'll go get something for myself later."

The doorbell rang and a most attractive trooper stood in the doorway when he opened the door. The name tag identified her as "Batiuk." "Hello, Investigator Girard, I'm Trooper Xenia Batiuk from the Ogdensburg barracks. They've sent me over to sit with Mrs. LaRose until all the details are worked out for tomorrow. Captain Telfer says it's just an overnight, so we'll wait for her health aide to come in the morning, and then take her over to the barracks, and then the courthouse in Canton for her arraignment tomorrow morning at 10:00 a.m.."

For a moment, Girard was dazzled by the blue eyes and soft blonde hair—where did *she* come from? And in the State Police? This beauty belonged on the runway for Miss America! Fortunately, she was too young to hold his interest for long, he knew, though she probably knew all kinds of karate and martial arts moves, and could beat up an old duffer like him with one hand tied behind her back if he forgot himself and got fresh. He wished he'd known her years before, though.

His professional face took charge. "Okay, thanks, Batiuk. They're putting me up, probably at the Quality Inn on Route 37. I'll call Captain Telfer to confirm that. You up to doing an all-nighter here?"

"Sure, I'm *young!*" she responded with a broad grin. Was she tweaking him about his age? he wondered. Surely he didn't look old, did he? Not *that* old!

"Okay, Batiuk, I'll be back at 9:00 a.m. and we'll take her to the barracks and arraignment then. Sound okay?"

"Roger, that," she replied.

"I'll see you again tomorrow, Mrs. LaRose," Girard offered, and let himself out. The little boy's empty tricycle stood at the end of the short sidewalk. Wonder whose kid he was? he pondered.

Standing outside his car, he called the captain. Telfer wasn't at headquarters, but Lt. Lou Gregory took the call, confirming that reservations had been made for him at the Quality Inn outside Ogdensburg, and that Trooper Batiuk was to accompany him and Mrs. LaRose first to the barracks for a booking, then to the next day's arraignment at the courthouse where DA Clark would meet them at 10:00 a.m..

Girard got into his car and headed out to Route 37. He reflected that in the old days, after such a stress-filled experience, he'd have felt polluted and roiled by the emotional horror of a wicked crime investigation, and would have ordered a thick steak and about five quick shots of Black Velvet to numb the conflicting feelings that always assailed him. Tonight, however, he was pensive and somewhat sad, and not inclined to eat much at all.

He pulled into the motel parking lot, but instead of entering the building to register, walked over to a picnic table on the lawn, dropped his overnight bag, and sat. The day's heat was receding and he welcomed the opportunity to simply sit and ruminate in the early evening breeze. Traffic was light on the highway and he found his first peace of the day in just sitting, looking at the darkening sky. The evening stars were just emerging and drew him to reflect on the Maker of those celestial lights. He found himself in a silent attempt at communication with that Great Mind, which had purposes beyond *his* comprehension.

"What is she?" he asked the Creator out loud. "When I just left there, I was almost sorry for that lady. And yet, she let her own kid be used by a man who certainly threw away the child in the end—and all for her selfish gratification! Isn't Darlene an unforgivable sinner? You can't really have a place for her at Your table, do You?" Someone gently placed a hand in the middle of his back. He spun around—who was it? He hadn't heard anyone approach.

"Hi, kid." It was Timmy, standing in the half-light, wearing his ridiculous red cowboy hat, flopped back over his shoulders. "There's a whole lot of different people at that table—you'd be surprised who gets fed." This older version of the brother he'd known and grieved for now stood with a broad grin on his face.

"Oh, no. Timmy, you can't just sneak up on a guy like that! Come around here and let me look at you. How can I see you? Didn't you go to Heaven, like the priest said?"

"What makes you think I'm *not* in Heaven, Denny?"

"You know that's over my head! I'm so screwed up since I got shot, Timmy. I talk with ghosts, I see strange lights—there's nothing normal in my life anymore."

"Normal? Denny, seeing and hearing beyond the narrow world that most people choose to live in *is* normal as far as I can figure out." Timmy leaned against the opposite end of the table. "When we were little squirts together I loved my kid brother. So, it's normal now that I get to work with you on stuff that will raise us *both* up. When I woke up here after my accident I was taught a whole lot about life, and that death really doesn't need to be scary. I meet lots of old friends and relatives here, too. Remember Grandpa Kelly? I see him from time to time and even sit on his lap—he likes that. He tells me about his recent fishing trips, but you and I know how long ago he died. But he's *alive* here, Denny! And I really do believe he goes fishing—somewhere.

"And remember Mama's sister, Aunt Kitty? She still sits and drinks tall beers on her shady porch, just because she likes to. Someday, when she's ready, she will look around to see what else there is, but right now, after all her years working in the hot textile mills, Heaven is a cool beer. They didn't teach us that in Catechism class, did they?"

"Timmy, I don't know what to say. Nobody ever told me I'd get to see you again. Nobody ever told me I'd get to see murdered ghost children or strangled ladies, or would get anything good out of all that. I just don't think I can handle all this. Why can't the angels leave me alone and let me get back to the old days?"

"*Angels*? You got to see *angels*? Wow! I haven't done that yet."

"Well, that's what he says he is. Some wise guy named Israfil. And you can't outsmart him. He's like a walking, talking earthquake and lightning storm; scares the hell out of me." He reflected on those last words for a minute. Why had he said *those* words? They really seemed so absolutely true. Maybe that was part of Israfil's job. "Damn, Timmy! Why didn't somebody tell me I could see you again? It isn't fair. Death is supposed to be so gruesome and final. And it *is*—I've seen it up close! Now, you're telling me it's just like walking from one room of a house into another. No sweat?"

"Yep, that's the way I got it figured, Denny. I'm not going to stay long this time. Do you understand that I'm going to be your point man on this patrol?"

"Point man? Where'd you get that lingo? You weren't with us in Nam!" Dennis looked at his brother, who stood grinning. "Oh, shit, you mean you *were*?"

"Denny, wherever I have loved ones, I just am. And that's how it is with many of the people I've encountered in my new place. To you it was more than 30 years ago. To me, it's just five minutes past. One great thing about not having a body is that you can be almost any place where someone you love needs help, although most of the time those loved ones just won't work with what you give them. Usually we have to get to them in their dreams. Remember outside Hué, when your enemies were shooting RPGs at you? Remember how most of those kept tailing off to your left?"

"I *do*, Timmy! Almost nobody in our position got hit, and later we joked about the shitty workmanship in those NVA tunnel factories. You mean that was *you*?"

Timmy beamed. "Yep. That was really my first time diverting solid objects and I didn't think I could do it, but it wasn't your time yet, anyway, so I was able. Maybe someone was helping *me* too, I don't know.

"Now listen up. This broken lady today was a present, and you have to see her as that. It's a part of your conversion, my friends here tell me. When you have such difficult experiences, don't turn away from them— one day you'll see they really are gifts. Where I am now, I learned that that hot rod '48 Mercury that ran me down and killed my body was a gift. It kept me from having to die slowly and more painfully from polio the next year, which was the only other option on my schedule. And that quick exit put me in this better place to guide you in high school. I was the 'wind at your back' when you broke the 1500-meter record at the Sectionals in Albany, and when you got the gold at The Empire State Games the next year. And they couldn't put *that* in the record books—ghosts aren't 'wind assisted!'" he laughed.

Dennis Girard felt the bottom drop out of his stomach and all his former certainties went with it. As he attempted to fathom Timmy's words, his brother simply blended into the night sky and was gone. Timmy's musical belly-laugh lingered for a moment longer before wafting away in the evening breeze. Girard sat at the picnic table for another 20 minutes, wiping the tears from his eyes.

Every one of his old truths no longer held—about people and about things—even about the horrors of death. He was pretty sure that he had also lost his capacity to take care of himself, and in his present dangerous business, that could be fatal. Slowly, he rose and walked into the motel to register, then to dine on a cup of mandarin orange tea and a good Caesar salad.

CHAPTER THIRTY-ONE

His alarm buzzed at 7:15 a.m. and Girard arose, showered and dressed in yesterday's clothes, which retained a trace of the previous day's perspiration and Darlene's cigarette smoke. From that stench, it was impossible to believe that he, himself, had once been an inveterate smoker. Fortunately, the motel had a razor and shaving gel in a courtesy basket in his bathroom, so he could at least look presentable in court—oh yes, and in front of that gorgeous trooper.

Checking out, he drove to a nearby restaurant and had a light breakfast. There was a special of spinach quiche, goat cheese and a drink, so he also had a hot cup of coffee and pondered the day's work.

At 8:55 a.m. he left the restaurant and drove the few miles to Paterson Street, where he parked and went to the door at 399. He buzzed the bell and Trooper Batiuk answered. What a delightful face and form so early in the morning—not one hair out of place! Ushering in the investigator, she informed him that the home health aide was with Darlene in the bathroom, cleaning her up and making her presentable. "I told her she should get a lawyer, but Darlene's stubborn, and said she'll defend herself. I helped pick out her nicest dress, although it hangs on her bony body like a shroud now," said Trooper Batiuk.

The aide spent a few minutes coiffing Darlene and then presented her to the two officers. Batiuk took the portable oxygen tank in tow and they placed Darlene in the backseat of her cruiser. Girard followed Batiuk's car on the short drive to the State Police barracks on Cedar Street. The booking only took 15 minutes, as the sergeant was forewarned and ready. Then came an 18-mile drive to the St. Lawrence County Courthouse in Canton. Exiting their cars, the small party moved slowly once in the front handicapped parking area, as Darlene was clearly frail and sagged once she got to her feet. Girard wondered if they might need an ambulance gurney to transport the woman inside, but the prisoner kept mumbling about "keeping my appointment" and adding, "I'm damn well capable of taking this last walk."

Entering the courthouse side door, the trio went to the elevator and punched button 2A, and in a few seconds they were on the second floor and entering Courtroom A. There they met the DA himself, Chris Clark. No Assistant DA was going to do this high-profile arraignment. Clark wanted this for himself, as he was up for re-election in the fall, and the *Ogdensburg Journal* and the critical *Watertown Daily Times* had already contacted his office for detailed information about the arrest in this baffling case.

Girard shook hands with Clark and introduced Trooper Batiuk. The DA motioned them to a front table, and in a matter of minutes Judge Loren Brown appeared to begin the proceeding. The charges were read, and Darlene was charged on a Manslaughter One count. Before asking for her plea, the judge cautioned Darlene that she should have counsel, but the prisoner declined and pleaded guilty. A tentative sentencing date was set, although everyone present knew that Darlene LaRose would never keep that appointment. Judge Brown then remanded her to the custody of the DA's office, a highly unusual step, and it was all over in just eight minutes. Clark fully expected Darlene LaRose would die at home.

As the small group turned, reporter Larry Goodwin of the *Watertown Daily Times* leapt from his seat and began peppering Mrs. LaRose with questions. She averted her eyes and ignored him. Goodwin then asked Girard and Batiuk to comment, but the senior investigator referred all questions to DA Clark, who had suddenly vanished. Goodwin was noted for his incisive reporting style and had been nominated for a Pulitzer Prize for a hard-hitting exposé of alien smuggling along the Canadian border. However, this was not his day to get an interview.

As they left the courthouse, Darlene suddenly stumbled, and only the firm grip of Batiuk and Girard kept her from falling flat. She began coughing up blood and Girard called 911 for an ambulance to Canton-Potsdam

Hospital. In three minutes the Canton Fire Department ambulance arrived and Darlene was placed on a gurney for transport to the hospital.

"Girard, if you don't mind, I'd like to accompany you to the Emergency Room, as I'm still pretty new at this kind of thing, and I never want to miss a chance to learn," the trooper said. "Besides that, I got to know this woman fairly well last night, and even though the press will portray her as a monster, I like some inner part of her." Then Batiuk grabbed the lapel of his blazer tightly and implored, "You won't tell anyone I got my head involved with the prisoner, will you? They'll think I'm a softie." She released her hold on his jacket and smoothed it out. Girard also stroked the lapel with his fingers and smiled to himself.

No matter how hard the state trains us to be businesslike and stoic in these gut-wrenching cases, he thought, some emotional part of each of us does respond to the people we deal with. Glad I can keep that under control, he reassured himself, but he wasn't sure that the recent developments in his life would allow him to sustain that impassive wall. "Sure, Batiuk, follow me."

Using no siren on his car, the trip to Canton-Potsdam was 20 minutes for Girard. He knew that the outcome of the journey had now passed from his hands. Whatever could or should be done for Mrs. LaRose would have to be done by the EMTs and doctors now. Following the ambulance closely, he noticed that they switched off their siren as they came into Potsdam, and he wondered why. Girard reflected on the strange turn of events in the case. It seemed that some part of Darlene had waited for this arraignment before completely falling apart. She'd been as white as a sheet when they'd loaded her at the courthouse.

When the ambulance stopped at the Emergency Room entrance he realized that something had radically changed. The crew no longer acted as if there was an emergency; no running to open the vehicle's rear door, and when the stretcher was withdrawn, he noted the sheet pulled over Mrs. LaRose's face. Inside the Emergency Room he was told that Darlene had apparently suffered a ruptured aortic aneurysm and died in the ambulance shortly after leaving Canton. There would be an autopsy, to be sure, but her sudden loss of blood pressure could not be overcome, leading the crew to their hypothesis as to the cause of death.

Girard and Batiuk chatted for a moment and decided that a Higher Power may have given their case a better conclusion than any earthly court could. Batiuk went to her cruiser to call Headquarters for reassignment, and was sent back to the LaRose house to secure the property and to notify County Social Services that they had lost a client. She shook hands with Girard and departed.

Investigator Girard reported to Troop B Headquarters on his cell phone and it was decided that he should stay at the hospital pending the signing of a death certificate, take a copy to DA Chris Clark's office afterward, and then return to Ray Brook. It was 2:10 p.m. when he made his delivery to the District Attorney's office, and since he hadn't eaten, Girard stopped at the Town Line Diner before heading home down Route 56.

It had been months since he had seen his old friends, Bill and Sal Smith in South Colton, and he needed friendly, non-job banter and pleasant company. The pair was steeped in Adirondack lore, and Bill, folksinger and lecturer, was a charter member of the Adirondack Liar's Club, the tellers of tall tales. Girard liked being in their company, and finding them in, chatted and drank coffee with them for a couple of hours while inspecting Sal's production line of souvenir stuffed black bears until 6:00 p.m. Though the Smiths invited him for supper, he chose to be alone and drive slowly south. In his head he tried to compose his final report on the LaRose case. Some issues had gotten solved, but other problems remained.

At Sevey Corners he absentmindedly pulled off the road to watch traffic. He realized that there was now a growing vulnerability within him, and the contacts with Israfil, Timmy, and even Darlene LaRose, to say nothing about her ghostly daughter, seemed to have weakened him. He concluded that he was now overly sensitive to the people around him, almost as if he could anticipate what they were thinking. He'd also found something within Trooper Batiuk that was deeper than his old libido lust. It was as if he knew her from somewhere before, but where? They were a generation apart, and he couldn't have run into her in any previous Troop B activity. As he mulled the events of the few weeks he'd been back on the job, he realized that this increased sensitivity both helped and hindered his job performance. At present, however, it didn't totally incapacitate him, so he could afford to be patient and let this new self emerge.

Dennis Girard watched passing traffic on Route 3 and gradually became aware that, instead of his car's windshield, he was looking through a circular opening, something like a ship's porthole. Inside, with his back to the window, a man could be seen hammering or chopping something on the metal floor before him. In an instant, Girard was inside the room and noted that it was a murky ship's hold. Immediately, he knew what he was watching and tried to avoid it, but was unable to turn away.

A small forearm with clenched fingers skidded along the floor to the left of the man, who reached out, snared the member and brought it in front of him again, where he made another chopping motion. "Good God!" Girard cried. "Why do I have to watch *this*? Why do I have to know the end that this child came to? Merciful God, let me not see this!"

The scene faded and he found himself once more seated in his car, drenched in perspiration and with tear-filled eyes. He cried like a baby for perhaps five minutes before regaining control. As he sat staring blankly ahead, a child's soft hand stroked his brow. "So that you will never mistake love," the child's voice said. "So you will fully understand where all violence leads. *Ma-as-salaamah*." And that was the end of it. He couldn't make out the last word, which sounded foreign, but it did bring peace to his soul.

Night had fallen by the time he started up again and drove across the intersection to get a pack of mints at the small store. Afterward, turning south toward Tupper Lake on Route 3, he intended to return to Ray Brook via Saranac Lake. Recollecting all the day's events, he almost missed the sudden activity on the left side of the road as he sped past the hamlet of Piercefield. Swinging around the curve, he saw the blinking yellow caution light of a road crew's van. Telephone company repair truck, he estimated. Girard was vaguely aware of two workers in hard hats and another on a ladder up the pole. He drove on by. Now, where was I? he probed his memory after the distraction.

"Where were their cones?" came a voice from the rear seat, startling him. He checked the rearview mirror but nobody was seated behind him. My imagination? he asked himself. "Where were their traffic cones?" the voice demanded again, as if tutoring him. He pulled over to the shoulder and made another quick scan of the rear seat. Nobody there. Okay, his mind said, where *were* their traffic cones? That's State Law—repair crews had to set out traffic safety cones when working on the edge of the highway, and there hadn't *been* any, or he'd have spotted them on the turn. He swung the car around and drove back, but the repair crew had vanished. Good thing for them, he decided, or I'd have given them a citation. Then it dawned on him that he had not seen the company's logo on the truck either; his memory was just of a plain white van. But, this wasn't necessarily suspicious, as utility companies sometimes leased unmarked vehicles.

Girard stopped where he estimated the repairmen had been working, turned on his emergency flashers, and exited to look around. Seeing only trampled grass, he looked up the pole. Nothing out of the ordinary was visible in the darkness. Nevertheless, he wrote the pole number in his notebook; he'd call the phone company in the morning and let the workers' supervisor know that the men had not taken all safety precautions. He realized he was now wearier than he'd thought, and at Tupper Lake he turned south toward Chestertown instead of returning to Headquarters.

One more workday tomorrow, he thought, then was asleep without dinner when he stretched out on the bed.

CHAPTER THIRTY-TWO

Senior Investigator Girard spent three hours preparing his final report on the LaRose investigation on Thursday morning, then turned it in to the captain. Taking stock of his inner self, he discovered no real elation at cracking another "cold case," though several of his fellow investigators stopped by to congratulate him. For whatever reason, none of them asked *the* question: How had he gotten Darlene LaRose to confess? If they'd asked, he would have had to pass it off as a spontaneous act of remorse on her part, though his official report contained no speculation as to her motives.

The state of New York really didn't care *why* she'd confessed, or even that she had died; only that she had been discovered as the malefactor, and that a likely hypothesis had been established for the girl's disappearance. Whether to pursue the matter with Lithuanian authorities or not, he'd leave up to his superiors and, ultimately the Feds. Although he'd intuitively witnessed the disposition of the little girl's body, nobody could ever subpoena his vision into a court of law. Management seemed happy that there was a comprehensive ending to the case. He was sure he'd never forget the dismemberment scene of little Janet's body.

Capt. Telfer stopped in the break room while Girard had his third cup of coffee, and they chatted. "Anybody ever find that lost UPS truck?" Girard asked. More serious than usual, the Captain responded, "Negative." A minute later he said, "You watching the national political scene, Girard?" It seemed that the Captain had something on his mind besides the politics.

"Nah, I can't get worked up about government, Captain. It's all about which gang of robbers is going to pick our pockets for the next four years," he responded. "I don't concern myself with politicians."

Telfer seemed surprised, but offered no response.

"We're going to have to help with some big political project soon, Girard. Secret Service has already been in touch with Division about some VIP visiting northern New York State before the national political conventions, and before the election in November. No details as yet, it's still hush-hush, but it's on the job board. Your Secret Service liaison on the JTTF will probably fill you in, just in case it involves many of our boys."

"Okay, sir, I have one call to make to the phone company," he told the Captain, "then I'm at your disposal."

After the Captain left, Girard walked back to the Headquarters garage to catch the noon breeze, and made the call on his cell phone. Reaching the phone company repair service, he identified himself, and spoke with John Barnes, supervisor of repair services. When the investigator asked for the identity of the repair crew working along Route 3 on the previous night, Barnes consulted his work logs and responded that there was no repair work scheduled in that area, and that none of his crews were logged out to that line. Girard's stomach reflexively tightened. "On top of that," said Barnes, "we almost never put a repair crew up a pole after dark; it's too dangerous and they might hurt themselves or someone else."

Something's *very* wrong here, Girard thought, but he didn't ask Barnes anything else and, thanking the supervisor, hung up. Who would be tampering with phone lines in a literal "no place" within the Adirondacks?

Filling his travel mug with coffee from the break room carafe, he headed westward along Route 3 to the curve in Piercefield. He checked his notebook to be sure of the pole number, located it, and parked along the shoulder of the road, setting his emergency flashers before he exited the car. He walked down into a small roadside ditch, then up onto the higher ground at the foot of the telephone pole. It all looked the same as last night; nothing seemed out of the ordinary. He went back to the car, got a pair of binoculars from his kit in the trunk, and returned to the foot of the pole. His stomach immediately sank when, at the top of the pole, on the side away from the road, he spotted a black box with a thin, 8- or 9-inch antenna rising from it. This is way out of *my* league, he surmised, and returned to his vehicle. What now?

He called Headquarters on his cell phone and they gave him the number for Jim Loricchio, head of the State Police Electronics Surveillance

Unit in Albany. Girard then briefly outlined his dilemma to Loricchio and, for a moment, they speculated about who might have reason to tap those rural lines. Intrigued, Loricchio agreed to dispatch his best man, Harland McAvoy, first thing the next day. "We'll get to the bottom of this real quick," he told Girard, but something in the investigator doubted this would turn out to be just a hacker's job or a simple prank. It had "big time crime" written all over it. "Just to be safe," Loricchio urged, "let's keep all calls about this matter on our cell phones and stay off the landlines."

Back at Headquarters, Capt. Telfer agreed that Girard had plenty on his plate and should concentrate on getting to the bottom of this phone tap mystery. Someone with money and sophisticated, technical employees or contractors had gone to a lot of trouble to tap a telephone cable in order to relay information to another remote site. Later, when Girard chatted about the particulars of the mystery with Investigator Joe Hill, the two concluded that there could be no legal use behind the surreptitious installation. It seemed certain that someone was intercepting vital voice or data transmissions for criminal purposes.

The next morning, Girard arrived at Ray Brook to find a rusty 2001 Ford Econoline van in the parking area. It looked like a big V-10, plastered with decals and hand-painted sunsets amid mountains, images straight from Woodstock and his youth. A long ladder was secured on the top. If this was the Electronics Unit, Girard had never seen such a state truck before. As he pulled in, a grey-bearded, middle-aged man in a pork-pie hat slipped out the door. He strolled over to Girard, saying, "You Investigator Girard? Jimmy Loricchio sent me. I'm his spook, Harland McAvoy."

The technician was quite a sight in his coffee-stained Hawaiian sport shirt and scraggly beard—a combination Santa Claus and beach bum. "Yeah, I know, you think I'm some kind of ruffian; some kind of derelict," McAvoy smiled. "I *like* it that way. After folks take one look at me and laugh, they never look again, so I can go most anywhere and do most anything and not arouse suspicion. Once in a while I just dive into a dumpster for fun. People take one look at me and think that's where I *belong*— I just love to play with their heads!" Girard agreed with that. McAvoy lifted the front of his sport shirt to reveal a lineman's tool kit on his belt, obscured by his gut overhang and the long shirt. There was also a service pistol there.

"Come on inside, Harland. Let's get some coffee. Have you ever been up to Troop B before?"

147

"Nope. We have enough crooks down Albany way, though not *all* of them are politicians," he said with a grin, "so I don't get up to vacation country like you guys. Do you really get *paid* to work up here in these beautiful mountains? And who do you catch, skiers at Whiteface Mountain who haven't paid a big enough tip?" Girard knew he was going to like McAvoy—a right-in-your-face kind of guy who dared you to like him immediately or go to hell.

Inside, Girard took McAvoy to meet the captain, then Lou Gregory, Frank Whitson, Alice Gaudreau, and a few others. Investigator Girard knew his new associate was going to do miracles, and wanted his friends and superiors to meet the man before the mystery began to unravel. There was also the nagging insight that he had known McAvoy somewhere long ago. Girard picked up some report forms and signed out a zoom lens camera and some evidence bags, in case they were needed.

Together they rode in McAvoy's van to Piercefield, and on the way Girard discovered that his associate had also served in Vietnam, but as a counterintelligence officer in Saigon. "Yeah, I never shot nobody, but I sure as hell made some special packages that took a lot of them VC to Commie Heaven," McAvoy said grinning at Girard. "We made sophisticated booby traps for the places where the Cong were sure to try cutting into our wires. We had taps on a lot of their long lines in the north, installed by Special Forces units, and we could hear them ordering out for dinner. Right at the end, before the ballgame ended, we had taps on NVA Headquarters lines, but the game was lost, so we didn't get to capitalize on those."

"When I got back stateside I was so goddamn mad at all the politicians, Democrats *and* Republicans! As far as I was concerned, they *all* lied to us, and I lost lots of good young friends who believed the government's crap about saving the South for democracy. They were all bullshit—even our supposed friends. Bullshit! So, I discovered hashish and got wasted for months on end down in New Orleans. Then I went to Hawaii and became a beach bum and smoked dope until I couldn't see straight anymore. I was so mad at the government that I was killing *myself*! Now does that make any sense?

"It wasn't until 1985 that I pulled out of it, recognizing that I was trying to kill a body that no enemy ever touched. I was destroying myself a little more each day, I realized. So I got into an AA group in Hilo, and Jules, my sponsor, got me into computer training. And I just *loved* that! I could use my wits to outsmart the slimy bastards in government or industry who use the little people, lying to trusting ordinary people just to enrich themselves. It was a real, genuine 'payback' for the sonofabitches who believe they can steal big time with impunity. I'd just *love* it if that's what we're running into in this case—some greedy *illegitimi* who are fleecing ordinary folks. I'd love to send them to prison for the rest of their misbegotten lives. Enough of that, Girard, what you got here?"

Investigator Girard filled McAvoy in on what he'd observed four nights before, and what he'd seen on the pole in daylight yesterday.

"Yep, already sounds like I'm gonna like this one," said McAvoy as he followed Girard's gesture to pull off at the tap site.

"Harland, I'm going to take a telephoto picture of the pole top before you go up, just for evidence."

"Sure enough, Girard," said McAvoy, who went to the rear of his van to remove the paint-splotched aluminum ladder. Girard took three pictures from various angles. He had a good lens and could read some of the small white numbers on the black box.

When Girard had finished, McAvoy went up the pole, staying on the road side in order not to touch the tap unit with his ladder top. "Aw hell," he said as soon as he reached the top, "this isn't much. It's just a WMT-18, not that sophisticated, but it must be doing its job. That antenna has a range of a mile or two, so their repeater or link must be fairly close by. From there, they're funneling the data or voice to another distant site, probably by landline. Wanna know who they're listening to?"

"I sure as hell do!" said Girard. "That's why I got you this paid vacation up in Olympics country, McAvoy. Once we know who they're tapping, we can begin to guess who they are and what they're after."

"Okay," said McAvoy, preparing for another climb. "I think that group the other night was either doing an installation or replacing a battery and sent three men in order to look like a regular telephone repair crew to any casual observer. One man coulda done it, but three looks better. It's likely a ni-cad battery in the box, just enough to push the voice or data into their local receiver. McAvoy took a small device that looked like a Palm Pilot from the back of his van, and went up the pole. As he climbed, he whistled "My Darling Clementine," causing Girard to grin at the bohemian nature of his new friend.

The technician spent about five minutes atop his ladder, listening through earphones and chatting with somebody on his cell phone. Then he folded his phone, closed the small computer, and descended the ladder. "What you got here, Girard...are you ready for this? What you got, is

149

somebody tapped into voice communications at both the Troop B Headquarters and the Department of Environmental Conservation right next door. Now who do you think is *that* scummy? What kind of crooks would want to know what EnCon and the State Police are talking about?"

"I don't know, Harland. I'll have to ask some questions in the right places. Who do you think? Who do *you* suspect?"

"Well, I'll tell ya, Investigator Girard, I think we'd better leave that tap in place, real nice, you know? So that they won't know we're onto them. All this stuff can be figured out if a man's brave enough to face that answer when it appears. I been doing this job for too many years to be surprised at what *that* truth might be. One other thing—if I was you, I'd have all my conversations about this case on your cell phone or through a pay phone. Don't want to tip off these slimy folk. Then we'll figure it out, if you want my help."

Girard joshed McAvoy again. "Sure, I *want* your help, Harland. Troop B is where they station all the dim-wit investigators who can't make it in the other troops. Hell, we have trouble deciding whether we should ticket speed skaters for going the wrong way over at the Olympic Rink in Lake Placid!" He had a big smile on his face, and McAvoy responded. They reattached the ladder to the van and drove back to Ray Brook.

Back at Headquarters, they parted. McAvoy had to head over to I-87 and south to Albany; Girard promised to call him the next day. The investigator was thankful to have a dinner date that night with Tommy Delehanty and his fiancée, Janice Howland. He could run some ideas past Tommy and still let down from the stress of the past weeks.

In his office, Girard received a call from the St. Lawrence County Assistant DA, Bill Getz. The Holochuck grand jury would meet on Tuesday, the 8th, after the long Fourth of July holiday, and the investigator logged it in his appointment book. He felt emotionally at loose ends, perhaps because of the continually intense situations he'd been involved in since returning to work. The damned angel stuff just compounded the job's difficulty.

I think I'll need some time off pretty soon, at least a few days, he ruminated. Ever since his chat with Father Bernie McCabe a few months ago, the idea of taking time to go on a spiritual retreat had captured his imagination. Maybe the church can help and maybe it can't; I think I'll ask Capt. Telfer for a little time to get my head and soul straight.

CHAPTER THIRTY-THREE

That Friday night, the finalists for the Republican presidential nomination dominated the evening news. The party was divided philosophically and things had gone sour for the party since the American misadventure in Iraq split the party and nation. America's people had finally tired of a war that couldn't be won, but that could only drain America of its bravest young men and women, to say nothing about its money. Likewise, the disclosures of corruption among high administration officials in 2006 had soured many voters, and there was increasing bitterness about officials who lied to Congressional committees, all of which had showed in the mid-term elections in 2006. Then there was the waste of billions of dollars both in no-bid war contracts and in the Hurricane Katrina relief failures.

President George W. Bush and Congress had failed to deal effectively with the porous borders and many Americans now feared that terrorists were entering America at will. Additionally, the job situation had not improved significantly since the last national election in 2004, and American firms were outsourcing more and more production overseas, leaving workers desperate. And on top of it all, the issue of Iraq was still unresolved, daily draining the blood of America's young men and women.

Hoping to gain from the patriotism of the Labor Day celebration, and at least to reinvigorate its own dispirited and flagging membership, the GOP was preparing to convene in St. Paul, MN, in the heartland of the American Republic. The finalist Republican nominees for President and Vice President would be known soon—whoever!

In the morning, before Girard's Regular Saturday Morning Hike, there was a surprise on the television news. Yes, the Republicans would choose their candidates, as would the Democrats, but it mattered little to Dennis, as he knew all politicians serve at least two masters. Though George W. Bush appeared a broken man in this last year of his second term, his father, George Herbert Walker Bush, the former 41st President, now seemed a new and younger man at age 84, and had publicly promised to make a July whistle stop tour of America to unite America's Republicans, even before a specific nominee had been chosen.

At Akwesasne the previous night, Dark Eagle had turned away from the CNN convention coverage, and smiling grimly, had said, "These corrupt robbers must not remain in power for four more years—they *will* not!" Outside, a car could be heard arriving, crunching its way through the driveway gravel. There were two horn beeps and two door slams, the signal for "friend" and the group relaxed its vigilance. Louie "Two Claw" Charbonneau lowered his pistol.

The man, to be known as "Black Crow," entered the dim repair shop and Dark Eagle introduced the stranger to those assembled. Only Dark Eagle knew the man's real name—Faust Hetzer. And *this* bird figured to make them all rich.

Black Crow shared with the group his hatred of the greedy and corrupt American government, especially the Bush family. Shifting his stance constantly, the man seemed irritated or frustrated and desperate for the group's help. Hetzer informed the Indians that he had a network that could destroy forever the oligarchy that dominated the American economy, while making the citizens think that their votes and paltry political contributions really mattered.

"We can't use my own network here in the U.S. because we think the FBI is observing it. We have what we call *tools* that have to be delivered now into New York State, and I talked with Jim, er…Dark Eagle, about using your cigarette operation to move these items into position. Let's call them "war clubs," and, if you men agree, you will be well paid. We have our own warriors to swing those clubs. And," he looked each man in the eye, "you can watch the government that humiliates you suffer a *great* blow; what your warriors used to call a 'coup.'"

The assemblage murmured, first about the power they would have, and second about the money that they'd gain. "How do we know we can trust *you*?" asked Hibou Blanc. "You're not Mohawk—you're a goddam foreigner! Nobody in *your* organization is Mohawk, are they? How do we know you're not state police, trying to shoot us down again? How do we know you're not FBI or Border Patrol, just trying to lure the last *real* Mohawk warriors into a final death trap? We're not going to have a goddamned Wounded Knee here at Akwesasne! How do we know we can trust *you*?"

Black Crow smiled, then took a small recorder from his pocket. "Listen to this," he had said. For five minutes the group listened to a recorded phone call from Lt. Gerard Michaels, the State Police officer working inside the Mohawk Nation Casino in Massena. The conversation provided surveillance and financial information to Major Edwin Sincavage at Troop B Headquarters in Ray Brook. It was all carefully guarded state data and secrets. Michaels signed off by noting that his regular weekly report would go to Albany. He also wished Sincavage well on his 35th wedding anniversary.

"How'd you get *that?*" demanded Iron Spear, jumping to his feet. "The State Police killed my brother at the barricades in 1990, and I *know* they have guarded and very secret communications."

Black Crow smiled and waited for everyone's full attention before responding. He knew he now had the group in his hands and that meant power and authority and success in destroying the fascist Bush. He knew these men would open their cigarette smuggling network to him because he'd shown big medicine power over the State Police.

"My network is powerful, as are the experts our organization employs," he began. "Maybe we can help you have greater efficiency in *your own* smuggling operation if you help us. But it is imperative that we move our 'tools' *now*. Will you help us? I'm going to step outside and have a smoke. Let me know what you decide." And with that, Hetzer stepped out the door of the chop shop garage. Leaning against the corrugated steel wall of the building, Hetzer lit his imported Samsun Turkish cigarette and took a deep puff under the moonless sky.

The seven Mohawks inside had become excited, asking questions of Dark Eagle and jabbering at the same time about new strength and profits for their organization, which was not supported by either the traditional chiefs or the Warrior Society. Dark Eagle revealed that Black Crow's network would pay $250,000 for their help. It took the conspirators only 10 minutes to agree on helping the stranger. Hetzer then called Dark Eagle aside and told him that a stolen UPS truck would be brought to the garage for a small repainting job at 3:00 a.m. on Saturday morning. At all times, except when the crucial serial numbers were being repainted, it must be covered with a tarpaulin. Hetzer handed Dark Eagle a paper containing the new numbers to be painted in gold.

Girard had slept fitfully on Friday night and really needed his Saturday morning walk on Graphite Mountain in order to focus his professional and emotional priorities. At the North Pond Parking Area he sat in prayer on the guardrail cables. Help me to handle all this new stuff, God…please. Help me do it right, and please help me understand all the spooky stuff that's going on. Most days I can hardly keep my head above water."

It took him an extra hour to make his return journey westward and down through Brant Lake to home. Girard walked sluggishly, and when he returned, he sat on the white iron bench in Mrs. Morgenstern's side yard, as if expecting a cosmic response to his prayer. Her few remaining peonies looked beautiful and smelled like a perfume factory, and it no longer surprised him to see wispy energies, some resembling miniature people, darting among the leaves and stalks. He settled back and relaxed. Wish my own life smelled as sweet as her flowers do, he mused. I've *got* to handle that anger, I know.

At 5:30 p.m. he went upstairs, showered, and made a light supper, then read some more Jung until bedtime.

On Sunday morning he drove eastward to Bolton Landing on Lake George and wandered the streets, looking at the tourists' faces, as if he might find profound answers there. He needed to be among people, but not feel the necessity to interact with them. He visited his old friend Cornelia, owner of the Trees Gift Shop and Bookstore and looked over her framed Adirondack prints, though he didn't buy anything. It was good to be a tourist, a nobody, just mingling with a mass of vacationing humanity. For a moment he recalled summertime jaunts to resort villages that he and Irene had shared, and felt sad that those days were long gone.

Returning to Chestertown, he had a light supper and hit the hay at 9:00 p.m., listening to a Public Radio concert of flute music by a young North Country musician named Sarada. Then he was asleep.

CHAPTER THIRTY-FOUR

When Girard returned to work on Monday morning, he asked Capt. Telfer for a half day off on Friday. "I have some personal business to attend to—emotional stuff left over from the stress of these recent cases."

"No problem, Dennis. You'll continue to supervise the Hetzer surveillance, right?" There he goes with my first name again, mused Girard.

"Yes, sir. There has been nobody visiting and nothing happening in Port Henry so far."

"You headed to Potsdam tomorrow?"

"Yes, sir. This Assistant DA over there, Getz—do you know him? I only met him at the arraignment," Girard said.

"Not well" replied Telfer. "He's an unknown factor, but tough on crime, I do know that, so I'd call him friend. He's relatively new to politics, and you know St. Lawrence County—always a lot of surprises over there. I do know that he always has a lot of pretty women around him."

"Thanks. See you later, Captain," Girard offered, and headed for the break room carafe to fill his carry cup. Recently, he'd heard that drinking coffee is good for one's health. Sounds good to *me*, he concluded.

The investigator finished additional LaRose paperwork, then sat for a while in the garage. Out of nowhere, he heard an inner voice suggesting that Hetzer was the person who had installed the wire tap in Piercefield. Did that come from within me or from outside? he wondered. But what if it's true? All his operation is in Port Henry...or *is* it? Returning to the building he stopped at Capt. Telfer's door. "Sir, do you have a minute?"

"Sure, Dennis, come in." There it was again—the use of his first name. What had changed?

"Captain, I wondered if Hetzer was running some big operation that might cause *him* to tap that line out in Piercefield. What do you think?"

Telfer paled. Only he and Major Sincavage knew the totality of confidential business that took place over those lines. "I've got one line with encryption, you know, but enough of *this*," he said, pounding his fist on the desk. "I'm going to get Jim Loricchio on the line right now. We'd better encrypt everything here, even calling out for pizza, from now on. Loricchio can get one of his boys up here to install the hardware for our entire commo system."

"As I say, sir, it's only a guess, but it horrified me. If he's the one listening to our secret communications, the whole investigation will blow up."

"Thanks, Girard, it's well worth following up. I note on my calendar that you take off next Tuesday for a doctor's appointment. Still with the psychologist?"

"Yes, sir, she's helped me put a lot of things into perspective."

"Good."

Girard returned to his desk to complete more paperwork and to prepare his notes for the Grand Jury testimony the next day.

When he returned home that Tuesday evening, the yellow and purple fairies, or whatever they were, were dancing for joy among Mrs. Morgenstern's flowers. Her irises were blooming, as well as the tall marigolds, and she had planted a border of red celosia around the perimeter. The entire plot looked like a cozy fire. He sat for a while on the bench, smiling at himself. Girard, you're a wreck, you know it? Six months ago, if someone had told you that you'd be seeing fairies among the flowers, you'd have put in for early retirement and a free ticket to the funny farm. At what point did all this crazy stuff just become *normal*?

He sat staring vacantly and smiling to himself for another half hour, as if comprehending the immensity of his involvement in the world's spirit. He didn't know where his emotional juggernaut was headed, and it seemed that the only course was to hang on until the end. Girard looked up and spotted a squirrel intently looking at him from an overhanging branch. Forget it, rodent, I don't even want to *know*, he said to himself and went upstairs to fix dinner.

When he entered the office Wednesday morning, Girard found Lou Gregory just arriving, and the two exchanged pleasantries. From time to time Lou liked to tease Girard about his poor command of French and the pair had a friendly discussion about languages and why some people pick them up easily and others have to labor. Lou often wasn't easy to talk to, though Girard never understood why.

Trooper Joe Ellington called from the Skippy's stakeout to inform Girard that a panel truck had pulled up at 9:05 a.m. and, using a key, the driver had gone inside where he remained for an hour, then exited at 10:10 with a clipboard in his hands and drove away. "We got photos of the whole thing, along with the plate and we ran it sir. The vehicle is registered to a J.M. Miller Enterprises over in Champlain. I have close-up photos of the guy who entered, although if he had a key, it must have been legit, right?"

"Let's see those pictures at day's end, Joe. Bring what you have when you change shifts. I think we also need some ears inside that building. Good job. Hang in there," Girard said.

At that moment, the phone on his desk rang and, picking it up, Girard heard Joe Zarr's voice. "Girard? Zarr. Free to meet at noon, today? A new development to talk about."

"See you at noon," Girard replied. Finishing up some of yesterday's messages and e-mails, he left the office at 10:00. The drive to Albany was an uneventful trip, and at noon he entered the JTTF meeting room in the FBI building. Agent Cindy Parker of the Secret Service announced, "Former President George H.W. Bush has set a tentative agenda for his whistle stop trip, and it involves New York State. He's full of pep with his hip replacement and ready to break all the old niceties of politics. Mr. Bush fully intends to return New York State to the Republican Party fold in this fall's election. It looks like his first speech and rally around the end of the month will be in Plattsburgh, then Glens Falls, then Watertown, then on to Buffalo, and finishing in Binghamton, all in a three-day tour. "Secret Service will be doing its usual vetting of troublemakers anywhere within 50 miles of these venues. We'll have a lot of them in for 'questioning' while the former Prez is here, but we thought it necessary to increase the surveillance on Hetzer immediately if you can find him. He's wanted for assassination and that makes the Service *very* jumpy, so we can't give him any free rein. He's only a few miles north of Glens Falls, and we want to know for sure what Hetzer or Ohnesorg, his real name, is up to, even though he must have an agenda other than a former president. Girard, you up to the increased activity?"

"Yes, Agent Parker, I'm on Hetzer full time now. No more fun and games in the mountains." He was irked by Parker's attitude, but couldn't fathom the reason; maybe all federal authority irritated him, but why? "We have at least one man on his store at all times and one on his house; though he has been absent for over a week. I'm coordinating the whole circus, getting ready to take a more active role myself," Girard replied.

Just then, the phone rang and Zarr summoned Girard to his desk. The call came from Capt. Telfer at Troop B Headquarters. "Dennis, I don't know if, or even how, this might relate to your project, but you know the man in question you're working on?"

From Telfer's guardedness, it became apparent that the encryption devices had not yet been installed. "Yes, sir."

"Remember the Nathan Hale case?" Telfer asked. "Well, I'd like to talk to you on your cell as quickly as you can call back." He hung up.

As he punched the call-back button, Girard tried to remember the full story on Nathan Hale from his history studies. He reached Telfer's cell phone and asked who it was that had only one life to give for his country. Telfer replied, "They found young Hochlitzer hanged in his cell at the Essex County Jail this morning. Nobody saw or heard anything. It appears to be a suicide, but something tells me the ante has been upped in the Hetzer case. It might have been a hit, but, if so, somebody in the jail had to be in on it because the boy hasn't had any visitors, not even his uncle. What do you think?"

Girard was stunned. He had hoped that young Hochlitzer might give up some information on Hetzer, maybe in exchange for a more lenient sentence. It had been his intention to visit the young man that Friday morning, to see if young Hochlitzer might have anything to say. Now what? "If this is a hit, sir, then the stakes seem to be *very* high, and Hetzer must be playing for something bigger than we thought. I can't think of anybody but Hetzer himself who had the money or power enough to engineer a hit. Okay, thanks for the info. We'll talk when I get back."

He clicked off and shared the new development with the other Task Force members. All agreed that Hetzer, if he did the deed, or arranged it, was working toward an extremely large payoff, one in which even family members were expendable. Agent Parker frowned. This wasn't good, she said. No, it wasn't good at all. "Keep me posted if Hetzer even sneezes, Girard, right?"

"You got it, Agent Parker."

Later, back at Troop B Headquarters, Telfer and Girard conversed about the case. "Girard," the captain said, "I want you to visit Essex County Sheriff Jim Parillo on this tomorrow. If it's Hetzer-involved, I think it's all one big ball of wax, and it's your case. Check it out. See what Parillo's official investigation has turned up so far. It's his ballpark, of course, but we need to know who's involved and where it's going. Give him a call and get over there in the morning, okay?"

"Yes, sir. You mentioned to me a while back about 'getting a feeling' about certain matters. That's what I have here. I feel certain that the boy knew something—something so dangerous to Hetzer that the nephew had to be shut up. I'll have something for you before the end of the day tomorrow, sir."

As Girard exited the building, he saw a stranger leaning against his car. Seeing him coming, the man stood and turned sideways. He wore a red cowboy hat. "Damn, Timmy! Now you're following me to work!"

"Yep," said the older brother, again pleased with himself and smiling broadly. "You should see this mess from *my* side. You wanna do this the hard way or can I save you some time?"

Girard smiled. What could his life have been if this older brother had lived? What a pair of Batman and Robin types they would have been. "Okay, Timmy, save me some time."

"Denny, there is a guard at the jail named Ernie. He has been paid a large sum of money to execute that boy. A man who looks like a black crow handed over money two days ago. I know birds don't really pay money, but that's all I'm allowed to see, and I want to share it with you. I don't know his name and they aren't showing me who he is. This man paid—when the autopsy is done, you'll find a sedative in the boy's system. Ernie gave it to the boy with his meal last night, then when the deputy got off duty at 7:00 this morning, he went to the boy's cell and arranged the hanging. The kid never stood a chance because he couldn't resist—he was in a stupor. It was kind of a cosmic balancing of the scales for Paul Michael anyway. That's it for now." Timmy faded away.

Girard stood in the parking lot exasperated. Goddam cases! Goddam ghosts! Sorry, Timmy, I didn't mean you. He wanted to yell after his brother, but Major Sincavage had just exited the building and walked toward the parking area. "How's everything Girard? Everything going okay?"

"Yes, sir, just fumbling for my key. I thought I'd misplaced it, but here it is," he dissembled, showing the key ring to his superior. Sincavage came nearer.

"Girard, I really am glad to have you back on board these past months. I don't know how you're doing it, but you've resolved some *very* difficult cases, and as a professional, I admire your work. You know, there was a time there when I was going to put you out to pasture."

"Yes, sir, I know that, and I probably deserved it," he said seriously. Then his inner comic asserted itself. "Sir, I was just *dying* to be a better trooper, and now, look at me!" The two veterans looked at one another and, in spite of himself, Sincavage smiled. Later, Girard realized it was the first time he had ever seen the Major smile. Each man saw a respected professional looking back at himself. Sincavage reached out his hand and Girard silently grasped it. Girard then got into the car and drove out of the parking lot. Instantly, his cell rang and he pulled to the shoulder to answer it.

Capt. Telfer was on the line, informing Girard that an Essex County Jail guard, Deputy Ernie Landrio, had just crashed head-on into a large tree on Route 9N, west of Elizabethtown. EMTs were on the scene but Landrio was dead. "He works at the jail, Girard, do you think he's involved?"

What could he say? "Yes, sir, I suspect *everybody* who works over there. I'll see Sheriff Parillo first thing tomorrow."

CHAPTER THIRTY-FIVE

On Thursday, at 9:30 a.m., Girard parked at the Stewart's Shop in Elizabethtown and got a small coffee. It was only his third cup of the morning and he knew intuitively that he needed to be sharp for the coming interview. Strange, I just never miss a cigarette anymore, he mulled; in the old days I couldn't sip a coffee without having a weed in my other hand.

Finishing his drink, he entered the courthouse and went directly to Sheriff Parillo's office. The Sheriff was expecting him. "Hello, Investigator Girard," he said, "I knew you'd be here early. I also know your questions. Let me lay it out for you, the way it looks right now. Ernie Landrio was full of heroin. I went out personally to the crash site. No skids or anything—straight into that tree. While he was still in the ambulance, the EMTs showed me punctures on Landrio's upper arms and thigh. The man had to have been out of his head. There was powder on the floor, and in the glove box was an envelope with $8,000 in it. We already printed the envelope, but it's clean—only Ernie's prints on it."

Parillo scowled, "It's strange that nobody here even *suspected* Landrio of being a user. It's almost as if he picked up the habit recently. Who knows? Maybe somebody gave him some free samples and he liked it. He has no family and lived by himself over in Keene, so this is such a dead end! I've got a deputy interviewing his landlady. Landrio may well have had a hand in Hochlitzer's death, but how can we prove it? And what are we going to do for a *motive*? And who set up Landrio's death?"

This summation mirrored Girard's thoughts. With Timmy's help he had already come this far. With Hochlitzer dead, the young man would never squeal on his uncle. Now, Landrio was dead too, and he'd never squeal on anybody else either. Timmy said a black bird gave the dope to the deputy. How can anybody ever put *that* in an official report?

"Yes, you're right, Jim. It looks open and shut, but it isn't very satisfying, is it? Why? Why? Why? Was Landrio your weakest link among the jail guards?"

"I never thought so, Girard, but what can I say? There's a part of everyone that *nobody* knows about, don't you agree? And I guess many of us get through life without our cover being blown, but most folks have something festering inside, don't you think? I've discovered that during my 30 years in law enforcement. In a way, I'm glad I'm near the end of my road. Gonna retire in August and go do some marlin fishing off Florida. You fish?"

"No, not for fish, just for understanding," said Girard, suddenly serious. He had had such hopes in this case—the kid was greedy and unpredictable, and maybe I could have turned him. Now, we'll never know. "Guess I'll leave it all in your hands, Jim. Keep me posted if something shows up, will you?"

"Yes, thanks for coming over, Dennis. Landrio's blood samples went right to the State Crime Lab, so we'll know soon what was cooking inside him. Same with the kid. His samples went down there yesterday. You going out to pasture soon?"

"Yeah, I think so. I only have one more real problem to solve, then I'm going to find a cave up near Rainbow Falls, walk in, pull the rocks across the opening, and sleep for a hundred years…like what's his name, down in the Catskills—Rip Van Winkle?"

Leaving the courthouse, Girard chose to fortify himself with another large coffee at Stewart's on his way back to Headquarters. When Ginny was working there, she always let him stir in a dollop of chocolate sauce from the sundae fixings. Homemade mocha!

Back at work, he wrote up a report on the facts as he knew them about the Hochlitzer case, including his suspicions about Landrio's involvement that could never be fully proved, though there was the matter of the glove compartment cash. He faxed a copy of the document to Joe Zarr in Albany, as Telfer told him that landline communications were now secret; the encryption devices were installed. Somebody out there, watching and listening, must be having a fit that their commo is all messed up now. Wonder if Harland did the fixing?

He dropped reports in Capt. Telfer's office on the way out, then caught sight of Tommy and they chatted another 15 minutes. Girard asked if the stolen UPS truck had been found. Tommy answered that no, it hadn't, and it was a strange case, wasn't it? Who'd want a UPS delivery truck, FedEx? Girard wanted to know if there was any news about Two Claw. "No, Denny, you know I'm working on it," said Tommy. "I have snitches all over the place and nobody knows a thing. Louie has to be on the res."

The next day, Girard finished more paperwork on outstanding cases, said goodbye to Tommy, and headed for the retreat center in New Hampshire. Four hours later, driving south on Interstate 93 from St. Johnsbury, VT, he exited at Littleton onto Route 302 South. Looming in the east was Mt. Washington, the highest peak east of the Mississippi River. As he drove southeast, Girard caught the sun's reflection on the U.S. weather station antennae and mountaintop observatory. He stopped in Bartlett to refuel, got another cup of coffee, then continued on to the intersection with Route 16, swinging north toward Jackson.

Girard pondered the lab results that had come in before he left Ray Brook at noon. Hochlitzer had enough Vicoden in him to make him sleep for a thousand years. Landrio had extremely toxic levels of heroin in his blood and may even have died before hitting the tree. Who was the mastermind, the ringmaster? It had to be Hetzer! What activity of his was worth two deaths?

CHAPTER THIRTY-SIX

Following Father McCabe's rough map, in Jackson, Girard turned toward the Tyrol area, and soon spotted the small sign for Holy Cross Friary, where he turned off on what appeared to be a seldom-traveled gravel road. Upward and upward the road twisted, with sheer drops of several hundred feet on his left. Then suddenly, there it was. An abbey and residence appeared, looking as if they were set in the English countryside, and a patch of green grass alongside a parking area filled with mostly out-of-state cars.

Checking his watch, Girard noted it was almost 5:00 p.m. and past time to be registered. He grabbed his small overnight bag, locked the car, then paused to reconsider that action. Who or what might pilfer his vehicle in this holy place? Habit! He trudged up the gravel path toward the chapel entrance, where a glowing antique light beckoned retreatants to enter.

As he walked past a border of evergreens, Girard heard a distinct "psst!" Turning to his right, he saw an elfin face peering through the greenery. More of the man emerged and Girard could see the brown robe of a white-haired Franciscan beneath a broad, impish smile. The friar beckoned with his forefinger, "Here, over here. Come on, in through the trees. This is the shortcut to what you are seeking." Puzzled, Girard concluded the priest was an unorthodox part of his welcoming committee; perhaps the man who greets latecomers. The diminutive figure disappeared in the boughs and Girard followed, parting the greenery and pushing through to the other side.

With the arborvitae behind him, the investigator could see two stone benches set at right angles with one another on the border of a beautiful flower garden. Along the sides of the building was a colonnaded walkway, bordered by rose blooms in their full array of summer color. A bit of paradise, I'd say, thought Girard. The small priest, who stood only five feet tall, motioned him onto a bench. "Hello, I'm Father Anselm Sweeney," he offered, sticking out his hand for a shake, then rearranged his wispy white hair.

"Nice to meet you," Dennis replied. "I'm here for the retreat. Father Bernie McCabe in Chestertown, NY, thought I could use a good dose of what you friars offer."

"Oh yes, McCabe. I worked with him for a short time some years ago, to help him get on his track."

"Pardon me," Girard replied, "I think I'm late, and it's almost five. I came to see Father Don Lee, a Vietnam vet turned monk. Father McCabe said he'd understand some of the particulars of my need."

"Yes, of course. All of us who have been in combat have returned scarred in some way. Do you mind talking with me for just a few minutes?"

"Sure, why not?"

"You have had much help in getting here," Father Sweeney said, "and I see you've met your angel."

Girard's heart seemed to stop and his mind reacted with shock. Stunned, he said, "What? How can you know *that*?"

The friar smiled, raising his eyebrows. "There is a special something that shows around you, like a light that someone has illuminated. When a person has seen or met their angel, such peoples' lives are never the same again. With you, there is a resonance of deep purple, with what seems like red flames spurting through it. This shows me you are on a path of deep purpose. And, of course, visiting the land of the dead wasn't harmful to you either."

Again, Girard blanched. Who *was* this guy? Some kind of psychic priest? It was almost as if his entire life was now known to the little man. "How can you know I've been dead, then brought back?"

"In time, I think you'll understand some of these issues. Let's start off with something huge. I can know these things about you because there really is *no* time, and *everything* can be known to those who are prepared.

The past, present, and future are all taking place right *now*—in God's love. How do you like them apples?"

Girard was silent for a moment, taking the measure of the grinning, small man. A leprechaun, if ever I saw one, he concluded. Grandma Kelly sure would have loved meeting this guy.

"Father Sweeney, I remember how we used to talk about Einstein's theories at Syracuse University. A lot of us students got very interested in the possibilities of time as an illusion, but in the end, we concluded that being alone in an Adirondack forest on a beautiful summer day was about as close as any of us would ever get to experiencing timelessness."

"Your grandmother was a beautiful woman, Dennis. From County Cork, I believe."

Damn! This guy's even reading my *mind* now, he exclaimed inwardly.

"Dennis, it doesn't matter that your thoughts are revealed. There is but one road for you, and that is oneness, integrating your individuality with everything else that is. Where time and space meet, there is a truth available for anyone who is prepared to know it. Your work now is that of preparation for great events.

"In a sense, all mortals have to travel the same path, though each one has his or her own peculiar twists and turns. Nevertheless, the goal is the same for us all. Look over there," he said, indicating the summit of Mt. Washington, now backlit by a setting sun. "I met a Japanese Buddhist monk once who showed me an overhead photo of Mt. Fuji, just outside Tokyo. On the rim of its crater, in the center of the picture, was a Buddhist shrine. He then showed me the many pilgrimage trails winding up from the many different points around Fuji's base, though from overhead they could all be seen to head toward the center. He noted that the goal for all pilgrims is a summit, the same summit, but not all pilgrims can follow the same trail. Each must follow the one that leads him or her higher. And if we love another person, we must allow them to take *their* unique path, too, even if it isn't ours.

"Later, when I was in India, studying with Father Bede Griffiths, I discovered that that is what it was really all about. Father Bede set up an *ashram,* a spiritual learning center, where Christians could work and study with the Hindus and other eastern religions. And there I found the basic principles of all religions to be essentially the same. You know, *religion* means 'to reconnect or rejoin.' In our western Christian tradition we have placed too much of a separation—a dualism, between God and man. This split obscures true spirituality, which shows God *yearning* for us to work intimately with Him, as co-creators, not as fearful, joyless drones, but as co-equal partners."

"That's strange to hear those words from you, Father. I just heard of this partnership idea for the first time a few months ago in church. It was the first time in years that I'd gone to Mass, and it really shook me up that an all-powerful Maker of the universe has such a role for each person to play. Father McCabe said that Jesus's role, as redeemer, was mainly to show us that we too could play the role that He played—nobody ever told me that before. Why have the clergy of so many Christian denominations emphasized retribution and punishment over God's love for us?" Girard demanded earnestly.

"It's fear, Dennis. Humans have a weakness for power, and seldom use it unselfishly at first. Too many religious leaders fear that the visible world is all there *is*, and strive mightily to retain and strengthen whatever earthly power *they* seem to have in that realm, even if that means denying brotherhood with those who are ruled. Most people, especially clergy who wield power over others, *really don't* believe in a loving and just God. Jesus, and certainly my order's founder, St. Francis, taught the role of joyous servanthood.

"Our church has long ago fallen into this behavior, and its fearful leaders have chosen to overpower their neighbors throughout recorded human history. You must forgive them their shortcomings. Too many clergy believe that fear of punishment is a better motivator for change than is love.

"Buddha warned that humankind walks around asleep, so our life's main obligation is to awaken to the truth of our existence and purpose. *You* are awakening from your soul's slumber, so it's disturbing to you and some people around you as you see life in its greater dimensions. And you will soon enough have your own tests with power.

"But, something wonderful has changed in the universe in recent years, and the effects of this process continue to speed up. New energies are coming into play in the earth, and it's happening first in individuals such as you. This is truly a time of change and challenge, which many call a new age. Never before has it been so possible for so many who accept the idea of a co-creator role and to fulfill it. You had to die for a short time in order to be open to this possibility."

"Yeah," Girard answered glumly, "I sure have had some unique after-effects from that!"

"You were transported out of so many of the earth's illusions to experience its truths, which lie just above the surface."

"Father Sweeney, why is there death? And why do people so many times die ugly deaths? Why does God seem to snatch good people from their families and friends? I don't mind Him taking the creeps and criminals, but why *children* like little Janet LaRose, or Walter Bortiatynski, and other innocent people?"

Sweeney paused for a moment, staring down at his sandals, then, raising his face, the twinkle reappeared in his eye. "Dennis, what soul that has come into the earth is *truly* innocent? What we know as life is a cycle, and that which appears here has appeared in another form in an earlier time. Jesus told us to call no man good, as *only God* is good—think about that for a minute." Sweeney sat silent and Girard, not daring to break the silence, tried to comprehend the priest's words. Nobody innocent? *Everybody* with some flaw or defect to face? That's almost what Sheriff Parillo said just yesterday.

"Part of your learning now involves the truest love," the priest continued. He ran the white rope cord of his belt through his fingers several times, then continued, "Love, *unconditional* love, is the answer to your question. It's the answer to *all* of life's questions. Humans cling desperately to what they think is their one life and their only loved ones because it's all their conscious mind knows. But, as an energy, love keeps right on after a person's body dies. Death is an illusion, and Jesus knew that! The Bible doesn't say that He joked with the crowds on His way to Calvary, but in the East, that event was recorded.

"A dead person doesn't suddenly stop loving those who remain alive. And though they grieve, the living can't suddenly stop loving the dead ones either—your brother told you that—don't you believe him? Life exists outside the body, too, though we never seem able to get that across to sorrowing people. I'm here with you now as a testimony to that truth—soon you'll understand what I mean by that. A loving God would not, will not, condemn *any* soul because of the twists and turns of its pilgrim trail as long as we keep climbing. Nobody can walk straight to the summit—even the Master had his *Via Dolorosa*. God keeps on giving and giving unconditionally, opportunity after lifetime, so in the end, you *will* reach your son-ship with Him."

"Lifetimes? Are you serious? Isn't that some of that reincarnation punishment stuff? Don't tell me you believe in *that* crap?"

"It's not a matter of believing, Dennis. It's the certainty of knowing *and remembering.* As your learning progresses, you will have many occasions to ponder this principle, which is based on the Creator's love, not punishment. You have been allowed to forget your many lives and deaths so that you can strive anew, with a clearer mind, if not emotions. Deep within your unconscious mind, the truth of your many past life experiences is recorded, though you are unable to remember even your teachers in elementary school. Yet, these are taking place just yesterday, today and only tomorrow."

Girard looked westward at Mt. Washington again, and noted it was presently backlit by an orange sky, now that the sun had set. Yet, the heavens seemed just as light as when he'd looked 15 minutes before.

"Now, how and why did you enter into your life's work this time?" Sweeney inquired, pushing a strand of white hair from his forehead.

"You mean police work?" Girard responded.

"The law enforcement to be sure, but also the lifelong contact with nature, as if at any moment you might finally comprehend its workings. And of course, to help sharpen the focus, there were those years in military life."

"If you're looking for something philosophical or profound, I guess I can't answer that," said Girard. "These are simply things I was drawn to, or they were drawn to me, or maybe *out* of me, I don't know. All of them seemed like good ideas at the time I began them. Now, this work defines me."

"Exactly—drawn to them, and them to you! That is what the gift of each life involves. In some instances these attractions stem from uncompleted lessons from what we call 'long ago.' In other cases, they represent new avenues of exploration and opportunity for the soul that you have merited. For lifetimes your soul has been seeking to regain its rightful role as healer—as transmitter of the golden light or life force. Before too much longer, these past life experiences will begin to unravel and return to your consciousness. Then, with new understanding, you will be faced with taking new paths. At present, you must decide whether you are more fit to *give* life than to take it. Sounds ominous, eh? Now, tell me this—were you more alive when you were dead than you are now?"

Dennis Girard sat silently, glumly staring once more at the vibrant orange of the setting sun, which seemed to have fallen no lower than when he last looked at it. There's not a whole lot left from my former life since I died, he realized, and now this little guy wants to take away even *that* certainty of my being alive here and now. He's talking about me being other places and other people in other times—all the while learning lessons that are supposed to be leading me somewhere. So, where the hell *am* I? And, how the hell can I answer these questions? He scuffed the dirt and grass at the base of the bench, and noticed several whitish-green star-shaped flowers. Sorry I kicked dirt on you, he thought to the plants.

"Pretty, aren't they? They don't mind the dirt though, it gives them life." Father Sweeney's words brought Dennis back to the present. "I'll let you in on a real little miracle. Most places in New England you can't find these flowers after June. They're called 'Star-of-Bethlehem' because of their shape. Here, in *this* garden they last until the end of September. Nobody knows why, but we say it's the result of Friar Dominic's nurture.

"You know, there are a lot of seeming miracles in our lives, but most of us are so terribly asleep to the wonders of this world. We pass through and wonder why life is so ugly and dull, though most of us have never taken the time to seek its beauty. You have been gifted to return to the appreciation of so much in nature that you once held dear. The Lord is allowing you to peer more closely into *His* garden. But you have to want to do so, if you're going to gain from it."

For a moment, the dismemberment scene of little Janet LaRose's body forced its way into his consciousness, and Girard tried to cast it out.

"That's okay, let it come," said Sweeney. "Let it stay for a bit—don't let go of the precious gift that little Janet sent to you and others. She now understands why such a thing *had* to be—indeed, her soul chose a life path that could only lead to her murder at a young age. She wants you to know and understand that. You still have a hard time seeing her soul at work in all this right now. And right now, you'd have an even greater difficulty in understanding how a Christian crusader butchering a small Muslim girl in Jerusalem long, long ago has led to this. But her soul has not forgotten the deed *it* once performed in the name of absolute religious certainty.

"In the world of the dead, lit by the eternal light, she has now come to peace with it all, understanding what she long ago inflicted on another little girl, and thus was allowed to help her mother *and you* in this life on your own paths to wisdom. How do you think it happened that your superiors assigned Janet's case to *you*? It was a gift within a gift, and your soul assented, though your mind was too concerned with proving yourself that day."

Fr. Sweeney then related a long, complicated story of his own past, episodes that he discovered only when he became grounded in the deep meditations at Fr. Bede Griffith's ashram. Girard could only gape as

Sweeney narrated scenes from an ancient island to civilizations in Greece, then Rome and on to the forests of Germany, then to the lands now comprising the Netherlands, and finally England. All at once the priest uttered a strange statement without explaining it—"and you and *I* companioned on the St. Lawrence, you know. That time I provided a foothold to boost you, but today I'm trying to *pull* you up," the little man said with a grin. Girard didn't dare ask the meaning of that remark.

"Now, look at this beautiful garden. Friar Dominic planned and planted it with great love. And you and I derive much pleasure from his vision and work. Love promotes love…cause and effect. And though it can be covered over and disappear at times, love can never be extinguished…it is a part of our eternal identity. Human beings are all struggling to remember their true identity and have to tread many false pilgrim trails before they find *their* unique holy path…a path that looks different to each man and woman, but is the same in purpose."

Girard stared again at Mt. Washington, still backlit in orange light. The friar interjected, "Dennis, see that mountain? A great symbol for man's obstacles, yet also his yearnings. Some part of us always wants to climb to the top and see the earth below. What do you think *that's* about?"

"Well, my talk doctor, Bernice, would probably say it symbolizes my inner need to elevate my consciousness, to rise above the earth and its dirt."

"Oh, dirt isn't bad either. These children beneath your feet," he said, indicating the flowers, "*need* dirt to stabilize and strengthen their roots. We can all draw sustenance from the dirt in our lives. Dirt makes us yearn for something more, however, and eventually to seek our sustenance from above and not below. Dennis, the highest mountain you'll ever climb is not *out there*. It's *inside you*—overcoming and discarding the heavy negative garments you have formerly worn, so you can now ascend.

"It is in the surmounting of base passions that served your earthy self in former life experiences. But in that overcoming, to now turn our faces to the warmth of He Who Is—the "I Am," just as these children beneath your feet do in their simplicity each day. Using our feelings, our knowledge and reason, we can set ourselves free from the 'lazy sleepiness' that The Buddha warned against."

Girard once more turned his gaze to Mt. Washington. He observed that the formerly orange sky was now tinged with blue and, as he watched, feathers of white clouds appeared and the sun now shone from behind him, and onto the mountain's eastern face. He turned to Sweeney and apologized, "Look, I really have enjoyed our talk, but I came to hear Father Lee, and I think I missed an hour of his retreat already. He glanced down at his watch. It read 11:00 a.m. Sunday. He shook his wrist—something was wrong with the watch. Looking up, he saw Friar Sweeney grinning and was irritated because the little man knew something that *he*, Sr. Investigator Girard, did not know.

"Yes, Dennis, it *is* time to go now, but I'll be available if you want to talk again. Here, let me usher you out through this door," said the little man, rising to his full five feet of stature, "so you don't have to scratch your way through the bushes this time. You'll soon have *a lot of bushes* to deal with. They shook hands and Girard walked to the left, toward the sanctuary, where he heard the assemblage singing, "*This is the day the Lord has made, let us rejoice and be glad.*"

Recognizing that he was hearing the closing ceremony of the retreat, Girard was puzzled. This shift in time made no sense, and he turned to question Fr. Sweeney, but the elf had vanished. All at once, men much like himself, some grey-haired and some young and virile, walked from the sanctuary to the outdoors, each surrounded with a brilliant mist. He rubbed his eyes to focus them and banish the fog, but the mist remained, forming a bright cocoon around each of the seekers. "Oh, no, more damned angel stuff!" Girard sputtered.

Returning to his car, he was a deeply troubled man. He'd taken the weekend off to attend a religious retreat, but hadn't done so. Instead he'd gone through some time warp with a little man whose philosophy aggravated and irritated the hell out of him. These ideas seemed too insane for his mind to grasp, much less believe, so what had he gotten out of it all? His head was swimming with both excitement and apprehension. He was *not* at peace, yet he had to return home even more confused than before.

He started his car and, heading south then west, tuned his radio to the New Hampshire Public Radio classical music station and found himself in the midst of a great choral work, one he'd never heard before. Fortunately, it was in English, and he tried hard to pick out the words. First, the voices sang, "*He watching over Israel, slumbers not nor sleeps, slumbers not nor sleeps*" over and over. Then, "*Shouldst thou walking in grief, languish, He will quicken thee.*" Well, I don't know about walking in grief, he said to himself, but I'm sure driving in a very boggled condition.

As that section passed, Girard tried to process those lyrics and their theme…it sounded like Old Testament stuff, about the Jews, the Chosen People. A woman then sang a solo, but he couldn't pay attention, as he fought to comprehend the first passage. Suddenly, his ears were drawn to the beautiful strains of an alto solo. The woman sang, *"Oh, rest in the Lord, wait patiently for him. And he will give you your heart's desires. Commit thy way unto Him and trust in Him; refrain from anger and forsake wrath."* Something in his heart suddenly gave way. He pulled over to the side of the road and burst into tears as the singer concluded her piece. "Oh God, what's happening to me? I haven't got any guts left, I'm wide-open to anything and everything, and I've lost control. When a bullet couldn't kill me, I'm getting destroyed by *music*! How can I go back to being a cop?"

He sat for half an hour on the roadside of Route 302, his car rocked by the wind gusts of passing traffic, though he was hardly aware of the effect. The music poured forth from the radio; some of it he distinctly heard and some vanished into his unconscious mind. Then he became aware of a final, majestic *"Amen,"* and it was over. Girard exhaled deeply. Amen—didn't that mean "So be it?" Is that a message for me? Was all that stuff about putting away wrath for me too? he wondered.

The applause began for what apparently had been a live concert from Chicago, and in a moment the announcer informed listeners that they had just heard Mendelssohn's *Elijah,* performed by the Chicago Symphony and Chorus.

That guy Mendelssohn again. And just who was Elijah? He made a mental note to look that up at home. Drying his eyes and adjusting his sunglasses, he hit the turn signal and moved out into traffic and the long ride home.

CHAPTER THIRTY-SEVEN

The act of returning to work on Monday required much self-discipline. Girard's head swam with images of his fellow troopers, criminals he'd brought to justice over the years, living and dead members of his family, murdered children, an impish Franciscan, Tommy, Luc, Bernice, Charbonneau and others. That little friar had said that it was all interwoven—that it all was integrated on a higher level. For a moment, Girard became enraged. What kind of Creator would deal with His progeny in such a secretive manner? Isn't God supposed to be Truth? Why would He *hide* things from us—why not just tell the open truth? "Just like the government," Dennis concluded—"from top to bottom, they're *all* lying to us," he muttered in exasperation.

Rising from his desk, he walked to the break room for a second cup of office coffee. Capt. Telfer arrived a minute later and asked him how he was doing. I can't let down and get weepy with Telfer, Girard decided. I've gotta keep my guard up, put on my investigator face, and get my act together. For the next 10 minutes they talked shop, then Girard had to know the answer to an issue prompted by Fr. Sweeney. "Captain, do you remember why you gave me the *LaRose* case to work on?" His superior looked up, startled. Telfer studied the floor tiles for a minute before looking deeply into Girard's eyes.

"I'm sorry, Girard, I can't tell you *exactly* why. You know that we have numerous cold cases here." He looked at the floor, then at Girard again. "After you solved that Bortiatynski case, I was really happy to have the old Investigator Girard back. Denny, you know I'm a prayerful man and a deacon in the Baptist Church, and I believe that Someone Higher often directs me in my thoughts and actions, and that's what I call God, or the Holy Spirit. My eye caught the LaRose name in the files and I just knew that was the one for you. Don't ask me to explain it; sometimes a man just *knows*. Does that make sense? Sounds nuts, doesn't it? But many times I believe that I'm led by the Spirit. You aren't a churchgoer, I take it, so I won't lay a lot of heavy spiritual stuff on you. But, you're a good man, Girard, and you've returned from the dead, and that amazes me— someday I hope you'll tell me what the other side is like." Suddenly self-conscious, Telfer looked at his watch and stood. End of tale, Girard surmised.

The captain offered his hand. "Denny, I'm glad you're back. Now take care of yourself, will you?" Telfer strode out the door. The captain was often crusty and officious in manner and this glimpse into his spiritual beliefs was as if a window into the man's soul had momentarily opened. There was more paperwork to do and Girard walked back to his desk.

By 10:00 a.m. he had completed six different reports and, fatigued, he looked out the window at the sun's glare over the mountain to the south. What a beautiful mountain that one is, he mused. Why haven't I ever noticed it before? Then the term *the same summit* came into his mind. Who said that? Sweeney, that little Franciscan leprechaun! What was it about? He couldn't remember now, as so much of that weekend retreat seemed a foggy memory. Hey, it's a piece of cake—I'll just call him up and ask; he said I could. Girard found the Abbey's main phone number in his notebook and called.

"Holy Cross Friary," a pleasant male voice answered.

"Yes, can you connect me with Friar Sweeney?"

There was a pause, and the other voice asked, "Er, what Friar Sweeney would that *be*, sir?"

"Why, the little guy, Anselm Sweeney, he said his name was," Girard responded.

Then came a long pause. "Sir," the voice on the other end said, "Friar Anselm Sweeney died in 1988. Is there anyone else you'd like to speak to?"

"No, no, wait a minute! There's a mix-up. The guy I want is a little five-foot-tall guy—white hair and goofy smile. Friar Anselm Sweeney!"

"Sir," the other voice said, "I knew little Friar Sweeney. He died during my first year here. I was at his funeral Mass. You can see his grave in the burial ground if you wish."

Girard hung up his phone and stared once more at the distant mountain. "What did that little guy *say* about highest mountains?" he said aloud.

Lt. Lou Gregory responded, "What's that, Denny?"

"Aw, nothing, Lou. I'm just talking to myself." He filed all his papers, cleared his blotter, and locked the desk. He knew he needed to drive. Maybe over to Skippy's.

Oh God, he complained to himself as he exited the building, now you give me a ghost priest!

At home that evening, having taken the next day off, Girard kicked his recliner chair back and picked up a copy of the book on symbology that Doc had loaned him at their last meeting. He found potential meanings for fire, water, certain animals, as well as colors and numbers. Then, there it was.

MOUNTAIN: An elevation or height; an obstacle; in many instances a barrier or obstacle to be overcome. An exaltation or highest expression. A "high place," often a site of transfiguration or sacrifice in dreams or religious scripture. A place of higher vision or revelation.

I guess a mountaintop is about the highest place where a man can stand on this earth, especially if it's the earth's highest mountain. Maybe that's why so many are drawn to the Himalayas, Mt. Everest, and K-2. Maybe the highest understanding that I'm capable of is what it's all about.

Now I remember what Sweeney said—that such understandings aren't outside us but rather *inside*. We can't find what we're searching for on an *earthly* mountaintop, but inside ourselves instead. Man! What a mess *I* am inside—how will I ever find any answers in there? The damn angel stuff is like driving in a thick fog! How the hell could I spend two days with a *ghost* and come away inspired?

Recalling Eugene Sprague, Girard remembered talking with his Albany friend about an old guy who Eugene knew, a friend who lived on a mountain top—an elder that "knew things." The investigator picked up the phone and called BCI Forensic Investigative Support Services in Albany, requesting to speak with Sprague. The operator replied that Sprague was not at work today, but after Girard identified himself, the woman provided Eugene's home phone number.

"Hey, Eugene, taking the day off?" Girard asked genially when Sprague's phone was picked up.

"Hey, Dennis Girard, you old scoundrel! Yeah, I'm not feeling well, so I figured I'd sit home and watch infomercials on television all day," he said jokingly. "Actually, I have an appointment with my cardiologist in an hour and was just about to head over there. What's up?"

"Hey, Eugene, I'm sorry about the ticker; hope it will all be okay. The reason I'm calling is that after I got out of Albany Med and stayed with you, you mentioned a weird old guy who lives on a mountain. You said that you thought he was closer to Heaven, and that was probably where he got his information. What was his name?"

"Oh, you mean Mr. Malcolm? Yes, he's in his late 80s. Lives up in the town of Hartford, not too far from Fort Ann. Do you know the place?"

"Oh yes, I sure do. I remember back in '82 when the local dairy farmers went on strike because of low milk prices. They were really angry, pouring out tanks of milk all over Route 4 rather than sell for low prices, so we spent some time keeping order over there when I was in Troop G. Yep, I remember how tough it was for them to make ends meet. Hasn't gotten any better, and a lot of them have sold their herds and just have city jobs now. My heart went out to the dairymen, but we didn't want violence there either. What part of Hartford does Malcolm live in?"

"'*Mister* Malcolm' is what everyone calls him; I don't think I know his full name. He lives up on Gilbert Hill Road, last house on the left, right at the top of the mountain, so you can't miss it. Let me see if I have his number in my book." For a minute there were rustling sounds, then Sprague returned to the line. "Yep, here it is." Eugene gave Girard the number and suggested that he call the old man for an appointment. Girard once more gave his best wishes to his friend, then signed off. For a moment he closed his eyes and asked that Eugene be healed of whatever was wrong.

Picking up the phone again, Girard called the number that Sprague had provided. After six rings, a gravely voice came on the line. "Ayuh?"

"Mr. Malcolm?" Girard asked.

"Ayuh. Who is it?"

"Mr. Malcolm, you don't know me, but I'm an old friend of Eugene Sprague from Albany. He says he has consulted you several times in the past, and maybe you could give me some insight about living on a mountain."

"So you want a reading, huh?"

"To be honest, sir, I don't know what I want. I have had a very unsettling year so far, and it's only half over. Could you give me some time so I can ask questions?"

"How's tomorrow morning at 10?"

"Fine, sir. I'll see you then." And he hung up the phone.

It was now 11:00 a.m. and time to spruce up for his now-monthly counseling session with Dr. Epstein.

CHAPTER THIRTY-EIGHT

Malcolm Viktor watched the approaching car negotiate the rutted dirt road to his home. High atop Gilbert Hill, he had built a home 60 years before, overlooking the beautiful Wood Creek valley off to the west. He already knew this Dennis Girard, who had made an appointment yesterday. Malcolm Viktor, who everyone locally called "Mr. Malcolm," knew many things—often a lot more than he wanted to. He knew when the Ryder family's house was going to burn down, had known when Barbara Creighton was going to have a girl, and, on the day his grandson left for Afghanistan, Malcolm had known that Mitch was going to die there, just as he had known the Iraq War adventure would end in misery and decline for the U.S. He knew that the dark energy of multinational corporations would assume leadership in the United States, and that it all *had* to be, because darkness was attracted by the darkness in the hearts and souls of too many Americans, and that few of them would ever own up to their inner darkness, so there's not going to be a Nineveh *here*, he mused.

His death and sudden revival in a German prison camp in 1944 had irrevocably changed his own life. Malcolm had arisen from that prison sick bed with the capacity to know people's thoughts and feelings, and, often, their futures. Now, using a dowser's pendulum, and with proper concentration, he could tune in on people's current difficulties and past lifetimes, seeing the errors and strengths that had propelled these individuals into their present situations. Malcolm had also discovered his capacity to heal others with prayer and touch.

Returning from the war, although he joined local groups and held local government offices, he also had maintained his essential apartness in order to be of greater help to his fellow humans. Now another individual, one he knew from his gladiator days in ancient Rome, had returned to him, though he doubted this Dennis Girard needed to know of their past association.

Sparky, the Viktors' miniature collie, met Girard at the parking area and gave him a friendly, yapping reception all the way to Malcolm's door. Only at the porch did the dog allow Girard to scratch her under the ears, and then she sped off, having spotted a woodchuck crossing the road.

The door opened and Girard introduced himself. The two shook hands and Malcolm's broad grin bid the visitor to enter. Girard had the uncomfortable feeling that he *knew* this man, though he'd never been on this road before, he was certain of that. The old man motioned Girard to the kitchen table, which was the seer's work space.

There were a few pleasantries, as Girard remarked on the beautiful view across the valley, all the way to Hudson Falls in the west. He also marveled at the wild birds that swarmed to Malcolm's feeders, even in the summertime. The phone rang and Malcolm asked Girard's pardon in order to answer the call. "Yes. Oh, that's okay. Uh-huh. Uh-huh. Ayuh, that's right—Fujiwara. Tuesday. Sure, that's okay. Bye now."

Malcolm looked sheepishly at Girard, "Sorry, that was a man in Japan's government who regularly calls, though he should know better than to phone between 10:00 and 3:00 our time because it's when I meet people here. I get lots of calls from people overseas, all of them seeking help or healing of some kind. The old man paused and inspected his guest before resuming. "Many times I just send healing to them while we're talking on the phone, and there have been some remarkable results, though I never know who is going to be helped. I leave all that to the Great Spirit."

Girard recognized that this name for the Creator matched the numerous portraits of American Indians on the walls. That's Chief Joseph of the Nez Perce over there, he mused; I know that profile.

"Yes, so many of these great peacemakers are here in spirit each day—they help me to assist others," Viktor said, watching Girard's eyes. "Well, Dennis Girard, how can I help you?"

"Eugene Sprague, my friend at the State Police Headquarters in Albany, suggested I come to you. I shared with Eugene a few of the strange events that have occurred in my life over the last six months or so, since I was shot and killed, then revived."

"When were you shot?"

"In February, during that awful cold spell."

"Let's see," said Malcolm. He lifted the small pendulum from the table top and dangled it over the edge. For a moment the device swung clockwise then stopped. Two seconds later, it began a counterclockwise movement. Abruptly, Malcolm looked up and stated, "You *knew* this man."

"Yes, I had arrested him some years ago, up near Chazy. Caught him smuggling untaxed cigarettes. He shot and wounded me at the time, but I recovered. This time he couldn't miss," Girard explained.

Mr. Malcolm grunted and lowered his chin upon his chest. He mumbled to himself and looked as if he might fall forward onto the floor. Girard braced himself to catch the man if that happened. The pendulum suspended from the seer's forefinger rocked sideways for a moment, then stopped and began swinging counterclockwise for almost another minute. Suddenly, he straightened and wiped moisture from his eyes. "Peronard. Étienne Peronard, that was his name when you last saw one another. Then slowly and deliberately, Malcolm peered into Dennis's eyes. "Girard, do you believe that people can live a succession of lives? Do you believe in reincarnation or the return of souls?"

"I sure didn't expect *that*," Girard responded. "I just wanted to know about catching Louie Charbonneau, and I wanted to know what is happening to me inside. I have lost so much of my old drive and certainty. I see visions and hear voices, and I think I'm in contact with an angel named Israfil, who bugs the hell out of me. And I haven't believed in angels since sixth grade."

"In due time," Malcolm responded, "but you have a score to settle first with this Peronard, or Charbonneau, as you call him now. The last time you met was in Canada in the year...he paused, closing his eyes for

177

a minute, then definitively finished with, "17…50…and 9. For the last minute or so I watched as you, at least a man I take to be you, all suited up in a red uniform, reached the top of a bluff or cliff. A man, a Frenchman in grey uniform, was surprised to see you and your fellow soldiers rushing at him, and as others fled in panic, he fired one shot. It struck you square in the heart and you died instantly, still filled with hatred and loathing for the French. It's immaterial now that your British army beat the French army at the place called The…Plains…of Abraham. That hatred and loathing has now come full circle and must be dissolved. Why is it so hard for you to speak French now?"

Girard sat silently, thinking, remembering, and struggling with immense doubts. All these crazy people! Izzy, Fr. Sweeney, and now Mr. Malcolm, all talking about life and lives as if *everyone* should know we have hundreds of them. His shoulders sagged and he looked beseechingly at Malcolm. "Well, what do I *do*?" The two men sat quietly, each in his own dimension of thought. Two blue jays squabbled noisily at the feeder outside Malcolm's window.

The old man was the first to break the silence. "See those birds? They love to fight. So do people, apparently. Always have. If a man's been raised all his life to believe in enemies, then how and when can he learn the *oneness* of all life? On the way to that learning, people have to first learn to value something fairly simple, like their families. Then, after enough life experiences, they have to grow in allegiance to towns and cities and the different people who live in them. And then take part in nations and armies to find a greater measure of togetherness and devotion to an identity and ideals beyond themselves. But all of us have to watch the idolatry in *each one* of those illusions fade away. And boy, that usually can only fade away after you've had enough painful failures in attempting to make those illusions real. Cheer up, though, in the end there's only one Pure Light. And when that's *all* that's shining on you, you've found Heaven," he smiled.

"Humanity is so divided—mainly because we believe only in what we can *see*. For thousands of years we have struggled against one another to be sure we, or our family, or our country comes out on top. On top of *what?* Did you ever ride a Ferris wheel? Where's the 'top' of *that?* All those who think themselves great and powerful *have to* fall. You know, one of my favorite quotes, from the Italians, I think, is this: 'At the end of the chess game, the king and the pawn both go into the same box.' Why can't people see that?

"My guides tell me right now that your recent path has two purposes. First, to show you there is not just *a* world, but *universes* of reality outside what we call normal! You have been initiated by an angel—few people are ever afforded such tutelage, my boy, and you'd better be responsive. This is important stuff that's facing you. You've got to think beyond this Charbonneau fella.

"The second part of all this new stuff you're experiencing is a path that you chose after you died in Quebec. The last conscious thought of Captain Howe, that was you back then, was 'Damn—what a waste! Jimmy (I think he was your commander and friend) and I worked so hard for this victory and we both got killed. Killing is such a *waste*!' So, here you are, my boy, it's put up or shut up time. You have had a rendezvous with your soul. How's it all going to end? And just to make the learning thorough, you've got that Jimmy back, still fighting, still a kindred soul, but now against you, as a *new* Jimmy."

Both men resumed their silence. Girard was almost totally lost within himself, confused and yet excited. What the hell did Malcolm mean? Something vague had just been illuminated within him, though he couldn't say what it was right now. He momentarily felt as if the weight of the world had fallen onto his shoulders.

Malcolm also cogitated. He knew what he needed to do, but this guy, this Girard, didn't appear to be ready yet. Shams, his Persian spirit guide, began prodding Malcolm and, in the end, the old man surrendered. "Girard, do you want to try an experiment?"

"Hey, what the hell do I have to lose? I lost my sanity some time ago—about the time I lost my life. Now, I see all kinds of ghosts, angels, spirits...you name it! I see plants and trees moving—some *talk* to me. I get light shows out in the bushes and mountains, I talk to birds—it can't get any weirder. I don't have any more fight left in me, Malcolm. All this crap since February has essentially killed me, the Dennis Girard I tried so hard to be. Now, you've got something crazier for me? That right?"

Mr. Malcolm smiled. "Well, boy! So you *are* ready to look into the beyond...this time without dying. It's your damned independent nature that has made things so tough for you. I'd like to try what I call a 'reverie,' a time of relaxation, and see what happens inside you, okay?"

"Hell, yes. Like I said, there's nothing more to lose. And maybe I can find something new that makes sense."

"Okay, boy. Come over to the couch and sit, and just lay your head back." The pair moved past the kerosene stove to the afghan-covered

179

couch. Kirby, Malcolm's tabby cat, stretched out on the carpet and, extending her forepaws, watched the two men pass. Girard sat and lay back.

Malcolm pulled up a chair in front of the investigator, asked Girard to close his eyes, and began to talk slowly...first about the house, then the nice weather outside. He spoke about Girard's gratitude to have life restored and urged his visitor to draw long, slow, and deep breaths. After a minute, Girard was no longer in Malcolm's house, though it didn't seem at all strange. He was with a large group of men in boats, approaching a high cliff at nighttime.

The general, his friend Jimmy, quietly recited a poem that had consumed him for months. It ended, *"the paths of glory lead but to the grave."*

"A terrible thing you say, General." Girard heard British-accented words issuing from his long-ago mouth. "Talk like that can doom us in this battle." Jimmy smiled, then once more grabbed his stomach. He'd been doing that so much lately, and it was clear that the general was a sick man. Yet, this officer, Wolfe by name, was a shrewd man...indefatigable. The wooden boat heavily bumped the narrow, rocky beach. Leftenant Jones quietly spoke the words, *"Anse de Foulon,* everyone off," and the men quietly and quickly disembarked.

More and more watercraft bumped the stony shore and soldiers moved onto the beach, formed into squads and companies, then began seeking the animal trail upward that their observers had spotted during daylight. Thick and stunted bushes obscured their route for a moment, and Wolfe ordered a Private Peterkin to remain posted at its beginning as a human marker.

Captain Howe, who was both a distinct *other* and yet Dennis Girard himself, looked into the eyes of the private, barely visible in the murk. Something—an energy? A sudden recognition passed between them in a second, as if each man was fulfilling his preordained task. He *knew* this man, though he didn't know him. Shouldn't he have white hair? A brown garment? For an instant it was as if they had always known one another. Then, the men were away—Howe stretching upward, silently waving his short sword, and up the rocky path they scrambled, sometimes slipping, and all of them quietly hushing the others lest the Frenchies hear them coming.

Capt. Howe feared they would be spotted from above because the disembarkation had taken so long that dawn's first light now appeared over the St. Lawrence River flowing to the east. Then, onto the summit they leaped. Ahead, snoozing around a small fire, were several guards. One sentry suddenly cried out, "*Qui vive!*" and Howe shot him dead with his pistol. Girard could feel the recoil of that pistol against his hand. There was panic throughout the small camp. Random shots were fired by fleeing sentries, one of whom kicked the fire momentarily into a flare of light. Kneeling directly before him, Capt. Howe saw one unafraid sentry. The man's musket was centered on Howe's white cross belts. In an instant, their eyes locked in the predawn gloom. They, also, knew one another! It was *time*!

And the seated Dennis Girard became absorbed in a profusion of motives, memories, feelings, and energies as life suddenly departed from the bleeding, dead body of Captain Howe. For a moment his essence drifted, then was pulled down to his present body as he heard Viktor's words, "Now, let there be peace in your mind and soul, forgiving those who harmed you and asking forgiveness from those whose lives *you* took."

For a moment, Lt. Lou Gregory stood beside him in spirit, begging recognition as the man whom Howe had shot at the campfire. The bottom fell from Girard's stomach once more, and he felt devastated, not knowing who his friends were, or the identities of his true enemies.

"Well?" Mr. Malcolm softly questioned Girard. "What did you see? What did you feel? Does any of this make sense now?" Dennis Girard, drained of energy, sat dumbly on the couch. He kept trying to focus his mind on a single period in time, but the images kept flickering between long-ago scenes of the St. Lawrence River, State Police Headquarters in Ray Brook, the frozen fields at Chilson, and the Viktor house. Scenes of ancient gladiators mingled with images from a convent. All at once he saw himself recently on the LaPorte Bridge entering Quebec City, and instantly understood all those physical symptoms from his past. Some part of him had remembered the battle and was afraid to die again at that spot because death felt like utter failure.

At that point, Girard was overcome with scenes from all his purported lifetimes and was unable to respond to Mr. Malcolm. His senses were stunned, and it took minutes of quiet before Sr. Investigator Dennis Girard was able to corral the energies and ideas that were now incorporated into his present person. All he could mumble to Mr. Malcolm was, "Sister Concordia would have had a *very* hard time with all this!"

He sat for a while in silence, and then looked directly at Malcolm. His benefactor now sat with a different face, naked from the waist up, and wearing only leather cuffs of some sort. He had jet-black hair, appeared to be about 50 years old, and seemed for a minute to be scolding, "Get it right, you peasant! *Ave, Imperator, morituri te salutamus!* Yell it out so those in the highest rows can hear! Can I teach you nothing?" Then the kind brown eyes of the present Mr. Malcolm were there again. A great hush came over the room, as if time had suddenly been suspended, and Girard felt 10,000 years old.

Malcolm arose from his straight-backed chair and stepped slowly to the couch. "My son, I love you now as I loved you then. I just couldn't show it at that time. The sorrow of wars and both of our losses now permit me to rejoin you as a brother. Can you understand *anything* of what I tell you?"

Dennis Girard straightened on the couch and as he did so, a tear came to his eye. It was as if he suddenly comprehended all the workings of the universe, and this sudden revelation had burned out his emotional wiring system. It seemed that the infusion of images and ideas had removed a hard spear point that had been lodged in his heart since birth.

CHAPTER THIRTY-NINE

The next day at work, Girard found a note from Capt. Telfer on the desk. "See me soonest," it said. Walking down the hall, Girard found his superior, who informed him, "I'm taking you off all other cases today; I want you on Hetzer full time. Any problems with that?"

"No sir, I think the JTTF expects that anyway."

"It's time for you to supervise a round-the-clock surveillance on the cycle shop, do you agree?"

"Yes, sir. I've got Simmons and Friskin working the night shift already, and am going to drive over this morning just to size up the situation and see how Tomlinson and Ellington are doing. Tommy Ellis is still watching Hetzer's house. In any case, you know the JTTF got federal approval to install a wire inside the shop to listen for anything suspicious. Jack Tomlinson said the installers were in and out like grease, 10 minutes, and we're recording any and all phone calls on that line. Strange thing, Hetzer never closed out the phone service there."

"Keep me posted, Girard."

"Yes, sir."

He left the building to drive down to Port Henry and immediately got a call on his radio. "Action, sir," said Trooper Jack Tomlinson. "We have movement at this site. A van just pulled in and two guys have opened the store. Doesn't look like a break-in. Want me to approach them?"

Girard answered, "No, that's okay. I'm on my way over, Jack, and I'll drop in for a friendly chat. Hang tight."

Forty minutes later, he swung into Skippy's parking lot. He observed two men carrying cardboard boxes into the shop from the van outside, but they paused when Girard exited from his car. He showed identification and introduced himself. The two young men, apparently in their mid-thirties, seemed to be Mediterranean types, though each spoke English very well, though their accent seemed French, which prompted him to ask, "Are you gentlemen Canadian?"

The one who identified himself as Augustin Corbeau responded, "*Ah, oui,* we've come down from Montreal and have a contract to re-open and operate the motorcycle shop."

"Oh," responded Girard. "And did you buy this place or are you leasing it, and if so, from whom?"

The other, Yves Marteau, held out a paper that appeared to be a lease agreement negotiated through J.M. Miller, a Champlain, NY, recreational equipment company. Taking the paper, Girard made a note, and asked about their plans for the business.

Marteau said they had purchased the shop's entire inventory and were buying the building on time. Marteau told the inspector that his expertise was mechanics and he intended to increase the parts inventory to turn the operation into a first-class repair shop. Augustin Corbeau would be in charge of sales. Girard shook both men's hands and as he did so, there were two small, icy nudges between his shoulder blades.

Retaining the lease document, he asked if he might photocopy the document and return it to the pair. "Business registration, you know," he added. The two men seemed taken aback by the request but, as Girard folded the paper and put it into his folder, the duo was left with no option but to agree.

He wished them well in their enterprise and, in a reference to Hochlitzer, the former manager, joked that the new owners would do well to keep their hands off people and more on the machines. Within weeks, Girard would rue that suggestion.

Leaving Skippy's and moving north, the investigator gave a subdued wave to the telephone repair truck that sat at the roadside surrounded by traffic cones and blinking lights. Trooper Jack Tomlinson, in his repairman's attire, returned the greeting. This was the same spot where a dump truck had sat broken down for three days before, and just south of a driveway where a carpet installation truck had parked during the previous week. Trooper Ellington, also dressed as a repairman, exited the truck and began a tedious and strangely unproductive digging near a roadside junction box, spending more time glancing at Skippy's than at the ground in front of him.

As Girard sped north, the two cycle mechanics grumbled about interference from cops. Once inside the shop, however, they laughed and Augustin, turning toward the parking lot, shouted, "*Sharmout!*" at Girard's departing car. The digital recorder inside the phone repair truck caught each syllable. Girard returned to Ray Brook and dropped the Miller Company document on Frank Whitson's desk. "See what we can identify in the prints on this document, will you Frank?"

"We'll get this on the SAFIS system immediately," the FIU officer responded.

Girard worked on more paperwork until Whitson informed him that SAFIS couldn't identify the prints and they'd gone to the FBI and would then go on into the Criminal Justice Information System (CJIS) if there was no hit in the FBI database. Finishing his paperwork, Girard went home, feeling the need for a double chocolate cone at Main Street Ice Cream Parlor. He watched the evening news, read another chapter on Carl Jung, and then turned in.

In the morning, Girard reviewed the previous day's Skippy tapes at Troop Headquarters and was puzzled at the term that the one young man had shouted after his departure, which didn't sound at all French and certainly wasn't an English language expression. He made a brief note.

The phone rang and Girard caught the voice of Cecile Sprague, Eugene's daughter. Weeping, she informed the investigator that her father had suffered a major heart attack and had died at 6:35 that morning in Albany Medical Center. Although arrangements were still incomplete, the family planned a wake on Monday evening and a private family funeral on Tuesday, as Eugene had requested. Girard offered assistance but Cecile simply asked for his presence at the wake.

Hanging up, Girard went to the break room and, pleased to find Tommy just pouring a cup of coffee, did likewise, informing his friend of Sprague's death. They recalled the good times all three had had as young troopers in Troop G, and Tommy asked to ride down to the funeral home with his friend after work on Monday. Girard quickly agreed, noting that, as friends, they had few opportunities to get together socially unless Tommy's fiancée, Janice, arranged them.

Delehanty also informed his pal that there had been a credible sighting of Charbonneau near Plattsburgh on Tuesday, but the trail had gone cold when he investigated over there on Wednesday. "So, Two Claw is back in the game," Girard observed aloud. "So, where *is* his game?"

Frank Whitson entered and informed Girard that the prints on the Miller document had gone to CJIS, where they'd also be run through Interpol's database.

So, who is this J.M. Miller outfit? Girard pondered. Everything is covered here, so I'll pop up to Champlain and check them out. Two hours later he rolled into the company parking lot and saw a large warehouse with six loading docks far back from the highway. He parked in the visitor's lot, and observed the company's sign: "Recreation is US," and then entered the small office. Once inside, he identified himself and asked the secretary if he could speak to the manager.

J. Frank O'Connor, the manager, emerged from the warehouse and shook Girard's proffered hand. "Please come in, Investigator Girard. This is a matter that still makes my head spin. On Monday, the 7th, we were approached by a gentleman named Faust Hetzer, who told me he was in distress about a family matter, had to close his enterprise in Port Henry, and was returning to Germany immediately. He handed me a list of his inventory along with the property deed, the store's books, and a recent credit rating. It looked like a profitable operation, certainly worth taking a chance on, but we chose to check it all out, putting our lawyers and accountants immediately to work on the offer.

"Last year they netted $211,000, and Mr. Hetzer said that because of the urgency of his need to wind up affairs here, he'd take a cash payment of $95,000. Well, you know we import Canadian snowmobiles and do a lot of over-the-border sales of recreational equipment, especially ATVs. This deal was too good to turn down. I called Tom Hopkins, our business manager, and he coordinated and verified our appraisal of the details. Hetzer gave us a key and I visited Port Henry on the 8th, checking out his inventory. With the growth of Lake Champlain Gateway tourism, I'm sure we can make big money there.

"Hetzer came in on the 10th and signed the necessary papers and I wrote him a check. It looked solid, and I guess he departed for Germany. Then on Friday, the very next day, the 11th, two young men from

Montreal came in and said they heard Skippy's was on the market and asked to lease the operation for a year, to see if they'd like to buy it from us. To test their sincerity, we asked them to take a one-year lease. Tom Hopkins wrote it up and within four hours, they paid us $15,000 security, signed the lease, and we notarized it. We made out very well on that deal—no down time at all. Bought it one day and leased it the next! Those two guys are intense and expect to be in operation by the end of the month. Good for us and good for them, right?"

"So, it's an up-and-up deal, then?" Girard inquired.

"Our company lawyer looked it over inside and out and couldn't find any way we can lose. So we jumped on the opportunity. Yes, that document is the one we signed with the Canadians."

After a few pleasantries and an exchange of business cards, Girard headed south, looking forward to the weekend, but not for a second believing that Hetzer had returned to Germany. Cruising down the Northway, he got a call on his cell phone. Trooper Joe Ellington was preparing to turn over the stakeout to troopers John Simmons and Peter Friskin, the night shift, but had noticed that their roadside vantage point didn't allow them to see much of the backyard at Skippy's, a plot of land that bordered the lake. "Do you think we should have some kind of water surveillance here? If these Canadians aren't legit, they might move stuff in and out of the back door that we might not observe. And there's a dock back there on the lakefront," he noted.

Girard promised to make a decision on Monday and asked if Ellington and his partner had worked out their schedule for the weekend. Ellington responded in the affirmative. "Okay, I'll check in with you guys every day, maybe a couple of times each day, just to be sure we have it all covered. We don't want these guys putting anything over on us." This whole transfer from Hetzer to two unidentifiable Canadians stunk. Back at Ray Brook, Girard put in a call to *Sûreté* headquarters in Quebec City, asking for Luc Gosselin.

When his old friend came on the line, Girard asked Luc to run the names Augustin Corbeau and Yves Marteau through the *Sûreté* data system. Did either man have a record of any kind and, if so, did they have prints on file? Luc promised to have the information faxed to Girard's machine before 9:00 a.m. on Monday morning. "So, *mon ami,* is it good to be back at work?"

"*Oui, Luc, c'est formidable.* We're sitting on some real bad guys and should have them all in the slammer or buried by the end of the summer," he laughed. After a few more words, Girard inquired about Marguerite's well-being, then hung up.

One more thing to take care of before heading home—a call to the JTTF office in Albany. Girard updated Agent Zarr on the twists and turns of the lease and related the most recent surveillance observations. Zarr promised to notify Homeland Security about the two strangers. Promising to keep all the other taskforce members informed also, he hung up.

CHAPTER FORTY

That night, at 8:20 p.m., farmer Joe Tessier hitched the manure spreader to his John Deere 4640 tractor and drove northward from his barn almost two miles toward the boundary of the farm outside Clinton Mills, NY. His property bordered both the Flat Rock Gulf state wilderness area on the east and Canada to the north. Like his father and grandfather before him, Joe had moved many a contraband shipment across the Canadian border over the years.

Grandfather Simon Tessier had begun the smuggling during the lean Prohibition years of 1926-27, and there was always good money for financially strapped border farmers in transferring items both ways. Farming and haying no longer paid even the maintenance costs of the farm, but Tessier wanted to retain his family lands and such "transfers" were a way to accomplish that goal, no questions asked.

There'd be rain for sure tonight, he surmised, because the sun was already obscured behind dark clouds gathering over western Clinton County. Tessier had been approached the previous week by his friend "Louie the Indian," as he called the man, to do a special operation that would net him $500 for less than an hour's work, and tonight was the time to follow through. Approaching the border of his northern fields, Tessier swung the rig into the forest and along a well-traveled dirt path. At the big boulder he stopped and shut off his engine, then restarted the tractor as a pre-arranged signal to the hiding smugglers.

Sure enough, six shadowy men emerged from the trees, each carrying the end of a six-foot-long bundle wrapped in heavy black plastic. Each pair dumped their load into the slop of fresh manure within the spreader. "Okay, that's it," one of the men said. "Don't turn around. Drive this load into your barn as you were instructed, and a truck will come by to pick these up on Monday morning at eight. Be sure you're ready. The driver will pay you upon delivery." Uttering these words, the Indians merged with the forest.

Rain began to fall in sheets, and Joe Tessier did as instructed. He always did—that's why Louie the Indian trusted him. The barn door stood open and Tessier drove into the interior, shut down his engine, then closed and barred the door. Inside, he hauled the bundles from the spreader, sprayed them clean with a hose, and left them to dry on the hay-covered floor. The Indians always included a case of Molson's with each delivery, and he carried the plastic-bagged case to his house where he always drank alone. As he trudged to his back door, he reflected on the irony—this time it's the Indians giving the fire water to the *white men*!

Saturday morning's rain ended about 8:30 and Sr. Investigator Girard was anxious to head onto Route 8 for his regular hike. Maybe the eagle will finally be up there today, he hoped. Maybe I'll get some bird talk along with the angel talk and then I can watch the fairies out in the garden! He smiled broadly while slapping the right side of his head. He set a pot of coffee to brewing and scrambled three eggs, while making two slices of wheat toast to accompany the liquid into his stomach.

The day's first job was a drive to Ray Brook, to see if Luc had sent a fax regarding the two Canadians a bit early. Filling his travel mug with a second helping of coffee, he walked to the driveway, waved a big "Hi" to Mrs. Morgenstern, who was weeding the flowerbeds, and got into his vehicle, setting the car's radio to North Country Public Radio. The NPR morning interview was with British baritone Stephen Varcoe, who had just recorded a new album of Ralph Vaughn Williams's music. The happy selections played after the interview were a peaceful vehicle to usher Investigator Girard toward an inevitable rendezvous with dark forces.

At Headquarters, he checked the fax machine and found the transmission from Luc. It was a curious document, indicating that neither Corbeau nor Marteau were on any RCMP or Sûreté wanted list. Neither were they found on the National Health Insurance database, nor Canadian tax or insurance files. And, Luc noted his certainty that the names were aliases—a definite indication of skullduggery. "If you can send prints," he wrote, "we can run those too. Those are harder to fake, as you know." Luc closed with a jibe in French that brought a smile to Girard's face. Before leaving, Girard went to the FIU office where Alice Gaudreau had the weekend assignment. She pulled the prints from the SAFIS sheet and he faxed them to Luc with thanks and some intentionally misspelled French. Maybe we'll know about these guys on Monday morning, he mused.

He checked his mailbox for Tomlinson's photos and notes from Friday. They were nothing special, but the report did jog his memory about the strange words spoken by one of the two Canadians. When I get to Eugene's wake on Monday, he concluded, I'll ask the superintendent. He's sure to be there and he's really a linguist; he will know. Back in the car, he headed for home, east on Route 86.

So, what have we got here? He slowed the car to allow two gorgeous women hikers in short shorts to cross over the highway at the Hurricane Mountain Trail on Route 9 as he headed east to I-87. Boy, I wish…he began mentally, then stifled himself. Soon enough, he was on the Northway and headed south, leaving the goddesses behind. Gee, I wonder why is it that I see *most* women as goddesses? Doc and I have to talk some more on that one. Why didn't Irene cure me of that tendency for good?

Parking in Mrs. Morgenstern's driveway, he went inside to change clothes and check for phone messages. Strangely, his cell phone was silent this morning. He heated up the remainder of the morning's coffee and took a swig, then changed into his hiking suit, which today was shorts, boots and a cut-off Syracuse U. sweatshirt. The outside temperature was 87 degrees at 12:45 p.m. and the day was as beautiful as a Warren County summer day could be.

At the Northway Bridges, going east, he spotted a large, black dog sitting on the opposite side of the road, as if waiting for him. Good naturedly, he summoned the dog with a clicking sound of his tongue. The dog looked at him but remained seated. Oh well, no accounting for taste, he thought, and continued onward. After Girard had passed, the animal then rose and also ambled eastward on its side of the road, neither walking faster nor slower than Girard.

Passing the southern end of Brant Lake, Girard noted the dog continued to match his strides, keeping him company. Past Point of Pines and all the way to the foot of the mountain, the animal kept its pace measured to Girard's. Though the investigator spoke to the dog, it looked neither to the right nor left, almost as if the beast was making its own pilgrimage to the top. Looking far into the distance, above the mountain, Girard could see a lone eagle soaring and riding the thermal currents. Gotta *go*, he decided and took up a marching pace, onward and upward.

At the North Pond Parking Area, Girard scanned the hillside and its surrounding trees. No bird. He turned to see where the black dog had gone, but it had also vanished. Here I am alone on the mountaintop, he thought, kinda like Friar Sweeney's mountain, I guess. The afternoon heat increased and beat directly upon him as he headed westward and downhill back to Chestertown. At the foot of the hill, he spotted Joe Parker, a longtime resident, and asked him who owned the large dog, but Joe said he had never seen such a creature in the neighborhood.

Saturday night's dream involved Dennis plowing soil with a primitive sharp stick. He experienced a struggle in trying to withdraw seeds from a pouch in order to toss them onto the plowed ground. For some reason, in the dream he felt great anxiety about whether the seeds would sprout, or whether the ground was too hard. The dream became repetitive. He'd rouse, go to the bathroom, then fall back into bed, only to revisit the same dream sequence again and again.

In the morning, drained of energy, he staggered from bed to the coffee pot and began brewing his true Sunday sacramental drink. Maybe a drive over to Skippy's, he decided. After finishing breakfast, he drove up the Northway to the Ticonderoga exit. Slowing at the Route 9N intersection, he radioed the surveillance van. "Just checking, Joe," he said to Trooper Ellington. "All quiet today, General," Joe responded. Always a wise guy but also a dedicated trooper. Girard was sure this man was headed for BCI—maybe if one of us old-timers got out of the way, he considered. He reminded Ellington that the van was to move two miles north at 8:00 a.m. on Monday morning because a State Police "surveying crew" would be doing the eyes-on surveillance for the next two days outside Skippy's. Their van would continue to monitor phone calls and conversations in the garage's interior.

From there, Girard drove over to Black Point, the Ticonderoga Town Beach at the north end of Lake George, and finding an unoccupied bench, sat. The sun was moving now to the southwest, creating a reflective surface on the lake in the direction of Rogers' Rock. The rippling water had a hypnotic effect and, in a moment, Grandma Kelly stood beside him. "Hi, Lovie," she gave her old salutation. "How's it been with you?"

"Hey, Grandma," he said, or thought he said. "You know I miss Grandpa and you. Hey, I also wanted to tell you I've seen something like the little people." Grandma Kelly gave a big grin. Then, sobering, she said, "Dennis, you know it's almost time now. You know they've been getting you ready for it, and I'm helping as much as I can. It is all going down, as you say, at the Fort, so be ready." Then she blended into the lake's reflection and vanished. A small boy digging in the sand nearby gave Girard a very strange look, as the child had also been party to the interchange. The youngster kept turning to see where the lady had gone, then gazed at Girard, as if *he* would supply an answer. Time to go, Girard decided, and stood to return to his car.

He drove back to Chestertown, parked, and then walked from Knapp Hill Road to the ice cream parlor on Main Street. Gotta get a double chocolate cone so my brain can understand all this stuff, he decided. Someday, maybe I'll start my own religion based on chocolate ice cream and coffee. Returning home, he sipped his orange mandarin tea and read until 9:00 p.m. Then he made one last call to the stakeout. Nothing moving.

Girard's adventures didn't cease there, however. In his sleep, he found himself walking a paved, yet dusty road toward a distant city that gave off a brilliant white light. As he approached the city, he could see a large, jeweled, and golden gate through which he must enter. There were intimidating guards at the gate, standing with ferocious, chained lions to impede easy entry. To the left of the gate, seated beside a well, was a man dressed entirely in black. As Girard came nearer, he noticed a sign on the side of the well saying "Life." From time to time, the black-garbed man put a dipper into the waters, then drew it forth to give to a traveler in exchange for a gold coin.

The water-server smiled at Girard exposing a mouth filled with dirty, rotten teeth. "See? *All* must pay me to receive the water of life," the man said smugly, then stood to face Girard directly.

"How can you *sell* water?" Dennis inquired of the man, who now, curiously, was wearing the white Roman collar of the clergy.

"People are afraid to enter this gate unless they buy the water of life from *me*," the man purred unctuously. "All people have fears, and most rely on someone else to ensure their safe passage into the city of light. In fact, I myself am afraid to enter this gate even though I have drunk of this water."

Girard felt his dreaming self becoming enraged. "Water is a gift from *God* and should be given *freely!*" he shouted at the man.

Then a woman who looked like Mrs. Morgenstern walked up, clad in a deep purple dress that touched her feet. She smiled at Girard, ignored the black-clothed man, and continued toward the gate guards. She raised her right hand, whereupon the guards and their lions vanished. Beneath the arch, she paused and turning toward Girard, pulled a pink veil from her sleeve, tossing it upon her shoulder. "See?" she said, "there are no lions at the gate of love." She smiled and, walking through the jeweled arch, vanished.

Dennis Girard sat up in his bed. It was pitch dark and he trembled, as if he had just ventured into a forbidden area. Peering at the alarm clock, he saw the time was 1:01 a.m. He staggered from the bed, went to his dream notebook, and recorded the imagery, resolving to share the experience with Dr. Epstein on his next visit.

Exhausted by the effort of reliving the experience and writing it, he fell upon his bed, dropping immediately into a deep and dreamless sleep.

CHAPTER FORTY-ONE

Dennis Girard awoke at 5:00 a.m. filled with anticipation. Something *big* is going to happen today, I just know it, he assured himself. Showering and shaving took minimum time as the coffee brewed. He chose to skip the solid food, and filled his travel mug with coffee. Maybe I'll get some junk food from the machine at Headquarters, he decided.

At 6:05 he was on the road and headed for work, and gave a radio call to Trooper Friskin, finishing out the night shift in the surveillance vehicle. "All okay over there, Peter?" Answering in the affirmative, Trooper Friskin signed off quickly, first noting that Corbeau had just showed up at Skippy's, quite a bit earlier than his usual daily appearance. "Hang in," Girard told him.

Up north, a P700 UPS van with repainted gold ID numbers passed through Churubusco, headed east toward the turnoff into the hamlet of Clinton Mills. Six minutes later, at precisely 8 a.m., the van backed into the long driveway at Joe Tessier's farm. The bulky driver in the brown deliveryman's suit, his braids tucked up under the cap, emerged and walked quickly to Tessier's door. This is my biggest day in a long time, Louie Charbonneau, exulted. And nobody in hell is going to look past this uniform and see *moi, Charbonneau*! All that people ever see or remember about others is their suit, so today is the day I shine!

Tessier, waiting on the porch, moved quickly to the barn and unlocked it. The two men lifted the three plastic-covered parcels into cardboard boxes in the van, and Charbonneau gave Tessier an envelope containing 10 fifty dollar bills, which Dark Eagle had provided. *"Ça va!"* he called out to Tessier, then started the truck and quickly drove off. My day, he thought. *Mon jour! Ecoutez, viellard?*

His father had been on Charbonneau's mind all week—the father whom he could never please—the man who beat him with the buckle end of a black leather belt because he was such a lazy boy. The man who barely scratched out a living in the mines around Saguenay, and the man who finally died, *gráce a Dieu!* Now Louis Philippe Charbonneau was his own man and was about to bring down the mighty ones. He was a warrior, he kept reminding himself. Slowing, he made the sharp turn onto Plank Road and headed south and over Route 11 to Hammond Corners, where he'd pick up Route 190. In under three hours his delivery would start the process of bringing the rich government assholes to their knees. Hell, not their knees, but right onto their fat *asses!*

CHAPTER FORTY-TWO

Shortly thereafter, Trooper John Simmons, the stakeout man, notified Girard that Marteau had also arrived at Skippy's—awfully early, they agreed. "Get pix," he told the trooper and, asking to be kept fully up to date, Girard signed off. He again filled his coffee mug at the break room carafe. Something's about to pop, I just *know* it, he exulted. Knowing that Trooper Simmons would inform him if anything novel occurred, he returned to a pile of paperwork at his desk.

Five minutes later, his cell phone rang, and the stakeout at Skippy's said that Corbeau had emerged from the building, peering anxiously up the road at 8:55, then had returned inside. Trooper Simmons, wearing a khaki hat and slacks, stood in his orange day-glow vest at the roadside after making the call out of sight of the cycle shop. Emerging from his cover, he gave a hand signal to Trooper Friskin, standing 80 feet away in cutoffs and with a red bandana around his head. The pair looked to all the world like local surveyors. Two hours later, Simmons called Girard once more to relate that a UPS truck was just arriving. The stolen van registered immediately in the investigator's mind and he told Simmons to check the UPS vehicle serial number against that of the stolen van: 1088769. Simmons replied in the negative—this van's number was 2444301, thus Simmons neglected to note the van's license plate number.

As a burly driver dismounted from the UPS vehicle across the road, Simmons toggled the digital camera suspended beneath his theodolite—three quick shots. Corbeau emerged from the shop and helped the stout driver to transfer three long cardboard boxes inside. The driver held out a clipboard to the mechanic, who made the motions of signing a paper. Trooper Simmons realized that UPS drivers now used electronic gadgets to log a delivery and also recognized the strange quality of the delivery, as if it were all for show. Are they on to us? he wondered. He made a few more hand gestures to Friskin, who held the prism pole, then captured another image of the UPS license plates and a good frontal shot of the driver as he remounted his cab. The surveying crew appeared quite busy as Louie Charbonneau turned right, out of Skippy's driveway and headed north into the village.

Simmons called Troop Headquarters once the site was quiet and, finding Girard awaiting FBI fingerprint data, gave his update. "No action at the store now," the stakeout reported. "Corbeau and Marteau are inside, but we don't hear much noise on the mike—just shufflings and bumps, and once there were a few loud laughs." Girard asked to be notified of anything new that happened, then signed off.

Frank Whitson came in the office door, waved hello to Girard, and entered the FIU office, only to emerge less than a minute later. "Girard, this item came in early this morning. The *Sûrete* has no identification of the prints you forwarded, neither does the RCMP. Something slimy is underway, I'm sure."

Girard immediately called the UPS regional office in Plattsburgh and provided them the serial number of the Port Henry delivery truck. In ten seconds, Jim Graves, the transportation supervisor, told Girard that there was no such numbered truck anywhere in New York State or Vermont. Thanking Graves, Girard hung up. His stomach tightened and the old pre-battle feelings returned. He called Friskin at the stakeout, made sure of the truck's direction of departure, then put out an APB bulletin to be on the watch for, but not to intercept the truck, instead to immediately report its location. He also told Friskin to download the morning's photos into the van's computer and send the images immediately to Ray Brook.

The rest of the morning Girard waited, nervously attending to paperwork, looking countless times at the phone on his desk, though it remained mute. Sheriff Parillo called to inform him that the autopsies and toxicology reports were finished on young Hochlitzer and Deputy Landrio. "Hochlitzer died of asphyxiation, and you know that means hanging, I'm sure," Parillo said. "His toxicology showed him to be full of Vicoden. How he got that stuff, I can't begin to guess, unless Landrio was his supplier. Now, on Landrio, he died of a massive heroin overdose and was probably dead before he collided with that tree, but the result is the same, only he didn't feel the impact. Too bad, I liked Ernie. You'll get a hard copy of both reports for your files, but I can't see where to go from here with my part of it. I wonder who is pulling all the strings here. It sure wasn't the kid or Landrio. Let me know if you turn up anything on your end. Take care, Girard."

Capt. Telfer emerged from his office and, to assuage his jumpiness, Girard filled him in on the new information in the Hetzer case. Then he called Trooper Tom Ellis at the Hetzer house. "Anything, Tommy?" The stakeout answered in the negative. Even with the office air-conditioning, Girard was sweating profusely. Something *had* to give—but it wouldn't, so he walked over to Agnes Simonds's snack shop for a sandwich, keeping his cell phone on the outdoor table as he finished off a turkey melt sandwich.

He returned to the Headquarters building just as Trooper Ellis called in from Westport. Hetzer's Navigator had suddenly appeared in front of his residence and slowed as it approached the driveway, but then he had apparently spotted Ellis's '06 Chevy pickup truck, recognizing it as a stakeout. Hetzer barreled off northward, but Ellis lost him in the pursuit. "I think he ducked into some building in Wadhams, maybe an open garage somewhere along the road. I can't understand it, Investigator Girard, he just vanished. I back-tracked the route twice, but can't figure out where he's gone. Do you want me to continue at the house?"

Girard replied, "No, come on in, Tommy, he knows he's on our menu now, and he'll try hard to stay hidden. It's not likely that he'll come home again." For a minute, Sr. Investigator Girard had a vision of Hetzer's evil face beside a hand-held scanner, and it occurred to him that Hetzer must be monitoring all State Police channels. "Use your cell phone from now on, Tommy," he cautioned, and hung up.

By now it was 2:00 p.m. and Girard knew he and Tommy Delehanty were due at Eugene Sprague's wake in Albany soon after 7:00 p.m., which meant being showered, dressed, and on the road by 5 p.m. Frank Whitson popped into Girard's office with a small pile of printouts from the stakeout camera. As soon as Girard reached to take the prints, his inner vision filled with the image of Louie Charbonneau's ugly face. Thus, the investigator wasn't surprised to recognize the bear-like form in the second photo. Two Claw! So, he's part of this goddam production—tied in with Hetzer! He hurried to the dispatcher's office and asked Dispatcher Ginny Rovelli if there had been any new sightings of the UPS van, but there were none. Just the way this damn case, or should I say these *two* cases, have gone all along—now you see 'em and now you don't!

In his nervousness, he called the Skippy's stakeout, but the only new information was that Corbeau and Marteau had moved two new motorcycles into the front driveway—the way a normal cycle shop might do on a normal business day, in order to catch passing drivers' attention. His mind was churning a mile a minute; what did it all *amount* to? Where was the connection—the common link that could tie untaxed cigarettes to foreign bad guys, one of whom was a former assassin? By 4:30, having made calls again to the evening stakeouts to be especially watchful, he headed down to Chestertown to shower, dress, and be ready when Tommy came by for the drive south at 5:00. On the trip home, Girard made several queries aloud to Israfil, Timmy, and whoever else might know the hidden truths, but his backseat remained silent.

CHAPTER FORTY-THREE

Delehanty picked up Girard in Chestertown and the two men, each in dress uniform, talked about the implications of their two cases now being joined, because Hetzer and Charbonneau were certainly linked. But how, and to what end? What was their ultimate goal? What would it mean to each of *them* as troopers, as far as personal responsibility went, and as far as responsible decision-making went? One thing for sure, they'd see plenty of brass from Division at the funeral home. At the end of the Northway, Tommy swung eastward, toward the city, whose state government buildings loomed in the distance. Within five minutes, they parked at the LaPierre Funeral Home and went inside.

Eugene's death had been no surprise, despite remaining active at the crime lab, resisting disability retirement until that last day of his life. There were sorrowing family members and many members of the State Police, some known and others unknown to Girard. He made his way across the viewing room to Cecile, Eugene's only child. She gave him a long and silent embrace and told Girard how happy she was that he could be here at her father's wake. "I'm so glad you came to his big send-off," she smiled. "He used to think you were a strangely wonderful man, Dennis, and he prized your love of adventure."

"Well, Cecile, I'm off on another one of those escapades, probably my last, right now. Maybe your dad can help me out from the other side," he quipped. Cecile smiled, "You know, there will be no funeral, as Dad detested religious formality. He'll be cremated and we'll scatter his ashes on the slopes of Mt. Greylock, over in Massachusetts, which he loved. Thanks, Dennis." She smiled, and then turned to shake hands with Tommy and the others in line, and Girard walked to an empty chair at the rear of the seating area. He sat in silence until another man, from behind him, said, "He looks pretty good up front, considering everything."

Vaguely recognizing the voice, Girard didn't turn around for a minute, but absent-mindedly responded, "Yeah, pretty good for a dead guy. But, you know, Eugene loved nature, so I hope the real Eugene is out climbing his trails in Rensselaer County."

"Just did that this morning," answered the other, giving Girard's shoulder a squeeze. The investigator turned to see who would speak and act so intimately with him. Just for a moment, he saw the smiling face of a younger and healthier Eugene, much like the fellow he'd first met during the 1980s. Then, the image was gone. Now fully turned to look behind his chair, Girard had to contend with the fact that there was no space there at all—only a blank wall eight inches away.

There was a rustle toward the front of the room. Delehanty looked Girard's way and touched the top of his head, an old signal from Bravo Company—"heads up!" Lt. Lenny Mueller walked into the room and offered condolences to Cecile and her daughter Amanda. Then came the superintendent. It had been years since Girard had seen the superintendent in dress uniform, and the man still cut an elegant swath in the crowd wherever he went, appearing almost as an historic figure, with his white, cropped mustache and silver hair and a ramrod-stiff military posture. After offering his regrets to Cecile and her daughter, O.H.P. Simcoe shook hands with many other troopers, but shot a look in Girard's direction, and Girard knew that was a command: front and center, Girard.

He rose from his chair and walked slowly toward Simcoe, and in a few minutes, the large hand was extended to him. "You appear to be in much better shape than the last time I saw you, Girard," the smiling man offered.

"Yes, Superintendent, being back at work again has sharpened some inner part of me. I just want to finish this Hetzer case right now, and then I think I'll head for the pasture." Simcoe quickly turned to see who was in earshot. Finding no one close by, he whispered to Girard, "My papers are already in. September first and I'm gone. I've overstayed my welcome," he said obliquely. "They've had enough of me over in the Governor's Office, and now they want new blood. So, I bought an almost-new Piper Saratoga II, with only two hundred hours of flight time on it, and the wife and I are going to do some air traveling before this body wears out.

"Also time for *you* to go, too, Girard—do you know what I mean? I think you've outlived at least six lives, and although your recent work has been superb, set a date, okay?" The comment was both friendly advice and a warning of some type. What did the superintendent know? Or didn't he? Maybe it was just friendly, professional advice.

"Thanks for your concern, Superintendent," he replied, "I won't have to be pushed. But first, I have to get Hetzer and see old Louie Charbonneau behind bars too. And I think it is all coming together long before autumn. Then something occurred to him. "Sir, I know you're good with languages, and I wonder if you can solve a little mystery that has popped up in a Port Henry investigation. What does '*char-moot*' sound like to you?"

Simcoe was motionless for a second, then his head snapped around and he almost hissed, "Where in hell did you get *that*, Girard?"

"Sir, we have listening devices inside a motorcycle shop in Port Henry, and one day, after I left the place and they thought they were all alone, one of the two employees shouted something like that, though I couldn't quite get it on the recording—sounded like a celebration. Do those words mean something to you?"

"Jesus, Mary and Joseph, Girard, you're talking Arabic! It is spoken as *shar-MOOT*! And it's an exclamation that calls you a male prostitute! What the hell are *Arabs* doing in a motorcycle shop in Port Henry? *Are* they Arabs?"

"Sir, they appear to be French-Canadian nationals and their business lease from an American company looks legitimate. Nevertheless, my friends in *Sûreté* and RCMP found no record of them in the Canadian national databases there, and the FBI and SAFIS don't know them down here either. And, of course, I'm no connoisseur, but although their French sounds pretty darned perfect, it's not genuine *Quebecois*."

"You're our man on the JTTF for this case, right? Get that to them *immediately*. Who's running the operation, Zarr?"

"Yes, sir."

"Good man. You got his cell?" the Superintendent queried intensely.

"Yes, sir."

"Call him right *now*. This type of thing only boils over unless you can put out the fire immediately. Get that done before tomorrow and copy me the outcome through channels, Girard."

"Yes, sir," Girard responded as the superintendent linked up with Lt. Mueller and the pair left the room.

Arabs in the Adirondacks? Sounded odd, although he knew George Salem, the merchant, in Star Lake, whose grandfather had come from Lebanon in the 1800s. And he knew Ibby Yousef in Malone, a Syrian-born engineering professor at Clarkson University. Sure, they were Arabs, but *our* Arabs, some with families having roots in America even longer than his own. But if these Canadian guys are connected with a former East German assassin, there couldn't be any satisfactory explanation. And how does Two Claw figure with these people? He hasn't the brains to help anybody but himself.

Girard dialed Agent Zarr's home emergency number and the man responded instantly. After Girard provided his new information, Zarr scheduled a 9:00 a.m. meeting for Tuesday morning in Albany and thanked Girard for what might be a crucial break.

CHAPTER FORTY-FOUR

At 9:00 a.m. sharp, FBI Agent Joe Zarr convened the JTTF meeting, asking Sr. Investigator Dennis Girard to update the team on the sudden convergence of the Hetzer case and the search for professional smuggler Louis Charbonneau. The team then began its analysis of the matter. A dangerous European assassin who had been dormant for more than a decade and a half had suddenly appeared as the owner of a legitimate business in Port Henry. The man, whose identity was recently discovered, had now gone underground and sold his operation to two bogus French-Canadian citizens who had no documentation and who spoke Arabic in private. Essex County had two recent, unsolved murders, and Hetzer was strongly implicated in both crimes. Then, Hetzer had eluded his stakeout and his present location was unknown, making him a dangerous wild card in the game underway in the North Country. The man was clearly working on some criminal activity. Girard interjected that Hetzer must be involved in the purported suicide of his nephew, Paul Hochlitzer, and tangentially, in the death of Landrio, the prison guard. This guy had 'dangerous' and 'high stakes plotter' written all over him.

In the meantime, a wanted felony escapee, Louis "Two Claw" Charbonneau, had surfaced with at least one new charge on his dossier, grand theft auto, and he had delivered an unknown cargo to Skippy's Cycle Shop. Discussion then shifted back and forth, with Agent Kuenzel arguing that the entire Port Henry operation be taken down immediately. That way, Charbonneau's delivery could be identified, suggesting the nature of the combined gangs. But what, Agent Parker inquired, was the link between two such disparate groups "Okay, Charbonneau is linked to smugglers—cigarette smugglers and small timers," she said, "so let's assume that, because the State Police haven't been able to interrupt *his* network, that Two Claw has successfully moved some items into Port Henry. But what is the nature of those items?" Kuenzel countered that a warrant and a quick raid would dispel all doubt. Girard caught Parker's dig at the BCI and noted it for future reference.

Secret Service Agent Parker then stroked her chin, pondering all the issues, then added, "Maybe, just maybe, I see something here. Girard says the pair at Skippy's seems to speak Arabic, so that likely is their primary identity, and in the Secret Service we know that identity often leads to purpose. Smuggler Arabs on Lake Champlain, and they're not likely transporting duty-free motorcycles, so then what? Now here's my concern. In six days, former President George H.W. Bush is traveling from Kennebunkport, ME, to Plattsburgh, but his flight path will bring him directly over Port Henry later that afternoon.

"Here's what I see: unknown individuals, criminals all, positioned directly below the former prez's flight path, and one of those has a record for assassinating a German government minister. These things don't just *happen*; there has to be an extensive network to set it all up. What does Hetzer plan to do and who are his friends? Is there still a third network behind Charbonneau's and Hetzer's? Is its ultimate purpose to shoot down Bush's plane? By the way, Bush's code name in this operation is 'Voodoo.' What would Hetzer gain from that act? What would the Arab agents gain unless they're serving some larger ideological organization such as Al Qaeda or Hezbollah? Is it simply a revenge issue? If we can perceive their final goal, we can perhaps short-circuit not only this plan, but also expose an underground network, or maybe two, of which we were unaware."

FBI Agent Joe Zarr interjected, "But here is the issue: we have the two Arabs under surveillance, so they're not going anywhere because we can pick them up in five minutes and know the contents of that shop, but they certainly are only the tip of the iceberg. Many terrorists and professional criminals tend to use a sideshow of some kind to distract law enforcement from their primary goal. Maybe all these Arab guys are is just a sideshow, trying to put us off the scent."

The CIA's Hershfield interjected, "Well how much bigger a show can we have than a foreign assassin of government figures on the loose?"

"What I remember about the Red Army Faction that Hetzer, or Ohnesorg, worked in," Zarr said, "is that the main schemers were never caught; they still exist somewhere in Europe—or have some come to North America too? In almost all of their operations, they let little people, which Hetzer was in the old days, do the shooting or bombing. Most of the time, it was the little guys, the pawns, that got caught. Those who financed those operations and those who made the master plans were never found. If those individuals are still operational, what is their aim *today* and how is it different from their antifascist rantings of the 80s? And how, and why do they now link up with Arab terrorists? Who is serving whom? What common goal can the two groups have? Okay, let's look at the issue of terrorism." Sue Wilson, Zarr's secretary, interrupted silently to hand him a memo, which Zarr glanced at, then stuffed in his pants pocket.

"Aside from his oil interests and longtime contacts with the Saud royal family in Saudi Arabia," Agent Zarr continued, "the whole of which Al Qaeda deems corrupt, why would Arabs want a *former* President dead?"

"Easy answer," Homeland Security's Brainerd offered. "He And Schwarzkopf dusted the fannies of Saddam's army's in the Gulf War. Our generals beat the best that Saddam had in 1990 and 1991. President Bush, the father, helped the Al Sabah family stay on the Kuwaiti throne, and prevented the ouster of the Sauds. And neither of those royal families is very democracy oriented. We all know the low role of women and their treatment of non-Islamics in their societies. But in the process, Bush, Senior, negotiated long-term positioning of U.S. air bases on what Muslims are taught to consider the 'holy soil' of Saudi Arabia! That huge peninsula is where Islam began, and the Saud family claims to be the protectors of the holy sites there. In a sense, then, the Islamists say the Sauds gave away holy soil to the infidels. So the terrorists would like to be rid of all the Sauds and Al Sabahs and anyone else who helped defile Mecca or Madinah, and anyone else who helps them stay in power, specifically George Bush, Sr.. And that would certainly include the present administration, too! And, don't forget that both Bush men are oil men, and the militant Arabs see only imperialistic greed among the American oil merchants."

"How can we be sure this is an Al Qaeda operation?" ATF Agent Kuenzel queried. "I think this might be something else. Isn't it possible that the Mohawk smuggling network is simply that—a cat's paw being used by Hetzer's people to pull Hetzer's chestnuts out of the fire? Maybe the Indians are just being exploited for his personal profit."

"Well, if we have illegals walking around at will in New York State for any reason, it's our job to *arrest* them!" sputtered a red-faced Curtis Brainerd. Girard gave the man a 'Duh?' look. It took a second for the investigator to remember that not all Homeland Security's people were experienced professionals. Brainerd seemed like another of the present administration's political hacks—maybe his name should be Brownie, Girard silently smirked. Politicians have handed out jobs to incompetents forever, and that was their right, as long as it doesn't kill a current or past President of the U.S.

Agent Zarr, who had obviously had previous dealings with Brainerd, put his calming hand on the man's arm. "Don't worry Curtis, the good guys always win, you know that." Brainerd wiped his brow and, relieved, sat back in his leather chair.

"Well, here's the Secret Service input," said Agent Parker. "To do *our* job, we're going to have everything locked down tight all along Voodoo's route as of Sunday noon. All suspected troublemakers will be in custody, in for questioning, or otherwise tied up. We don't want anybody on the loose, and I repeat, *any-body*, who can harm Voodoo. In any case, he'll have a restricted air corridor along his route. So our group has five days to figure out and to act on the implications of this plot, or two plots, if that's what we've got here."

Brainerd reported that Homeland Security operatives at Akwesasne had observed no new or suspicious activities on Mohawk lands. He said his links to *Sûreté* and the Mounted Police likewise had observed no immediate threats north of the border, which jibed with New York State Police intelligence from Montreal. CIA concurred, as did ATF's Kuenzel.

Nothing big or bad seemed to be moving on either side of the border. If anything, indeed, *was* up, Brainerd suggested it might be a rogue operation cobbled together by international malcontents.

By noon, it was clear that they all needed to keep watching and see if the more intricate details of the plot would be exposed. "Let's meet here at 9:00 a.m. tomorrow," Zarr said. "Each of you will provide a status report. It was noon and Girard felt in need of a coffee infusion. The carafe near Secretary Sue Wilson's desk was just filling with a new brew, so Girard liberated a foam cupfull to take with him. Zarr entered the office and, thinking Girard had exited, was a bit surprised to see him. "Oh, hi Girard, thought you'd left." Absentmindedly Zarr dug in his pocket and fished out the secretary's memo. Scanning the words, he raised an eyebrow and showed it to Girard. "You know, Investigator Girard, I have a hunch this note might involve *us*."

Dennis scanned the brief notification from Russ Roberts, FBI resident agent in Plattsburgh. The Secret Service in Burlington, VT, just notified his office that the NBT Bank in Ellenburg Depot, Clinton County, NY, had received a counterfeit $50 bill. A customer named Tessier from Clinton Corners had deposited two hundred dollars in 50s, of which one was counterfeit. Secret Service out of Burlington, VT, had gone to the bank, verified the bogus bill and had gone to the depositor's house to question the man. Upon arrival at Joe Tessier's house, the agent had found the man roaring drunk in a front porch chair, boasting about being the local Indian agent. In a short time, after further questioning, Secret Service arrested Tessier, notifying the FBI's Plattsburgh resident agent. After the arrest, Tessier had been read his rights, then brought to the Federal Building in Albany for booking on accessory to counterfeiting charges, because no federal judge had been available in Syracuse.

Although there was more interviewing to be done, it seemed clear that Tessier had been smuggling with the aid of Indians unknown to him, except his contact, known as "Louie the Indian." The name didn't escape Girard's notice. As the case likely involved international smuggling and the potential for involvement of Indian Affairs, Roberts had copied Zarr's JTTF office and the Bureau of Indian Affairs about the matter, as well as the FBI's liaison agents at Akwesasne. As Girard read these words, the familiar phantom hand was laid upon his shoulder. "Yep, Agent Zarr, I think you're right," he said. "I'd like to question this Tessier fellow, if it's all right with you." Zarr agreed, making a phone call to the U.S. Attorney's Office as to where the U.S. Marshal's Office had transported the prisoner. Girard then departed for the Albany County Jail, where Tessier had been incarcerated after his arraignment in front of Federal Judge William Shaw.

As he drove, Girard had a sudden vision of old Grandmother Thompson at Kahnawake in Quebec. Why *her*? Why now? His inner voices remained silent as he turned into the Albany County Jail parking lot.

CHAPTER FORTY-FIVE

Yves Marteau worked on the exhaust system of an old 1978 Harley while his partner, Augustin Corbeau, discussed the sale of a used Kawasaki Vulcan 1600 with a customer out front. Both men waited patiently for their destiny. Hetzer would call, they were assured, when the prize was in sight. *He* would give the order to do their work because *he* had the intelligence network. Wiping the perspiration from his brow, Marteau pondered the events that had brought him to this place and time.

Born on August 12, 1972, in the Shatila Palestinian Refugee Camp in Beirut, Lebanon, in the name Khalil Abu Nasr, Marteau had been present on the 16th of September in 1982, when his grandfather was machine-gunned by Lebanese Phalangist soldiers supported by the Israeli army. Grandfather's brains and blood had splattered on young Khalil's clothing, horrifying him with deep psychological wounds that still troubled him. Grandfather represented wisdom and continuity with his forefathers. That day, all ideas of the past, peace, and a meaningful life vanished for Khalil forever. He could no longer believe in a just or loving God and became a political activist aimed at destroying Israel, whose army he held responsible for the Shatila massacre.

As a teen, he learned welding and rudimentary electrical skills in the U.N.-sponsored schools at the camp, but never held a full-time job until 1991, when he joined Hezbollah as a soldier. Hezbollah, "the Party of God," he decided, would be his deity, his substitute for a god—the living wrath of what was, to him, a mythical Allah. The organization helped him improve his verbal and mechanical skills, making it possible for him to emigrate to Lyon, France, where he eked out an existence while polishing his skills in the French language he had studied in Beirut. Attending the new and beautiful Grand Mosque of Lyon, he joined a political study group led by Imam Hussein, which aimed at the destruction of Israel. He took part in daily prayer only because it linked him with other passionate men seeking a better world. Marteau remained untroubled that such guerilla activity could succeed under the cover of a religion that taught surrender to the will of God. In Lyon, he adopted the French name, Marteau, or "hammer."

His partner, using the name Augustin Corbeau for this operation, was likewise a Palestinian with a grudge to settle. He had been born Hassan al-Nabulsi in Baqa'a Refugee Camp in Jordan, and being bright, took advantage of U.N.-sponsored schooling at that site, learning mathematics and electricity skills. At age 20, he was hired as an electrician at the Doha power plant in Kuwait. Making a good income, he had sought the hand of a young woman named Ru'yah, and she was promised to him. The young couple survived the Iraqi invasion of Kuwait, only to have Ru'yah perish in an American rocket attack on the second day of the Gulf War in August 1990. After the attack, when the Americans learned he was Palestinian, al-Nabulsi was expelled from Kuwait by the American forces, and not even allowed to attend his beloved's funeral. Hassan grew bitter, vowing revenge on George Herbert Walker Bush and his minions who were spreading a satanic social value system, while attempting to dominate Middle Eastern oil resources. They have so much, he reasoned, why do they want to seize our *oil* too?

Returning to Jordan, Hassan joined a Hezbollah action group, then moved to a guerilla camp in Syria, where he learned to use explosives. With forged papers, he subsequently traveled to Canada in 2004, linking up with other Hezbollah "sleepers" and awaiting a call to action. In 2006, he met Khalil while preparing for insertion into the United States for special missions. Like Khalil Abu Nasr, Hassan al-Nabulsi was prepared to give his life in a strike at the American greed machine. Unlike his partner, however, Hassan deeply believed in a God of justice, a supreme being who would bring righteousness into the earth with help from believers. When he received word that his guerilla cell would make an attempt on former President Bush, himself, Hassan was overjoyed. The day of divine wrath was coming, and soon! Meanwhile, to keep up appearances, there was a cycle shop to run and, perhaps, some money to be made.

At his barn on Youngs Road, west of Wadhams, Buck Stouffer backed his old Ford L8000 packer truck into the driveway. His new "renter" needed a place to hide a stolen UPS truck and a Navigator SUV, and for $3,000 cash money, Buck was willing to provide it. From time to time, a network contact named Ace called him with requests to transport or hide items. And it was only these under-the-table payments that allowed Stouffer to keep his three garbage trucks on the road and to pay his two drivers. The trucks were old and worn out and continually needed parts or repairs. The repairs he could usually do by himself, but he couldn't manufacture those parts.

The grey-haired stranger sent by the network handed over money for "one month's storage rental," then requested the use of Buck's company pickup truck for a few days, and the use of the barn's small kitchenette for no more than a month. Buck's drivers usually got hot coffee in that room during their winter runs, but in the summer's heat, the place was now a refuge for the stranger and his husky friend. In exchange for the money, Buck, who lived alone, also agreed to bring two fold-up cots from his house and to feed the two men for two weeks.

The renter never gave his name, but did use a code word that Ace often supplied, so Buck knew the stranger was a network member, and dedicated to changing the American economy that kept him in poverty with endless regulations and high taxes. It was also agreed that, upon their departure, both of the stranger's vehicles would be his, though he would have to make some "adjustments" to them, in order to put them on the highway again.

Faust Hetzer continually checked the rearview mirror after driving the pickup onto the Adirondack Northway at Exit 31, though nobody seemed interested in following a truck with "Stouffer Refuse" painted on the side. His intention was to check out the cycle shop and make sure the two shooters were ready; however, if the place was under observation by the FBI, he'd continue on past. Exiting at Exit 29, he went over the mountain and turned on to Route 2, to arrive in Crown Point. There, he turned north on Route 9N. Approaching the turn into Port Henry, he saw the garage on the right, and it looked okay. But then, in one blink of the eye, he spotted a surveyor's van with multiple antennae. It was an electronics unit and he recognized the vehicle instantly, and understood that the two men standing behind it only pretended to be surveyors. He knew at once that they were a police stakeout, likely FBI. Trouble! Hetzer realized the shop and its occupants were under observation and were thus compromised. The network had sent him a couple of amateurs who would never be able to get their missiles out of the building without being seen! Now, if the task was to be done, after all the trouble he'd gone to, it would be up to *him*. Without slowing, he drove into and through the village, then northward to his new Wadhams hideout.

Returned to his lair, Hetzer made a cell phone call to his contact in Frederick, MD. Alderschild wasn't in, so Hetzer left a message that the Arabs were compromised, and asked for immediate instructions, because all other elements of The Plan seemed to be in place. Leaving his cell number, he switched off.

Charbonneau was asleep on his cot, having complained of stomach pains during the night. Whatever it was, was going to kill the man, Hetzer decided, because Louie was continually coughing up blood. If he's on his way out, maybe he can help further The Plan, and a variation on the scheme began to form in Hetzer's mind.

CHAPTER FORTY-THREE

Joe Tessier had been committed to the Albany County Jail pending his arraignment on the federal charges. Showing identification, Girard was ushered into the jail visiting room after securing his pistol in the outside office. Shortly thereafter, Tessier was brought in, accompanied by a guard, who then, after the prisoner was seated, moved a discreet distance from the interview table. Sr. Investigator Girard identified himself to the prisoner, whom he seemed to remember from some long-ago North Country foray. Getting down to brass tacks, Girard asked Tessier to identify the man he called "Louie, the Indian." Immediately, the description left no question that it was Charbonneau. The investigator then questioned the prisoner as to the details of the Indian business deal: what was in the plastic wrapped packages? Tessier, however, though he spoke freely, had no idea of the contents. "It felt like something metal," he said.

"Metal, like what?" Girard questioned.

"Oh maybe metal like a tractor tow-bar, but not as heavy," came the response. "Maybe like 10 or 12 pounds and round, but long, like a cylinder—that's all I know. You know, Mr. Trooper, I was just trying to save my farm," he pleaded.

Girard then plied the man with questions as to the identities or descriptions of the Indians who loaded his manure spreader, but again, Tessier pleaded ignorance, as he'd never directly seen the men who moved the parcels. "How do you contact those men?" Girard asked. And again, Tessier said he didn't know, stating that he never contacted them, that *they* always called him when they needed some work done. "I only wanted to keep my family farm," the prisoner whined again.

The investigator stood. "Now, it looks like you're going to lose it for sure, right?" he asked. Signaling the guard that the interview was concluded, Girard left the room, picked up his pistol outside, headed for the parking lot, and was away to Exit 4 on I-87, then north to Ray Brook. Moving his state car along, he reached the Troop B Headquarters parking lot in just under three hours.

Inside, he met Tommy Delehanty at the coffee machine, where Tommy was dropping ice cubes into his cup before filling it. Girard brought his friend up to date on the affair. For 10 minutes the pair speculated how and why their two cases had converged. How and why could Hetzer be involved with Indians, and where had he gone? It had to be that the Indian group was moving some kind of contraband for Hetzer, but what was it? Why had the road patrols seen neither hide nor hair of him? And where had Charbonneau disappeared to? What was the secret hidden inside Skippy's Cycle Shop? Was it now time to get a search and seizure warrant and find out? As they drained their cups, Tommy gave Girard's forearm a friendly poke. "Want to hear something really weird, Denny?"

"Sure, go ahead buddy. You don't know the meaning of weird, and I'll tell you someday after I put in my papers, but not right now."

"Den, at the wake last night, I *saw* Eugene Sprague. I don't mean in the box, I mean walking around and looking at people in the crowd. He kept grinning at the superintendent while he was there. I'm not nuts, Denny. I really *saw* the guy!"

"Tommy, I'll tell you some of my thoughts. Yes, I believe you. I saw him too, and I've come to believe that, even though a person is dead, that his energy or his soul or whatever it is, can be seen, at least for a while. Man, when I die, I'm going to walk around the funeral home and listen to what people are saying about *me*!" Grinning, the two stood and returned to their desks. Tommy was to follow up two sighting reports of Charbonneau near Beekmantown.

As he approached his desk, Girard briefly saw a large wooden cross lying on its top, a construction with blood smeared at its center. Then, abruptly, it was all gone. What the hell? he thought. Sitting for a few minutes, he relived his own crucifixion scene from a long-ago dream, which seemed like just yesterday. Damned angel stuff! he fumed, and dug out photos of yesterday's UPS delivery at Skippy's to study. Then came a series of phone calls unrelated to the current cases. At 5:00 p.m. he called it a day and headed south.

Rolling down the car windows, he let the warm afternoon air blow through his car, bringing the sweet scent of pines to perfume his car as he drove down I-87. At the North Hudson exit, he left the superhighway and pulled to the shoulder, calling the stakeouts at Skippy's for an update, but nothing new was going on. Both of the shop's operators had gone home early. Girard headed west, uphill toward Blue Ridge, where he spotted a wild turkey hen scurrying across the road. He envied the creature's ignorance of all the important goings-on of humans. Or, maybe in God's eyes, he speculated, none of it was really important. From there, he drove over to Route 28, where he turned south. Tonight was a good time to catch the early-bird special dinner at Lucy's in North Creek.

As he pulled into the restaurant's gravel parking area, Girard saw a large number of cars, and reckoned he'd be lucky to get a seat. Yet, once inside, he found his old corner booth had just been cleaned. Something was wrong, however. The normal jolly atmosphere at Lucy's had been replaced by that of last night's wake, and he couldn't understand why. Had someone died? Juanita, the waitress, came to take his order and he asked her about it.

"Yeah, we're all pretty sad here today," she told him. "Some stupid sonofabitch from the city came in this morning and killed Oscar when he flew to the guy's table. So much for hospitality! When the morning regulars realized what had happened, they ran the guy out the door, but the poor bastard never understood why. 'A goddam *fly*?' he kept screaming. What'll you have, Inspector?"

Dropping his menu, he said, "I think I'll do the chicken pot pie, tonight, Juanita. You okay?"

"Yeah, Inspector, you know. Oscar was a real part of this place for so long. Maybe he was my only friend here. Not like my old man, who's always complaining about something."

"Well, Juanita, I have it on good authority that flies go to heaven, too," Girard said with a grin. The woman looked at him and opened her mouth as if to ask the obvious question, then glancing at Girard once more to be sure he wasn't kidding, abruptly closed her mouth and went to put in his order.

As she departed, a teenager with multiple piercings sat into the opposite side of Girard's booth. Instantly, the investigator recalled the time when Israfil had appeared in such an abrupt manner. Somehow, it all didn't surprise him. "That you, Izzy?"

The young man brightened and smiled. "Good of you to be so perceptive, Dennis," came the response. "I think you're really learning."

"Why *this* get-up, Izzy. Can't an eternal creature such as you do any better? Maybe a Brooks Brothers suit? Even that armor was cooler than this outfit."

"I'm here to be joyful today, Dennis," the angel said. "If there is any quality in the Kingdom, Dennis, it's joy. In the end, it's all a big hoot—haven't you figured *that* out yet? There is so much overflowing joy in the Kingdom that a lesser being than I couldn't stand it. Anyway, here is where we're at. I'm proud of you, for all the progress you've made. At least you are asking all the right questions now, if not arriving at all the right answers. We're about there, you know?"

"Yeah, I figured that. I ran into Grandma Kelly over in Ti a while ago, and she told me. At the fort. Which fort, Izzy? Fort Ti? Crown Point? Fort William Henry?"

"You will know when the time arrives," Israfil told him solemnly. "The important thing is that you think about your eternal task of brotherhood with all beings. Don't be stampeded by "official thinking," see? That's why this will be your last case, you've outgrown the need to be directed by others. You should see what lies ahead for you." he commented. After a few seconds of reflection Israfil smiled and added, "Well, probably not. You won't believe me if I tell you."

"Look, Izzy, I don't care if this case kills me because I now know there is more, but will I *succeed*?"

"In the end, sure," the angel said, with his long earrings swinging slowly. "In the end, *all* of you will succeed, but on this case—who knows? Even God doesn't know how your soul will choose—remember that. He gave you the choice as to how the story ends, and even when. And the Kingdom's definition of success is much different from that in this limited world. If you don't make it in what you call 'this time,' you will have other shots. But, the fate of many, even your nation itself, may hang in the balance right now. And your nation is in deep spiritual trouble as it is. Is *that* important enough for you? In any case, you've come through the needle's eye and don't need me any longer. Remember, the answers are inside *you*!" As Juanita brought his order, the other side of the booth emptied. Goddam angel stuff! Girard grumbled, and popped his fork into the pot pie.

It was a bit after 8:00 p.m. when he returned to Chestertown. The sun was dipping toward the mountains in the west, but he chose to sit on Mrs.

Morgenstern's white iron bench in the garden for a while before going inside. Her irises were fading now, and she kept the dead tops clipped, though the celosia still looked fresh and sassy, and the marigolds were fully open. Looking downhill, he spotted a strange creature slowly trudging up the road in his direction. At first, the man resembled a movie image he remembered of Robinson Crusoe. As the stranger approached, Girard noted that the figure actually wore a coat that appeared made of fur or animal skin. Who the hell would dress like that anymore, he wondered, and in this *heat*?

The character left Knapp Hill Road and walked slowly across the lawn toward him. Instantly, Girard went on guard—it all looked like the old hippie days, with shaggy oddballs wandering the country roads. The man came to a halt directly in front of him and asked genially, "May I sit?" After having been in Izzy's presence so recently, all Girard could say was, "Sure," though the bench was only five feet wide and not enough space separated the two for him to feel secure.

"My thanks," the man replied, reaching into his pocket and popping what seemed to be a small twig into his mouth. Girard noted that the stranger had piercing green eyes. "I'm John," the visitor said.

"Dennis Girard," he responded without extending his hand. "You live around here?" The other didn't answer the query. This time, as John took another snack from his pocket, Girard could see it was a dried large grasshopper or locust.

"Nice little stream down there," the man said, pointing to the foot of the hill. "Life is a stream, and streams have always played a part in my lives." Girard immediately went on guard. Lives? Sounds like more damned angel stuff—Oh God, here we go *again*! "What do you do, John," he inquired, knowing he'd be better off if he hadn't asked.

"You could say that I take care of alumni affairs, I guess, that's why I've come to see *you*," the man said charmingly and softly. "It's what I did among men that now defines my work. Last time, I did advertising, I suppose you'd say—I was a publicist for my cousin, who was a great man. It was work I needed to do for him and for myself, though in the end you could say I lost my head over the job."

Instantly, Girard thought back to having pondered that concept of beheading a bit further down Riverside Drive several months before, near the Catholic Church. "I know I'm going to regret this question, John, because I know none of this is real, but in what way did you lose your head?"

"Broadsword," the other said matter-of-factly, "that's how they usually did it back then."

Sweet Jesus, Girard begged silently, I know what this is and who this guy is, and I know I'm not ready for any more of this stuff. Please make him go away! The two sat in silence. Two sparrows flew to the ground in front of them, as if seeking discarded crumbs, and finding none, flew off.

"I had to come to an understanding of not only what one believes, but what one *does* about what he believes," John told him. "You know I was Elijah, also? Oh, I was so close to the One at *that* time." John was lost in his memories for a minute and he smiled. "I had heard Him as a still, small voice while hiding in the desert. I was amazed that He came not in thunder nor in the whirlwind, but as a soft, inner prompting. And I took that connection as a license to kill those who were not called at that time. Oh, the stream ran red with blood, *their* blood, that day! Only later, did I come to understand that The One loved those priests of Baal as much as He loved me. By then, what could I do to atone for my ignorance?

"I could become John and that next time, to announce the coming of Him into human flesh. My righteousness was still something that I wore on my sleeve, as you say today, so I fully accept my end there, because of the One whom I could usher in. I have briefly returned to the physical world now to love and serve those whom I once caused to be murdered, and who have since risen to listen to their own inner promptings." He looked squarely at Girard.

After a pause, Dennis Girard could no longer stand the thoughts and feelings that welled up inside. "What the hell do you want me to do with *that*, Mister John? You want me to hear your confession? I'm no priest!"

"No longer, and not yet," John replied with a peaceful smile. Now, Girard could no longer hold a single thought in his consciousness. Ideas, pictures, and feelings flooded his being. What was this guy saying? What did he *mean*? Girard knew he couldn't face the answer to that question, yet his head filled with images of a burning pyre atop a hill, and a bearded, wild-eyed man, along with other wild-eyed men pursuing him downhill toward a stream. Then, darkness. What *was* all this? Oh God, I can't *stand* it!

"Dennis Girard, I come to make amends and to fully replace my ire and violence of long ago with the mission I next came to fulfill—to grow into love. You, my friend, have longed to return to serving the Creator of this world as an intermediary, and your desire shall be satisfied. Please remember *me*. Please remember that, no matter how much a man believes and knows, he knows *nothing* of the full Truth! No man alive today has commanded the morning, nor shown the dawn its place. No man alive today remembers when the morning stars sang together in chorus and all the Sons of God shouted for joy. And yet, we have, and still *do* kill one another over ideas. Live now in love and understanding of those whose view is limited. He watching over Israel, the seekers, neither slumbers nor sleeps, you know." Instantly, the other side of the bench was vacant.

Dennis Girard put his head in his hands. His body seemed to burn in the single ray of the evening sun that shone upon him. He could no longer even summon his standard complaint about angel stuff. It was as if the marrow had been suctioned from his bones, and he had no more fire or strength left. A cool breeze began, rustling the green leaves overhead, and a ruby-throated hummingbird visited the flowers in front of him, tapping their nectar. After a half-hour more the sun was down, and he rose slowly, gently slapped the side of his head, and resolved to ask Lucy what she put in her chicken pot pies.

Returning to his apartment, he showered and sat in his skivvies and tee-shirt with his eyes closed for another hour. Eventually, it came to him that he had been in deep, reverent prayer for some time. His contact with the Divine hadn't been a formal wording, but more a pouring out of his heart, placing his cares upon an altar for the Creator to bless. At nine o'clock, he turned in, though, during the night, he awoke to hear the words, "false gods!" shouted by a strange voice. Sitting up in bed, he found the room empty and otherwise quiet. The alarm clock read one minute after one. He fell back upon the bed and into a deep sleep.

CHAPTER FORTY-FOUR

At half past five the next morning, Faust Hetzer's cell phone rang and he roused from a troubled sleep to answer it. "Clear?" asked the voice he associated with Alderschild.

"Yes," Hetzer responded deliberately in English. He was tiring of the game for some reason, and felt manipulated by people he'd never met. It was as if The Plan now required more from him than he could manage. Action used to be sudden and then finished; this matter seemed to drag on forever. He was tired; revolution was an exhausting business because the forces of greed were so powerfully entrenched.

"You have quite a situation," the voice said accusingly. "I suggest that you use your two allies to draw fire and take the responsibility for finishing their part of the job, even though they are under observation. That should make it easier for you to do your part. We're sending one of our own to the airport in the north, so you both can take out the target as soon as possible. Your helper will have a job at the gate and will help you through, but you must find an innocuous vehicle to transport the emergency package. Two blinks is the gate signal. You still *have* the package, don't you?"

"Yes, I have it safe," Hetzer replied, disturbed at the implied lack of trust. "No one would suspect its present location, but I'll need someone to pick it up for me because such a move might put *me* in danger. I still have enough funds, however, so I think I have a likely pawn to do the job."

"You'll be interested, Dieter," the voice said, calling Hetzer by his given German name, "to know that I've discovered another plot right where I work, at the military installation," he laughed. "The Americans here have their own schemes for seizing power from one another, but more about that another time. With your package we supplied remote detonators; are they still there?"

"*Ja*, still in plastic," he replied.

"Use those then, to get yourself clear of the site. The package will take care of everyone within five hundred feet, so just get close to the speaker, park the vehicle and get out of there. Once outside the gate, use the remote. Is that clear?"

"*Jawohl*," Hetzer responded. "Is there more work to be done on this issue after my activities?"

"You may expect to be on vacation for quite a while afterward, as the fascists will have their hounds scouring the countryside," Alderschild told him. "Just do your part, then go to ground in either the Illinois or Georgia sites. After enough time, we'll move you to a greater arena." The phone clicked off.

Hetzer put on a pot of coffee, pondering that all participants—those friendly and those who were not—were probably having their morning coffee at that very moment. Except old Bush is probably drinking a finer brew than this stuff.

As the coffee perked, Charbonneau rose from his cot, groaning. Hetzer knew the man was no longer reliable, and thus had become expendable. It seemed better if this dope could be sent to work with the

Arab pawns; they could all sink to the bottom together when the FBI spotted them. Louie had served his purposes and was now a weak link in a chain that had to be strong, Hetzer resolved.

"Come on, Louis, rise from your pallet and partake of this wondrous brew, instead of the licorice," he said sarcastically. He set a mug of coffee in front of Charbonneau, who was bent over, grasping his stomach. Louie straightened and accepted the proffered cup.

"Louis, I've been thinking that the Arabs need expert advice. Up until now, you haven't needed to know further details, but today I'm appointing you, as a true warrior, to supervise them." Hetzer knew that flattery would win the man over. "There is another $2,000 in it for you to take command, money that you can either keep for yourself or take back to your friend Jim's group—your choice." Hetzer opened the valise he had carried from the pickup truck and handed the wrapped bundle of $100 bills to Charbonneau before the coffee-sipping man could make a decision. Once Charbonneau felt the smooth texture of the currency, he was convinced, and felt like an indomitable warrior, and a well-paid one at that.

"Louis, I want you to use the cover of darkness to find a very fast boat tonight and 'borrow it.' Understand? Keep it under cover until I tell you how to use it. Do you know how to operate a power boat?"

"*Sure* I do," Two Claw retorted. "I often ran high-speed boats on the St. Lawrence when we moved cigarettes. If I wanted to, I could be a professional speedboat driver, but it's not a warrior profession."

"Good. So find a fast boat and have it gassed up and ready, out of sight. I have details to take care of right now, so be sure you're not caught. Move like a stealthy brave," Hetzer instructed.

He knew the general plan, which was to have the Arabs in position just north of the Poultney Street Bridge down in Whitehall, at the southern end of Lake Champlain. Small aircraft, such as Bush uses, tend to begin their descent into Glens Falls Airport at that point and, when flying Visual Flight Rules (VFR), are cruising at only about 5,000 feet over the village. Monday's weather promised to be clear, so VFR was a certainty. The missiles should be effective at that point if the pilot isn't flying higher, and, if events at Plattsburgh don't go as expected. Albany Approach Control usually keeps small planes low at that spot so they don't interfere with east to west commercial traffic in the area. Hetzer relished the thought of Bush and his cohort not only crashing but also drowning, should they survive the fiery fall. He didn't want to give full instructions to the Arabs yet, however, it was time for them to prepare. He decided to call them on their cell phones just in case the FBI was listening in on their office phones. These Middle Easterners would do as they were instructed, and at the appropriate time.

Another arrangement to put in motion today was to secure the package from his home in Westport, and that task would be tricky, especially if the FBI was still watching. It all had to look normal. His trump card in this part of the game was Buck's poverty, and that would do the trick, he assured himself. As Stouffer gassed up his packer truck, Hetzer went outside and asked him if he'd like to make another thousand dollars. Stouffer's heart beat rapidly, as this money could help pay his back taxes and get the IRS off his back. "What do I have to do for that chunk?" Buck asked suspiciously.

"I have some garbage to pick up at my house in Westport. You make runs in the village anyway, and this is an especially stinky can, so nobody is going to take it away from you. Here is the key to my garage. What time do your other drivers finish on Friday?"

"They're done and out of here by 4:00 p.m.," Stouffer answered.

"Good. Inside the overhead door of my garage, on the right, are two garbage cans," Hetzer continued. "At the end of your last run on Friday afternoon, stop at my house, pick up the cans, but don't dump them. Put them in the back and bring them along back here before you dump your load. How's that for easy?"

Buck Stouffer thought about the deal from many angles and couldn't see how he might be screwed, so he responded, "I'll do it."

"And the payoff will be right here Friday night when you return from the landfill," Hetzer said. One thing about Americans, as well as most of his fellow countrymen, he decided, there was no principle higher than an increased income, especially if one could secrete it from the tax man. Greed *will* be the end of the United States yet—Lenin was right!

Stouffer pulled out from the driveway and began his day's work. Hetzer returned to the kitchenette to fill another cup with the less-than-gourmet coffee. When I return to Germany, I'll get some really *fine* Turkish coffee, he reassured himself.

CHAPTER FORTY-FIVE

Sr. Investigator Dennis Girard spent his first hour at work that morning conferring with Delehanty. As they reviewed the implications of their accumulated information, a call came for Delehanty from Tom Ellis in his Chevy truck, who was driving Essex County roads as a roving stakeout, specifically searching for the UPS truck and any sign of Hetzer or his SUV. Trooper Ellis informed Delehanty that he had briefly seen a figure much like Charbonneau in front of the hardware store in Westport, but after parking and walking to the store to investigate, the individual was gone. He entered Cole's Hardware and asked the clerk about the man, showing his ID and a photo of Charbonneau. The clerk confirmed that Louie had been in, buying wire cutters and several lengths of nylon rope. "What do you make of those items, Lt. Delehanty?" Ellis inquired.

"I don't know yet, Tommy, but keep looking. Sooner or later, the S.O.B.s have to take to the roads," Delehanty replied, hanging up his phone. He then sat and scratched his head. "Wire cutters and nylon rope. That ring any bells to you, Den?"

Girard's cell phone rang and he broke off his conversation with Tommy. "Investigator Girard," Trooper Peter Friskin said, "there's something strange going on down here. Marteau came in briefly at 9:15 and exited at 9:28, posting a 'closed' sign on the front door. Thirty minutes later, a customer came by, a guy I know named Charlie Johnson. Charlie read the sign, then left. I had the road patrol stop him a bit south of here, asking what the sign said. Johnson told Trooper Ramirez that the sign said, 'Closed. Death in the family.' What do you make of that?"

"Looks to me like the pair are getting ready to do something, Peter. Looks like they're going into hiding to prepare for something. Keep a sharp eye out," Girard instructed. "You know that a car carrier is going to replace you at 2:00, right?"

"Yes, I got that at my briefing. He's going to watch the place from the south, where he has a 'breakdown.'" The two chuckled, and Friskin added, "Gee, Girard, I was really liking the surveyor's life, but my wife's tuna fish sandwiches don't keep well in that hot van, so thanks for the reprieve." Friskin and his partner slowly began retrieving their tools and road markers, preparing to return to Ray Brook at 2:00.

After he hung up, Girard shared the new developments with Delehanty, though neither one could guess where it was all headed. Girard returned to his desk and shuffled papers, waiting for new developments. Should they get a search warrant for Skippy's? If so, based on what probable cause? He couldn't decide. There was likely some evidence, perhaps even contraband, in there, so he didn't want to scare the pair away when they returned to pick it up. But, if there was anything really valuable inside Skippy's, would the pair simply abandon it?

Girard departed from Ray Brook at 5:30 p.m., and headed south on the Northway. There were the usual radio calls and chatter, but nothing dramatic. His head was working overtime, trying to draw some meaning from the numerous details in the case. He called aloud toward the rear seat of the car, "Timmy? Izzy? What do you guys know? Where's it all going?" No response. At the Chapel Pond trail on Route 73, he had to slow almost to a stop because two gorgeous female hikers were sauntering across the highway, both chatting on cell phones and unmindful of oncoming traffic. This time, Girard concentrated on their infractions and not the beauty of their legs. He gave a big honk of his horn and the two ran like frightened deer, one dropping her backpack at the road's edge. One of the princesses turned and gave him the finger as he sped by. Ah, American womanhood, he sighed.

At home, he ate a dinner of fresh green beans and a thawed fish filet, then drank a cup of mint tea while watching the news on CNN. Will program host Lou Dobbs ever give up and realize this country has *already* gone to hell? he wondered. Then, strolling into the garden, he half expected to see green-eyed John, the locust-eater, on the bench, but no one was visible. Girard sat staring at the children biking on the road below his hill. Wish I could go back to those carefree days, he thought. Aha! Maybe the solution to America's problems is to eat more ice cream, he concluded, and began a slow walk over to the ice cream parlor on Main Street. Tonight was Wednesday and Mikki of the strong dipping arm was working.

Approaching the Catholic church, he spotted Father McCabe just entering, but held back so the man didn't see him. How could he tell that nice guy what had transpired in New Hampshire? The best news of his day was that Mikki hadn't lost her strength, and he ended up with almost a triple-dip cone for the price of a double. The walk home was uneventful, and he read until bedtime. Twice during the night, he awoke to what sounded like howling wolves, though he couldn't determine whether they were dream sounds or real.

In the morning, North Country Public Radio's news broadcast carried a brief mention of George Bush Sr.'s visit to Plattsburgh on Monday. As Girard scooped the last of his shredded wheat from his breakfast bowl, he felt the light touch of the spirit on his shoulder. "Hey, Timmy!" He spun around, but nobody was visible. "Hey, Timmy, where have you *been*? I need help in sorting this stuff out. Come on out where I can see you!" But there was no sound or presence. He was apparently alone again. Showering and dressing, he drove north to Troop B Headquarters, failing to connect the phantom touch with the Bush news story.

At work there was still nothing new, although there was a message from Trooper Ellis for Investigator Delehanty to call a cell phone number, and Tommy made that his first task. Ellis had been cruising at the northern end of Schroon Lake, when Dispatch notified him of a complaint at Blaauboer's Blue Man Marina in Westport. A big boat had been stolen, along with auxiliary gas cans. The steel mooring cable had been severed with a cutting tool. Ellis quickly remembered Charbonneau's purchase of the previous day.

At the marina, Ellis spoke with the owner, who was livid. It was not just any boat that had been stolen, but a brand-new, 23-foot Bayliner Trophy, which he had just bought in May with a big portion of his retirement savings. "I've got a big 250-horsepower outboard on it, a Mercury Verado, and that boat *sails*. Now some idiot has it!" Blaauboer agonized. "What can you do to help me?"

Ellis gave the standard responses without sharing his suspicions. The State Police would need a copy of Blaauboer's bill of sale, the boat's state registration numbers, a copy of the boat's insurance contract, and a photo of the boat, if one was available. The owner filled out a complaint and Ellis asked to see the mooring site. The plastic-coated, braided steel cable had been cut cleanly. Ellis noticed the cut end had a slight curvature toward its center, and he could almost visualize the cutting tool. "Twenty-three feet is a pretty big boat to hide," he told the owner. "I'll bet somebody spots it. In the meantime, I'll put in a call to all the county sheriffs' marine patrols on this side of the lake, and get a message over to the Vermont State Police to watch their side. I'm sure you'll have it back as good as new next week." Blaauboer thanked Ellis and, mumbling, went off to collect fees from a new tenant. Ellis made his initial report to Delehanty by phone, as this was part of the priority Charbonneau case, or he'd miss his guess. The FIU would come in quickly, of course, and see what they might find.

At Ray Brook, Delehanty shared the new development with Girard.

"Denny, we've got Charbonneau buying ropes and a wire cutter. Within hours, and only a half mile away, a braided steel mooring line is cut, and a high-powered boat is stolen, almost certainly by a known smuggler. I guess the only questions now are where Two Claw is going, with whom, and what is the cargo that he's trying to move at 45 miles an hour on the lake?"

"Okay, assuming the Arabs are working with Two Claw, and assuming that Hetzer is in on it too, what are they moving? Too much money and too many deaths are involved for it to be just cigarettes this time. It has to be a big score, so what can it be? Something transported across the Canadian border by the smuggler, Tessier, carried by Louie to Port Henry, probably still stored inside Skippy's—do you think it's dope, Tommy?" Delehanty scanned the bulletins, seeking news of a recent hijacking. Nothing. He called FedEx and UPS requesting information on any upcoming high-value shipments. Nothing. So, what *is* it? Again he checked the bulletins, seeking information on any recent high-value thefts, but only two stolen autos turned up. One was a 2007 Mercedes S-550 Sedan and the other is a strange one, an antique 1940 LaSalle convertible sedan.

"Look, Den," Delehanty responded, "we know Hetzer made his reputation by assassination. The Red Army Faction killed government officials and leaders in the capitalist German economy. Is that little group going to knock off some major drug dealer? A businessman? Who else is there who's worth hitting—some politician? This is an election year—who might those anarchists want out of the way? One of the major candidates? On the other hand, is it possible that they're just going to steal, repaint and re-sell high-power boats? That Bayliner and outboard motor must retail at more than $60,000 with all the bells and whistles the owner installed. But why would an anarchist assassin make that his work—unless he's tapering off a career?"

Girard was quiet for a moment. "Hetzer is the one I'm really scared about," he began. "With the exception of Charbonneau and his Indian cig smugglers, covert Arabs in Essex County almost certainly mean something political or terrorist-inspired is going on. Hetzer was a terrorist of sorts in West Germany. His kills were politically motivated, and he was slick enough to get away with every one of them. Last time I met with the JTTF, FBI agent Parker theorized that, to escape Germany and to lay low for over 15 years, Hetzer had to have big-time help. Is there some kind of international organization that the NSA or FBI, or even the CIA hasn't yet discovered? Whoever they are, they're not amateurs, and they must have funding from somewhere. And, if any or all of that is true, then what is their purpose—mayhem and terrorism just for the sake of scaring people? From what I can see of the Middle East developments, the terrorists no longer have any aim over there except to exterminate people unlike themselves. And most of the people on earth *aren't* like them!"

Delehanty sat for a moment, lost in thought. "Denny, remember Professor Mike Gonroff at Syracuse? Remember when we took his history course on the rise and fall of the Third Reich in Germany? What the Nazis did in the 20s and early 30s was to destroy confidence in the new democracy of the Weimar Republic by creating terror throughout German society. Fear became so widespread that democracy couldn't and didn't work, or keep the German people safe or fed. And it couldn't restore Germany's dignity among other nations. After 10 years of chaos, their citizens were ready for someone who would provide order in the country at whatever price, so enter Hitler as their savior. Is domestic terrorism going on here, and if so, how can it benefit these foreigners? The answer might be that someone in the *U.S.* intends to pick up the pieces after society learns to live in fear. Maybe more safety in exchange for promises of rigid government control?

"Look what's happened in the last 5 years, with communications and mail often being intercepted without a federal warrant. Maybe it is someone's goal that *our* citizens will become obedient followers like those Germans, just so we can have order by turning all important decisions over to a strong government. How many more Patriot Acts will it take to achieve *that* end?"

The two sat in deep contemplation. Might it be that certain elements in the U.S. were in league with the terrorists or smugglers, intending to literally enslave the American people in exchange for the illusion of safety? If so, the Bill of Rights would vanish, especially because few Americans can list even four of those rights. Might there be government figures who had that goal even *before 9/11*? For another half hour, the apolitical pair chatted about the end of American democracy coming not from the outside—where the threat seemed to originate—but from big money, multinational corporate interests working from *within*, and protected by the favorable federal laws which they bought.

Girard stood and kicked his chair—such a prospect scared the hell out of him. All the damned angel stuff had already made him paranoid enough, but this prospect for the end of America…! And what had the eagle said to him about saving the nation? Good Lord, was *that* it? So what *was* such a network of conspirators? Who were they, and what was their ultimate goal? And where were they located? Or, is it possible that they had no national identity at all? A chill ran down his back.

"Look, Tommy, maybe we've gone nutso. Maybe it isn't that at all," Girard said. "As BCI investigators, we can't go off half-cocked, chasing something that investigative intelligence can't confirm. We've got to stick with what we *know*."

At that moment, FBI Agent Zarr called with notification that a JTTF meeting was scheduled regarding the situation at 9:00 a.m. on Friday. As it was now lunchtime, Girard hiked over to Agnes Simonds's snack shop to have a Philly cheese steak sandwich and sit at a picnic table. The sun was bright, the day was warm, the sky was blue and, seeing the birds and squirrels, it struck him that the other creatures in nature couldn't survive in chaos. A dozen sparrows walked attentively beneath the tables, picking at the remains of cold fries and burger buns. The investigator hoped something new would happen, but his cell remained quiet. His mind seemed to itch, as if an already-formed idea was struggling to claw its way into consciousness. Girard closed his eyes, took a deep breath, and listened.

Although he heard nothing, when he opened his eyes he knew the stakeout had to return to Hetzer's house. Back at the office, he asked Capt. Telfer to reassign Trooper Jack Tomlinson to the Hetzer house in Westport. Telfer was glad to do so, as it seemed to him that the Charbonneau/Hetzer cases were coming to the crisis point.

Girard called the Skippy's stakeout, Trooper Joe Ellington, seated in the cab of an apparently broken-down, empty car carrier, just south of Skippy's. The truck's flashing lights and the reflectors in the road told passersby that the truck was disabled. It was such a sore thumb spectacle at the roadside that no passerby would suspect it being a stakeout vehicle. Ellington sipped from a cup of cool iced tea, just poured from his Thermos on the seat. He told the investigator that nothing had moved at Skippy's since yesterday morning. The little rise on the roadside partially obscured his vision, but Ellington could clearly observe the front of the shop and its large overhead door. There had been no customers during the day and no lights inside at night. Ellington expected to be relieved about 4:00 p.m. With a caution to stay sharp, Girard hung up. Something has to give...something!

Frank Whitson and his Goo Crew were just returning from the Blue Man Marina and Whitson expressed a certainty that the prints he'd lifted along the dock and on the mooring line were Charbonneau's, but he'd send them to SAFIS to be certain. Alice Gaudreau, passing Girard, reached up and gave his cheek a gentle tweak and told him to smile. "You're not the ringmaster, Dennis, you know that. Somebody bigger than us is calling the shots," she joked. He thanked her for reminding him of his true role in the universe. It was hard to just do nothing when one didn't even know what was going on, he told her with a smile.

By 4:00 p.m. Girard decided to head south to Chestertown. He needed time to think, and maybe Timmy or Izzy were on duty somewhere along his route and might inspire him. He reached home with no help, however.

In his apartment, he showered, pulled on his cut-offs and sleeveless Syracuse U. sweatshirt, and walked up Knapp Hill Road, keeping his cell phone handy. By the time he reached the hilltop, he could see an orange mist accompanying him, about 20 feet back in the trees. When he got past the houses, he spoke to the mist, asking its identity, and whether it was a force that could help him. As he did so, he felt he'd completely lost his sanity because there was no response, other than a brightening of the color in response to his questions. After a mile, he turned and went home. Damn lights! Why won't they talk to me?

There was some cold chicken in the fridge, which he made into a sandwich, and downed it with some mandarin orange tea. After cleaning up the kitchen for the first time in a week, he sat to watch CNN, before switching over to MSNBC, seeking some meaning to life's events in the day's news. But the national and international news was just as chaotic as that in the Adirondacks crook hunt. At 9:00 p.m. he gave up his search for understanding and dropped into bed.

He dreamed of a large black crow, walking unimpeded through the streets of a small village, killing and tossing aside the inhabitants who dared to show themselves. And behind the giant crow, a flock of vultures was descending to feast on the mutilated bodies. He felt powerless and tossed and turned throughout the night as the dream kept recurring.

CHAPTER FORTY-SIX

Up early, Girard started the coffee, showered, dressed, and was out the door with his carry cup at 6:45 a.m. The morning of the 25th had broken sunny and mild, and he was exhilarated to see the sun in its ascent over the eastern mountains near Lake George as he sped south on I-87. Though national political candidates would soon be traveling throughout the northeast, Brian Mann, reporter for North Country Public Radio, reported that the biggest upstate event so far in 2008 so far, would be the appearance of a former President at the old Plattsburgh Air Force Base. In addition to his rousing speech, Bush was expected to dedicate a plaque, officially naming the old base The Plattsburgh International Airport. It was an ideal spot in the North Country for international travel and trade connections, and was already attracting many small businesses to the area, which had been in something of an economic slump since the Air Force departed in 1995. Now, something good was finally coming from that seeming disaster, the reporter said. As Girard mentally processed the story, he heard an "Ahem!" from the backseat.

He checked the rearview mirror and half turned around, but nobody was there. Who? Why? he wondered. It's got to be Timmy, he concluded, and reflected on the first time Timmy had appeared to him, announcing their upcoming "work together." Suddenly, it dawned on him—he was supposed to pay attention to the *Bush* issue, which so far had occupied only a small part of his consciousness. I'd better be prepared to play my part at this meeting, he concluded, as he turned off I-787 into south Albany.

The gist of the meeting was that "someone high-up" in Washington had taken a personal interest in the Hetzer case and had ordered that the FBI now take the lead on the case. "Of course, we'll expect the State Police to continue fully supporting us, Girard," said Agent Zarr. "The State Police is vital in this effort, as is Homeland Security. For the FBI's part, we're reinforcing our details at Plattsburgh and Glens Falls, the first two Bush stopovers, with 20 extra agents and will follow up on all leads, even though that means going over a lot of your separate investigations again," he continued. "Let's also remember, we aren't separate agencies once we become TFOs, and it is the protection of our nation and its leaders that is now paramount."

Secret Service Agent Parker questioned the meaning of the decision. "*We're* still the agency that protects the Presidents," she emphasized. "That's *our* job from the beginning to end of Mr. Bush's tour."

"Right, Agent Parker, your task hasn't changed, but the FBI is providing the ground forces starting at Plattsburgh and throughout Bush's trip. His travels have become entangled in our case involving a terrorist potential. You've stated several times that, among the Secret Service's agents, Mr. Bush is the most beloved of ex-Presidents, and that isn't going to change. It seems clear that Mr. Bush will not cancel his tour, so all we can do is keep him safe wherever he goes. Girard, we expect the State Police to provide an overlapping ring of protection outside the FBI perimeter at Plattsburgh, and then it all shifts to Glens Falls once he is airborne again. And that is going to require a Troop G assist. We've got TFO Kurto already working on that end." Zarr then provided the frequency for an operational satellite radio link, which all agencies would use beginning on Sunday at 6:00 a.m.

Girard sat quietly. In a sense, he was relieved that the FBI was now top dog in the operation, but, on another level, he was irritated that any other agency would be peeking over his shoulder, reviewing the BCI handling of the Hetzer/Charbonneau issues. "Roger all you said, Agent Zarr, I feel confident that we can all do our jobs. Then, I'm retiring when it's over. I sure will miss all this fun," he said with a sardonic smile.

For the next hour, all participants anted up their latest information. More and more, the information pointed to a showdown at Plattsburgh, and Agent Parker offered that Secret Service Headquarters had warned the former President that there was a likelihood of danger there. Bush, however, was full of fight and wanted "the garden plowed even before the convention," as he said, "and I'm the man behind *this* plow."

So, the Secret Service was at its highest state of readiness and would have both airborne and ground units involved in the Bush journey. It suddenly occurred to Girard that Parker was very uneasy, to the point of resentment, that the Secret Service's best efforts might not be good enough because of what she considered political grandstanding. For her part, she appeared to sit coolly in her leather chair, but inwardly, she was pondering whether or not she should follow Girard's example and go hike the Rockies for the rest of her life.

It was agreed that the State Police would add extra road patrols on both I-87 and Routes 9 and 22 throughout the eastern part of Troop B and down into Troop G. The FBI would have vehicle checkpoints outside the base, visually inspecting all who entered the main gates. As a former Air Force installation, its perimeter was fenced, so all access was controlled, with only two gates open to the public and an emergency or escape gate available to the Secret Service. Every federal and state officer within two hours drive of Plattsburgh had recent photos of Charbonneau and Hetzer, as well as additional artist renderings of their likely disguises. The evidence was very strong that the two men were collaborating. Everyone at the JTTF meeting also agreed that Hetzer or Charbonneau, or perhaps both, were likely to try a hit on Bush, and all agreed that any such effort was *not* going to be successful.

In Westport, Buck Stouffer neared the end of his day's work and relished the prospect of making an easy pile of money that night, simply for picking up two garbage cans on Sisco Street in Westport. He suspected that the police might be watching the house, as he knew that Hetzer was deep into law-breaking, but he also knew he could take the "I was only following instructions from a customer" route if there was trouble at the house. Nearing Hetzer's home, he could see nobody watching. There was only a telephone company truck a few doors away, but that couldn't be the cops. Stouffer backed his truck into the driveway, opened the garage door with Hetzer's key, stood the two cans into the back bay of the truck, then closed and locked the garage. He dropped the ram onto the can tops to secure them for the rest of the journey. Easy as pie, he said to himself, and turned toward home.

If all went as he hoped, Hetzer knew what he must do. With the package in his hands, he'd plan Monday's work, and there must be no slip-ups. He stood in front of the large barn as Stouffer drove in, did a half-turn, then backed toward the building. A telephone company truck drove slowly past, likely searching for an address.

Back from the JTTF meeting in Albany, Girard sat at his desk as 4:00 p.m. approached. Somebody *had to* see or hear something, and he knew it. An attempt on the former President's life would have to be done in the open and everyone in law enforcement would be ready to stop any such effort dead in its tracks. Agents Parker and Zarr indicated that there would be armed helicopters ready, but out of sight at the speech site, in case an attack came by air. Burlington, VT's tower would watch the skies over the lake and Plattsburgh.

Trooper Jack Tomlinson, in plain clothes, turned off Sisco Street and onto Main Street in Westport before stopping his telephone company truck to call Girard. "Here's what transpired at Hetzer's. A refuse service from Wadhams picked up garbage cans at Hetzer's garage," he began, "but the truck was backed in, so I didn't see what the guy loaded. Probably just a regular garbage collection. The company is Stouffer Refuse from Wadhams, and I followed the truck to its base. Again, the vehicle was backed in when I went by, but the driver was talking to someone out of sight behind the truck. I didn't see anything out of the ordinary. Probably just a regular weekly pickup. Do we have anything on Stouffer?"

"I'll get back to you on that one, Jack. Return to the Hetzer house and continue surveillance. That refuse truck might have been a decoy to pull us away, but you were right to follow it. Stay at Hetzer's until you're relieved. I'll have someone there soon because I know you're working into another shift. He signed off and found Trooper Simmons available for relief, and gave the officer a call to be at Hetzer's by six. "Gee, maybe the FB almighty EYE would like to come and take some of this grunt work off our hands," he groused. Turning to his video terminal, he consulted the database regarding Stouffer, but there was no hit. He called Tomlinson back and informed him.

Buck Stouffer raised the ram that held the two garbage cans secure in the truck's back end, and as he did so, a cover fell off one can; it almost seemed that Hetzer had deliberately hit it. "Am I gonna get my pay soon?" Buck Stouffer asked his companion. "Real quick, Buck," Hetzer replied, lifting both cans from the bay. Then he added, "Get that cover that fell inside, will you, Buck? It's very important to this job." Stouffer climbed up onto the truck, extending himself fully into the bay, and reached for the metal cover amidst Essex County's garbage. Hetzer hit the emergency ram drop lever on the side of the truck and the ram came crashing down onto Stouffer, almost cutting him in half.

"Sorry, Buck," Hetzer murmured, adjusting his steel-rimmed glasses, "but there's little enough payoff for any of us on this job. You'll be happier where the smell is better." Leaving the two cans in the driveway, Hetzer drove the truck behind the barn, where Buck's body wouldn't be discovered until Monday. And by then, the game will be well underway, he concluded.

Hetzer hadn't seen Charbonneau since the previous night and hoped the man had succeeded in stealing a fast boat. Hardly had those thoughts crossed his mind, than Charbonneau turned into the driveway in Stouffer's yellow pickup truck. Hetzer greeted Louie, telling him that Stouffer had "gone home." He invited Charbonneau into the small kitchenette and opened up a map of southern Lake Champlain. "Okay, Louis, you know what you're looking at. See here, at the bottom of the lake, this narrow area just at Whitehall—the waterway becomes almost like a river there. Your instructions are to be underneath the Poultney Street Bridge on Monday morning with the cargo you're going to pick up at Skippy's," he gestured to the site. "That's the first bridge you come to, and you'll have the two new friends with you—the guys you met on delivery day at the

227

cycle shop. Underneath that bridge, out of sight, is where you'll set up to shoot. It is imperative that you be in position by noon. The men with you are going to shoot down an airplane. You'll like this, as an old UPS driver—it's a FedEx plane, and it must not get past. It's carrying government stuff and it will be the only plane on that route between 11:00 a.m. and 2:00 p.m., flying at about six thousand feet. Your job is to drive the boat after you pick up the two men and their cargo at the Port Henry cycle shop. Make sure the boat is stable when your friends are ready to shoot, and not bobbing up and down, you *got* that?"

"Sure, I can do that! I *told* you I used to drive fast boats and never got caught doing anything wrong," said Charbonneau. He was starting to not like Black Crow, despite all his money. Crows had always been too clever for him, he mused, and he didn't want to get screwed by this guy, even for all the money in New York State. This Black Crow seemed just like his own father, always insinuating that he, Louis Philippe Charbonneau, was incompetent.

"You'll be able to get off three shots, and when you have fired your missiles, using the bridge as cover from prying eyes, leave the boat and start walking westward to the main street. There will be a pick-up van there to bring the three of you to safety. Got it?" Hetzer demanded sharply.

"Yeah, I *got* it!" Charbonneau threw back testily.

"What did you get for a boat?" Hetzer inquired.

"I got a big Bayliner with a large outboard motor, and it can move at almost 50 miles an hour wide open, so it will get us where we're going, *Seigneur*." He threw in the French title to show both contempt and distance from the man who seemed to taunt his competence.

"Okay, good enough," Hetzer replied. "Clean out the refrigerator here in this kitchen—make yourself lots of sandwiches and…where did you hide the boat?"

"There's an old deserted boathouse at the Clifton Estate. It's been up for sale for several years without a buyer, I learned, so nobody is going to just drop by," Charbonneau responded. "The building looks like it's going to fall down soon, but it's deep enough for me to hide a 25-foot boat."

"Okay, good," said Hetzer. "So get yourself some food now. Maybe it would be a good idea also to get some shut-eye until midnight, then start figuring out how you're going to move the boat—a little farther south each night, maybe. Your pickup is going to be at the cycle shop in Port Henry before dawn on Monday morning, so find a place above town to hide out on Sunday night. Probably you can just pull into the marina there after dark, but do it without lights. Then you can head down to Port Henry before 4:00 a.m. that morning. It figures to be stormy, as there is a big low-pressure area moving in on late Saturday or on Sunday morning and lasting all day and night."

Charbonneau fished a licorice stick from his shirt pocket and popped it into his mouth. Great stuff, licorice, he decided, it keeps down the stomach pain. "I'll go out at midnight and see if I can locate a hiding place for tomorrow night," he told Hetzer.

CHAPTER FORTY-SEVEN

Hetzer had left the garbage cans in the driveway because, if there was any chance that Stouffer's was under surveillance, he expected someone to drive in and make a fuss. But no one apparently was interested in garbage cans sitting in the garbage man's driveway. A few minutes after nine, Hetzer went out to the cans and brought them into the front of the large barn, and there, he opened them. The aroma brought tears to his eyes. Both cans had been deliberately topped off with the smelliest concoctions of decay that he could find, just in case his home was searched. Any investigator would have had to poke through some awful-smelling stuff to discover the packages he now retrieved.

The assassin walked toward the rear inside the barn, past his Navigator and the UPS truck. He didn't even think about the vehicles anymore, because they were expendable; too hot to put on the highway again. Raising the back door, he exited and dumped each can in turn into the rear bay of the open packer truck, from which Stouffer's legs still extended. The vile-smelling waste was just enough to cover Buck's pant legs and shoes. Then he hosed off the package to remove as much as possible of the waste and smell.

Returning inside with the black plastic-wrapped parcels from inside each can, Hetzer closed the overhead door and returned to the better-lit front of the structure. Slowly, he opened the more tightly packed carton. A label caught his eye, "Potter's Clay," it said, though Hetzer knew the malleable material inside was Semtex, a plastic explosive favored by terrorists in years gone by. This batch had been sent to him because the network had acquired it cheaply, as it could no longer be used to sabotage airplanes or vehicles because it could be sniffed by high-tech sensing machines. Hetzer's intent, however, was to use the material outdoors, where sniffers would be powerless. All he needed now was the telephone call as to which airport gate he'd enter on Monday at noon. Trusting that Alderschild would make the call, he walked to his cot in the kitchenette to plot his next move. Charbonneau was already asleep, probably dreaming of the glory to come.

Dennis Girard woke at 6:00 a.m. on Saturday the 26th. The sky was dark and the weather service was promising driving rains late that night and all day Sunday. For a moment, Girard wondered whether or not Bush's ceremony would even be held in Plattsburgh if a crowd was unable to gather on the airport apron. Well, that's their problem, he decided. My problem is Charbonneau, that weasel—and Hetzer, the cold-blooded killer.

Coffee…he decided, and rose to begin his daily brew. As the machine bubbled, Girard turned on the television, watching a special report from the racetrack at Saratoga Springs, where the thoroughbred racing season had begun again, attracting the glitterati of American society. He blotted out old memories of rich folks who he'd been required to escort there in the old days—guard duty for millionaires who were rich enough to hire their own security detail, but instead mooched off the taxpayers and career troopers of New York State. "Bah!" he exclaimed.

It wasn't typical for Girard to be mellow on Saturdays, but he poured the coffee into his carry mug and, slipping on his walking shoes, sweat pants and t-shirt, he chose to sit first on Mrs. Morgenstern's garden bench. The village below him was quiet, with almost no traffic on Riverside Drive. It was good to just sit and let his mind drift, though it quickly skidded to a stop at the present reality. The eagle had warned him—the time seemed to be at hand. Grandma Kelly had warned him, and his work in the JTTF seemed to indicate that the matter must soon break open. Then there was the apparition of John on this very bench, but it was unclear what he wanted to communicate, though it seemed urgent. It was all about protecting another rich American, he realized, but this one was a former American President. However, our nation's soul might also be involved in making this protection successful, he concluded. And, most important, he realized, was whether or not the corruption of power, symbolized by Hetzer and Charbonneau, was going to win out.

His own new battles, if there were any, would not be at Plattsburgh, but somehow involved Skippy's and the absent duo of fake Frenchmen.

Where did they go and when would they return, if ever? He called the broken-down car carrier on Route 9N. All was quiet, Trooper Friskin told him, and a tow truck would remove the big vehicle at noon, as scheduled. The next surveillance would be by two troopers, Noah Vincent and Francis Petrosky, already camped on the forested hilltop opposite to the cycle shop. Both men had high-powered rifles, if those would be needed for the upcoming denouement. Those two men, whose radios were on Girard's tac channel, would see the operation through to its end.

Girard figured he could get a better intuition on it all by commencing his Saturday Morning Hike up Graphite Mountain. By occupying the body, his mind often was liberated to seek beyond its human container. It was early, but, picking up his hand-held radio, he set his cup on the bench and headed across town to commence the Route 8 hike.

In her Plattsburgh apartment, Dr. Bernice Epstein sat pondering a dilemma. There was no question that she despised the former President who would visit her city in two days. She had firmly opposed the Gulf War and the man's other efforts to lift America's elite even higher while the poor of the nation sank lower. She was a liberal in every respect, she acknowledged. But, she also had enough Buddhist instruction to realize that continued animosity to any human would become an anchor that pulled her soul into the earth again and again until she acted to release it. If my life and profession are about anything, she considered, it is about the ability of people to change and grow, and I'd betray that possibility if I couldn't permit a politician to do likewise. Bernice resolved that, as every soul can begin each new day reborn, she would rise and go to the airport on Monday and hear what the man would say about the nation's future. She was not too proud to learn from *any* person, she concluded—and to refuse to at least listen would be a mistake. Epstein finished her cup of green tea and returned to the cross-stitching that was both a hobby and pacifier to her inner fires.

Irene Karamanlis lifted her sized, eight-square-foot canvas onto its large easel in her North Bennington, VT, apartment. This was another new day, and after receiving second prize at the Boston Minimalist Art Show in April, she was buoyed with a newborn self-confidence. This new work, she had decided, should have an animal theme. She had once seen an ancient Chinese painting of cats, and decided to model this new work on the black, grey, and white shades from that masterpiece—the barest representation of feline energy. This would be a good one, just three brief lines, and then, ready for the Philadelphia show in October.

Patrick Girard, Dennis's youngest son, said a final goodbye to his now-ex-wife, Giselle. The divorce was final this morning, and he had moved from the city of Rochester, NY, into the nearby hamlet of Kent, where he had an apartment. There he could remain close to his two children. He had taken a month off from his job at Kodak Corporation and decided to give his father a phone call in Chestertown, perhaps to reopen an old relationship. Maybe soon, he'd take his children to visit a grandfather that they'd never met.

Clara Girard finished her night shift at Children's Hospital in Philadelphia. Pediatric nursing was such a physical and emotional drain, especially with the suffering little ones who couldn't sleep at night. Tonight's shift had been especially difficult, as she tried to ease the pain of a six-year-old who had been hit while riding her small bicycle. This morning, for some reason, Clara suddenly remembered that her father had also been hospitalized months ago, and she'd never even sent a card. Maybe I can at least send a "keeping in touch" card now, anyway, she decided. Maybe something with flowers on it, though I don't think flowers are his thing.

Joey Girard, long estranged from his family, walked slowly down the open-air porch at Ten Broeck Psychiatric Hospital in Louisville, KY. Breakfast had been another predictable disaster—the food was swill and the cooks needed more occupational therapy than he did. It was awful garbage, unpalatable when compared to the gourmet meals he'd once enjoyed in Atlanta. That's when times had been good and easy, and his life as an investment counselor had brought him easy living and easy women. It wasn't his fault that Red Morton had set him up to fail. Morton had always been jealous of his genius, so it had to happen sooner or later, before he, Joey Girard, eclipsed the fool and became office manager. And it wasn't *his* fault, either, that the move to Louisville had ended so badly, at least for the present.

He couldn't understand why the lawyer didn't return his telephone calls—another incompetent! Here he was, locked in with crazy people! And it was the stupid judge's senility that caused him to rule that I be involuntarily committed to this state hospital, he grumbled to himself. I'll get out, I know, and then I'll finally show the world! Right now, however, there was the morning anger management session—more morons! If the idiot lawyer ever *did* call him back, Joey was tempted to sue the state of Kentucky for cruel and unusual punishment.

Hannah Morgenstern knew the pain wasn't going to stop. The MRIs and blood tests were conclusive and she knew the Stage Three intestinal cancer would end her life before winter came. Pain medication could make only a few more months a bit more bearable. Perhaps today would be a good day to tell her wonderful upstairs tenant that he'd soon need to find new lodgings. Hannah had dreamed of a beautiful golden gate last night, and felt that it represented her exit from this old body, and *that*, she looked forward to. In the meantime, if her strength didn't fail her, the last of the irises needed dead-heading. I don't suppose that the flowers in Heaven *ever* wilt or die, she smiled.

FBI agent Martin Donahue finished his sketched plot of the barriers to position outside the main gate at the Plattsburgh International Airport. The loaded concrete barrier trucks had just arrived, the backhoes were ready, and the airport maintenance men would have all the obstacles in place by noon. The sky was graying up and he figured there'd be rain by nightfall. This was a good security detail and he hoped to see the former President in two days, as his father had been both an admirer and large contributor to the man's 1992 campaign. Donahue liked working for the government. He'd been a cum laude history graduate at Notre Dame University, and had deliberately sought out work that would ensure the continuation of the best government on earth. As a member of the advance contingent of agents at Plattsburgh, he intended to ensure that Monday's celebration went off without a hitch. Then, afterward, back in Albany, he'd pop the question to Amanda, his dream lady.

The phone rang in the Durand Street apartment of Sally Reid in Plattsburgh. The unknown voice asked if she had received her new clothing. She answered yes, that the Clinton County Sheriff's Department uniform had arrived two days before. By now, Reid said, she was entirely familiar with the security procedures at the airport and understood the time at which to cut the chain securing the old rusted gate on Route 22, which had been padlocked since the Air Force left. There, she'd post herself as a regular member of the day's security detail, work that she had done for four years in the service when stationed at Lackland Air Force Base. As her gate was so far from the main event, she was certain that nobody would take the time to question her, even though she wouldn't have an official car. She knew all the official lingo, however, and was confident she knew how to bullshit most male security guards, federal, state, or local.

Reid also knew that the FBI was already crawling all over the old air base, and that Secret Service agents were coming in tonight. From the airport layout, she ascertained that the main security would seal off the FBO buildings, more than a half-mile away from her gate, but she had no problem with her part of the bargain—she'd be there. Sally Reid would do her part for the network, and she'd find a package filled with 50 one hundred dollar bills in her mailbox when she returned home. Open the gate, let the pickup truck through onto the trail behind the Passenger Terminal, which faced the huge concrete apron, and she was done. The driver would find his own way out, the voice in Maryland said. "That's good enough for me," she had responded and hung up.

Juanita Perez hustled to do second refills of coffee for the summer tourists in booth 4 at Lucy's that Saturday morning. It was a good day for tips, and she hoped against hope that Inspector Girard might come by today. Whenever he visited, she experienced unnerving emotions, not romantic ones, though. There was always some mist in his booth, and she hoped he could explain it to her, so she didn't have to consult a head doctor.

At the North Pond Parking Area, Dennis Girard looked over at the dark evergreens that screened the pond's southern margin. What a beautiful sight, he thought. Now all I need is my eagle. Almost noon, he reflected, and gave a call to the Skippy's stakeout. "Just changing hands," Trooper Friskin responded. "We have two apparent lumbermen measuring trees on the hill across the way—looks like they may be there a while," he said jokingly. Girard thanked him, switched off the tac radio, and began his walk west, pausing once or twice to look over his shoulder and see if his bird had returned. It hadn't.

CHAPTER FORTY-EIGHT

At home, in the shower, Girard realized that the next two days were what he had been working and living, and perhaps even dying for, during the last six months. A major event, likely involving either international criminals or a former President of the United States, or both, was the focus. Drying off, he impulsively grabbed for his hand radio and called Trooper Noah Vincent at the Skippy's stakeout. Identifying himself, he asked Vincent what was taking place across the road. The stakeout responded that everything inside was quiet, and that they'd heard no interior sounds since assuming watch at noon. The parking lot was empty and the "closed" sign still hung in the window. "These guys may be gone for good," the lookout warned.

"Watch them tighter than tight," Girard instructed. "I *know* there is some mystery in that place, and if we can't solve it by this time tomorrow, I'm going to get a federal warrant and go in. Keep looking at their backyard too, what you can see of it. They might try to sneak in by boat or at night." He signed off. The tension was too great, so he brewed a fresh single cup of coffee, poured it into his mug, and then drove to Troop Headquarters. He knew Tommy was on duty and, like himself, monitoring all the tac channels, while hoping for even the smallest lead on his quarry, Charbonneau.

Investigator Delehanty watched his friend and fellow officer, Sr. Investigator Dennis Girard, striding down the hall to the BCI offices. His friend was scowling, and Delehanty realized that he also was developing a set of permanent wrinkles in his own forehead. How could Charbonneau be *nowhere*? Where could he be hiding? It was almost certain that he had copped the boat at the Blue Man Marina, so what was his destination, and why? What did that excuse for a human intend to do? Tommy waved to Girard, who was looking through his e-mail messages, then listening to telephone messages.

"What a bummer, Den," he said to his friend when the two men were no longer occupied.

Girard asked his friend, "Tommy, do you think Louie is going to try to hit Bush? Is he smart enough to do that? Might Hetzer be using him in some way to do that? Do you think he stole the boat and intends to go to Plattsburgh by water? I can't help but think that the old air base isn't that far from the lake. Might Louie or Hetzer be trying a water attack, and if so, how can they hope to breach the airport fence and all the patrols? Secret Service and FBI must have motorized patrols all along the fence. They have absolute control over the parking area, checking all cars and drivers who enter for the event. What's left? An attack by air? There's no evidence that Hetzer or Charbonneau know the first thing about airplanes. And, besides, we're going to have armed FBI helicopters ready to dust off any threat."

"You've said it all, Den," was Delehanty's reply. He sat, tapping a Ticonderoga pencil on his forehead.

"On the way up here, I had another brilliant idea and requested a State Police helicopter to be available over lower Lake Champlain from dawn to dusk on Monday," Girard continued. "If there is a boat attack and it's down there, we'll have a gun in the air. But what is there of value to attack around Port Henry? Are they going to try recapturing Fort Ticonderoga? He smiled, then said, "Jimmy Spulnik will be aboard the chopper with his sniper rifle. Gordon Nesselbank will be piloting, and Gordon has worked the lake and Lake George too. If anyone can identify a boat by make and model from a thousand feet up, it's Gordon. That Bayliner Trophy can't be on the water for five minutes without being seen. And Gordon will sit right on Louie's head if he spots him.

"The other thing, buddy, is that I'm going to get a federal warrant for Skippy's tomorrow if nothing happens down there today. There is no indication of a current threat at Skippy's, because nobody has been home for several days, but I can't stand the suspense any longer. I've got to know what they're hiding, so we can know what to defend against. We've got two spotters with sniper rifles on the hill across the road, if they're needed. They're tied into the listening devices inside Skippy's but there hasn't been a sound for days," Girard concluded. "Nobody here to make coffee tonight?"

"Naw," Tommy responded, "Alice usually has the pot perking when she comes in, but she's off this weekend, so we'll just have to suffer. I'm headed over to Janice's tonight, so let me know if anything pops."

Each man headed home. Girard to fall immediately fast asleep, and Delehanty to make love to Janice for a few hours before surrendering to Morpheus. During the night, the worst electrical storm in years blew into the Adirondacks, knocking out power in many towns and mountain hamlets as far south as Warrensburg. The only other incident in Troop B that night was a fire in Tupper Lake, but the road patrol took care of that investigation. Throughout the night, thunder boomed and lightning flashed.

"I'm glad this storm was so predictable," Marteau said aloud as he and Corbeau slipped and slid up the soaked, grassy bank behind Skippy's at 4:00 a.m.. Rain pelted down from above, and for just a moment, Marteau reflected how well such a rainstorm might replenish the wells at home in Palestine. Corbeau waited for a lightning flash, then inserted his key into the back door lock by the illumination, and turned the knob. It was as still as a tomb inside and the pair dared not risk a light, navigating only by the indirect glow of the lightning's flash.

Amid the booming peals of thunder, the two made their way to the couches in the small reception office, being careful to stay away from the windows. This was not the luxury that they had enjoyed for the past few days down at the Stepping Stones Motel in Diamond Point, but it would have to do. In case their lives were about to end soon, both men had used almost all of their Skippy's income to enjoy a few unstressed days in Diamond Point. They had hitchhiked both down and back without incident, telling drivers that they were Canadians seeking help for a broken-down car. Both agreed that ignorance and gullibility of the average U.S. citizen would be America's end.

This building would be their lair for a final 24 hours. By now, they suspected that the police might have listening devices inside the shop, but it was too late to seek those out and disable the microphones, so the two men moved only in the crashes from on high. Before dawn on Monday, the Indian would come to move them and their cargo.

"This is just about *my* kind of miserable," Trooper Francis Petrosky mumbled to himself as he peered through the binoculars at the front and sides of Skippy's across the road. He listened carefully through sensitive earphones for sounds from inside, but he knew the effort was useless with the electrical storm raging around them. This slow-moving low-pressure area was predicted to remain almost motionless over the Adirondacks and Green Mountains for 24 hours, so all that he and his partner could do was their best. Trooper Vincent, now asleep, would be revived at 2:00 a.m. to pull his shift. Look and listen, Petrosky told himself, while adjusting the earphones. Look and listen.

CHAPTER FORTY-NINE

The cold rain of Saturday night had raised a fog over the warm waters of Lake Champlain, and only a few inveterate fishermen were afloat, as the rain continued to drench the countryside. Louie Two Claw Charbonneau peered from beneath the tarp on his stolen boat. Nobody had come near his anchorage and he didn't expect anyone to do so during today's downpour. He had a large box of Twinkies that he'd purchased before leaving Wadhams, and they kept him satisfied, though his eyes now itched terribly. His stomach also hurt badly, so he alternated licorice sticks with the Twinkies.

The sounds of rain on the canvas overhead frequently lulled him to snooze, and he imagined the long-ago sounds of rain on a teepee's sides, though the Mohawks had lived in bark longhouses. It all was exciting, and this adventure gave meaning to what had for so long been a life of miserable failures. Now, lying low, he imagined himself as a young Mohawk brave waiting to charge from the brush and scalp a family of settlers. Yes, the thought of red blood spurting from a scalp sure was exciting. He popped the last of an unwrapped Twinkie into his mouth and swigged from the bottle of water beside him. This Puro brand of water was supposed to be good for one's health, he'd heard. Then, he dozed once more under the cadence of rain on canvas.

Voodoo Ground Unit of the Secret Service arrived at the Plattsburgh International Airport at 6:00 a.m. sharp, with four black GMC Yukons in a file. Agent Sharon Fiedler, driving the lead vehicle, glanced through the sheet of rain at the radiation detectors, already installed outside the main gate barricades, devices that would have meant nothing to a casual observer. Slowing at a barrier right-angle turn, she saw the tall bomb-sniffer tower, which looked more like a lamp post—the FBI had it all set. "Looks good," she said to Agent John Cunningham in the shotgun seat. He returned a silent grin, adjusting his glasses.

Cpl. Bruce Swearingen, New York State Police K-9 officer, led "Puffer," his explosives-sniffing German shepherd through the last doorway in the FBO building, completing his daily sweep of the facility. He had begun the early morning search in the new passenger terminal at the north end of the airstrip, then the nine former National Guard hangers, though there was no place to hide anything inside those arched and open-ended structures. Continuing southward for a half mile, he had checked all the facility's buildings. Now, outside the FBO door, he saw FBI Agent Martin Donahue welcoming the Secret Service, who would have the final say about procedures until Mr. Bush was airborne again on Monday afternoon. Feds! Swearingen muttered to himself. He didn't like the audacious attitude with which he felt Secret Service took over every operation with which they were involved. Nevertheless, he checked that impulsive thought with the recognition that a former President's life and well-being were at stake tomorrow. Puffer was loaded in the State Police SUV and they departed until their return early Monday morning.

Secret Service Agent Peter Alvarez set up the communication center in the unused airport control tower. Tomorrow, he reminded himself, he'd have to share the space with two other agents, each armed with a scoped rifle. Alvarez did a quick radio check, making sure the satellite link was up and running, and then radio-checked each of his comrades who had just arrived. A secondary radio was tuned to the single tactical frequency that united all law enforcement units in the Plattsburgh area, so coordination would be instantaneous. Then he awaited direction, helping himself to a Powerhouse energy bar that he took from his backpack. From the tower, there would be excellent visibility of all those in tomorrow's crowd that would come onto the apron from the parking area on Idaho Avenue, and seat themselves in temporary bleachers immediately next to the FBO building.

Agent Jimmy Kearney checked briefly on the sleeping accommodations provided by Clinton County in the former Nose Dock Building Number One, built for B-36 bombers back in the 1950s. Large, obvious signs designating the ladies' and men's rooms had been posted inside the huge building. Inside one Nose Dock building, women from the Clinton County Republican Women's Club had just set up an ad hoc kitchen and serving line to provide meals for the security teams during their duty in Plattsburgh, and pancakes and sausage were to be served starting at 7:00 a.m.. All of the volunteers wore hologram security badges issued by the FBI. Kearney wasn't quite sure how good the Swiss steak would be for lunch, but it was food, he concluded, and gourmet cooking is not what this operation was about.

The old airstrip was covered with a mist as the driving rain moved across its surface in liquid curtains. It would be messy, Kearney observed, but he'd seen worse, even at Andrews Air Force Base, where he'd often served on the Presidential Detail. He popped a mint into his mouth and sauntered toward the old Day Room to further explore the facility. Nothing is going to land today, he realized, because all general aviation is being diverted to other fields until 5:00 p.m. tomorrow.

"I'll give you until noon to make my life interesting, Izzy," Girard said aloud in his apartment. This waiting was unnerving, because he knew an explosion of some sort was certain. When you've got angels helping you, that takes all the doubt out of it, he reasoned, but where was Izzy when you *needed* him? And where was Timmy? Those two guys were his backup, and he was uncomfortable without their counsel. For just a second, he recalled that Izzy had signed off a few days ago, and the angel had told him long ago that the time would come when he'd have to get his answers *from within*. But surely they wouldn't abandon him to his ghosts, visions, and sensations. How would he know what was *true*? "Damn, this is uncomfortable," he murmured. He went to his well-worn recliner and sat, placing his feet on the floor and, sitting as erect as he could, he closed his eyes. Dennis Girard could form no words consciously and could only send a plea for guidance out into the universe.

It was after 9:00 a.m. when he finally stirred, and there had been no report from anyone. Tommy was undoubtedly back at Ray Brook, monitoring Sunday's communications and calling his sources. Would he, himself, be better off up north, or should he stay available for events at Skippy's if they should erupt? Girard placed a call to Trooper Vincent, who had taken over the day shift in Port Henry, but the stakeout had little to report. The crashing thunder during the night had left him and Petrosky nearly deaf, as all sounds were greatly amplified, not just those from within the apparently empty cycle shop. Frustrated, Girard was nevertheless courteous with Vincent, and thanked him for his help and discomfort. Here was another "foot soldier" in service to his nation.

Not even my eagle can fly in this rain, he told himself. Then he became resolute—enough is enough, dammit! No action, and I can't *stand* that! He called the Division of State Police Headquarters in Albany. To get a strike team and get one fast, would require a directive from the top— the Superintendent's Office. No BCI officer, even an ad hoc member of the JTTF, could make such a decision on his own. Maybe, he pondered, I should go through Zarr, over at the JTTF, but nevertheless, he called the Division. The operator gave Girard Lt. Lenny Mueller's home number and, in the day's deluge, Girard was not surprised to find Mueller at home. It was a lousy day for skeet shooting. Briefly, Girard explained his decision and told Mueller he intended to immediately contact JTTF, then request a federal warrant because one would issue rapidly, as he was a federal TFO. Mueller asked for ten minutes, took Girard's cell number and told him to sit tight.

Five minutes later, the cell phone rang and Mueller told Girard that a Mobile Response Team would be assembled and ready at 5:00 a.m. Monday. "Just tell me the assembly point, and is that quick enough, Girard? You're sure you'll have the warrant?" Answering in the affirmative, Girard asked that the team assemble at the intersection of Route 9N and Bridge Road, north of Crown Point, just four miles south of Port Henry. The team should be armed, armored, and ready at 5:00 a.m., and Girard would meet them in the roadside pull-off there. Lt. Mueller also notified Girard that the MRT would be under the leadership of Lt. Bill Cole from Troop G. "A good man," Girard recalled, "an old veteran like me—I remember him well." The men signed off and went about their respective duties. Glad to know the Big Man is still on my side, Girard reassured himself.

It was now 9:45 a.m. and Sr. Investigator Dennis Girard realized that he was still in his sweats. He'd need a federal warrant and was sure he could secure one, but wanted JTTF's FBI Supervisory Agent Zarr to get the ball moving. He called the agent on his emergency home phone and informed Zarr that the last hurdle was about to be jumped, unless Zarr disagreed. "We'll know what's in that building before six o'clock tomorrow morning," he told the agent. "It may well relate to Mr. Bush up north. I've never gotten a federal warrant before, though I have no problem appearing in front of a federal magistrate, but I'd like you to open a door for me."

Zarr responded, "That is a go, Girard. I just saw Federal Judge Bill Shaw in church an hour ago, and I know he and his wife are playing canasta at home this afternoon, so I'll set it up. I have your cell number in the office, but give it to me again, then get on the road down this way, and I'll call, telling you where to go. Good job, Girard," the agent said, "Maybe we should have initiated that raid a few days ago, but there is still time. Talk to you shortly."

Girard jumped into the shower, shaved, pulled on slacks and a sport shirt, and stepped without socks into a pair of loafers. In five minutes, he was in the car headed south without coffee, although he had thawed a frozen piece of French toast in the toaster and nibbled it as he drove. His life blood pumped with a new vigor inside him—here was a resolution to lots of badness. He no longer cared for his reputation or career. Too much was at stake, and he didn't even consider proving himself to his superiors anymore. This was the last big one. Solve it, get Charbonneau and Hetzer, then go to Hawaii—or wherever.

Just south of Malta on I-87, Zarr called back and directed Girard to the Federal Courthouse on Broadway in Albany. Judge Shaw was excited about the potential of the events and would meet him at his office in the courthouse. "Use the front door on Broadway; the guard is expecting you. Keep us informed, because despite this storm, the big show is going full speed ahead in Plattsburgh." Zarr hung up.

Most of the traffic was headed north to Saratoga Springs that morning, as the season's first big stakes race was scheduled that afternoon. Little traffic was moving south, and thus Girard made excellent time. At 11:00 a.m. sharp he was jogging up the slippery marble steps of the courthouse. Inside, the guard directed him to Judge Shaw's office. Girard had never met the judge before, but there was a closeness and familiarity about the man that, for a moment, almost caused Girard to embrace him. That's a hell of a way to ask for a warrant, he stifled himself, and instead, held out a hand. Judge Shaw did likewise, then inquired, "Have we met before, Investigator Girard? You seem familiar."

"No, sir, for all my years in Troop G and now B, this is the first time I've even been in this courthouse."

"Okay, what have you got? Special Agent Zarr briefed me, but I like to hear it firsthand," Shaw said.

For the next 10 minutes, Girard revealed the specifics in the case. With the impending arrival of former President Bush in Plattsburgh, the timing now was critical. The troopers needed to know precisely what was inside the cycle shop. It might just be a state matter, but there were huge federal possibilities, and Girard said he wanted all the judicial protection he could get. Judge Shaw filled out the affidavit in longhand as Girard spoke. Such documents were usually typed when the secretary was working, but as this was urgent and a Sunday; it would stand up. When the document was complete, Shaw asked Girard to raise his right hand and swear that the information was as complete and accurate as it could be, and Girard did so.

Shaw then produced another piece of paper, a warrant that permitted the search and seizure of any incriminating items within the cycle shop. This document would also permit the arrest of any person or persons inside, if evidence of a crime seemed likely. And, Shaw noted, since the two bogus Frenchmen seemed to be working and traveling in violation of federal immigration statutes, they were fair game to be grabbed immediately if they showed up. Judge Shaw completed the warrant with a flourishing signature and held out his hand. "I always admired the first George Bush. He was a Navy flier, you know. He served his country and almost died," he stated. "The second one can go to hell, as far as I'm concerned, though. My nephew died in Fallujah in a needless war and it wasn't necessary. It just wasn't necessary," he said sadly. For a moment, the judge was somber, then looking out his window at the grey skies, asked, "You ever play canasta, Girard?"

"No, sir, I'm not much of a game player."

"Try it sometime," Shaw said. "It's kept my wife and me together for almost 50 years." Both smiled, and Girard thanked the judge for convening the hearing on such short notice. He reflected that even canasta could never have kept him with Irene for that long. Shaw reached for his cap and umbrella, and the meeting was over. They shook hands again, and Sr. Investigator Dennis Girard left the building. As he ventured out onto Broadway, there was a crack of thunder and the deluge recommenced. It was a wet walk to the courthouse parking lot.

Now, with something finally cooking, he called Tommy at Ray Brook, informing his fellow officer that he had his warrant for Skippy's. Delehanty told his friend that he'd been cleared to ride with the State Police helicopter over the lake on Monday morning, taking off from Glens Falls Airport at 5:00 a.m., if that would work into the plan. "I wanted to be looking for that Bayliner on the water at dawn, Denny. The weather service says the rain will be moving out after midnight tonight."

"Go for it, Tommy," he said. Hanging up, Girard called and updated Capt. Telfer, who had been hanging around his headquarters office, expecting such an eventuality. In fact, though Girard didn't know it, the superintendent had called Telfer more than an hour before, to make sure all the components would work together. O.H.P. Simcoe had carefully questioned the Troop B captain, "You're confident he can lead this charge, Captain Telfer?"

"Yes," Capt. Telfer had told Simcoe. "We have a new man in Girard now, and I feel confident he'll be a credit to the Division. Besides, I hear it's going to be his last cavalry charge. Did you hear of that, Superintendent?"

Though Telfer couldn't see the superintendent's smile, he could hear it. "Yes, Captain, I was *sure* that would happen." The two men rang off. Simcoe called Lt. Cole, an old-time friend, and asked him to watch out for Girard. "He has the damnedest tendency to get himself killed, Bill." Cole laughed and assured his boss that he'd watch Girard's back all the way.

CHAPTER FIFTY

Something intangible told Charbonneau that the building was under surveillance, and he cut his motor 50 yards north of the dock behind Skippy's. A blanket of mist covered the landscape and the smuggler felt confident that he could pick up his new associates and their cargo and be out on the lake before dawn's early light made him visible. His stolen Bayliner gently bumped the weathered pilings beneath Skippy's old dock, which had seen better days. He tied up snugly and, using the wharf as cover, looked around—visibility was no more than 20 feet. He climbed the ladder and slipped his way across the weeds to the cycle shop's back door. Charbonneau gave two knocks, then two more, which was the agreed-upon signal. He waited.

On the hilltop across Route 9N, Trooper Vincent stiffened. Had he heard knocks? There were no further sounds, however, and the observer relaxed.

It seemed like an hour before Corbeau's head peeked out of the doorway. As they recognized one another, Corbeau raised his forefinger to his lips. He pointed toward the roof of the interior and, though Charbonneau didn't quite understand the gesture, he was wary enough to remain silent. Marteau pointed to the three long cardboard boxes on the floor, then quietly opened them. Inside each, encased in plastic carry cases, were launchers for shoulder-fired missiles. Marteau signaled that these objects were to be moved to the rear of the boat, one at a time, with one man on each end, so there would be no slip-ups. Charbonneau and Corbeau nodded their assent, and reached for the first item. Charbonneau found it difficult to see the missiles clearly in the gloom, but there was one long projectile for each launcher. Each missile was approximately two feet long, and painted red, which was probably not the original color. A thin band of white encircled each one, and the smuggler wondered whose job it was to paint missiles.

Marteau hefted the first explosive charge, while Corbeau and Charbonneau hoisted the launcher. Slowly and quietly they moved each load into the rear of the boat. Corbeau then brought a shoulder bag and backpack containing three old TEC-9 pistols that could shoot on full automatic, along with a dozen 50-round magazines. The back door was left open, perhaps as a taunt to the police who, when they finally came to investigate, would realize that their quarry had flown, and would have to guess in which direction they had gone.

Charbonneau moved to the driver's seat and encouraged the two Frenchmen to shove off mightily but silently, as he didn't want to engage the engine until the boat was hidden in the mist. Slowly the big boat moved offshore until the buildings were lost in the swirling fog. The three long launching tubes lay on the padded rear seats. Marteau had placed all three missiles in a large, plastic case with Blaauboer's name on it. Charbonneau turned the engine over and, at slow speed, they ventured out onto the lake, moving slowly and deliberately to the south. Marteau glanced at his wristwatch. It was 5:05 a.m. and they had plenty of time to reach Whitehall, even at half speed.

Ten minutes later, two large black vans and three SUVs, along with

Girard's car pulled down into Skippy's parking lot. Instantly, all doors opened, and Girard, in body armor and with pistol drawn, joined the charge. Two state policemen dressed in black assault uniforms, hit the front door with the battering ram, and the portal flew inward and off its hinges as officers streamed around each side of the building, completely encircling it in the steady rain. Once inside the building, Girard moved quickly into the repair shop and was startled to see officers already inside. Lt. Cole, who was among the group, dejectedly told Girard that the back door had been open and the occupants, if there had been any, had fled. He had spotted many footprints in the dirt and wet grasses between the building and the dock.

The 12-man team scoured the interior, looking for anything that might give a clue to the former contents. All that remained, beside the cycles, workbench, and strewn parts, were three long, unmarked cardboard cartons on the dirty cement floor. Beds in the small lounge looked as if they had been recently used, but there was no apparent evidence of who the occupants had been. Girard was beside himself with anger, and was about to spout off, when a hand pushed him from behind, back into the garage. He was angry enough that he turned quickly to reprimand whichever officer had shoved him, but no man was closer than 15 feet. "Under the carton," said a voice. Girard leaned forward and, beneath the first cardboard carton, retrieved a packing label. It read, *SA-7a*, with some additional Cyrillic script. He knew this was an old Soviet surface-to-air missile tag. A small red hammer and sickle was stamped in the lower left-hand corner of the label, removing all doubt as to the package's origin. He'd heard enough about the SA-7s. Division explosives expert, Sgt. John Murray used to talk about them, and instantly Girard knew the entire plot.

This was it! He called Lt. Cole to his side and showed him the sticker. There was no question now about the former contents of the boxes, and Girard began inwardly to berate himself for being so short-sighted. *Of course*, they're going to be using missiles, he realized, how else to reach Bush's plane? Are these guys Russians? Who are they? Our team got in, did a thorough search, and almost missed the most important clue, but of course we had expected a fight. Girard thanked Lt. Cole and his men, telling them that it all had *not* been for nothing. "Include this tag in your report as *your* find, Bill. You guys deserve the praise and promotions." Girard took his tactical phone and called Zarr in Albany. "Zarr, it's missiles. The place was empty when we got here. There is strong evidence that those guys have shoulder-fired missiles. Looks like old Soviet jobs—

SA-7s. My guess is that they're headed north from here to hit the former President, probably from somewhere on the lake."

"I'll get that right onto the line to Plattsburgh. What have they got for transportation?" the agent inquired.

"They're likely driving a big Bayliner Trophy, probably about a 25-footer with a big outboard motor, 250 horsepower, as I recall," Girard responded. For a moment, Agent Zarr was in animated conversation with someone else on his end of the line. There was a rapid and almost heated exchange, and then Zarr returned to the line.

"We estimate about an hour's travel time for them at top speed, and that will give them plenty of time, certainly, to set up and catch the Bush plane on its descent into Plattsburgh. What are the lake conditions?"

"I don't see how they can travel flat out, Zarr, the lake is quite calm but has *a lot* of fog or mist on it, and they'll have to move cautiously so they don't hit a Monday morning fisherman or someone who's been anchored overnight," Girard responded.

"Bush is scheduled to speak at noon," Zarr ventured. "I'm convening an emergency meeting of our Task Force within the hour, and I'll get that information on the tac frequency right now, to all *our* officers, and the Secret Service. We'll also copy State Police, Border Patrol, Homeland Security, and ICE and the Vermont State Police. Be sure you notify your captain. Now, because explosive devices are definitely involved, I'm sending our FBI explosives expert, Ray Vadnais, up to Plattsburgh too—fast, to head up that part of the defense; I hope he's in time. In any case, we know what their weapons are; the only question is—where are they going to use them? Looks like Plattsburgh, for sure. Good work, Girard. We'll get those bastards yet! Keep us up to date." Zarr hung up.

Girard then called Tommy, who was still waiting on the ground at Glens Falls Airport. "The ground fog makes the pilot hesitant about going up until some of it burns off," Delehanty said, "because he wants to fly at one thousand feet and doesn't want to look at just the top of the mist. We won't be able to see any boats from up there until some of this stuff clears." Girard told his friend that all evidence pointed to the bad guys heading north, and that all available security was rushing to Plattsburgh. Essex County Sheriff's Marine Enforcement Unit was on the tac frequencies and already knew what their quarry would look like.

Tommy's problem was likewise Charbonneau's, Girard reminded him. There was almost no visibility on the lake at Port Henry, and this wasn't the St. Lawrence, where a boat driver could make a single, point-to-point high-speed run. It was also a bet that Charbonneau didn't know Lake Champlain's waters, so he, too, might have to proceed slowly, whether or not he had charts. Before he hung up, Girard notified his friend that the forensics investigation at Skippy's would be run by the Feds; however, unofficially, he'd asked Troop B's FIU to send a man, and Kenny Quinn would be there in 15 minutes. "Knowing Kenny, he'll probably push the envelope and bring his buddy, Shaloub, also. I'll wait for them, to see what those wizards turn up, and then I can call you or jump on it myself. Hey, take care of yourself, Tommy," he said.

Driver Lucky Stotz arrived at Stouffer's Refuse Service garage in Wadhams at 7:00 a.m. and was surprised not to see Buck unlocking the gas pump. In any case, I know where the key is, he assured himself, and reached inside the kitchenette door toward the hook on the right. "Funny, where's Buck?" he asked aloud. He started his truck, drove to the fuel pump and began gassing his vehicle for the morning run. Then it occurred to him that Buck's truck was missing. Maybe he's already out on an early run, Lucky figured. At that moment, Sandy Bognar pulled in, also ready to begin his day of refuse hauling. "Where's Buck?" he asked, unlocking his truck door.

"I don't know, Sandy. He must have left early, maybe some special run. But, now that I think about it, there were no tire tracks in the driveway mud after two days of rain. Maybe he's out back doing something. I'll go see," Lucky offered.

Within a minute he was back, his face as white as a sheet. "Aw shit, Sandy, you're not going to believe this." He vomited on the driveway dirt. "Buck's truck is back there, and Buck is *inside*—underneath the ram. He's *dead*, Sandy!"

"Under the ram? How the hell does a guy like Buck do that?" Bognar asked, sidestepping the pool of vomit between himself and his fellow driver. "God, it can't be an accident. I'd better call the Sheriff." With that, Bognar stepped inside the kitchenette building and placed a call to the Sheriff's investigators.

It was almost 40 minutes before Essex County Sheriff's Investigator Mark Stubblefield arrived. He took a few notes from both Stotz and Bognar before asking to see the body. From the outset, the investigator ruled out suicide, as no man can trigger the packer truck's ram from inside the bay. He called for the State Police Forensics Unit, but was told that it might be noon before the team could come—a priority request had just come in from Port Henry. Stubblefield courteously thanked the trooper, but inwardly cursed his luck. It was going to be a hot day, once the mist burned off, and that garbage, including Buck, was not going to be smelling very sweet by the time the FIU showed up. Wadhams was not killer country, and this crime scene needed interpretation immediately, he reasoned, kicking at a plastic bag that blew across the parking area. He put in a call to fellow investigator Sherwin Bowen to come as soon as he could, to help assess the situation.

Resuming his questioning of the drivers, Stubblefield discovered that Stouffer's light yellow, three-quarter-ton pickup truck was missing. "You shouldn't have any trouble finding it because it's got Stouffer Refuse painted on the side," Lucky informed the investigator. Stubblefield called the office and reported the stolen vehicle, now potentially being driven by the murderer. He turned once more to study the horrible-smelling, dead fish parts that partially obscured Buck's legs. This guy and those fish have been here a long time, he concluded.

CHAPTER FIFTY-ONE

Finished filing his flight plan, Capt. Mike Jeppesen strode across the tarmac outside the Operations Center at Portsmouth International Airport in New Hampshire. It was a fine morning on a day that promised beautiful flying weather west to Plattsburgh. It would be nice to see his former duty station again, he realized, not having been there since his Air Force service days from 1981-83. He loved coming in over the northern part of Lake Champlain, then doing his final approach onto Runway 16. His plane, a Gulfstream 4, leased from Conoco Oil Corporation, sat on the apron, fueled, pre-flighted, and waiting. His copilot, Jimmy Morzillo, waited inside the cockpit, attending to small details until the Bush caravan arrived.

Precisely at 10:15 a.m., two large, black limousines pulled into the FBO parking lot and three men and a woman dressed in black emerged from the first vehicle. Another man dressed in black emerged from the Operations Center and greeted them, giving the thumbs-up signal that all was clear. Secret Service Agent Tim Lagoe walked quickly to the second vehicle, gave the thumbs-up, and the 41st President of the United States, George Herbert Walker Bush, emerged. He had just celebrated his 84th birthday, and appeared vigorous and enthusiastic about his new role in the Republican Party. "So, we're off to plow some new ground, Michael," he said to Jeppesen. Dressed in tan slacks and a blue and white sport shirt, and carrying a briefcase, Bush entered the plane and took his customary rear seat. Glancing around, he remembered the days when the planes were bigger and the role more demanding, but he tossed the thought away with a sigh. If I'm anything, he mulled, it's adaptable!

Secret Service Agent, Joan Convery entered the cabin, followed by Agent Crayford Hattlee. The last man in was Agent Robertson Baker, crew chief on the former President's tour. Briefly, Baker spoke to Jeppesen regarding the increased possibility of a missile attack. The State Police along Lake Champlain had verified that the enemy had missiles. Then Gulfstream 526 began to roll, with Jeppesen requesting taxi and takeoff instructions. He was given permission for immediate takeoff on runway 34. Minutes after its 10:28 a.m. takeoff, as 526 went through 2,000 feet, the tower called, giving him a vector to the west:

"Gulfstream 526 you're okayed to 6,000 on a heading of 280. Contact Departure Control on 132.3 and then contact Boston Center. Good day, sir."

"Portsmouth Tower, thanks, and see you again soon," Jeppesen returned, switching his frequency and making contact with Boston Center, which would direct him to Plattsburgh through Burlington, VT's air space.

Boston Center immediately responded. *"Gulfstream 526 you are cleared to flight level 200."*

Once they reached their assigned altitude, Agent Baker made a call on his satellite phone: *Voodoo ground, this is Voodoo air. How do you read?"* Agent Gerald Bloom, with the Secret Service ground unit at Burlington, responded that all was well, though his detail had learned of the heightened assassination potential. He was in touch with the security detail at Plattsburgh and it promised to be a clear day by noontime, but again, the danger of attack was heightened. The Clinton County Sheriff's Marine Enforcement Unit was clearing all civilian boats 10 miles away from the Plattsburgh waterfront to the north and south, Bloom related, and a call had just gone in to the Vermont State Police lake patrol to do likewise until further notice on the eastern lakeshore. In essence, there would be a 20-mile, no-go zone on the surface of Lake Champlain until Bush finished and moved south.

Baker responded that Voodoo had been informed of the enhanced threat, and felt certain that the large security force would protect him.

"That's what *he* says, but when things are going too well, that's when I'm most suspicious," Baker muttered. He had the ultimate authority to call off the flight, but was persuaded by Bush's confidence and determination to continue a bit farther.

Spectators began showing up at Plattsburgh International quite early for the noontime rally. There had not been a national political figure of note in Plattsburgh since Mrs. Clinton came to campaign for the U.S. Senate in October 2006. At the outer barricade off Route 22, a state policeman from the Plattsburgh Barracks looked closely into each car's interior, asking if the driver was at the airport for the Bush rally. If so, they were directed through the manned radiation and explosives detectors into a marked corridor leading onto Idaho Avenue, at the far end of which was the rally parking lot. At that point, an FBI agent instructed all passengers to leave the vehicles. All visitors were then to walk around the end of the FBO building, and through the gate. From there, they were escorted to the temporary seating grandstands that had been erected near the base of the control tower. Carol Monroe and her Dixie All-Stars provided jazzy music for the event from a small bandstand nearby, creating a festive atmosphere. Four Secret Service agents, directed by Agent Donahue, patrolled the area between the grandstand and the FBO building's podium.

At the north end of the airstrip, facing east from the northernmost National Guard hanger, a single New York State Police cruiser stood watching the gap between the hangars and the large maintenance building five hundred yards straight ahead, even though no civilian traffic was expected at that end of the runway. Trooper Phil Shepherd, from the Plattsburgh Barracks, was informed that official airport vehicles, each sporting a yellow caution dome light, might on occasion move down the flight apron, but all were instructed to pass in front of the trooper's car. Neither could any vehicle, official or not, approach within two hundred yards of the speaker's podium, as tack strips blocked the route.

Three hundred yards closer to Bush's podium, to Shepherd's right, was the first Secret Service vehicle of Voodoo Ground, with Agent Cunningham likewise parked facing the facility's buildings. Another one hundred yards closer on the apron, near "the throat," the old passage into the Nose Dock buildings, was a second Secret Service van, with Agent Fiedler on watch. Any vehicle would have to pass in front of all three positions, and any dangerous car or SUV could be quickly rammed, pushed and cornered against the buildings. Beyond Agent Fiedler's position was a series of tack strips to puncture any vehicle's tires.

At the south end of the airstrip, near the tower and the pad where Bush's plane would park, sat Agent Norman Frederick in another of the black Secret Service vans. Such surveillance patterns had always worked—limit the area in which the crowd can move, and always have an established escape route if something goes wrong. The greatest danger to the former President, Frederick surmised, would most likely come from someone in the crowd, and not a vehicle. His orders were to prevent people on foot from passing his position in either direction.

Agent Alvarez stood in the control tower, monitoring the communications channels. He could hear the Vermont State Police Marine Patrol just giving their "all clear" from the eastern side of the lake, and Clinton County Sheriff cruisers affirming the push-back of all surface boats to the south of Valcour Island and north of Algonquin Park Road above the city. Two Secret Service snipers had joined Alvarez in the tower and were already at work with field glasses, scanning the growing throng from above. If there was any question about a visitor's handbag as she approached from the parking lot, these observers called to an agent on the ground to do an inspection before the person came within the gate. All backpacks were given a cursory inspection also. The snipers hoped their rifles wouldn't be necessary.

At Glens Falls Airport, pilot Gordon Nesselbank lifted off at 10:02. Trooper James Spulnik checked over his sniper's rifle, making sure it was ready if the need arose. As he always did, Spulnik licked his left thumb and pulled it across the rifle's front sight. He grinned at passenger Inv. Tommy Delehanty, "Gives me luck," he said. On the intercom, Nesselbank asked Delehanty where he wanted to start his search for Charbonneau. "He's got to be headed north toward Plattsburgh, Gordon, and I'm guessing that he'll try to stay in the just-offshore traffic to the east, now that the mist is almost burned off."

"Sounds good to me," Nesselbank returned, moving his craft to one thousand feet as they passed over Dresden. "How about I head straight to Port Henry and follow his trail northward from there?"

"Sure, go ahead," Tommy said, and the trio laughed in anticipation of a quick arrest. Nesselbank moved his stick slightly to the left and the big Bell helicopter sped north.

Quinn and Shaloub, from the Troop B FIU, had quickly reached Skippy's at 9:10 a.m. and photographed the scene. They did little other forensic work because of the federal boys arriving soon. FBI forensics arrived at 10:05, having hurried north from Albany. The FBI team invited

Quinn and Shaloub to accompany them. FBI Agent Joe Cochrane soon hunched over the first cardboard container, which Girard had kicked and underneath which he had found the SA-label. Cochrane's "aha," echoed in the silent building, as each investigator worked quietly in photographing scenes or taking scrapings. He called Quinn to his side and asked, "Ever see this stuff before?" Quinn looked at the off-white trace of powder. "Looks like the high explosive that was in our mortar rounds when I was in Vietnam. Cordite?"

"You got it, Quinn," came Cochrane's answer. "One of those missiles, assuming they have three rounds, has got a slight leak—it must have been dropped or something. Part of the solid rocket propellant has broken away inside. So now, there's no question what you're up against. We'll have this at the forensics lab in Albany within hours and do the chemical tests, but I'm sure that's what this is. There's a smell to cordite, even when it's not exploded."

For another hour, the two forensics teams measured, scraped, vacuumed, and dusted for fingerprints. To Girard, it was all part of the big opera going on around him, but, glancing at his wristwatch, he could see it was now 11:23. The big show was going up in Plattsburgh in a bit more than a half hour.

"Cochrane, tell me what you know about the SA-7a's," he asked.

"Well, almost nobody uses the early models anymore—not even the Boy Scouts—because they really can't pick out a specific heat source very well. They're heat-seeking missiles, as I'm sure you know. If you have a lit candle closer to the shooter than a jet plane, you're likely going to kill the candle before the jet. And the shooter has to lead a fast plane, or they'll never hit it, so the operators have to have some practice to be good. A good pilot can outmaneuver such a missile, if he knows one is on the way. That's why the Ruskies have made lots more advanced models. They and the Chinese have stuff today that you don't want to mess with, and I don't care what the news says, neither of them are our friends."

Then Cochrane smiled again. "Of course, we have *our* good stuff too. And, Girard, one of those missiles is damaged in some way. Somebody must have somehow dropped it or banged it, so it has lost some propellant. See, here I just showed Quinn some of this stuff—it's cordite, the explosive inside. How much has leaked out during its transportation, I can't guess. But there's still enough explosive to mess up a plane pretty good if it's a direct hit. And, they've likely got two more good ones. Depends on which one they pick up first. Whoever supplied this batch of missiles and launchers must have bought them online—discount models. Someone else must have thrown them away. Nevertheless, they're dangerous in professional hands."

CHAPTER FIFTY-TWO

At 11:38 a.m., Capt. Jeppesen again called Boston Center:

"Boston Center, this is Gulfstream 526 special, on flight plan Voodoo from Portsmouth, requesting a route to Papa, Bravo, Gulf."

"Gulfstream 526 special, turn left on heading 225 and descend to 16,000," came Boston's reply. One minute later came: *"Gulfstream 526 special, Boston Center. Go to a new heading of 340 degrees and descend to 10,000. Contact Burlington Tower on 121.1."*

Twenty miles ahead, the flight crew could see America's sixth Great Lake coming at them fast, and 526 began its passage through the air space of Vermont's largest airport. Switching his radio communication to Burlington, Jeppesen was given a new vector, and then the tower transmitted: *"Good afternoon, sir. You're on VFR, and do you have the runway in sight?"*

Co-pilot Morzillo noted the ASOS wind, weather, and altimeter at Plattsburgh and called, "Burlington Tower, this is Gulfstream 526 special, I have Runway 35 lined up. Thanks and good day."

The prevailing winds had changed and Jeppesen didn't get his favorite runway, but the scene of Plattsburgh's white buildings along the deep, blue lake still inspired him. Aware of the danger by water, he was surprised to see almost no boats for miles to the south. Apparently, the government security folks had chased them all out of what looked like a 20-mile space. Descent was rapid and Gulfstream 526 was quickly on the ground, rolling out leisurely to taxi way Alpha, near the site of the old National Guard hangers. So much for missiles off the lake, Jeppesen reassured himself.

He taxied quickly to the Fixed Base Operations building apron, where the large crowd was gathered. Stragglers were still entering the gate and onto the concrete apron near where Mr. Bush's platform had been installed in front of the FBO building. Secret Service had chosen to have a solid structure at the former President's back. Democrats and

Republicans alike were happy to see a vigorous, octogenarian former Chief Executive, a man whose retirement energy had only been equaled by the recently deceased former President Gerald Ford. Bush's ceremony was scheduled for noon.

Jeppesen taxied to the pad just two hundred feet from the podium. It was decided to bring the plane in fairly close to the podium in case of a quick departure. As all engines stopped, the onboard Secret Service detail deployed from the plane's door first, and then, on a signal from Agent Baker, Mr. Bush descended to the ground. The Dixie All-Stars broke into "The Yellow Rose of Texas." A great hurrah rose from the crowd and the former President began shaking the hands of dignitaries.

Dr. Bernice Epstein closed and locked her car door at the rear of the Idaho Avenue parking lot. She figured she'd be late, simply because of the security checkpoints coming in. Now, as the roar arose, she knew Mr. Bush was on the ground, though it was only 10 minutes until noon. She made sure her straw hat was on tight, and semi-jogged toward the FBO gate. Directly in front of her stood a uniformed New York State trooper, and for a minute, she didn't recognize him, but it was Dennis Girard! "Well hello, Dennis, it's good to see you, I didn't...."

"Go home now, Doctor. Turn around, get in your car, and go directly home. This is no place for you," the figure said. He then vanished in mid-air. Bernice stood amazed. Strangely, she also knew what it was. It was a bi-location, sometimes performed by the holy men and women of the East. How it worked, she didn't know, but she also understood the phenomenon to be a profound spiritual event. I'll have to ask Dennis how he did that at next month's session. "Well, Mr. Bush," she sighed, "I guess I'll have to get to know you another day." Turning, she doffed her hat, and got into the car, driving out Idaho Avenue and turning right toward the exit gate. The FBI Agent stationed there signaled for her to stop. "Have you been in the Idaho Avenue parking lot?" he asked.

"Yes, but I suddenly got sick, and have decided to go home," she replied. Agent Eddie Phillips felt something was fishy and ordered her to pull to the right, turn off her engine, and hand him the keys. Dr. Epstein knew she was in some kind of trouble, and asked, "Is it the peace rally I attended in Burlington back in '92?"

"Lady, I don't know what you're talking about, but please give me some identification," Phillips countered. Dr. Epstein fished in her purse and brought out both her New York State drivers license, and also her membership card for the American Psychological Association, an organization of psychotherapists and researchers. "This is me," she said, "I'm a doctor and counselor, and as you can see, I have an office here in Plattsburgh. I have to go home."

Phillips inspected the documents, then stepped away from the window and walked behind the car. Checking her rear plate, he stood in the car's "blind spot" and called in the license tag number. New York State Motor Vehicles confirmed both the license and registration. There was no plausible reason for him to detain her further, so he stepped to the car window and returned her documents, thanked her for her patience, and pointed the way out of the gate. "I hope you're feeling better, Doctor," he called after her.

All the way back to her apartment, Bernice mumbled to herself. "'Harm no living thing,' the Buddha said. Boy, that FBI man is lucky, or I'd have popped him. Well, the *former* Bernice would have, anyway. I'll go home and watch it all on the local news," she decided, having seen the WPTZ, Channel 5 broadcast van in the parking lot.

Gordon Nesselbank turned to his passengers and yelled, "Well, we're pretty far north of the city and haven't seen a single big Bayliner between Port Henry and Plattsburgh. He can't be on the lake, or the three of us would have spotted him. Either he's gone to shore and is in some vehicle, or he didn't go north from Port Henry. All we can do up here is burn fuel. You wanna go south and look again as we go? We can also go south from Port Henry, although if those guys went south, they're probably long gone."

"We have no other choice, Gordon. Turn it around and we'll keep our eyes peeled," Delehanty called back. The big Bell 430 turned and headed south at 140 knots. Delehanty felt an energy drain—had he failed his partner? Had he somehow let the bad guys escape? And, if the enemy had missiles, as they surely did, how could their chopper prevent the assassination of a former President?

The truth, however, was less disastrous. Two miles south of the Crown Point Bridge, about 35 miles short of his goal in Whitehall, Louie Two Claw Charbonneau was in trouble. Travel in the fog had been slow at best. He was not familiar with the southern, narrower part of the lake, and after passing beneath the bridge, had hugged the western shore, looking for landmarks. He knew that the village of Crown Point would be coming up on the right. He asked his passengers to be spotters, but distracted, they continued to jabber away in some foreign language that he couldn't understand. And not understanding a conversation always angered him because he felt dumb. And he couldn't *stand* feeling dumb!

So intent had he been in sighting the village, that he didn't realize he was running out of water. Suddenly, just after he raised his speed to 25 miles an hour, there was a great sigh beneath the hull and the boat was instantly surrounded by vegetation—rushes, cattails—whatever they were called. The propeller of the big outboard motor suddenly stopped, its motor's drive shaft wrapped tightly in grasses and other vegetation. The boat was dead in the water and he was aground on a mud flat. He realized what had happened, and knew that completing his mission would be a big problem unless his two shipmates immediately helped him untangle the propeller and the engine could be restarted. "And here's hoping I didn't break the shear pin when it stopped," he groaned. For the past 30 minutes the trio had sat in the boat, angrily disputing which of them was to go into the water to begin the arduous task of cutting away the reeds from the propeller and its shaft. Marteau was the one with a stiletto knife—*he* should be the one to jump overboard, Louie argued. The water was only two to three feet deep in spots.

Charbonneau considered himself the captain of the boat and his passengers were the hired help. A warrior of his stature didn't go into the water, but as the time passed and it was now after 11:45, he knew that he had to swallow his pride and go over the side. His stomach hurt badly, and he grabbed for another licorice stick. There was only one piece left in the pack, and he needed to resolve the tension. Grabbing at Marteau's knife, he jumped into the muck and sank almost to his knees. The grasses seemed like wire, and he could only cut one strand at a time when he could even pry a section loose from the motor's drive shaft. It was hot, and now the sun was rapidly dispersing the fog. If a plane came overhead, they'd spot him and radio for help...unless it was the FBI! Then *they* would swoop down and arrest or kill them all. And Charbonneau had resolved never to return to jail; so such an attack would mean his death in any case, he knew. Then, the worst thing happened. A helicopter did swoop down from overhead—it was the State Police, and here he was with a jammed propeller. He cut furiously, thankful for the moment that a remaining cloud of fog obscured him from the helicopter that was coming around again. With the last of the rushes off the shaft, he turned the propeller and was gratified to feel resistance; the shear pin had not broken.

In Port Henry, Sr. Investigator Dennis Girard was numb. So near, and yet so far, he grumbled to himself. He'd found the bad guys' weapon of choice, he knew where they'd gone, how they'd done it, and what they intended to do in Plattsburgh. Even though he was a member of the Joint Terrorism Task Force, here he was, reduced to watching a forensics crew pack up and head back to Albany. Whatever happens, it isn't going to involve *me*, he groused. Well, maybe that is as it should be. It's time to retire, I guess; hang it up and visit with Doc every month. All my battles are behind me, and I'd best get used to it.

"Delehanty to Girard. Come in!" his radio crackled on the State Police channel. This was not a Task Force call, but one made directly to him.

"What's up, Tommy?"

"Den, I found the bastards. I mean, I've spotted Louie's boat. He and his two passengers seem stuck in the mud just above Crown Point Village, where Putnam Creek enters the lake. We're overhead, but he's working furiously to get free. There! There! He just jumped into the boat. We're going to try staying overhead. Any way you can get here? They've got guns out and are shooting up at us."

"You bet there *is*, Tommy. Watch the bastards. I mean, watch those bad people—I've got transportation. Girard out." Without explaining himself to the others, Girard ran to his car, spun out of the parking lot, then took the first left onto Harbour Lane. His destination was Nicky Quatro's boat shop. He slid to a long stop in front of the old PT boat, jumped out, and yelled for Nick. "Nick, hey Nicky!" The proprietor came out of the repair shop, slowly wiping his hands on an oily rag.

"Hey, Nicky. Last time we spoke a few months ago, you said you wanted to know if ever you could go to war with me. Still mean that?"

Stunned by what he considered a joke, Quatro smiled and said, "Sure Dennis, who we gonna kill?"

"I'm serious, Nicky. Can you crank up that big boat and head us south?"

"You're serious, aren't you, Girard? Hell yes!" He dropped his rag, ran into the shop, got the boat keys, and trotted with Girard to the biggest, most frightening machine that the investigator had ever seen on the water. "Where we goin', Girard?" he asked.

Investigator Girard was just closing his car trunk, having grabbed his body armor vest and three clips of ammunition for his Glock from his carry bag. "Nick, we're going to aim for a swamp just above Crown Point Village. You know it?"

Quatro jumped into the cockpit, turned the ignition key and the monster boat, which Quatro had named "Tango Twelve," fired up. "Cast off all lines," Nicky instructed, and Girard hurried to comply. Slowly at first, the big boat gained momentum, heading directly eastward toward the center of the lake. "Hell, yes, I know that swamp. Right at Putt's Creek. Anybody who's ever run a boat on this lake learns where it is…one way or another!" Quatro turned to grin at Girard, then threw the throttles forward. "You're gonna need that seat, Girard," he said to his companion, motioning for his passenger to get fully into the left-hand passenger's seat. "You'd better sit and strap in, then I'll show you a trick. Is there going to be gunplay, Dennis?"

"You bet your ass there's going to be gunplay, Nicky. And, if that's *all* there is, you can consider yourself lucky! Too bad you don't have torpedos!" The boat shot through the water and Girard couldn't believe his eyes. The speedometer registered 80 and the needle kept climbing, yet there was almost no bounce on the waves. The big Fountain Lightning, a 38-foot-long speedboat with twin 600 HP engines, was literally boring its way through the wave tops. The RPMs kept rising, and the speedometer needle continued to climb. Now it stood at 98 miles per hour and the Crown Point Bridge could be seen across the bay. Moving toward the eastern half of the channel, Quatro continued to gun the engines, which left small rooster-tails behind them.

CHAPTER FIFTY-THREE

Faust Hetzer had taken every back road possible to drive from Wadhams to Plattsburgh. He had tried to stay off the major state routes and the Interstate, because he was sure Buck's body had been found, and a bulletin would be issued for either the truck or him, or both. It was five minutes before noon and he was agitated. He hated to be upset. Finally, he made his turn onto Route 22. The big water tower that marked Plattsburgh International loomed to his right. A sheriff's car zoomed past, going the other direction—had he been spotted? Hetzer watched in the rearview mirror—apparently not. He knew his truck was an attention getter, and he wanted to simply penetrate the base, get at least behind the passenger terminal, park the truck, and just walk away. There was the bogus deputy, standing with her hands on the old rusted gate. He gave her two flashes of the headlights, and she opened the gate onto the old air base "back trail." Good thing she's not real, he chuckled, and waved to her as he passed through. The large passenger terminal was now straight ahead, but it was 10 minutes after noon. Sally Reid walked away too, across the road to her parked Gran Prix. At that moment, the sheriff's car returned, this time to stop and chat with a fellow deputy who, for some reason, was driving a civilian car. She knew the ball game was over for her.

A half mile ahead, he could see the tiny figures of the throng. One of them was the oligarch fascist, Bush! Hetzer kept the terminal in front of him as a screen. To appear official, he even turned on his yellow flashing dome light—that might buy him some time. The concrete apron was just ahead, but there on his left was a State Police car. Yes, but he was pointed away, facing the maintenance buildings. Hetzer drove quickly behind the trooper. Either he'd been seen or not. He drove behind the line of hangers, which would screen him from the trooper's scrutiny for quite a distance. Now, he slowed, so the vehicle would appear as a regular service vehicle. The crowd was now more visible and he could make out the old traffic control tower above the farthest buildings. He was going to get this *done*!

A movement in his rearview mirror caught Trooper Shepherd's attention. Had something shot behind him as he watched a food service truck ahead of him? He craned his neck but nothing seemed to be out of the ordinary. Then, there it was again, just for a second, at the far end of the hangars. Whatever it was, it didn't belong! He turned the wheel and, flipping his lights on, began a rapid pursuit.

Agent Cunningham caught the bright light movement off to his left and wondered for a second what was up. Then he saw the yellow truck. It wasn't a service vehicle, and in fact, had the suspect Stouffer's Refuse on its side. He had just heard about it on the tac channel—this was an enemy vehicle. Slapping his big Yukon into drive, he shot forward to intercept the vehicle coming from his left, and which was now picking up speed. He had to cut it off or they'd *all* be refuse.

Hetzer realized he'd been spotted and recognized in an instant that he'd never walk away from this one. His remote detonators would no longer serve his purposes. The *Scheisskopf* Bush must not escape! He knew he had to deliver this message in person. Cunningham's vehicle came straight at his right side, and now there was a trooper vehicle in pursuit, red and blue roof lights spinning frantically. With the black SUV about a hundred feet away, Hetzer swerved to his left, toward the nearest large building. His passenger window was already open, and he hefted his M11-A1 pistol with oversize magazine, balancing it on the windowsill.

He fired intermittent bursts of five shots, blowing out the Yukon's windshield on the first volley, then killing the driver with the second burst. The big, black vehicle turned to its right and rolled over, skidding his way on its side, but Hetzer was losing control of his own vehicle.

The second black vehicle now came directly at him, with Agent Fiedler driving. She knew there would be gunfire and swerved to her left, then back to the right. Hetzer had just straightened once more, aiming his vehicle toward the podium in the distance, and attempted to fire at this second SUV, but his pistol kept bouncing on the window sill when it fired, and he couldn't hold it on target. She was getting closer—he was dead, he knew, and clicked a button on a lead cord, screaming at the top of his lungs, *"Ich bin die Faust!"*

Just as Fiedler's vehicle hit the pickup truck and drove it quickly ahead and into "the throat," a fireball engulfed the north central section of the airport buildings. Twenty-five pounds of Semtex had finally found its destiny. Then, two seconds later, a huge secondary explosion erupted as the jet fuel storage tanks at that location were touched off.

Secret Service Agent Kearney was the first to throw himself in front of former President Bush, who had just finished his speech when the first Secret Service vehicle had been hit. Kearney rushed from his position at the front left of Mr. Bush's platform to protect the man, throwing the 84-year-old to the platform and shielding Mr. Bush with his own body.

In a blur, several things happened simultaneously. The control tower windows popped open and long rifles were extended, pointing in the direction of the rolled vehicle. The force of the distant blast instantly shattered those panes of glass, causing the wounded snipers to dive inside, where Agent Alvarez was trying to make sense of the radio chatter. All he had heard clearly was the code word, "snowball," which signaled an attempt on the former President's life. Then the world blew apart. Screams from the assemblage filled the air. The bleachers had taken the full force of the blast, even though the explosions had taken place a quarter of a mile away. Bush's podium flew southward, just missing the parked jet.

The Secret Service team jumped to their feet and Mr. Bush, shielded by a protective phalanx of agents, was hustled in front of and away from the platform. The vehicle escape plan to the northeast gate was immediately vetoed by Agent Baker, and security moved their charge into the plane, which Jeppesen had already started. Agents Lagoe, Baker, Hattlee and Convery were inside when Baker slammed the door and yelled, "Go!" They rolled in a tight circle past the bloody and inert body of FBI agent

Donahue on the pavement in front of the speaker's stand.

Gulfsteam 526 special revved its engines and moved rapidly to taxiway Charlie, and without pausing, turned quickly right onto the runway. The captain threw his throttles full forward, and the plane shot down the runway like an orange and white dart, climbing into the air in the minimum space and time. Jeppesen didn't know fully what had happened, but the explosion's flying debris had missed his windshield by inches. This was big trouble, he knew, but the Secret Service had trained him well in evasive maneuvers, if such were needed. Nevertheless, those maneuvers only worked in the air!

"Burlington Tower, this is Gulfstream 526 in emergency, requesting altitude immediately en route to Glens Falls."

"Gulfstream 526, Burlington Tower. Go immediately to 10,000 feet on a heading of 210. Contact Boston Center on 124.52. Good luck!"

Burlington Tower had been notified by Voodoo Ground in Burlington as to the identity of the plane's occupants, and a note had been made on the flight plan. They were airborne, but none of the crew and passengers believed they were out of danger. Only Mr. Bush seemed unperturbed.

Agent Baker was immediately on his phone with supervisors, regarding whether the tour should be continued. Baker wanted the trip aborted and the emergency flight plan to be followed. Mr. Bush kept shaking his hand side to side in response to that suggestion. Voodoo Ground in Plattsburgh radioed that they had found enough of the Stouffer Refuse truck's side panel to presume that Hetzer had been the instigator. Baker's superiors told him he'd know soon enough whether or not there were co-conspirators. "If they have missiles, now is the time they'll use them against us while we're at low altitude," Agent Lagoe said grimly. "If there's more than one bad guy, there's bound to be a follow-up attempt." But headed west, Capt. Jeppesen saw nothing abnormal on radar. "Looks like we're clear," he called back to the former President and his retinue.

Mr. Bush was remarkably calm, trusting fully in the Secret Service's established protocols. "Well, I said what I needed to say before I was interrupted, though I don't think anybody can remember it now! From the size of that crater back there, the ground sure got plowed in a way that I never expected," he frowned.

Behind and below them, many of the Plattsburgh International Airport buildings lay in a shambles beneath the deep black smoke that rose to two thousand feet. On the emergency channel, Agent Convery heard a babel of calls for emergency vehicles for the dead and injured. "There's nothing we can do to help them but pray," she murmured. How to protect Mr. Bush was now her only concern, and that of her companions.

On the ground, they always had plenty of alternate routes to take, all determined before any event, so there was always a choice of escape routes when the crazies made their moves. But in the air, everybody can see you and where you're going. Without a fighter escort, there is nothing to do but hope. Unfortunately, the Gulfstream had no counter-measures capability against missiles. Two minutes later, Boston Center called once more, clearing the plane to flight level 250. *"You're safe there,"* the controller said to Jeppesen. Yeah, but I have to come down sometime, too, the captain thought. ETA for Glens Falls Airport was 1:05. With no tower, he was free to maneuver under Visual Flight Rules, and would do his best to get the craft down with all aboard safe.

At home, Dr. Bernice Epstein was astounded at the activity she saw on her television screen. Dumbfounded, she plopped into her easy chair, staring vacantly at the picture. Dennis Girard chased me away, was all that she could think with any clarity. If I'd have stayed there...her thoughts faded away.

CHAPTER FIFTY-FOUR

The northern end of Plattsburgh International Airport was essentially destroyed. The front of the new passenger terminal was entirely gone. The northern maintenance buildings were nearly demolished, while a huge airstrip snowplow truck was turned on its back 40 yards from its parking spot. The facades of both Nose Dock buildings were gone, and most of the volunteers inside were badly injured or dead. The Clinton County Emergency dispatcher was frantic, trying to field all the emergency calls.

FBI agents and Sheriff's deputies were hurrying uninjured visitors to the parking lot and off the airport grounds. Few of the cars had been damaged, as they had been shielded from the blast by the extensive building complex. EMTs and volunteers were trying to triage the injured. A dozen bodies were already recovered and shrouded in blue plastic tarps, while others were being pulled toward a temporary morgue in the spot where Mr. Bush's airplane had stood just a half-hour before. Though the Channel 5 cameraman, Jack Collins, was dead, Barbara Wilson, the station's reporter, had hoisted the camera to her shoulder and was doing a voice-over as she panned the scene of carnage. She was unaware that she was splashed with Collins's blood and had a cut forehead. What had begun as a "fluff coverage job," was now the biggest story in America.

City Police Chief Burt Valachovic huddled with FBI agents Phillips and Van Loan. Just getting help for the injured was a massive task. Valachovic's initial estimate was that there were 50 persons dead and at least 400 injured. Many airport staff were missing and the facility was inoperable except for emergency helicopters. Every emergency squad within six counties had all their vehicles on the way. Three rigs were on the way from Montreal, with special permission granted by the chief of the Border Patrol. There were just not enough hospital facilities available in the North Country, with the injured being taken a hundred miles in every direction. Ambulances were also crossing the lake from St. Albans and Burlington, VT, as quickly as the ferry could move them. This clearly was the biggest North Country disaster in years, and worst of all, it was a man-made one.

Nicky Quatro gunned his big Lightning beneath the Crown Point Bridge at 95 miles per hour. They were chasing a boat that was fast, but only by half. They'd catch the craft before it reached the Narrows below Ticonderoga, and they had to. When spotted by Charbonneau, Girard knew there would be gunfire. And to escape that, Quatro would need lots of maneuvering room, which wouldn't exist south of the Narrows. Faster and faster, the boat shot through the lower lake, and Quatro motioned Girard to come closer so he could hear. The driver told him to find the button on his seat and push it, while bracing his feet against the foot panel. Girard did so, and was amazed to find his seat rising and straightening him to a standing position, while wrapping itself around his torso. "If you're gonna shoot at them bastards, you at least ought to be steady," Nicky yelled and grinned. The position was wonderful for his shooting needs, Girard considered, but he'd need goggles to keep his eyes clear at this speed. But for now, he reasoned, I have nothing to shoot at.

"We just took a hit, Denny," Delehanty radioed to his old partner below. "Gordon got down too far, and they hit our fuel tank. We are losing gas fast and gotta go, but will set down as close as we can…maybe at the fort—that good enough? Drive them ashore there. Looks like you may even catch them before Ti, but try to push them into that Fort Ti cove." Girard responded affirmatively, thanking Tommy, Gordon, and Spulnik. The latter was fuming that he hadn't gotten off a round against the scum below, but was happy that they'd be caught.

Charbonneau rejoiced to see the helicopter suddenly fly off, and he continued to drive south. Before him was the Fort Ticonderoga Ferry, slowly running a green car across to Shoreham on the Vermont shore. On the long, flat ferry boat, a man and woman stood waving at his rapidly approaching boat. "*Canaille!*" he screamed at them. Suddenly, Corbeau hit Louie on the back, yelling something about a chase. Charbonneau dared only a peek to the rear, as he didn't want to hit the ferry that was dangerously close ahead.

Corbeau indicated a large, high-speed boat approaching rapidly from the rear. Louie was filled with a mixture of admiration for the size and speed of the craft, and a loathing for the man he knew was pursuing him— *le bâtard Girard*! The chasing boat was no more than one hundred yards behind him now and closing fast. Charbonneau turned his wheel to the right, beginning to zig-zag in case Girard fired at him.

The first bullet from Girard's Glock 9mm. came within a second of the Bayliner's turn. All three men in the lead boat heard the two slugs whiz past. Girard was firing in two-shot volleys and Charbonneau's stomach began to hurt. "Fire back, you fools, you've got *guns!*" he yelled at the Arabs. Neither Corbeau nor Marteau needed prompting, with both opening up with their TEC-9 pistols. Each had chosen the "selective firing" position, and their firearms pumped out three slugs at a time.

"Damn, Girard! You said we're going to war, and you meant it," Nick Quatro yelled over the engine's roar. He began to zoom forward in large arcs, never the same distance to either side, and the Arabs were clearly dazzled. One minute they'd have the Lightning in their sights, and the next, it was gone. Quatro reached into his carry bag and handed Girard a pair of skiers goggles, smiling as he did so. Girard waved, smiled, and immediately donned the gear. Sighting, he knew he had to disable the big Mercury motor on the rear of the Bayliner, and concentrated his shooting patterns on the motor rather than the boat's occupants at first. One, two. One, two. His slugs ripped through the air.

Girard became aware that a large peninsula was passing on the right and spotted a large American flag. There it was! Fort Ticonderoga, an American monument—he hoped Tommy and the chopper were able to set down there. Girard knew the big bay to the east of the promontory, which Tommy had mentioned, and resumed his firing. If he could kill Charbonneau's engine, he might force them ashore right in that bay. One, two. One, two. One…wow! As he closed with the quarry, Girard saw a plume of dark smoke blow from the engine.

As he fumbled with something in his carry bag, Quatro yelled, "You hit a hydraulic line, Girard. The top cowling of the engine blew off." At that point, Nicky revealed his own surprise, hoisting an old Army .45 from his bag. Holding the wheel with his left hand, he returned the Arabs' fire over the top of his windscreen. Girard looked, stifled any official thinking about the weapon, smiled, and continued to pour bullets into the Bayliner.

Suddenly, Marteau fell into the boat, apparently hit by Girard's shots or Nicky's. Corbeau then reached down and came up with a long tube. "Oh, shit, Nicky! He's going to use a rocket on us!" Continuing to zig-zag, Quatro noted that Charbonneau had apparently lost way. "We must have cut his rudder cable too," he yelled. The Bayliner continued on a tight starboard tack, seemingly unable to maneuver toward the opening of the Narrows which was now visible on their left. "One, two," Girard yelled, "One, two!" as he continued shooting, now at Corbeau, who was trying to load a missile into the launcher. His magazine empty, he snatched another from his carry bag and slammed it into place. "Fortunately, that missile is almost always a two-man job, firing that thing," Girard yelled at his driver.

Somehow, Corbeau did get his missile loaded. "Damn, I've been *here* before, in Nam!" Girard exploded. Then he remembered. "Timmy, if you're out there," he shouted, "divert that damn thing or I'll be having dinner with you tonight!" Suddenly, there was a flash, followed immediately by a scream. Apparently, Corbeau knew what to do, but not how. First, Girard and Quatro watched the missile jump from the tube, then begin to cork-screw while trailing smoke. Then it shot past Tango Twelve, to splash in the water behind them—there was no explosion. "Wow, *that* was the dud!" Girard exclaimed. "Thanks, Timmy!"

But the second sound was an unearthly screaming coming from Charbonneau. Corbeau had aimed his launcher without noting Charbonneau's position behind him. The rocket's back-blast had hit Two Claw squarely on the spine, burning away his jacket and shirt. As the boats closed, Girard could see Two Claw's bare, red back; Louie was in agony, and lost his grip on the wheel allowing the boat to head directly toward shore. Now they were below the battlements of the 250-year-old fort.

Bang! The Bayliner landed hard, running up onto the stony beach, where it stopped. Burning hydraulic fluid and engine smoke filled the air around the boat. Corbeau grabbed a launcher and one missile and jumped onto the shore, and Charbonneau, though clearly in pain and near losing consciousness did likewise. Nobody was going to jail him again! Girard looked on in amazement at what Two Claw could still manage to achieve.

With a steadier shooting position, both of the pursued men turned to pour rapid fire onto Tango Twelve. The windscreen shattered and Quatro yelled, mainly in fright, but then in increasing anger, "You sonsabitches! You can't do that to *my* boat!" He emptied his clip in the direction of the pair on the shore and kept pulling the trigger until he realized the .45 was empty, then threw it onto the floor.

Corbeau and Charbonneau, knowing that they were sitting ducks, turned and ran across the field toward the hill before them. Their path then slowed, as they had to climb toward the ramparts above. Girard kept firing at the two men, but the distance began to grow between pursued and pursuer. Quatro was not about to run his prize racer, winner of the 2006 Lake Champlain Poker Run, aground, and slowed greatly to avoid a crash. Throttling down from over 80 m.p.h. to zero in just fifty yards took skill, and then a quick reverse of engines at the end. With a bump, Tango Twelve made shore, and Girard jumped down. Turning, he yelled to Quatro, "Hightail it out of here, Nicky. I owe you, but don't die for your country here. I have friends coming. Get going!" With an empty pistol, Quatro decided that he'd had enough war for one day, anyway. "Take care of yourself, Girard," he yelled out, and reversed engines for a much slower trip home.

CHAPTER FIFTY-FIVE

As he passed the smoke-spewing Bayliner, Girard looked inside. There was Marteau, apparently dead, so the investigator moved quickly to close with his opponents. On the lower slopes to the ramparts, Corbeau knew he needed to gain the high ground, but every few steps, he turned to shoot a short burst at Girard, who had just reached the open field below. Charbonneau was lagging and not firing at his pursuer, as the effort to carry the launcher and rocket, and to climb at the same time, was taxing his last reserves of energy. With the pop, pop, buzz of the TEC-9s, tourists looked down from the picket fence barricade at the hilltop. "Must be some kind of publicity stunt," Tony Banchi said to his wife, Lori. The two smiled and, having paid their admission at the gate, headed leisurely toward the fort's main entrance. In the distance they could hear the fife and drum corps warming up.

Corbeau now encountered great difficulty because there were large blocks of stone, rip-rap that had been tumbled down the hillside to keep the soil from eroding. Wending his way through these obstacles, he could no longer shoot at Girard, who was just reaching the bottom of the hill. As he climbed, Girard was also having great difficulty. He kept reaching to his left hip for something. It seemed he needed it if he was to climb this hill. Well, what *was* it? Then he knew—he needed his short sword. And State Police investigators aren't issued swords! Part of his consciousness was back on the trail up to Quebec City—more than two hundred years ago! Damned angel stuff, he barked inside.

When I reach the top, *inshallah*, I will turn and kill him. Then I will watch for that airplane, Corbeau resolved. It's almost time.

"Gulfstream 526, this is Boston Center. Descend now to 6,000."
"Boston Center. Gulfsteam 526. 6,000, Roger and thank you."

Pilot Mike Jeppesen was now breathing normally. Most of the adrenalin had left his system and he smiled at copilot Morzillo. "I guess the rest of the day is going to be normal, Jimmy, what do you think?"

Morzillo responded, "Let's hope so, Mike. But we're ready for anything, right?" Jeppesen smiled and descended to 6,000 feet over Westport.

Corbeau now reached the picket fence barricade and pushed down a section of fence, receiving only stares from the summer tourists. It was a hot day and they didn't want to get involved with a vandal carrying a long tube. But Don Rave paid attention—he'd seen missile launchers in the Gulf War, and knew this was no part of the 250th Anniversary Celebration at the fort. He returned to the admission building to tell someone in authority.

Corbeau had the choice of waiting for Girard to emerge from the vegetation and strewn rocks below, or hurry to a *demi-lune* fortification and ready himself for a shot at the airplane. It should be coming soon, and he wondered why Hetzer hadn't been in contact all morning. Then, it occurred to him—Hetzer likely was dead. Once more, he scanned the slope and field below, and made his choice. There would be no repayment if Bush didn't die. Corbeau walked as nonchalantly as a man *could* walk, while carrying an automatic pistol in one hand, a missile launcher in the other, and a rocket under his pistol arm. Straight ahead was the perfect spot. He could get off a good shot toward the south before Girard ever came near. He would do this for Ru'yah, his beloved.

Charbonneau finally reached the top of the hill and was fortunate that someone had pushed down a section of fence, as he doubted that he would have had the strength. He had jammed his pistol into his belt and carried the launcher in his left hand, while barely holding on to the missile in his right. He turned and looked downhill. Girard was just reaching the rip-rap. Turning again, he couldn't spot Corbeau, so Louie headed for the main gate of the fort, following the tourists.

Jimmy Cook looked around the parade ground and enjoyed the admiring looks that he received in return from the visitors. Here and there, he stopped to answer a child's question about his dress or ideas. Cook had shaved the sides of his head and now sported a Mohawk haircut, which was only fitting, as his ancestry was three-quarters Mohawk. His grandparents in Syracuse had urged him to live the life of his ancestors for at least one summer after high school, and he found great pride in walking and talking of the ancient ways as guide and interpreter Standing Bear at Fort Ticonderoga.

A superb physical specimen at six feet and three inches, he was an imposing figure in leggings, breechcloth, and moccasins. His naked torso with a turtle tattoo had gained its normal deep bronze from the summer sun, and he took pleasure in the admiring glances from the girls. In his belt, he held a tomahawk, which he liked sharpening each morning at the parade ground whetstone. Cook moved through the large stone arch tunnel between the parade ground and outer works. As he emerged and turned once more into the open air, he was startled by a stocky man carrying a lot of apparatus, who wore his hair in long braids, almost as a Mohawk of old might. The tourist blanched and seemed near fainting. What the hell was *he?* One of the maintenance men? An Indian wanna-be? Go figure, Cook concluded. Mmmm, there is a pretty lass—maybe she needs interpreting, he ruminated as he moved out into the sunshine.

Louie Charbonneau had seen a ghost. A warrior of old had just passed him and he had tried his hardest to be nonchalant, but this truly seemed a sign that the ancestors were still with him. The people in the crowd likely didn't see the man, as ancestor spirits are usually invisible. So, perhaps this was a sign from his dead wife, Marie—an invitation to greater courage. Though his back was searing with pain, Charbonneau stumbled through the dark passage to the parade ground; maybe Corbeau was in here.

Dennis Girard gained the hilltop and passed through the broken fence. Immediately in front of him stood a New York State historic marker. "Fort Carillon," it said, "a French name meaning, 'the place of the bells,' and the name of the first fort on this site." Oh, shit, he murmured, remembering the prophecy of Grandmother Thompson at Khanawake. This sure was destiny day—saved from missiles by a dead brother and now it was his task to kill two bad guys if he could find them, thereby saving a former President for whom he hadn't even voted. He had hoped to see Tommy or Nesselbank or Spulnik on this hilltop already, but none of them were here yet. Well, between me and the spirits, he decided, I guess I know which party has the upper hand here. Girard started down a slope toward the fort entrance.

In the parking lot, three men, two in State Police uniforms, ran toward the admissions booth. They hoped that Girard had gotten his part of the operation done successfully. Each of these men carried a firearm.

The faint noise came to Corbeau first—the whine of jet engines, but he couldn't see the plane yet. It sounded as if the pilot were slowing or losing altitude. He knelt beside a large old cannon and placed his launching weapon on the ancient shooting tube. With his other hand, he maneuvered the missile into the rear of the launcher. This should be pretty easy—there *can't* be a second misfire. Suddenly the plane appeared, not out over the lake, but much farther to the west than he had thought it might fly, and suddenly almost overhead. Corbeau brought the viewfinder to his eye, but immediately realized the plane was flying too fast. He would have to shoot at it after it passed, and he turned slightly. Aim wasn't the main consideration here, however, because he knew the missile would follow the plane's heat trail faster than the plane could fly. He glanced at his watch—it was now 1:08. He readied.

Sr. Investigator Dennis Girard looked left at the people streaming toward him from the admission gate, then scanned straight ahead into the old defensive moat. Nobody. Walking slowly, he peered into each nook as he passed—Corbeau could be in any of them. Then he heard the plane. The Arab would have to shoot from out in the open—so where *was* he? Yes, there he was—behind the cannon on his right. Girard went into a shooter's stance and called out, "Corbeau, you sonofabitch, drop that weapon and put up your hands. This is the State Police!"

Cautious vacationers suddenly realized that the scene before them was no performance, and began to run away or dive for cover. Corbeau instantly switched his position toward the right as the plane soared overhead; he ignored Girard's warning. Corbeau pulled the trigger, but as he did so, he lost sight of the plane, which had vanished in the afternoon sun's glare. Corbeau knew no more, because somewhere in the plane's overhead roar, a bullet ended his life. By the time the second of Girard's shots hit the body, Corbeau was already dead, struck in the head by Girard's first precise shot.

Overhead, Jeppesen reacted immediately when Morzillo called out, "Incoming missile!" Glancing at the radar, he could see the blip approaching fast from the rear, and turned into a steep dive to the west—directly at the ground. If this maneuver didn't work, he knew that all passengers would become a metallic pancake. Down and down he went, almost to the ground, leveling off only two hundred feet above Route 22 in Washington County. He and Morzillo checked the radar again. There was just one blip and it was moving fast due south, away from them. The missile that Corbeau had fired was slowly losing propulsion and altitude, as it attempted to kill the sun. It would eventually fall to earth, without exploding, four miles north of Fair Haven, VT.

"Too late—shit!" Girard exclaimed. Corbeau had gotten off a shot. "I'm too goddamned late!" He looked up, expecting to see a plane exploding, but there was no plane at all. Maybe Voodoo Air had gotten away unharmed, because if there had been a hit, everyone in three counties would have heard it. When he realized what had happened, Girard said aloud, "Thanks, Izzy. You, too, Timmy." He walked rapidly to Corbeau's body and covered it with his jacket. Nevertheless, blood continued to flow from beneath the garment and down the steps. Did I take a life to save many lives? Girard wondered.

At that moment, drawn by the pistol shots, Tommy, Gordon, and Jimmy rushed up. "How's it *going*, lad?" Tommy asked nervously.

"Well, two down and one to go, Tommy. That bastard Charbonneau is in this crowd somewhere, and he's armed and he's got a rocket launcher. Two uniformed Sheriff's deputies arrived with drawn pistols and moved quickly to Girard's side. Quickly, the four troopers identified themselves and announced that there was one more criminal in the crowd and more shooting was a certainty. They gave the deputies a quick description of Charbonneau. "Let's get these people out of here," Girard commanded. "We're likely to have people hurt here, and probably some more dead if we have to shoot in such crowded conditions. You'd better call county dispatch right now and get us some ambulances." The deputies began rapidly herding people away from Corbeau's corpse. Girard pointed a direction to each of his trooper companions, sending each man to a different part of the fort's interior. "Two Claw is injured, but he's cagey and you guys know he's dangerous," Girard said. "Don't give him even half a chance to hurt you." He ejected his almost-spent magazine and popped in his third and last one.

As his fellow officers dispersed, Girard walked carefully to the main gate. Seeing his drawn pistol and the badge that he held aloft, tourists scattered. Because the parade ground was isolated from the activities in the outer fort, and perhaps because the fife and drum corps was performing at top volume inside, none of the crowd in that interior knew of the shootings outside.

Investigator Girard walked cautiously, keeping to the left in the dark passageway, which seemed all the more murky because of the bright sunlight at each end. There was a doorway inside now on the left, but it was locked. Now move ahead, he told himself. The music stopped.

Without warning, he lost his bearings and all reality fled. The fife and drum corps was coming out, and he no longer knew where, or even *who* he was. Girard couldn't have known that the corps was attired this week in the royal blue and red uniforms of the Royal Roussillon Regiment of French troops long ago stationed at the fort. This was the same regiment that Capt. Howe had faced on the French left at Quebec. Though the picture was not at all that clear in his mind, Girard reacted with the emotions of Howe, a man who no longer existed in physical form. All the cycles of history struck him at once, and he was unsure whether or not to fire at those apparent enemies who now marched toward him and beneath the arch, within four feet of his position. Fortunately, he let them go, as they proceeded into the outer works, the inner parade ground now was almost quiet.

Looking into the bright sunlight within, Girard could see children playing, visitors sauntering between doorways, and families taking photos. But where was Two Claw? He inched around a left corner and along the eastern wall of the large space. Bang, bang bang! Lead slugs hit the stone wall above his head, almost deafening him. Yes, Charbonneau was here. A little girl lay on the ground screaming near his legs. Crouching, Girard moved over to her to see whether the child was wounded or simply scared. She looked into his eyes in terror; just scared, he judged. The crowd had ducked into doorways or lay flat on the ground. Where *was* Two Claw?

Guess I'll have to keep drawing his fire, Girard decided, there's no other way—if not, he's going to kill everybody else inside this fort.

Unbeknownst to Girard, his three companions in law enforcement, drawn by the sound of gunfire, had assembled just outside the arch. Knowing that they might be targets, each man scuttled along the ground in the arch's gloom, moving slowly toward the fort's interior.

Bang, bang, bang! Again, stone chips flew from the wall above his head. He pushed the cringing little girl backward from his position and she ran into the archway. Girard could hear the reports were now coming from a doorway on his left, where a sign said "Museum." He knew that if Charbonneau was in there, that tourists within that room would be used as hostages before Charbonneau was killed or captured. Bang, bang, bang! Bullets bounced around the fort's stone parade ground. An elderly man lay against the western wall and Girard could see blood trickling from the man's ribs. A teenage boy lay crumpled and unmoving in the center of the parade ground.

The investigator half-turned, scanning to his right and was startled to see beaded deerskin moccasins right beside him. Glancing up, he saw Jimmy Cook, whom the investigator had only briefly noted on his way into the archway. Girard couldn't have known that, in his just-finished high school days at Salmon River Central High School, Cook had lettered in three sports, including one season as an unscored-upon goalie for the Shamrocks' hockey team. He was rugged and brave in a way that Charbonneau was not. And, it had just dawned on young Cook that he knew Two Claw from the reservation. "Get down, you young fool," Girard hissed. "That guy is nuts and he'll kill you as quick as look at you! Get down!"

"Who, *Louie*?" the young man inquired. "He's just scum; he's only an opportunist." And so saying, Cook stood tall and quickly strode to the center of the parade ground. Oh, crap. Here's another body we'll have to haul away, Girard grumbled. But Cook was too big for Girard to persuade in any physical way, and the investigator now understood that the young man wouldn't stop whether or not he flashed his badge.

Cook briefly touched the neck of the inert teen, then straightened and yelled out, "Two Claw Charbonneau, I command you to come forth from your hiding place!" Cook repeated his command in the direction of the museum. Charbonneau's bug-eyed, pale face appeared in the museum window. Who *was* this god-like man? Was he an ancestor? A spirit? Surely, others couldn't see him.

"Louis Charbonneau, in the name of the Mohawk Nation, I command you. Come forth!"

Yes, that must be it, said Charbonneau to himself. His back was on fire. His intestines were so sore he could no longer stand up straight. He hobbled to the doorway. Who was this figure? Is he calling me to the spirit world of my Mohawk ancestors? Yes, he must; he can't be human. Two Claw had never seen such a magnificent man on the res. He felt obligated to obey, and inched his way into the open doorway.

On either side, tourists cowered while, one step at a time, Charbonneau moved, as if in a trance, down the steps into the open space. Girard must be gone, Louie surmised. I can't see him. He raised the TEC-9 and chambered another shell. One step. One step more. Then a movement to Louie's right caught his eye—Girard hiding on the ground. "You sonofabitch, Girard," he yelled, pointing the pistol at his nemesis. Before Charbonneau could get off a shot, Jimmy Cook, former Shamrock halfback, tackled Two Claw. The pistol fell from his hand and Girard leapt at the pair, jumping onto Charbonneau's chest and placing the muzzle of his weapon between Charbonneau's eyes. This was the moment he'd waited for! Today it would be *done*!

Unbearable pain surged through Two Claw from his raw back on the gravel, and tears rolled down his cheek. A voice from behind Girard spoke softly, "We have taken the field together, don't you see? Let's run a bit farther together." Who was that? The kid? God, he knew, he *knew*! Girard couldn't turn, he didn't dare, for fear he'd see a bearded tourist dressed in a white robe. All anger vanished immediately, and he was once more atop the bluffs of Abraham outside Quebec City. Another useless killing?

Rolling his prisoner with young Cook's help, Girard spat, "Aw, shit. Get up, you lousy excuse for a human being. Get up!" Charbonneau sagged, near fainting. Instantly they were joined by Delehanty, Nesselbank, and Spulnik. The latter grounded his sniper rifle, muttering something about unemployment for crack shots, but Girard couldn't make it out. "Who are *you*, kid?" he asked the young Indian.

"I'm Jimmy Cook. I work here as an interpreter. I like this work and, after today, I may stay on permanently—this is a heck of a lot better than a soccer game!"

"*Gulfstream 526, Boston Center. Descend to 5,000 and contact Albany Approach on 123.0. Good day, sir.*"

"Boston center, this is Gulfstream 526 special. Thank you and good day."

"I want to shake your hand, Jimmy Cook," Girard said. "I never saw such a brave act, even among the Airborne in Vietnam." As he turned, he saw that several more people had been wounded by ricochets or flying pieces of stone. In the background he could hear ambulance sirens. The two deputies appeared with drawn weapons in the tunnel. The final count was a dead man at the cannon outside, a badly wounded man and unconscious teenager on the parade ground, two children bleeding from scrapes outside the Museum door, a woman crying near an elderly woman unable to breathe, and an old man who had passed out.

Delehanty and Nesselbank hurried among the hurt and wounded, assessing who had to get out first. EMTs were rushing through the tunnel and into the parade ground, ushered by the deputies. Standing, Girard realized that he, himself, was bleeding from the right thigh, though he never felt the bullet. His comrades took a handcuffed Charbonneau in charge and ushered him to the vehicles outside. "Read that bastard his rights right now, Tommy," Girard called after the officers.

"Yeah, okay, Girard," said Deputy Forgette as he walked forward, "he's taken care of, and they've loaded the dead guy. The other deputies just reported another badly wounded, but still-alive guy, in the boat down on the lake. They're transporting them all up to the hospital. That's where *you* belong."

"Okay, Deputy Forgette," Girard said, reading the man's name tag, "just give me a ride up in your cruiser." As they moved through the crowd toward the south parking lot, Girard unslung his radio and called Tommy on the State Police channel. "Tommy, on the way up, will you report in right now to Captain Telfer, and ask him to do an initial report down to the JTTF?"

"Roger that, Den. How you doing?"

"I'm okay, lad, I just sprung a leak, so they're going to drive me up to Moses-Ludington. I used to know a nurse there—maybe she's still around," Girard said with a laugh. "Are you taking Two Claw to the barracks at Crown Point?"

"Yeah, we'll book him there on fifty counts, and get him transported over to the jail. Then I'll come back looking for you, you bum!" Tommy replied. "Hang around at the hospital, and I'll be back, buddy." He signed off.

Girard sat in the front seat of Forgette's cruiser. The deputy grabbed a towel from the trunk and demanded that Girard immediately wrap his thigh and put some pressure on the wound. "I'll have you up the hill in a minute," the deputy said, hitting his lights and siren. Forgette made quick time driving past the crowd and out the entrance road, past historic markers and the old French trenches of Montcalm's 1758 defense. Girard recognized the big monument to the legendary Maj. Duncan Campbell of the British Black Watch, who died from wounds received there.

Forgette came to a short stop at the large, stone entrance gate and resident's house. On the right stood a young man with auburn hair, wearing a California Angels baseball cap and a white sweatshirt bearing the UNION inscription. The man waved and smiled. Girard elbowed Forgette and said, "Deputy, if you ever see that guy hitching through here again, don't stop. He's nothing but *trouble!*"

CHAPTER FIFTY-SIX

As they entered the Emergency Unit parking lot at Moses-Ludington Hospital, Girard could see two Ticonderoga village ambulances, one from the International Paper Company Ticonderoga Mill emergency squad, two from the Crown Point squad, and one from Hague. Most other North Country emergency units, he knew, were even now converging on Plattsburgh International.

Deputy Forgette assisted Girard in hobbling to the door. His leg was now stiffening after the few minutes' ride. Inside, he found the Director of Nursing, Pat Chamberlain, acting as triage nurse. Most of the seriously wounded were already in the trauma unit being treated. Nurses were maneuvering a stretcher into a treatment room, with the teenage boy covered by an Autopulse unit. She got Girard immediately into a wheelchair and beckoned to a young male LPN to assist him. The young man pushed Girard into the Emergency Unit hallway and, as he went, Investigator Girard turned and thanked Forgette. Down the hall they went and parked outside Trauma Room Number Two. "Sorry, I have to look at your leg out here," the young man said, "but, as you can see, we've got a lot of customers today." He tied a hospital gown around Girard's neck, covering the investigator's front, then asked him to drop his trousers. Girard complied.

For a minute or two, the nurse, whose name tag identified him as Ben Eli, LPN, pushed and poked at the wound. "Looks like it went right through," he said. Taking a Betadine sponge, he swabbed the exterior of the wound. "I'm going to give you an antibiotic shot and then we'll get you into the x-ray line as quickly as we can, just to be sure nothing's left inside. We just got a second radiologist in, so it should move pretty fast. I don't think the bullet lodged in you, though. Can you sit here a minute until they're ready?" Eli asked, withdrawing the antibiotic syringe. Girard nodded and after wrapping a thin blanket around Girard's shoulders, Eli left to attend to someone else.

I don't believe it, Girard mulled, that sonofabitch Two Claw got out of this whole turkey shoot without a scratch and just some burns. Well, I'm glad I didn't kill him, I guess—he was crying at the end. Abruptly, Girard heard strange sounds from inside Trauma Room Number Two and stood to look. The woman nurse was working on a badly injured man who was hooked to several monitors and had two drip lines into him. Looking up, she saw Girard observing. He peered in at the victim, and saw that it was Marteau, whom he'd long considered a dead man. Alice Bonville, RN, shook her head, indicating to Girard that the man was going. She walked to the doorway and asked Girard, whose badge she could see hanging from his neck, to enter.

"He keeps trying to say something, but I don't know what it means. Maybe you can help," she said. Girard hobbled to Marteau's stretcher. Faintly, the man kept repeating, *La illaha illa Allah. Muhammad-ur-Rasul-Allah. Atubu illa Allah.* Over and over, in increasingly quiet gasps, the dying man repeated the phrases.

"That's Arab talk," Girard said to Nurse Bonville. "That's all I know." LPN Eli then entered, took stock of the situation, and smiled.

"Even *him*," Eli said, gently grasping Marteau's right wrist. "Even this one, who would have killed many, is readying to come home." Girard asked himself what it all meant—why did Eli say "*come* home?"

Eli responded, "This man followed Islam once. He's just asking God to accept him back in spite of everything."

"Who would have thought such a thing?" Girard grumbled. "What did you mean by *come* home?" Ignoring Girard's question, Eli then placed his right hand upon Marteau's brow and suddenly the vital signs alarm went off—Marteau was straight-lining. The three recognized that Marteau's journey had begun. Nurse Bonville, knowing that nothing more could be done for the man, jotted the time on her chart and covered Marteau's face with the sheet. She turned off the monitor and stopped the drips. "It's amazing that he lasted as long as this—his wounds were so severe." She peeled back the sheet to indicate two bullet holes an inch apart on the man's chest. "I don't know what kept him alive," she marveled. Girard looked at his handiwork and knew it was time to hang up a career. Let the younger guys do this, he resolved, and stumbled to the doorway, dropping once more into the wheelchair.

There was a stir in the lobby at the end of the hall, and he could see Nurse Chamberlain pointing at him. A uniformed trooper thanked the nurse and walked toward him. "Investigator Girard?" the man queried. "I'm Trooper Bill Reynolds from Crown Point Barracks. You probably don't remember me, but you helped me years ago with my first case, a burglary. I heard you had some bad luck and asked to come over and see you. Looks like you've had quite a day."

Girard remembered the man, and suddenly felt older than he wanted to be. "Thanks, Bill, I do remember you. I'm okay. They're going to take some pictures of me, then turn me loose. I'm not hurt bad; just a through-and-through. Probably won't go out and boogie anytime soon, though. What I *will* need, however, is a ride to the boatyard in Port Henry, where I left my car. And Tommy Delehanty, do you know him? Tommy is outside somewhere and will need a ride down to Glens Falls Airport, to get his car. Watch for them to come in, will you, Bill? I'm suddenly so tired. I guess I need to snooze.He didn't realize that Eli had added a small dose of Valium to the injection.

Girard awoke to Nurse Bonville's quiet words. "Investigator Girard, are you ready for your closeup?" She smiled, and he remembered the punch line from the old movie, "Sunset Boulevard." She took him to x-ray, where two views were taken. The attending nurse asked who his family doctor was and Girard gave the name of Dr. Neil Gregory, his Hudson Headwaters physician. The nurse finished filling in several papers and reports on the clip board, then told Girard not to drive for two more hours, asking him to sign at the bottom of two sheets of paper. She signaled to Trauma Unit Doctor Scott McMahon, who walked quickly to the pair, looked over the paperwork, briefly inquired about Girard's state of mind, then released him to Tommy, who had just entered. "I'll have your x-rays and treatment all faxed to Dr. Gregory by noon tomorrow. Take care, Officer Girard," Dr. McMahon said.

On the way out of the hospital, Dennis again thanked Nurse Chamberlain for her care, and for all she was doing for the wounded. "Will someone claim Mr. Marteau's body?" she asked. "Do you know if he has any next-of-kin?"

"I really don't know, nurse. I'll put that to the Feds; they have a way of finding out those things. Put him on ice."

Tommy pushed Girard's wheelchair out to Trooper Reynolds's cruiser for the ride to Glens Falls Airport, and the trio got in. At the foot of the hill, Girard asked Reynolds to pull into the Stewart's Shop. "I think it must have been another lifetime since I've had any coffee, Tommy. Will you go in and get me a tall, two sugars and cream? He handed his partner a couple of singles. "You guys want java?"

With Girard contentedly sipping his coffee, Reynolds sped off south on Route 9 to Glens Falls, where Tommy would pick up his car. During the ride, Delehanty again called Troop B and informed Capt. Telfer of their situation, and Telfer asked to speak to Girard.

"Hi, Captain. We earned our state paychecks today," he chuckled.

"Girard, I'm glad you brought it to a conclusion. Things at Plattsburgh are horrible. We have a lot of men over there. Casualties are high—some were *our* boys, others are FBI. Lots of civilians are dead, I'm sure you know. But we'll talk about that tomorrow. You'll be in at the regular time, right?"

Girard was a bit surprised at Telfer's assumption, but agreed that there were several tons of paperwork to begin. "Yep. See you tomorrow, bright and early, Captain," he responded with a smile.

After signing off, Girard turned to Reynolds and glanced back at Tommy. "The first paper I write up tomorrow is my resignation. I'm all done," he said contentedly.

"Gulfstream 526 special, Albany Approach Control. Descend to 2,000. You are VFR to Glens Falls. Go to 123.0 and have a nice landing."

"Albany Control, 2,000 feet. Thank you, Sir. It's been an interesting day…Gulfstream 526 special out."

Captain Michael Jeppesen smiled at Co-pilot Morzillo, who gave him the thumbs-up sign. Jeppesen then looked into the rear of the cabin. Former President Bush sat, with spectacles on the end of his nose, sipping a cup of tea and poring over his notes. He looked up and yelled past his Secret Service detail to Jeppesen. "This time, I intend to say some profound things about this nation and the people who *serve* her." He tossed a salute to his crew.

Gulfstream 526 cut its engines at 1:28 and Mr. Bush emerged to do an impromptu news conference outside the Fixed Base Operations Building, and grabbed a sandwich at Sally's Briefing Room Café. By the time Trooper Reynolds pulled into the parking area at Glens Falls Airport, the black limousines were coming out, headed for the 3 p.m. rally at the Glens Falls Civic Center. Secret Service Agent Hattlee looked at the State Police cruiser entering the parking lot and elbowed Agent Lagoe. "I bet those guys are just starting *their* day's work."

Girard eased out of the State Police cruiser and into the front seat of Tommy's car. He thanked Reynolds for his act of kindness and friendship. "A trooper never knows how many friends he has until the chips are down, Bill. Thanks a lot."

Reynolds left the parking lot followed by Delehanty, straight over Quaker Road to I-87 and then north. On the way, Tommy told Girard that the past few weeks had left him wondering. "It's time I made some plans for *my own* future, Den. I'm going to ask Janice to set the wedding date and make me into an honest beau. What do you think?"

"Sounds good, Tommy. You two have been lovers for 10 years now. I don't think it can get any better. Take the leap now, then find something you two can do together." Then a sparkle came to Girard's eyes, "Hey, did you ever consider playing canasta?"

Delehanty gave an uncomprehending look at Girard, while the latter laughed riotously. Tommy, however, refused to take the bait and commented on the bright orange parasails in the air over Lake George.

When Delehanty dropped him off in Port Henry, Girard said goodbye and "see you tomorrow." His right leg was still a bit stiff, so he walked over to Quatro, who stood with a question mark on his face. "Did we win, Girard?" the mechanic asked.

"Yeah, Nicky, we won. The bad guys are dead. Is your insurance going to cover the windshield?"

"Oh yes! That was the first thing I thought about when I got home— got right on the pipe to my insurance agent. Hey, Girard, you know what? I never fully appreciated Tango Twelve until today. I'm pretty happy with that performance. In Dad's time, they painted little flags on boats that made a kill. What flag should I paint on Tango Twelve?" They laughed, and Quatro said, "Plus I know I'm going to win the Poker Run next month. Hey, did you get hurt? I see you limping."

"Oh, I got an Arab bullet in me. Or maybe it was Canadian, I don't know. I think it's going to be okay, so I'm going home to take a nap. The boss gave me the rest of the day off." He thanked Quatro profusely for being there.

"Hey, Girard, did you see that little angel on my control panel? I call her Wilda. Yeah, I knew we'd be okay. She helps me. You don't believe in that stuff, do you?"

Girard only smiled. He waved and left, driving south on Route 9, and over to Chestertown.

When he arrived home, he saw Mrs. Morgenstern squatting near the flower bed. He walked over to chat, and was surprised at the pain he saw on her face when she turned to greet him. "You okay, Mrs. M?" he asked, extending a hand to help her up.

"Sure, Dennis, I'm okay. I always *have* been okay, but I'm going to be leaving town soon. Come on over to the bench here and let's chat. Did I tell you I saw a cute little wren here this morning Also, tell me, do you know anything about dreams?"

EPILOGUE

On September 1, 2008, Sr. Investigator Dennis Girard officially retired from Troop B of the New York State Police. His plans for the future were hazy, but he knew for sure that he was going to indulge his love of travel and exploration of the unknown world.

His son, Patrick, had called and was bringing the kids to Chestertown for Labor Day weekend. His daughter, Clara, had sent a nice flowery card. After finishing the remaining paperwork and court appearances during the month, Dennis called his daughter and asked if he might come to Philadelphia soon, and she could show him the Liberty Bell. She seemed nervous, but agreed.

His August session with Dr. Epstein had been a fascinating one. They marveled at his out-of-body excursion or bi-location that likely saved her life. He had no awareness of the phenomenon that day, but it meant a lot to her. Girard mentioned his travel plans to "somewhere" for the future, and Bernice said that was also *her* hoped-for activity when she retired. "Just two more years," she said. "You *are* going to keep on with therapy?" she asked hopefully.

"Sure, Doc. This is my home away from home." They used the rest of the hour to explore a recent dream that he'd had, about seeing the planet Earth from high in space. The polar ice cap seemed to be vibrating, and he wondered about the Jungian symbology in such images. They laughed a lot, and she told him about a big Jungian dream conference to be held at a Prince Edward Island resort in June 2009. He wondered if she was inviting him.

In early September, and with the permission of the St. Lawrence Seaway Authority, Girard had a small memorial stone erected near the

Port of Ogdensburg. The engraved plaque read, "To the memory of Janet LaRose. Wherever the oceans flow, your love is there."

Apparently, Timmy and Israfil had also retired, as Girard never saw them again, though he often felt their warm presence in times of doubt. His experiences with voices and visions seemed to intensify, and civilian Dennis Girard couldn't wait for the future to unfold. What was it that little Friar Sweeney had said? It is all going on right *now*? Present, past, and future?

Mohawk interpreter Jimmy Cook entered the State University at Potsdam on September 1st, majoring in elementary education. He is also a freshman goalie on the Potsdam Bears hockey team. In late May 2009, he will return to his job as Standing Bear at Fort Ticonderoga.

On August 5th, following the discharge of the last Fort Ti patient, LPN Ben Eli disappeared. His apartment in downtown Ticonderoga retained his few possessions, and investigators noted that he even failed to pick up his last paycheck at the hospital. Sheriff's investigators, however, could find no evidence of foul play. Nurse Alice Bonville, RN, is now retired. Head Nurse Pat Chamberlain, continues as Director of Nursing at Moses-Ludington Hospital in Ticonderoga.

In Ray Brook, Maj. Sincavage and Capt. Telfer continue to administer Troop B of the New York State Police. Lt. Lou Gregory (*né Gregoire*) was promoted to Sr. Investigator, while investigators Quinn, Shaloub and Gaudreau continue with the Forensics Team.

In Elizabethtown, Essex County Sheriff James Parillo, has purchased a condo in Tarpon Springs, Florida, where he keeps his nineteen-foot Tyee fishing boat. Essex County Judge Diane Conlin retired on December 30, planning a retirement filled with watercolor painting and world travel.

Louis Philippe Charbonneau, after being indicted in federal court on sixteen federal charges, died of stomach cancer in Albany Medical Center Hospital on October 30, 2008. His body was returned to Akwesasne for burial, but was refused by the tribal council. He was laid to rest in an unmarked cemetery plot, purchased by Franklin County Department of Social Services.

The bodies of Marteau and Corbeau were claimed by the U.S. State Department and returned, through the auspices of the government of the Hashemite Kingdom of Jordan, for traditional burials on the West Bank.

Malcolm Viktor was found dead by his grandchildren in early November. Mr. Malcolm seemed asleep on his couch, and had a smile on his face. Kirby, his cat, sat contentedly, purring on the old man's chest.

DAVID J. PITKIN

In Frederick, Maryland, Willy Alderschild never reported to his job at Ft. Detrick on Tuesday, July 29th. His apartment had been cleaned out, according to a police investigation. Alderschild now resides under an assumed name in Albuquerque, New Mexico, and has used forged papers to get a security clearance at the Sandia National Laboratories. Unknown to him, the FBI continues to monitor the man's phone calls, mail, and computer activity.

The body of Paul M. Hochlitzer was never claimed, and received a burial in Forest Dale Cemetery in Crown Point at the expense of Essex County Social Services. There were no identifiable remains of Faust Hetzer, and there is no earthly memorial to his existence. Buck Stouffer was buried in Wadhams, and his business is now run by Lucky Stotz, whose trucks sport the motto, "Let Stotz dump your pots."

Plattsburgh International Airport has approved a design for facility reconstruction, to be completed in June 2010. All damage to the Passenger Terminal has been repaired, and commercial air business has resumed, with US Airways scheduling daily air service. The nearly-demolished Nose Dock buildings have been redesigned as cargo warehouses, and major freight carriers are waiting to move in, as soon as new construction is complete.

Freddy Holochuck, in exchange for sentencing leniency, disclosed the location of Walter Bortiatynski's burial in the foundation of the Clarkson University Alumni Hall. The University Board of Trustees approved an expenditure of $124,000 to remove the body and repair the excavation. Holochuck is now serving 25 years to life at the New York State Correctional Facility in Attica. Walter's remains were interred in a Potsdam cemetery.

Three State Policemen died in the explosion and were buried with honors in their hometowns. Two Secret Service agents died on July 28th: Sharon Fiedler and John Cunningham, who perished in the initial explosion. Six FBI agents received serious wounds or injuries. FBI agent Martin Donahue survived his severe injuries and is now engaged to Amanda Burns. The total casualties at the political rally was 98 dead, 159 injured seriously, and 221 were treated and released at hospitals. The *Press Republican* treated the Republican Women's Club, almost decimated in the blast, as "heroines," and Republican Party enrollments countywide are up, with a new 38-member Women's Club now formed.

JTTF Special Agent, Joe Zarr, was promoted to Assistant Director of the Counterterrorism Division at Washington, D.C. FBI Headquarters.

Channel 5 newsperson, Barbara Wilson, who received a national press award for her courage on the 28th, has been hired as news director at WREG, CBS Channel 3, in Memphis, Tennessee, which places her closer to her idea of Heaven: Elvis Presley's home at Graceland.

Plattsburgh received so much worldwide media coverage that the Chamber of Commerce was deluged by businesses hoping to locate at the rebuilt International Airport. Housing sales in Plattsburgh are brisk, and the city is now promoted as "Home of Heroes/Comeback City." Tourism, especially from Canada, is up, with two escorted tours of the airport, run by Mary Reed Tours, each day. The State University at Plattsburgh has expanded its Psychology Department to include a major in grief counseling.

Jim Tarbox, Dark Eagle, disappeared from Akwesasne on July 29th, and his present whereabouts is unknown, although there are occasional sightings at motorcycle races and antique car shows in the U.S. and Canada.

"Buzz," as he has been christened by the regular customers, is now the official greeter at Lucy's Restaurant in North Creek. The cooks and waitresses are amazed that Buzz now knows all of Oscar's old tricks, leading to speculation that houseflies might actually be able to reincarnate.

Hannah Morgenstern sold her Knapp Hill Road house to Dennis Girard two weeks before her last, brief sojourn in the Glens Falls Hospital, where she died at midnight, as the calendar moved into 2009. Neighbors noted a large flock of cardinals feeding in her snowy yard on that New Year's Day.

Thomas Colin Delehanty and Janice Suzanne Howland were married by Justice of the Peace Frederick Wickert on Halloween Day, with Dennis Girard as Best Man. The Delehantys live in Westport, following Tommy's retirement on November 1, where he operates a small private investigation service. The newlyweds continue to be amazed at the great peace that has descended on their friend, Dennis Girard, and they estimate that he has just begun his personal odyssey.

DAVID J. PITKIN

The Eagle

A Fable

An ecology professor hiked through the Adirondacks, studying and photographing the beauties of Nature, in which he found Truth. Not too far from Wanakena, on a back-country dirt road, he saw a sign, "Fresh Eggs: Chickens Are Us!" This business is pretty far off the main road, he mused, so guess I'll study his operation.

The proprietor, in straw hat and bib overalls stood at the wire fence, observing his birds as the professor approached. "Howdy," offered the farmer.

"How do you do?" the hiker responded. "You have a lot of chickens here."

"Yes," the man responded, "I got Rhode Island Reds, White Leghorns, Plymouth Rocks and a few Arucanas. They keep me supplied with eggs and even a little meat when they no longer can produce, and, most important, they make me some money."

The professor noted a larger, rather strange chicken in the back of the pen, a bird happily pecking away at the cracked corn that the farmer had strewn. Looking closer, the man noted that it was no chicken at all—it was an eagle! "Why, that's no chicken, it's an eagle!" he said to the farmer.

"Yup, I got him young and raised him as a chicken. He don't know no difference, and he's content to live on handouts."

"But that's not in accord with his nature!" exclaimed the idealistic teacher.

"Yup, but he don't know no better," said the farmer, grinning.

"But, he's got to be an eagle," replied the astonished professor, "everything in Nature has to be what it is, not what others want them to be!"

"Nope. He's too happy here. He'll never be an eagle; he thinks he's just like all the others in the pen," came the smug response.

"That can't be," said the hiker. "Why, I bet you fifty bucks I can teach him that he's an eagle!"

"Haw, haw!" replied the farmer. "You city-slickers think you know everything, but this critter is set for life. He'll always be a chicken. Nevertheless, I'll take you up on that bet," said the farmer. "Here—here's a carry-cage. Take him for a week and see what you can do. But, at the end of the seven days, you'd better bring him back—with the fifty bucks. Even if he don't lay no eggs, he's mine. He always will be, 'cause you

284

can't change him. His true place is behind the wire; that's how I raised him." The farmer reached into the pen, snagged the eagle and placed it in the cage. Promising to be back in a week, the professor strode off, back to his wilderness campsite.

Returned to his tent, the professor immediately set the bird free. At first, the creature was reluctant to emerge from the cage, but with coaxing, ambled out and stood looking questioningly at the teacher. The bird took a few steps and looked up again. He scratched the ground and made a few tentative pecks upon the soil, but found not even seeds. Again, he looked at the teacher. This won't do, thought the man. He gave some dried bread crusts to the bird, which gratefully gobbled them up. Putting the bird back into its cage with a canteen cup of water for the night, the man resolved to try an experiment the next day.

Arising in the next morning's pre-dawn darkness, the professor carried bird and cage to the top of a nearby mountain. At the summit, he opened the cage and placed the eagle upon his forearm. The bird's talons dug deeply into his flesh and the man was glad to be wearing a thick jacket over his sweatshirt. The light grew rapidly, and just before 6 a.m. the sun displayed its brilliance above the mountains to the east. The bird glanced at the illumination and, shuddering, turned away. Just briefly the creature moved its wings. Great! He's going to fly, thought the teacher. "Fly!" he urged out loud. Once more the bird moved its wings, but then jumped down onto the ground, searching for seeds. For a while it pecked fruitlessly at the ground, found and snapped up a cricket, then looked up beseechingly at the man. This is going to be a tough struggle, the professor concluded. He re-caged the bird and trudged back down the mountain to his campsite.

Early on the second morning, the ecologist once more climbed to the summit of the mountain, opened the cage, placing the eagle once more upon his forearm. As the sun began its ascent over the eastern mountains, the bird shuddered and extended its wings almost four feet, brushing the professor's head. Now he's going to do it, the man exulted. "Eagle! You are an eagle, the king of the Adirondack skies! Spread your wings and fly!" he commanded. But the bird again hopped to the ground, where he looked up wonderingly at the man. A field mouse ran by and the bird killed and consumed it immediately. Damn! The farmer might just be right, concluded the teacher. He re-caged the bird and took it downhill to its daily feeding of bread crusts and water, a sad diet for the king of the skies.

On the third morning, resolved to reach his goal or surrender bird and money to the farmer, the professor discarded the cage at the campsite and carried the eagle once more to the mountain summit upon his arm. A breeze was blowing from the west and the bird raised its head, facing into the wind. The sky in the east brightened and once more, stroking the back feathers of the bird, the professor said, "Eagle! You are an eagle and not a slave bird. You must no longer live on handouts from others. Spread your wings and fly. Become again what you always were!"

As the first rays of morning sunlight fell upon the bird's head feathers, the breeze stirred more strongly and the eagle shuddered to its core. The great wings were extended to their full six feet and the creature made a sharp noise, almost a cry of agony. The sun rose fully above the eastern crest and once more, the professor commanded, "Eagle—you are an eagle, not a tame bird! You are lord of all the earth beneath you—the skies are your true habitat. Claim your destiny and become again what you have always been!

The bird hopped briefly upon the arm, caught its balance and settled. Then it hopped more determinedly, spread it wings fully again and threw itself from the teacher's arm with an anguished cry. It glided down the mountainside on the freshening breeze, then caught a thermal current and soared up above the scientist's head and away into the skies. It gave three piercing shrieks and flew away into the light of a new day.

Brothers and sisters, we are all eagles. We have become too comfortable taking handouts from the power-brokers in our society. In the process, we have abdicated our true purpose, which has always been to look into The Light, discover the truth of our being, and fly toward that. Don't remain with the chickens. Fly today on your own wings!

About the Author

Retired history teacher David Pitkin has always been fascinated by events that cannot be explained. His personal experiences have taken him into a lifelong study of metaphysics, including his own spiritual study. A professional numerologist for 25 years, he has used his degree in Counseling Psychology to aid others in their spiritual search, and has served as a facilitator of dream study for 11 years.

He is regularly interviewed on television and radio throughout the nation, especially at Halloween, as he has authored four books of true ghost stories. His path has also taken him into many situations that involve overcoming fear.

The motivation for this book arose in 1988, when Pitkin attended a Spiritual Frontiers lecture by Tom Sawyer, a Rochester-area laborer who had died underneath a fallen truck 20 years before. After a half-hour of clinical death, Sawyer revived to a brand-new lifestyle. Four years later, Pitkin met Don Cherry, a retired District of Columbia detective who discovered his own psychic talents. The author wondered for many years what would happen if the two men were combined. *The Highest Mountain* is the result of his exploration.

DAVID J. PITKIN

Order Blank

The following titles can be ordered directly from the publisher and autographed
if the customer wishes. Please specify below.

Title	Price	How many?
Spiritual Numerology: Caring for Number One	14.95	
Haunted Saratoga County	17.95	
Ghosts of the Northeast	18.95	
New York State Ghosts, Vol. 1	19.95	
The Highest Mountain: Death & Life in the Adirondacks	18.95	

Subtotal _____

N.Y. State Sales Tax _____

Postage/Shipping _____
Shipping (all orders less than 5 books) Free
More than 5 books add 3.50
Total enclosed (check or money order) _____

To whom should the book(s) be autographed?

Mail to: Aurora Publications, Post Office Box 690, Chestertown, NY 12817